HESTER

HESTER

BRIAN CLEEVE

BOOK CLUB ASSOCIATES LONDON

This edition published 1980 by
Book Club Associates
by arrangement with Cassell Ltd.

Printed in Great Britain by
Richard Clay (The Chaucer Press) Ltd
Bungay, Suffolk

To
You

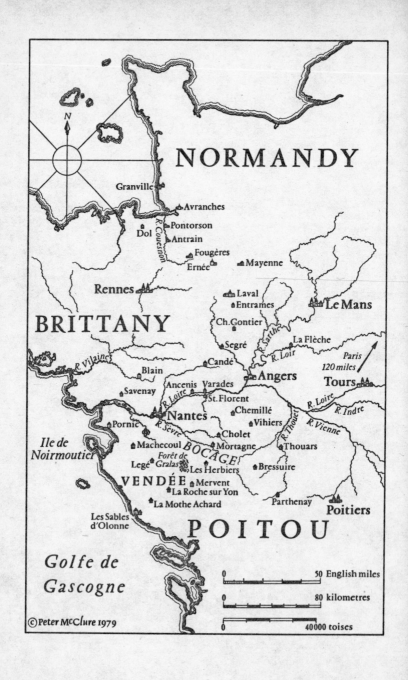

N

NORMANDY

Granville

Avranches

Pontorson

Dol

Antrain

Fougères

Ernée

Mayenne

Rennes

Laval

Entrames

BRITTANY

Ch.Gontier

Le Mans

Segré

La Flèche

R.Sarthe

R.Vilaine

Candé

R.Loir

Paris
120 miles

Blain

Angers

Tours

Savenay

Ancenis Varades

St.Florent

R.Loire

Chemillé

R.Loire

R.Indre

Nantes

Pornic

R.Sèvre

Cholet

Vihiers

R.Thouet

R.Vienne

Ile de
Noirmoutier

Machecoul

BOCAGE

Mortagne

Thouars

Legé

Forêt de
Gralas

Bressuire

Les Herbiers

VENDÉE

Mervent

La Roche sur Yon

La Mothe Achard

Parthenay

Poitiers

Les Sables
d'Olonne

POITOU

Golfe de
Gascogne

© Peter McClure 1979

0   50 English miles

0   80 kilometres

0   40000 toises

Prologue

Late September, 1768, Switzerland. The St. Gotthard Pass. The wind screaming down from the high mountain peaks as though winter had already come, flinging the early snow against the shutters of the inn; now snow, now sleet; billowing the smoke of the log fire into the bedroom, among the curtains of the bed, choking the couple who lay there.

'This is a damnable inn,' said Mr. Broadhurst. 'And a damnable country, and a damnable journey. I hope you are pleased, Fanny. Travelling is all very well for a young fellow who must make his Tour, and look at ruins, but for us! At our age! I am above forty, and you are as near it as makes no difference, and here we are scampering across Europe like a pair of lunatics.'

'Hardly scampering,' Mrs. Broadhurst said with a tired peevishness. 'We have been fastened here for four days in what you rightly call this damnable inn. It seems like four months. And if you had for once in our lives consented to listen to me we should by now be in Naples and looking forward to a winter of sunshine, and good society.'

'Naples!' cried Mr. Broadhurst. 'Thieves and beggars! Stenches and dirt and not knowing when one would be stabbed in the street. Was Venice not bad enough for you?'

'I was happy there for the first time in my married life. And if——' Mrs. Broadhurst began. A scream from the room next door cut her short. A high, lifting, agonized scream that competed with the wind outside, rose above it, seemed to break like shattered glass, and died away into long shudders of pain.

'It has begun,' said Mrs. Broadhurst. 'Poor wretched creature.'

'Upon my soul,' said Mr. Broadhurst, 'what a country, what people! In a public inn at——' He pressed the catch of his repeater, and the tiny chimes rang three times, and then gave five sharp little sounds in quick succession. '—at five past three o'clock in the morning!'

'A woman in labour does not take much account of the time,' Mrs. Broadhurst said. The scream came again, and Mrs. Broadhurst put the coverlet round her ears. 'Go to sleep for heaven's sake.'

'Sleep! What can her people have been thinking of? To send her off like a—like a delivery parcel! At such a time! Could they not count? Do these people not even know that a child comes after nine months, and one should not go lurching about the Swiss Alps in coaches or—what can her husband be thinking of? Is he a madman?'

'If she has a husband. Go to sleep, you are freezing the bed sitting up like that.'

But there could be no hope of sleep. The screams rang out again and again, hour after hour, until near morning they came swifter, nearer together. A coming and going in the corridor, heavy feet of servants carrying firewood, buckets of hot water. The midwife, the girl's own servants talking outside the door. A man and a woman. She had arrived in her own coach, her servants travelling with her. A tall, very tall young Frenchwoman, obviously near her time, trying to conceal it with her cloak. Needing to be helped up the stairs, a whispering and hurrying among the inn people as if they guessed the traveller to be of more than usual consequence. Although she was spoken of as plain 'Madame'.

For three days she had kept her room, her meals brought up to her, and mostly, Mr. Broadhurst had noticed, brought down again untasted. Always one of her own servants outside her door, as though she was being guarded from intrusion, although who in heaven's name would wish to intrude on her? And now she was giving birth. Mr. Broadhurst got up and paced the floor in his rage. Not a wink of sleep. Not a sign of the weather breaking. They might be trapped here all winter. All winter! All the hunting season! All the shooting! Trapped in this sink-hole with a young woman and a baby and not a human being who spoke English. Except Fanny. And after such a night he was not much inclined to class her among human beings. They should have brought their own servants, although he would have died

[2]

rather than admit it to Mrs. Broadhurst. At least he could have talked to his valet about something.

'Why did we come?' he said. 'Why did I let you persuade me? I am an imbecile, I deserve it, I am a weak fool, a hen-pecked lubberlumpkin. Pictures! Statues! Churches! I never saw so much trumpery in all my life!'

'Henry, you have woken me up again.'

The screams next door had died down, faded, become a gasping for breath, an exhausted sobbing.

'She has given birth,' Mrs. Broadhurst said, a shadow of bitterness in her voice. She herself had given birth three times, and lost each child within hours. 'Now will you come back to bed? It is over and finished, and if Heaven is merciful she will make no more noise.'

There was the sound of slapping, and the child began to cry.

'This is intolerable!' Mr. Broadhurst shouted, 'I shall go out of my mind. Is this place an inn or a lying-in hospital? When shall we get out of here?' He went to the window and flung open the shutters. Snow fell into the room in a great heap from somewhere, and the wind followed it, tearing at the curtains, the window, Mr. Broadhurst's nightshirt and nightcap. An ugly, leaden twilight, neither day nor night. Nothing visible, not mountains, nor rocks, nor road. Mrs. Broadhurst hid herself under the covers, shrieking.

'I shall die of pneumonia and it will be your fault,' Mr. Broadhurst said, kicking the snow away with his bare feet and trying to refasten the shutters. They slammed out of his hand against the outer wall, and he had to content himself with closing the window with its panes of horn and oiled parchment. Not even glass! What a country! What a damnable, damnable inn!

It was another four days before the weather changed. Waking to daylight, sunshine, the wind dropped, a snowy landscape, snow peaks glittering, black rocks, patches of grass between the dazzling snowdrifts that were already melting, sparkling like heaps of diamond.

A bustling of servants, of horses, the young Frenchwoman's coach being brought round, the horses put to it. Trunks loaded behind. Mr. Broadhurst watching through the dining-room window, if one could call such an ill-favoured, smoke-ridden, bacon-smelling hole a dining-room. What were they doing? They could not mean to travel with her? After scarcely four days? But they not only meant it, they were doing it. Her coachman, her postilion already mounted. Her two servants coming out of the inn supporting her. Muffled to the eyes, so that there was almost nothing to see but her tall figure, leaning on her manservant's shoulder, her fur-lined bonnet, her long fur cloak.

She seemed so weak that they needed to lift her into the coach. Climbed in after her. And the child? Where was the child? The coachman snapping his whip, slapping the long reins on the rumps of his four horses, the coach swaying. And from inside it another scream, 'Mon enfant! Mon enfant! Ma fille!' The coach swaying wildly, the young woman at the coach window, trying to open the door, beating at the glass, her face uncovered now, white and shocked and ill, her mouth opened as she screamed again, 'Ma fille, donnez-moi ma fille!'

The servants pulling her back between them, her face vanishing. The coach climbing the road towards the pass, towards Italy, her screams still ringing, and then cut off, as if they were being stifled. Mr. Broadhurst stood at the window with his own mouth open, shocked into momentary paralysis. What— what had they——? He began to run out of the room, and crashed into his courier, almost knocking him down.

'Joseph! They have gone off without that woman's child, what are they about? After them, man, stop them!'

The courier held on to him, half to save himself from falling, half to hold his employer back from a useless enterprise.

'Signore, calmo! Be calm, milor'. There is much complications there. Better not to notice anythings.'

'Not notice? When I've been kept awake four nights on end! And now they go off and leave—what complications?'

'Calmo, milor', vi prego. Many many complications. Is a young lady from a great family and she have no husband, much disgrace, so they send her away to Italy and her time is coming on her here in the inn too soon, e eccolo. Leave alone, signore, is much better always, the quiet life.'

'Let go of my arm, damn you.'

But the coach was almost out of sight, was out of sight beyond rocks, a bend in the villainous track that these Swiss had the impudence to call a road.

Mr. Broadhurst ran round to the back of the inn, thinking of getting a horse, of riding after the monsters. And met the midwife carrying a swaddled bundle that made mewling cries as she held it under her arm like a parcel. Hurrying, looking away from Mr. Broadhurst, as though the darkness and back stairs were her proper setting, and sunlight and the open air affected her uncomfortably.

'What are you doing?' Mr. Broadhurst shouted, 'Is that the child?' He made to take it, the woman was holding it in such an unwomanly fashion. The old crone began to run, like a crab, scuttling. Mr. Broadhurst seized hold of her, shouting, 'Fanny, Joseph, someone! Come here, this devilish old hag is going to murder the child.' He had no doubt of it as he said it although the suspicion had only entered his mind that second, as the woman began to run. She shook and trembled in his grasp, whistling through her blackened stumps of teeth, jabbering her incomprehensible language.

'Be quiet, you wicked wretch! Give me the child!'

She could not have understood the words, but slowly she relaxed her grasp as Mr. Broadhurst took hold of it. The innkeeper's wife came running, the innkeeper himself, bow-legged and squinting. The courier 'Joseph', whose given name was Giuseppe, late of Venice and praying only to return there as soon as he might, out of this country of mountains and ice and assassins and atrocious wine. Mrs. Broadhurst. The inn servants.

'She was taking the child off with her, she was going to murder it!'

'Signore, vi prego! Lascia stare!'

Babble of dialect, Mr. Broadhurst holding his prize cradled in his arms, still mewling like a cat. He uncovered the tiny creature's face. A red crumple of skin, a kind of bronze-gold, coppery down on the top of its head. Kitten mouth opening to shriek, tiny fists freeing themselves from the swaddle, lifting towards Mr. Broadhurst's cravat.

'Signore, I beg! Give it back to the old woman. Already they have killing the father, shooting him dead as soon as they discovered it. Give it back, milor', forget everything.'

'You ruffian! Fanny, Fanny! Take it, we shall——' He was going to say 'We shall find someone to look after it.' But just as he had known that the old crone meant to do away with the child, he knew now that he himself meant to keep it, that nothing on earth would get it away from him. They had lost three, and he had

[5]

wept for them more than Fanny had done. And now here was a fourth, put into his arms like an act of Heaven. 'Take her, Fanny, quickly!'

'I have no intention of touching it,' Mrs. Broadhurst said. 'If you insist on making an exhibition of yourself——' Turning to go into the house again. To stop as if she had been struck. 'And if you are thinking——!' she cried, clasping her hands together, 'if you are so much as imagining that we—that I——' And as she saw her husband's expression, 'Henry! I forbid you! I will not countenance it! Are you gone stark mad?'

But all her protests were useless, as were the outcries of the midwife; of the people of the inn; of Giuseppe predicting vengeance and death from the nameless 'great family' that had so wisely and honourably condemned this child to a swift return to Heaven. 'É una bastarda, signore, una niente. C'é l'onore di sangue, di famiglia! O signore, milor', I beg an' pray of you leave her be to these good people.'

Nothing served. By the expenditure of as much good English gold as might have brought Mrs. Broadhurst's maid and Mr. Broadhurst's valet with them for the entire journey, instead of hiring Italian creatures who did not know how to attend to hair or brush a coat, the thing was more or less arranged; a wet-nurse found; and the long journey towards France, and the Channel, and distant England was at last begun, with the small additional passenger sucking contentedly at a great naked breast, as the carriage swayed and bumped and shuddered down the mountain-side.

'I shall have her christened Hester,' Mr. Broadhurst said. 'After my mother. And I trust that you will never try to persuade me to set my foot outside of Sussex again so long as I live. Hester? Hester? See, she knows me already, the rogue.'

The wet-nurse changed the baby from one enormous breast to the other. Mrs. Broadhurst closed her eyes.

'It is a pity of course that she is not a boy,' Mr. Broadhurst said. 'But I shall teach her to ride, and she can come hunting with me. There is good bone there. Hester? Hester? Look! She is laughing, the villain. You hear her? She is glad to be coming to England.'

Chapter 1

The noise was savage, overwhelming. It filled the darkness with a bronze-throated roaring, a deep, continuing clamouring of bells. The night shook with it, the balcony under her feet vibrated, the tall, open windows beside her, the thick walls of the house, as if they were trying to ring in answer. Wave on wave of sound like a storm. A dozen, fifty, a hundred churches drowning their individual voices in the uproar and then one peal lifting high above the others for a moment, a high wildness of ringing; now one, now another and another; far away, near to, across the river, and again almost beside her so that the rooftops shivered. Every church in Paris sounding the alarm, gone mad with warning. Out to the distant Faubourgs and back again. Wild, deafening, making her blood sing with the excitement of it, as if the heart of Paris was singing the wildness of the Revolution. And under the clamour of the bells, the drums. Deep and throbbing, beating the assembly, drumming, drumming, drumming like blood. Far away, but calling, calling. Come, come, march with us! Ça ira, ça ira! Beat of blood.

She felt dizzy with the storm and throbbing of the noise, and had to grip the iron rail of the balcony to keep herself steady. Leaning over it, leaning into the dark, into the waves of sound as if they could support her by themselves, like the force of a gale. Shadows hurried in the street below, along the dark, narrow channel of the rue du Bac. A man keeping close to the wall beneath her balcony, his head bent as if he was afraid of being recognized. The glisten of steel from bayonets, two soldiers, the ring of nailed boots in an instant of almost silence, and then the bells drowning out their footsteps, seeming to drive them on like shadows on the wind.

'Messieurs! What's happening, what is it?'

But they did not hear her, or did not trouble to answer a woman's stupid questions at such a time. Lights in the houses opposite, candles, lamps lit, behind dark curtains. The silhouettes of people moving, as if they were hurriedly dressing, against Heaven knew what emergency. War? Invasion? She leaned out further still and looked towards Léonie's balcony. Surely she must also be awake? Even she could not have slept through this? But her window was dark and shuttered. Was she too frightened to open it?

Hester went back into her own room and knocked at the connecting door. 'Léonie?' No answer. She went in. Like a hot-house, scent of flowers, fruit, perfume, stifling in the closed heat of the room, of the August night. 'Léonie? Are you awake?' Lifting her candlestick to see better. How could anyone sleep in this atmosphere? She could feel the sweat start on her. 'Léonie!'

Her cousin's eyes opening, heavy with sleep, then widening, alarmed. 'What is that noise? The bells?'

'That is what I mean to find out. I am going to call Papa. I came in to see are you all right?'

Léonie reached out for her, gripped her wrist. 'Don't go! What is it? Where is Euphemia? Euphemia! Are they going to kill us?'

'Don't be a fool. No one is going to hurt you. It is only an invasion, the war has begun, something like that. I am going down into the street to ask someone.'

'No! Hester, are you mad?' Lifting herself from her nest of down and pink and blue and ivory satin, her hair falling like spilled honey on her shoulders; the scents of warmth and sleep and bed, and soft youngness and cream white flesh and womanhood seeming to pulse out of her, so that Hester wanted to shake her, her own puritanism, her own almost masculinity revolted by her, as if she herself was a young monk looking at a temptress. She had to turn quickly away; pull the curtains open, and the shutters, and the tall French windows that opened out like doors onto the balcony. The noise of the bells that had been muffled and yet loud enough came flooding in like thunder, and Léonie gave a small scream of terror, burying herself among the cushions and the silk sheets and the eiderdown. 'Euphemia! Hester, for pity's sake! What is it? Are they down below?'

[8]

'It must be the Austrians. Do you hear the drums? They are calling the army to defend Paris! Ça ira, ça ira! That is what they sing! Can you hear it?'

'Euphemia!'

The Negress came in by the other door, her eyes white-shining, pulling the belt of her nightgown round her waist, knotting it. Kneeling down by her mistress, putting her arms round her. 'Ma cocotte! Little sweet one, don't be afraid, Lalitté is here, Euphemia is here, I'll look after you.'

'Make her shut the windows. Make her.'

'Madame, please Madame Estaire——' She could not say Hester properly, 'Madame Estaire, please, my mistress is frightened.' Gently but firmly she took the handles of the windows from Hester and pushed the two casements shut. Then the shutters and the curtains, until by comparison there was almost quietness. The storm shut out. Léonie was crying, allowing the tears to fall like crystal drops. Euphemia dried them with her fingertips, whispered in Créole so that what she said was incomprehensible to Hester. Her fingers black against the white velvet of Léonie's skin, the honey-gold of her hair, smoothing, comforting, cosseting; round black head with its tight black curls that were usually hidden under a red silk cap, red satin nightgown tied tight at the waist. As if the two of them were making a picture deliberately, white and gold and black and scarlet. And the scent, and the stifling heat of the room, like a blood-beat of sensuality; and the cushions, and the curtains, white muslin and dark velvet; and the clothes scattered and heaped and piled on the chairs, the sofa. Silk chemises, satin gowns, scarves, ribbons, stockings, bodices, heaped and scattered where the two of them must have spent hours last night before they went to bed trying on new clothes in front of the cheval glass.

I could strike them both, Hester thought, and wanted to catch hold of the Negress and pull her upright and make her do something, even though there was nothing to do. And at least she was keeping her mistress quiet.

'I am going to call Papa,' she said. 'And then I shall go and find out some news.'

But her father was already awake, and half dressed, trying to pull on his boots, his thin grey hair on end and his waistcoat still unbuttoned.

[9]

'What a damnable uproar. Can they do nothing quietly? What is it, Hester, what are they about now?'

'I don't know, Papa. I am going down to find someone to ask. Do you hear the drums? I think it must be an invasion. What a sight you are, I'd best brush your hair before you let anyone see you.'

But she could not wait to do it and was at the door again before her father called after her, 'You are in your nightgown, child! What would your mother say? Put something on.'

But it was not a time for thinking about clothes. She ran through the ante-room that served them for a hall and opened the doors onto the outer landing. The stairs were a well of blackness down to the first floor where Madame de Richeteau lived in a welter of cats and clocks and remembrances of her husband, the general. There was not a sign of life from her or her servant, not a glimmer of light. Down the main stairs to the entrance hall. She had the chain unfastened and the bolts drawn back before she heard the knocking. The man's hand was still raised to knock again as she swung back one of the heavy leaves of the great doors. The shadow shape of a tall man in a riding-cloak and a beaver hat. As tall, taller than herself, his fist still raised as though he was about to strike her. She stepped back by instinct, and caught her breath.

'Do not be frightened, citizeness. I have a message for this house, for someone here. May I come inside?'

'I am not frightened. Who is your message for?' And then, as he came in still hesitating, perhaps in the natural fear of frightening a woman at such a time of night, or morning, and such a morning as it was, she said, 'What is happening? Why are they ringing the bells? And the drums? Is it war? Have the Austrians invaded?'

'No, citizeness. It is the people. Have you any light?' He had closed the door behind him and they were in the total darkness of the hall. He was no longer even a shadow. The bells themselves muffled again by the closed door. Growing quieter still for a few moments as the nearest churches stopped for breath or exhaustion, the sounds now coming from far off. Then surging nearer and nearer, filling the street outside, beating against the doors.

'What do you mean, the people?' At such an extraordinary

time it seemed quite ordinary to talk to a stranger in the dark of the hall, in her nightgown.

'They are marching against the King, madame. They are tired of him, even of a King who does nothing.' He sounded as though he was grinding the words between his teeth. But whether his anger was with the people or the King it was impossible to tell. 'But I am pressed for time,' he said. 'Otherwise I should not have—and I saw your light. Are you Madame Broadhurst, perhaps?'

'I am Miss Broadhurst. How do you know my name? And who is your message for? Who sent you?'

'If your father is above may we go up to him and I shall answer everything?' He took her arm without waiting for her agreement and began to guide her up the broad stairs as if he could see in the dark. He had begun to speak in English as soon as she had told him who she was. Not at all a Frenchman's stumbling and mangled English, and yet not an Englishman's. A strange accent that she recognized without being able to place it.

'Who are you?'

'Wait, madame.' Hurrying her, his grasp of her arm more powerful than polite. She tried to free herself but he held her without effort, without seeming aware that she wanted him to let go of her. On the landing above her father was waiting with a lit candle, his hair still on end, none of his clothes laced or buttoned as they should be, one of his boots in his other hand, the candle-stick raised up.

'Hester? Hester? Is that you, child? Fetch that damned rogue of a valet down to me. He can't be asleep in all this racket, devil take him. And get your girl up to make us some tea. What? Who's that? What the blazes? Who the devil is this fellow?'

'Inside, if you please, sir. Mr. Broadhurst? I have a message for you. From the Count St. André de Richeteau. Two in fact.' He brought both of them inside the apartment, closing the doors again behind him, and took out a folded and sealed paper from inside his cloak. Indoors he seemed even taller. A man of thirty or so, a dark, lean face, carved out by candlelight in strong shadows of cheekbone and nose and jaw. He looked at Hester and bowed. Not the elegant, court bow of those who still used it, nor a servant's bow, but a stiff bob of the head as if it was a waste of time to be got over quickly. 'You had questions for me? Who I am doesn't matter. I am a messenger, nothing else. I know your names from the Count.' He did not say 'The Count my master.' 'As for the bells and the drums, I told you, the people are marching. They are tired of having a King.'

There was something, in fact a great deal, about his manner that she did not like. Her father had turned away to a table in the small ante-room to read his letter and Hester became conscious of her nightgown, and the man's eyes looking her up and down.

'You called me madame,' she said, 'not citizeness. You are not in favour of the people, perhaps?'

He did not take it as a rebuke, nor a challenge, nor look surprised at such a remark from a foreigner. Instead, and to her surprise, he seemed to take the question seriously. He was stripping off his long riding gauntlets. His hands were dark-tanned like his face and he gripped his long jaw between a dark thumb and forefinger and rasped at the night's stubble of beard there. 'Not of these people,' he said at last.

Mr. Broadhurst turned round, waving the letter in his fist. 'Impossible! Nonsense! Forgive me, sir, I have not yet thanked you. Thank you, thank you, but this is the most foolish—Hester, the Count says in this that we are to return to England! Good grief, man, we are just come! I have business here, my niece's business. Does the Count not realize from my letter? Did he so much as read it? There are estates, an inheritance. I must see to them for her, in these times more urgently than ever. Go back to England? And without delay, he says! Does he think I am a madman to come all this way, leave my home, my wife, my niece's parents, put up with all we have had to put up with these past weeks, in order to go home again? "Without delay"? Is *he* mad? Or what the devil is it, sir?'

He had taken the messenger's arm in his excitement. The man detached Mr. Broadhurst's hand as if he was dealing with a child. 'If you will listen to me, sir. I have not much time to spare. I am to add to that letter. If you can leave Paris today, so much the better. Tomorrow may be too late. The Count wrote that more than a week ago. I have been delayed in reaching you and every day that has gone by strengthens the arguments for your leaving.'

'I have no intention——'

'Sir, you may do as you wish, but you must first listen. You have your daughter and your niece with you. Things may soon

[12]

happen here, *will* soon happen, that must put every family like yours in danger.'

'Stuff, sir! Who the blazes are you or that damned old ninny of a Count to tell me what I must do? Where the devil is my fellow? Hester, fetch him down, the French rascal. And that girl of yours. The deuce knows what they are at, you had best not go yourself, I will go. No, send up the black creature for them, let her give them a fright. What was I saying?' He had begun to brush his hair with the letter, making an odd crackling sound against the background thundering and pealing that had grown so constant Hester had almost put it from her mind. And suddenly, as she thought of it again, it stopped. Seemed to die like a wave receding, like thunder rolling farther and farther off to a dark horizon. Silence. And that rasp and rattle of the stiff folds of paper in Mr. Broadhurst's plump white hand. A clock ticking. All three of them listening, holding themselves still. A hush of quietness.

'You see?' Mr. Broadhurst said. 'They've stopped it at last. After waking the entire city and ruining my sleep, they've stopped it. Like this whole rubbishing Revolution. I tell you, sir, you haven't told me your name, but if you're the Count's messenger I assume you share his feelings. I don't like any of it, sir. It's nonsense. I came here full of sympathy. I believe in Liberty, in Constitutions. Privilege is a damnable immoral thing. I was prepared to see good here, to find you all taking a fine, sensible road towards the sort of government we have in England. I'm not one of your ruffian Tories with his head in the fifteenth century. I believe in change, sir, progress. But all this! Ringing bells, running about in the streets like mad creatures, shouting at your King, invading the Palace, the Tooleries or Tweeleries or whatever you call it, smashing the furniture like those villains did two months ago. By heaven, sir, they'll get nowhere like that. And you let 'em! You all put up with it! And the state of the streets! The filth! If I had your poor King's ear for five minutes, I'd tell him what he ought to do.'

'Let me shake your hand on that,' the messenger said, his voice and expression at once, by some alchemy, ironic and sincere. 'There are a great many of us share your feelings exactly. But the answer is less simple than you think. There is going to be a deal of blood spilled before we have a King again who does what he ought to do. And it is likely to begin today. That is why you should go home, and indeed without delay. Is there a window we can go to for a moment?'

They went into Mr. Broadhurst's room and stood side by side on the balcony. Dawn had come, turning the sky blood-red. And at first they could only hear the silence. Like emptiness, as if the sky and city had been emptied out, drained by the storm. And then, within the quietness, sounds beginning to make themselves heard, to fill the immensity of silence. A murmuring, indistinct, distant, formless. Like the sea.

'They have begun,' the stranger said. 'They are marching against the King.'

Hester leaned out above the street, as she had done an hour ago, listening. She imagined she could hear the rhythm of their marching, of the drums. Ça ira. Ça ira. It began to beat with the rhythm of her heart-beat, pulse with her blood.

'I think it is wonderful,' she said. 'A whole people marching, risen against tyranny: God grant they win!' She looked sideways to see how the stranger would answer her, but he was gone. After a moment the door opened and shut below her, and she saw his tall shadow striding away down the dark channel of the rue du Bac.

'Such damned nonsense,' her father said, and she could not tell for a moment whether he was referring to her opinions or the messenger's. 'Marching against their King indeed! Even this poor fellow won't stand for that twice. I think we should take a stroll across to these Tweeleries, thingummies. We'll go after breakfast and see what happens when these wretches come up against the Swiss Guard and see a few drawn bayonets. I'll wager you a guinea they'll march pretty fast in the opposite direction. And to make such a damnable noise about it! Have you sent up for that valet of mine yet? And for tea? John, damn you, are you there? Bring my razors. Telling us to go home without delay! Did you ever hear such rubbish? The fellow must be an imbecile.'

Chapter 2

Even now, at half past six in the morning, there were already crowds in the street, streaming across the Pont Louis XVI, into the garden of the Tuileries. All making in the same direction, towards the Palace. Poor people for the most part, workmen, tradesmen come from their shops. Butchers with bloody aprons and a cleaver, market women with baskets, some of them with red bonnets of Liberty on their heads like red snuffers clapped on dirty candles. Shop-boys and apprentices, women in bright rags with painted cheeks and haggard mouths.

It was not a pleasant crowd to be amongst and she needed all her energy of mind to tell herself that she was glad to be jostled by them, and stared at in that brutally offensive way they all had of looking at any stranger or anyone slightly different, as if he or she was not only mad to be different, but suspect of dreadful crimes as well.

'I am with you!' she wanted to cry out to them. 'In my heart!' They knew no better, they were scarcely a year freed from slavery, from brute beast oppression, how should they have manners, know any better, behave like English gentlemen and ladies? And Heaven knew, a London crowd was almost as bad. Worse. More violent, more unpredictable, more drunken. And without a glimmer of an ideal of freedom to excuse its violence. 'We are come as your friends!' she wanted to cry to a woman in a sacking apron with hell in her face and a knotted club sloped across her shoulder like a soldier's musket. 'Stare as much as you want, citizeness. That is your freedom, you have won the right to stare.'

But the woman stank like a drain and Hester had to cling to her father's arm to prevent him sending her away from them with his cane. Women like her had torn down the Bastille stone by stone and brought Tyranny to its knees. 'Ça ira! Liberty!' The woman spat, measuring Hester with her eyes. Her tallness, her cleanness, the gloss of her hair under her hat brim; as if all those things were an insult to a crowd of *sans-culottes*. Measured Mr. Broadhurst, from the high crown of his new London hat to the shine of his top boots; his gold fobs and flowered satin waistcoat, his English wool coat that stood out in this ragamuffin flotsam like a fragment of Pall Mall set down in a jungle.

'How they stink!' Mr. Broadhurst said, in his customary loud English, making no concessions to France or the French language. 'Get away from us, you rascal, how dare you push in front of me like that?' He lifted his cane pommel in threat against a man in a carpenter's apron with sawdust in his hair, and astonishingly enough the man did back away from them and lost himself in the crowd among the trees.

'Papa! They cannot help the way they smell. And you will get us into trouble if you——'

'Trouble? What trouble? I shall need to change my shirt when we get back. I am filthied already by them. Get away from me, madame, did you never see a gentleman before?'

'Papa, papa, be quiet! Someone here may understand English. You wanted to come out, and here we are. You even wanted to come the long way round, didn't you? And I am so glad! I would not have missed this for anything in the world.'

'The devil take them, soap is cheap enough. Where is Léonie? And that black savage of hers? If these creatures want to stare let them stare at her.'

Hester turned and looked. Even in that crowd, and although they had fallen far behind, she could see them at once. Léonie's great curly-brimmed hat with its ribbons and feathers, and Euphemia's red and white striped chimney-pot; like bright flowers drifting on a dirty flood, bobbing here and there, jostled, half swamped, now vanishing, now in sight again, seeming to form the centre of a still tighter swarm of people.

'Oh heavens! Papa! They are miles behind us. I must go back for them. Why on earth did we bring her?' Certainly she had not wanted to be brought. Not even to get up, and only her fear of Mr. Broadhurst and being lifted almost bodily out of bed by Hester had made her do it. 'She will be terrified!' Hester said, and

[16]

began cleaving her way back against the crowd like a powerful swimmer against a strong tide.

'Let me by, let me by, please.' She towered above most of them by a head and more and swept aside the last barrier of ragged starers surrounding her cousin and Euphemia.

'Léonie, what are you doing? You *must* keep close to us. Come *on*.' Grasping her by the arm, lifting her along. 'Take her other arm, Euphemia. Don't cry, there's nothing to be frightened of. But I told you not to dress like this, no wonder they are staring at you.' Blue silk and chiffon, as if she was going to Versailles, or to have her portrait painted. And Euphemia as bad, in a scarlet redingote, and that ridiculous, monstrous chimney-pot of a hat.

'She sets me off,' Léonie had said, as all of them were dressing. 'Do you want her to go naked because she is black? Am I a monster that I should not dress her properly?'

'Come *on*! Papa will be furious with you, we shall miss everything.'

'I want to miss it. I want to go home. Please, please, Hester, take me back to the apartment. Let me lie down, I feel so ill.'

'You don't. How can you not be excited? Such a day! Listen to the crowd outside the Palace, listen to them chanting!'

They could not make out the words, but it was like the tocsin of the early hours of that morning. A deep throbbing, and then a high voice alone, as if a street singer was leading a chorus. They reached Mr. Broadhurst again, standing with his back to a tree, like an English monument.

'Léonie girl, don't dawdle so! You are making us late.'

'My head is bursting with the pain. Oh Uncle, may I not go back to bed?'

'Stuff and nonsense. There's no such thing as a headache, it's all imagination, vapours. Take three deep breaths and it will go. Now, out of my way, you scoundrel, what are you looking at? Make way for these ladies, sir.' If the man did not understand the words he understood the fierce expression of Mr. Broadhurst's large blue eyes and stout, pink, shaven cheeks, and wilted away from before him like dirt before soap.

'These people should be at work,' Mr. Broadhurst said. 'What do they mean by flocking about the place like this?'

'But this is what we have come to see, Papa. These people *are* the Revolution, they are the new France.'

[17]

'If they are, then it is a damnable dirty augury for the future. Hold my arm, Léonie. *Hold* it, I say, take a grip of me, damnation, and you, girl, mind your mistress's whatnot before one of these villains makes off with it.' Pointing his stick at Léonie's indispensable, that Euphemia was dangling negligently from her wrist by its coloured string. 'Hold it properly, don't swing it about like that. Dear heaven, I shall tell Wilberforce to his face that he is mad, they are not fit for freedom. What are they shouting, Hester?'

They were at the railings of the Palace by now, those of the crowd who were closest shaking the bars, screaming, 'Down with tyranny, down with the Great Pig! Down with Monsieur Veto!' More of the crowd flowing round towards the Place du Carousel behind the Palace. The press so thick here that it was impossible to move except as the eddies surged and flowed. Stench of dirt, stale wine, sweat and filthy rags. Unshaven faces, women with streeling hair and black teeth in savage mouths, screaming insults at the blank windows and the balconies, the empty courtyards. Soldiers drawn up on the steps, more soldiers on the rooftops, at the parapets. The white coats of the regulars, and red of the Swiss. The grey-blue of the National Guard.

They had come to a kind of haven beside one of the massive gate pillars, sheltered there by Mr. Broadhurst's bulk and his free use of his cane. 'Get away from us, damn you, give these ladies air, cannot you see what you are doing, blast your eyes?' Fending off men, women, a hag with a basket of fish that even in that crowd stank astonishingly and who seemed determined to push her way in beside Léonie.

'Get off with you, madame, and your horrible basket.'

'Look at him!' the woman screamed suddenly. 'Dirty aristocrat pig! And his fancy girls. Look at 'em, citizens, some of the King's friends, come out to jeer at us!'

People began to turn towards them, make a circle.

'Three o' the Queen's whore-women! Here, friends, let's teach 'em a lesson, strip 'em naked, an' one of 'em's black like a devil. Here's a good fish to begin with!' She had her fist deep in her basket, pulled out a slithering, limp handful of bloody silver, and hurled it at Léonie. It struck her on the breast and fell, and Léonie opened her mouth in a pitiful scream of horror, staring down at her ruined silk, at the thing now lying at her feet. Hester leapt forward before her father could move and seized hold of the woman's basket, taking it out of her hands like a toy.

'Citizeness,' she cried. 'We are come as your friends, and are you going to treat us like this? Look, there is your enemy, in there!' She lifted the basket effortlessly and threw it over the railings, where it fell with a heavy thud and spilled its silvery mass like a declaration of war on the courtyard. 'Ça ira!' Hester cried. 'Liberty, Fraternity.' The woman stared open-mouthed, as if the sight of Hester, her height and size and foreign handsomeness, the suddenness of the attack, and the casual strength of flinging a loaded basket over a ten-foot railing, had taken all power of speech from her. Before she could recover it a man better dressed than most of the crowd, tall and stooping, had gripped the woman's shoulder and swung her round towards him. He bent down and shouted something in her ear, pushing her deeper into the mass of people by the gate, as if he had given her orders. Another eddy of the crowd pressed him almost into Hester's arms.

'You are foreigners?' he said. He steadied himself with one hand against the stonework. 'You have not chosen a good day for sightseeing.' Even shouting at the top of his voice his tone carried a sneer in it. His eyes were small, muddy brown and red-rimmed, close and deep set, his nose long and tilted upwards at the tip above a mouthful of crooked teeth. But ugly as he was he carried authority like a club, as if he had the right to question them. His coat was bourgeois black, and he wore knee breeches and buckled shoes and white stockings.

'We are not sightseeing,' Hester said, raising her own voice, while her father was shouting into her ear, 'What's the fellow saying, eh? What a damned ugly physog he has. Ask him what's happening.'

But before Hester could answer the man was torn away from them, the stooped, crow-black shoulders, tricorn hat, powdered hair tied in a queue, seeming to be lifted up for a moment by the mob like a black flag, and then vanishing into its heart again, but purposefully, as if the man had things to do there. And for a second Hester had the feeling that the crowd was not what she thought it was, a great ill-kempt and unwashed ideal of Liberty surging up from the gutters as flowers grow on dung, but something quite else and horrible, and the man in black with his crooked teeth and his sneer and his close-set eyes was the soul of it. But there was no time to think. A man's shoulder took her in the breast, hurting her savagely for a moment. Someone else trod on her foot, her father's hat was knocked over his eyes and she had to grip his arm to prevent his being sucked out into the whirlpool of the crowd round the gate, while Léonie clung to her in her turn, wailing about her skirts, her dress, the violence, and then simply weeping with terror.

The chanting of the mob lifted again, became a howl of expectation. Voices yelled, 'The King! The King! He's coming out! Kill the Pig, kill the Pig!' An organized tone about the chanting, a beat and rhythm to it like the bells. Under the shouting the tramp of marching feet, ring of steel. Hester twisted herself round. She could see through the railings and over Léonie's head a column of the National Guard making for the gate beside her. Men running ahead to open it. Military shouting, orders, crash of iron. The chanting died, gave way to isolated shouts of hatred, jeers of 'Where's the Austrian, where's the Whore?' 'Down with the Veto.'

The crowd staggered as the gates swung back and men with fixed bayonets made a steel hedge, a laneway for their comrades and the King. The column marched through the opened gateway. Hester forced herself forward, used her elbows and her great height and her strength until she was in the front rank of the crowd, her father beside her, still trying to beat his hat back into its shape, shouting, 'The villain! I'd like to break his head!'

She could see the King himself now, walking uncertainly among a dozen gentlemen of the Court, all of them in the hollow space between the lines of the National Guard, the King's velvet coat and white silk breeches, his dazzle of stars and jewelled orders like a mockery of his stout, somehow shambling figure, his heavy face, at once florid and haggard, his eyes peering about as if he was short-sighted, or could not understand what was happening, or why. A thin man in bourgeois black, obsequious and yet triumphant beside him, seemed to guide him along. And behind them came half a dozen ladies, and two children clinging to the hands of one of them. A girl of twelve or so and a small fair boy in velvet clothes and a frilled white shirt kicking up the leaves as he walked. Hester could see him between the marching guardsmen. A little boy of eight or nine tugging at his mother's hand.

[20]

Was it the Dauphin? The woman bent down to him, her face white, her eyes red with crying. Hester was so close she could almost have leaned forward over the barrier of men in front of her and touched the boy, and his mother. The woman looked up, met Hester's eyes, straightened herself with an habitual arrogance. The Queen. The Queen of France, the Austrian. Marie Antoinette. Her eyes red-rimmed, a slight flush mounting into the pallor of her face, as if something in Hester's stare had angered her. Perhaps to see a gentlewoman looking at her humiliation was harder to support than the jeers of the crowd.

There were not so many jeers now. A quietness, a tenseness spreading, a stillness, only the wasp-swarm murmuring and surging, the tramp of the soldiers, grinding nailed boots on gravel, an officer's shouted command.

'What's happening, where are they going, Hester? Was that the King?' Mr. Broadhurst nudging Hester, and then banging a young officer in front of them on his shoulder. 'What's happening, sir?'

The officer turned, astonished perhaps at the sound of English, and looked up first into Mr. Broadhurst's and then into Hester's face. A short, sallow-faced captain with lank black hair under a shabby hat, and such intensity in his dark eyes as was like being physically handled and shaken.

'My father asks you what is happening, sir, and where the King is going. We are English visitors. And friends.'

His mouth curled at that, in amusement, or contempt, or both. 'The King is going to the Assembly, madame, to put himself under its protection.' And then, as if he could not contain it, he said in Italian, 'Che coglione!' not to her but to himself, turning away like a man preparing to spit. Then he turned back to her and with scarcely a change of expression said, 'What part of England are you from?'

'From Sussex,' she said, astonished at the question, and even more at the business-like way in which it was put. And at such a time! 'If you have heard of it. It is in the south of England.'

'I know,' he said abruptly. And then, 'Are all the women so tall there?'

'What is he saying, Hester, what is he saying?'

'He is asking if all the women in Sussex are as tall as I am.'

[21]

'Good grief, is the man mad? I thought you were asking him about the King. What——'

She told him what he had said of the Assembly, and suddenly the officer gripped her by the wrist. 'Come, madame,' he said. 'Come with me. You say you are friends of France. You shall see how we bring a thousand years of history to an end. Come.' And began pulling her after him as if she could have no business in the world but to obey him.

'But, sir, my father——'

'Bring him. Come, sir. We will go to the Assembly.'

'And my cousin and——' Hester cried in protest, looking round for Léonie. But she was already beside her, not by her own efforts but by Euphemia's, and as Hester looked down at her the officer followed the direction of her eyes, saw Léonie, and gave that instant impression of being struck hard with a velvet-covered mallet that all men gave the first moment they saw her. As if the pith had been drawn out of him. 'Citizeness,' he whispered. His sallow cheeks flushed dark, went pale again. 'You will come too,' he said. 'Quickly. Follow us. Sir, take care we are not separated.' He renewed his grasp of Hester's arm, and began forcing a way through the crowd. He did not seem to use any violence about it but the crowd gave way in front of him like waves parting for the bows of a thin, impatient skiff, and he towed Hester along as if he was indeed a skiff pulling a tall yacht towards harbour. In their wake Mr. Broadhurst came grasping Léonie's elbow in one hand, with Euphemia at her other arm. They were almost on the heels of the rearguard of the King's column, and perhaps the crowd thought that they were part of it. Indeed, it soon became clear that it did. Seeing the young officer in his captain's uniform appearing to lead a group of aristocrats and their black servant towards the same destiny as the King and his family. Shouts began to lift again in the murmuring. 'It's Lamballe!' 'No no! It's the Polignac!' And 'Hang them, the leeches! Hang them!'

Hedged in by the crowd, pressed against, fists raised, more shouting, until it was as if they had really been arrested, faces staring, jeering, spitting insults, a woman reaching out to claw at Hester's face, the crowd behind surging forward to see what was happening, who was being led away. Shouts of 'They've got the Lamballe! Give her to us! Did you suck the whore's breasts last night? How did they taste?'

Hester scarcely understood the meaning of what was shouted, and yet she flushed with anger as if a bucket of filth had been flung at her, and wanted to answer whoever had shouted, clenching her fists. But the officer was pulling her faster, they were between lines of guards, crossing a roadway, climbing steps, going into a building.

'Here!' the officer said, allowing her to collect herself for a moment. 'Here is the heart of France. They used to break horses here. Now they break kings.' He looked at her as if he meant to draw her portrait from memory at some other time, and gave the impression that he could have done it, could have hit off the dark green of her riding dress, the copper-chestnut of her hair, the paler green of her eyes, the strong set of her mouth, without need for another glance. 'And the other young woman, your cousin? She is not English?'

'She is Créole. From Martinique. Her mother is my aunt.'

'Ah,' the officer said. 'Present me.' And suddenly glanced down at himself, at his uniform, at his boots, and gave the swift, dark flush he had shown before. And his uniform was indeed something to flush for if he was in any way concerned for his appearance. The coat was threadbare at the cuffs and collar, the boots were much too large, and cracked across the instep, and seemed to have been greased rather than polished. Their tops gaped like buckets round boyish, bony knees in ill-fitting white breeches.

'You have not told me your name, sir,' Hester said. Her father was occupied resetting his cravat and waistcoat, and making sure that his gold fobs and his watch were still there, unstolen. The young officer gave an impatient, downwards jerk of his head.

'Buonaparte, Captain Bonaparte at your service, citizeness.' Correcting the Italian of his name to French.

'Mademoiselle Léonie St. André de Richeteau,' Hester said, presenting her cousin. She scarcely knew why she did not say 'citizeness'. Perhaps for the sake of that vile shouting at her a few moments ago, outside, when the crowd had taken her for the Queen's friend.

Léonie had put out her hand to be kissed with her usual slow languor, her eyes taking in the officer's appearance, her eyes crinkling at the corners with amusement and malice. All her terrors of the past hour had vanished as if they had never existed.

[23]

She was safely in a building, there was no more danger that she could see, there was a man in front of her.

Dear Providence, Hester thought, she is a strange creature, and she watched for the melting of the young captain's bones, like watching for a candle to bend and melt in front of a fire. But Léonie's amusement was too open. His face flamed, grew very pale and he drew himself up to the fullest of his inconsiderable height.

'I have the honour to make you smile,' he said. 'Good day, citizeness.' And swung on his heel and marched away into the throngs of people already filling the hallway, his boot tops sagging and gaping so that he had to walk slightly straddle-legged, like a horseman on foot. Léonie laughed, clear and ringing and bubbling.

'He looks like Puss-in-Boots!' she said, her voice piercing the noise, the echoes, the clattering of footsteps. The officer's shoulders quivered as if he had been shot between them by an arrow. He almost halted, seemed about to turn back to them. And instead went on, deliberately, holding himself very erect.

'Léonie! He heard you!'

'What does it matter? Why are we here, where is this? And look at my dress! Look at what that woman did!' She held out her skirts, stained and silvered and bloodied, the hems torn where someone had trodden on them, the chiffon ruching hanging in rags. Beside her Mr. Broadhurst was staring round the crowded hall with open contempt. 'So this is their parliament,' he said. 'A damned circus. Well, since we are here, let us go in and see what sort of jackanapes nonsense they are making of it.' He began pushing his way towards where the crowd was thickest, around a great open doorway. Hester took Léonie and Euphemia by the arms and brought them along with her, Léonie protesting and yielding in the same breath, and Euphemia merely submitting to be led as she submitted to everything, in her body and not her mind. The sensation was, as always, both horrifying and aggravating. Horrifying because of the slavery, of the knowledge that the arm she held was as much Léonie's property as her spaniel dog or her parasol, and aggravating because of the falsity of the submissions. Like a malicious trick.

Mr. Broadhurst disappeared into the main Assembly chamber. When Hester managed to shepherd her two companions after him through the doorway, into a dark corridor and then into the vast open space of the manège, with its banks of seats and benches, its overhanging galleries and the high dais opposite the entrance where she was standing, she could not see her father anywhere. The benches were half-full of men who must presumably be members of the Assembly, but the floor in front of them, the corridors, and the galleries, were packed and crammed with people who looked like the advance guard of the crowd outside. Rough hungry faces, red freedom bonnets, lank greasy hair; women in rags and headscarves; fists and clubs shaking, voices shouting insults, men leaning over the bars of the galleries to scream down at men below.

As if the Assembly was theirs now, and not the elected members', the members almost crouching in fear, trying to make themselves inconspicuous, or to look like *sans-culottes*. Only on the dais two men stood out like at least symbols of authority. And one of them extraordinarily enough was the King. Hester recognized him even at that distance by his breast glittering with stars, and also by his fat immobility. A man shouting just above her head leaned so far out over the balcony that looking up she could see his face. It was the same man who had spoken to her by the gates of the palace, the same crooked teeth and yellow face, and narrow set, sunken eyes.

'Let's have an end to this farce of a monarchy!' he was yelling. 'That fat imbecile! Let him abdicate!' Beside and behind him other men took up the cry like soldiers shouting to order. 'Abdication, *déchéance*! Down with the last of the Capets! Down with the Veto!' Around Hester men and women were forcing their way into the chamber, pushing her forward. She was on the floor of the chamber itself, but no one seemed to care. If there were ushers whose business it was to keep the floor cleared of strangers they took care not to show themselves. A group of men were on their feet shouting, 'The King cannot sit with us? The King out of the Assembly! Out of the Assembly! Against the Constitution!'

She was almost below the dais by now, still holding Léonie and Euphemia by the arms. The man beside the King bent his head to listen to another man, whispered, turned to the King. The King stood up, pale and dull-faced, his eyes staring about as they had in the gardens not long before. He seemed to shrug in submission, and a man bowed and guided him down the steps and under the dais. Hester could see an iron grille there, cutting off a small room from the chamber. The room seemed to be packed with men and women and she thought she saw the Queen among them. Two men with a lever and a hammer were trying to break the grille away. And the noise in the Assembly was so great, so echoing, that the hammer blows and the ring of iron were almost lost in it. The grille came down with a crash and a cloud of dust that made the women beyond it cover their faces with handkerchiefs and choke.

At Hester's back a man said, 'Miss Broadhurst! God has sent you! Where is your father?'

She turned; it was the Count's messenger of the early morning. He looked exhausted, as if much more time had gone by since she had seen him than the few hours of the clock.

'I told you dreadful things would soon happen,' he said. 'They have barely begun. Where is your father?' He was looking round as he spoke, not only for her father, she thought, but for others, or other things. She had seen huntsmen with the same almost absent and yet concentrated expression as they studied a countryside, hills and woods and the run of a river, all while looking for the fox or a lost hound. 'There he is!' he whispered. 'Stay here, I'll fetch him.' He was gone with a long stride, and back on the instant, Mr. Broadhurst protesting loudly, 'What the devil, sir? Be quiet? Why? In this damned uproar?'

Until the messenger brought them together and thrust them into a corner under the dais. The noise continued round them, the broken iron grille lay at their feet and from where Hester stood she could see the King, the Queen and all their entourage crammed into the narrow room that the grille had protected or screened off, no more than two or three steps away from her. In the Assembly chamber itself the noise had grown more furious. The crowd jostled and fought its way here and there. Knots of men stopped to harangue one another, or the dais, or the galleries. The galleries shouted down to the floor, insults or encouragement, abuse or orders or defiance, although Heaven knew what they might be defying. The floor returned the shouts, and made enormous gestures of determination and fervour. But here in their shadowed backwater it seemed almost quiet by contrast, and the messenger's urgent whispering could make itself

[26]

heard easily enough against the yelling, the stamping, the banging of wooden sabots, the chant of '*Déchéance, déchéance!* Down with the Veto, an end to the Capet tyrants!'

'The King has destroyed everything,' the messenger was saying. 'In another hour, by tonight at latest, he and the Queen will be prisoners. They are prisoners already in everything but name. There is one chance in ten thousand of getting them out of this place and to safety, and you are the only people who can give it to them.'

'We?' cried Mr. Broadhurst. 'Get the King to safety? If he is not safe here——'

'I implore you!' the messenger said, clapping his hand across Mr. Broadhurst's mouth, and staring round him as if spies and worse were at their backs. 'If you shout like that we are all dead. Don't you understand what is happening?'

'I understand nothing!' Mr. Broadhurst said furiously, struggling to free his mouth from restraint. 'I do not know who you are, sir, or why you are telling us such rubbish, or what the devil is happening except that it is more French nonsense and I'm sick of it, sick to death of this damned kennel of a town. You should see London, and then you would know how a city should be conducted. Liberty, sir! If this is Liberty, give me clean streets instead.'

The man made a harsh sound of impatience, and swung round to Hester.

'They will have his head if they can. Would you help them out of here if it was possible? Would you dare it?' He had gripped both her wrists in his hands, so fiercely that he was crushing the sleeve buttons into her wrist bones and hurting her, and his eyes looked into hers as if they were burning. Blue, slightly bloodshot eyes, with leaden shadows under them. There was a stubble of dark beard on his cheeks and jawbone, and a nerve twitched at the tightened corner of his mouth. She had not liked him at first seeing and she liked him no better now. Heaven knew she had no prejudices of class, but he had not a gentleman's face nor a gentleman's manner, nor a servant's respectfulness, and she did not like to be handled by anyone, gentle or simple. It was the second time he had grasped hold of her that morning as if she was something to be dragged about. It seemed to be a French characteristic, and she did not care for it, in him or the captain.

'You seem to assume that we are friends to the aristocracy, sir,' she said coldly. 'We are not. We are friends to France and to the Revolution, and to Progress.'

He stared at her for a moment as if she had said that she was a cannibal, and then such exhaustion came into his face as seemed to dissolve his features into a grey despair. Even the burning in his eyes went out like embers, leaving grey blue ash. And then he recovered himself. His mouth hardened and curved in contempt, and not simply contempt, but pity.

'You are friends of *that*?' he said, jerking his thumb towards the chamber beside them. 'They are lice, girl, crawled out of the panelling.'

'And who made them into lice?' she cried, freeing her other hand. She began to say, 'That family in there!' and stopped midway. The King was looking at her, vacantly, as if he was looking at a tree. Someone had found him a chair and the fair-haired child had come beside his knee and was playing with a bandalore, throwing it down and drawing it up over and over again, absorbed in his game. The Queen, a score of ladies and court gentlemen, the other child, the princess, were crammed in behind the King like birds in a cage at market, with no room to move. The ceiling was so low that one tall man among them needed to bend his head down to avoid it. The boy looked at Hester and smiled, something patiently bewildered about the smile as if he was so tired of asking why they were there and what was happening that he had almost given up thinking about it.

'You could help them,' the messenger was whispering. 'I don't know what you've heard in England about all this, but I tell you it's nothing good that's happening. Hell is opening for all of us. Save their lives at least. And one day God will reward you by letting you understand what you have done. They could walk out of here with your party. If your father gave the King his coat and hat and you walked with him. You've been seen with a stout gentleman in English clothes, no one would think of it. And the Queen in your cousin's hat and scarf and the two children with your Negress. Please, for compassion's sake, do you want me down on my knees to beg you to be human? Another hour and it will be too late.'

'What is he saying, Hester? What is it, what does he want?' The messenger had fallen back into French in his urgency.

'He wants what is——' she began to say 'impossible' and stopped, as she had stopped a minute earlier in her accusation of the royal family. The boy was still looking at her. Almost as if he was saying, 'I am very tired and unhappy in here. Would *you* take me away?' It was the most stupid nonsense and yet she could hear the words in her head as if they had been spoken.

'It—it is ridiculous,' she said. She told her father as quickly and as quietly as his interruptions and the noise around them would allow, what the messenger had said. And all the time she felt the messenger himself trying to influence her mind, the tone of her voice, as if he was a burning glass to focus sunlight on her, until it was so painful she must give in to him.

'But this is his own parliament!' Mr. Broadhurst was saying. 'They are his servants! What do you mean, save him? Bring him out of here? If he is not safe here——'

'Look round you!' the messenger whispered, his grip now fallen on Mr. Broadhurst's thick arm like a hawk's talons into a plump brown hare. 'Whose servants do they look like? Not his. Please, I am begging you to help.'

'And if we were caught?' Hester said.

The man shut his eyes and again his face seemed to dissolve, grow leaden-dull with exhaustion. 'I know. He is not your king. It is not your country. I have no right to ask you and you have every right to be afraid.'

'Afraid?' Hester said in fury. 'For myself I am afraid of nothing. But my father? And my cousin? She has estates here, you know that, we are come to see to them. What would happen—— How can you ask me——'

'I know.' He put up a long hand and rasped it across his chin and up the side of his face as if he was trying to wake himself. 'And if you had agreed the King would not. He has failed us at every turn this past two years. It would be too much to expect him to make a right choice now. But I am so tired I am like a drowning man clutching at anything. I am sorry.' He looked at her as if he was already asleep with his bloodshot eyes still open, and she felt looking into them that she could see inside his head, into his mind and his soul. It was a strange, an extraordinary sensation for a moment. Like looking into the holes in a mask and seeing another face, quite different to the mask's. But the impression was so brief, his face altered again so quickly, that she

[29]

did not know what she had seen, was no longer sure of what she thought even of the mask. Like a Red Indian's face she had seen in a painting in the Academy in London. Hard. Contemptuous. Cruel? The same hawk curve to the nose, the long jaw, the tanned brown skin. Until she could almost imagine the headdress of eagle's feathers, the necklace of bears' teeth.

She wanted to say, 'I would help them if it lay with me alone.' But he was turning away, shrugging, self-mockery in the set of his mouth, and she did not want to make another claim to courage. She already felt fool enough. Instead she looked again towards the royal family in their cramped refuge, like a rat-trap with the grating fallen away. The King still stared vacantly into space. Behind him courtiers whispered urgently. A woman was crying, half-hiding great brown eyes with a lace handkerchief. The Queen sat like a statue, her arm round her daughter's waist. The Dauphin still played with his bandalore. It struck against the King's shoe buckle and the King looked round at him, seeming surprised to find his son there, or himself in such a place.

It was madness, Hester thought. How could that man have imagined—— The King of France wearing her father's coat and English beaver hat, escaping from his own parliament!

And as she thought of it there was the sound of cannon-fire. For a moment the shouting in the long Assembly chamber grew quiet, as the bells had done. And the cannon roared again. They could hear the crack of muskets, like iron hailstones beating on a roof far away. A man came thrusting his way past Mr. Broadhurst, his face livid pale, his cravat falling from his neck. He went on one knee to the King. 'Your Majesty, sire, they are fighting, the Swiss Guards—the people—they are attacking the Tuileries. They will—they will be massacred. They have no orders, sire.'

The courtiers behind the King had come swiftly forward, and caught the newcomer by his shoulders as if he had meant to attack their master.

'They must cease fire,' the King said, something like a ghost of energy in his face and voice for a moment. 'They must not fire on my people. No one must be killed. D'Hervilly, go—give me some paper—I will write and then you must take the order to them. No one must be killed, do you hear me?' Someone gave him paper and something to write with and he scribbled his order, resting the paper on his fat white knee. Hester could see over the kneeling man's head the scrawled, unsteady lines. Like a theatre. Only in a theatre one was not so close to the stage.

Her father was tugging at her arm. 'Your cousin is fainting,' he said. 'We must take her outside into the air.' He said it as though the fault of Léonie's weakness was partly Hester's. 'And we have had no breakfast. What are you gaping at, child?'

Outside the *Manège*, when they had succeeded in forcing their way through the chamber, and the foyer, the sounds of fighting had grown deafening. As if they were on a battlefield. Clouds of smoke, the huge crash of a cannon, the whistle of its massive charge. The bonfire rattle of muskets. And then in the smoke men running. White coats. Red. Blue. Men falling. She could see the roof of the Palace, the black stick figures of men on the parapets and balconies. She saw a man fall, his body turning through the air, imagined she could hear his screaming. She gripped her father's arm and could not move, could not say anything. Men fighting. Battle. She had read of it a thousand times, and thought, if I was only a man! How glorious to fight in a battle! And the stick figure that had fallen from a balcony was gone out of sight. Men were running along the street ten yards from her, and the gunfire, the iron hailstones seemed to follow them. Two of the men fell. Then a third, a fourth. They lay twisting on the stones of the street. And she could not move. To run. To go back, forward, anything. Somewhere, it seemed a long way off, she could hear Léonie screaming. A fifth man staggered, came to his knees and stared at her but he could not see anything, he no longer had a face.

She had to cling to her father's arm not to fall.

'They are fighting!' her father said. 'Good heavens! What next? Look at that poor fellow!'

A woman ran screaming with an axe uplifted over her red bonnet and struck the kneeling, dying, dead man a tremendous blow on the back of what was left of his skull. 'Liberty or Death!' the woman shrieked, and ran on, her rags flying, her sabots like gunshots on the paving stones. And someone's bullet caught her in the back and she twisted round and fell down facing her last victim, still clutching her bloody axe.

'What devils these people are!' said Mr. Broadhurst. 'Don't look, Hester. Léonie! Keep hold of my arm. You girl, support your mistress. Don't faint, child. Damnation, wait until we are home.'

[31]

Chapter 3

'We shall leave tomorrow,' Mr. Broadhurst said. 'I have never felt so outraged in my life. Fighting in the streets! What do they imagine visitors must think of them?'

'I doubt if they care, Papa,' Hester said. 'And I doubt if we shall find horses, either.' She had her cuffs turned up and was sponging Léonie's forehead with vinegar and water, while Euphemia held the basin and a towel, kneeling beside her mistress.

'I am dying,' Léonie said. 'Why did you make me go out today? I could have been still in bed.'

'You are still in bed, or at least on a couch. And there is nothing in the world wrong with you. If you don't sit up at once and drink your broth I shall lose all patience with you. Sit up!'

The great blue velvety eyes opened in shocked reproach, the lashes thick as fringes of dark gold silk, and such an utter lack of intelligence in them, Hester thought, as would have disgraced a doll. She put the vinegar sponge into the basin without much care whether it splashed Léonie and Euphemia or not, and grasped her cousin by her soft round arms. 'Sit up! Drink your broth or I shall do something violent. I have been nursing you for two hours at least and I am sick of it. Euphemia, make her drink it.'

'You hurt me,' Léonie was whimpering. Tears rolled. The Negress drew the golden head against her shoulder, smoothed the peach satin cheek, and gave Hester a look from her own jet and mother-of-pearl eyes that was impossible to interpret. Anger? Irony? But Hester had small inclination to try and went with long impatient strides to the window. The rue du Bac was as empty now in the late afternoon as it had been at three o'clock that morning. The fighting had ended long ago, at least of any organized kind, and even the occasional musket fire, and the screams of men hunted down and butchered where they fell, was no more than an occasional horror in the distance.

It had taken them three hours and more to make their way home, and another quarter of an hour to persuade the old servant to come down from Madame de Richeteau's apartment and let them in. Madame's garçon was gone, and so were their own French servants, and Madame was locked in her room, dead to the world and its terrors with a dose of laudanum. Only the old servant Anne was still shuffling about the house like a ghost. She had promised them a meal but except for the cup of chicken broth for Léonie it was still only a promise.

'Does the villain expect me to change my own shirt buttons? What am I paying him for? Gallivanting off like an apprentice sneaking to a fair. I knew I should have brought Thomas, and you should have brought Mary; it is insanity travelling without proper servants, and expecting to find some in a country like this. I remember with your mother——'

'Papa, it was you——' Hester began, but it was futile to remind her father of facts at times of difficulty, and there was a man running along the street, or rather limping than running, blood on his shirt, with no coat nor hat. He stumbled, and saved himself, leaning against a doorway. Looked back as if he was looking for pursuers, and then up towards the window where Hester stood leaning out over the balcony. It was their 'messenger' of the morning, and of the Assembly chamber. He made to lift his arm to her. His face was like wax, all blood and colour gone from it. He called something out that she could not hear, took half a dozen more stumbling, half-running steps, and collapsed under her balcony. In the distance she thought she could hear shouting, like hounds running a fox.

'I must go downstairs,' she cried. 'Papa, help me, there is someone, the Count's messenger, he is down below wounded.' She was already out of the apartment, and taking the marble stairs three at a time. 'Hester, you will break your neck.' She did in fact trip over her skirts, and fell the last six treads, breaking her fall with her outstretched hands.

'I told you!'

She took no notice of him and wrenched back the bolts that old

Anne had pushed home again when she had let them in. The man lay on the step. She picked him up by the shoulders and began to drag him inside. She could hear the hunt now as clear as a view halloo on the Downs at home. Running feet, sabots, nailed boots. 'Take his legs, Papa! Quickly!'

'What the devil?' But Mr. Broadhurst did lift the man's legs, and they were inside and she was closing the door. And saw the bloodstains on the stone step. Nothing to cover them with. She bent down and wiped them as best she could with her skirts. There was dust in the corner of the doorway and she scooped it out with her fingers and scattered it on what was left of the mark. They would still see it if they looked, but it was almost hidden. The door shut. The bolts. And the crash of running feet was within ten yards, five, outside the door. She leaned against it.

'Hester!'

'Be quiet, Papa!' she whispered.

A dozen, twenty, thirty hunters clattering and shouting by, checking ten yards further on at the entrance to a stable court-yard, hammering on the timber gates. 'Open up! In the name of the Section! Open up!'

Listening, holding her breath. If they turned back. More shouting, as if someone had opened a wicket door and was protesting, the sounds of the hunters forcing their way into the courtyard, a woman screaming from a window somewhere. More running feet outside. More shouts. 'This way! Down here, he must have gone down here! Follow me!' The sounds dying. On the black and white chess-board of the marble floor the man lay unconscious, blood spreading slowly from his leg.

'Upstairs, Papa. We must bind his leg and then find a doctor. He is bleeding to death.'

Mr. Broadhurst was bending down to examine him. 'Good heavens, child, it's the man who came here this morning!'

'I know, I know, Papa, but he will still bleed to death if we don't hasten. Give me something, give me your shirt-tail.' And before her father could object she had pulled his shirt front out of his breeches top and had ripped a long strip from it. 'We must bind above the wound, if we can find it.'

There was a ragged hole a few inches above the knee, on the inside of his left thigh. The blood was pumping from it with an ugly, urgency, dark crimson in the shadowy light of the hall. She

[34]

made a tourniquet, twisting the linen strip into a cord, and tied it as tight round the leg above the wound as she could. It needed to be made tighter still, but already the bleeding had lessened. They lifted him again by shoulders and knees and carried him up the stairs, Mr. Broadhurst cursing Frenchmen and Paris and the Revolution and the missing servants and the ruin of his shirt at every step.

'My breeches will be ruined as well, you cannot get bloodstains out of buckskin, it's impossible, what the devil has this man been doing to get himself shot? I knew he was a fool the minute I clapped eyes on him. Don't push me, Hester, I cannot climb backwards as fast as you can go forwards, I shall drop the fellow if you don't take care. What a weight he is, why the deuce could he not choose somewhere else to behave like this?'

They carried him into the apartment and for lack of anywhere else to put him laid him on Hester's bed.

'Euphemia!' Hester called, 'Someone has been hurt. You must run down to the floor below and get the old woman there to go with you for a doctor. At once, as fast as you can or he will die.'

The bleeding had become bad again with their carrying him up the stairs. It ran swift and terrifying from the wound. Hester had to lean against the bed-post for a second to prevent herself from becoming faint. 'Give me a spoon, papa. I must press some-thing——'

'A spoon?' cried Mr. Broadhurst, as though he had never heard of one. 'Look at your sheets! Poor devil, I'd say he's done for by the colour of him. I knew we should never have stayed in Paris, it was the sheerest madness.'

She could not answer him. She was searching for anything on her dressing-table that would serve to twist the tourniquet tight enough. A comb, the handle of a hairbrush? Behind her Euphemia was by the bed, quiet and dark as a shadow, touching the man's leg with her black fingers, whispering.

'I told you to run below, and fetch help.'

The Negress took no notice of her. She had bent down and was putting her ear close to the man's chest, laying it against his heart. From the next room Léonie was calling fretfully, 'Euphemia, where are you gone, what is happening?' The Negress loosened the man's belt. From her apron pocket she took a small knife and began to slit the cloth of the breeches above

[35]

and below the tourniquet. She pulled the last of it gently free. The blood gushed and then stopped. She had her black thumb pressed deep into the man's naked groin.

'You see this place, madame?' she said. 'Put your own thumb where mine is and I shall do something for him. Otherwise he will die.' She spoke so confidently that Hester did as she was told without even thinking it strange to obey. She had to shut her eyes against what was below her, not the naked sex, but the blood. She had not thought that so much blood could come from a wound and leave the man alive. Nor had she thought that it would make her feel faint. She began to count under her breath to control the nausea. One, two, three. She had reached forty-nine before the Negress came back with a cloth bundle and opened it on the bed beside the man's leg. Something that looked like a large hollow nut, stoppered with a bundle of leaves. Other leaves rolled up like fat green cigars and tied round with fibres. A glass jar. A glass tube of powder. And beneath the stoppered nutshell as the black girl lifted it out of the cloth, a snake. Green. Coiled. Flat viper head. The shock of seeing it was so sudden and intense that Hester slackened the pressure of her thumb. The blood spurted, bathed her wrist in warmth. She dared not look at it. Was ashamed of herself, and wanted to be sick, and was irrationally furious with the girl.

'That thing!'

'The deuce, a snake!' Mr. Broadhurst said.

The viper, if it was a viper, had lifted its head. Euphemia, who had gripped Hester's fingers and thumb, and pressed them down again, took the snake by its throat and laid it on the dying man's chest, on his bloody shirt. 'If Monsieur would fetch some milk in a little dish?'

It was a case of arguing or obeying, and Hester felt too sick to argue. 'Fetch her some milk,' she whispered. 'Please, Papa. Downstairs. And tell the old woman to fetch a doctor. For God's sake hurry.'

'No white doctor,' Euphemia said. 'He will tell other people. Then you will all be taken away.'

Hester almost lifted her thumb again in astonishment. The girl's black fingers held hers in place, gently, but with strength. 'I know how to heal him,' the girl said. 'Our kind of medicine. This is nothing. But please, the milk. Samedi must have to drink.' She had unstoppered the nut and was scooping paste into the palm of her hand. Bright red paste. She took a leaf and crumbled it. Grey dust. She palmed the two together and there was a sharp, bitter smell like herbs burning. When she opened her hands again the bright red of the paste had dulled to purple. A thin smoke seemed to be rising from it and the girl moved the large, soft pellet she had made from hand to hand as if it was become very hot. She laid it down on the sheet, took her knife and cut away the tourniquet and patted the unconscious man's cheek, twice, softly, and then struck him, stinging hard. Even in his unconscious state he opened his mouth and grunted. She pushed the rolled-up tourniquet into his mouth like a gag and his teeth clenched on it. And then so quickly Hester could hardly follow what she did she had buried her knife-blade in the wound. Was cutting, probing, slicing flesh. The man arched his back. His eyes opened. He tried to scream, and then clenched his teeth on the twisted linen so hard that they still seemed to grind together in spite of it. Something rolled out of the wound, lay between the man's legs, in a mess of blood. The musket ball. The girl took her lump of dulled paste and pressed it deep into the hole.

This time the man did scream, choked on his gag, and lost consciousness again. The girl was cutting strips from the sheet, making pads and bandages, pressing, twisting, binding, tying. And all the time her hands were moving the little green snake seemed to be following them with its eyes. Mr. Broadhurst was there carrying a wine-glass of milk. The girl took it, clicked her tongue at the sight of the glass instead of the dish she had asked for, hesitated, and ripped away the man's shirt, exposing his flat, hard stomach. She poured a little of the milk into his navel and with a quick rustling sound the snake's head moved towards it. His forked tongue flicking, triangle of head and jaws dipping into the white liquid, the cup of flesh.

The girl whispered. The snake lifted its head, turned it this way and that. 'Loa, loa Rada, come, Samedi, heal flesh, heal your friend, help the gros bon ange, strengthen him. You shall have much milk if he lives. Do not give him to Grand Bois, do not let him go down the Path.' She went on whispering, but in another language, not French, nor the Créole patois she spoke with Léonie when they did not want Hester to understand what they were saying. Her tone pleading, coaxing, talking to the little

[37]

snake as if she was pleading with a lover for a favour. Urgent. Then almost threatening. Wheedling again.

'Lift your hand,' she said to Hester, in French. The snake moved, hesitated, slid down into the man's groin, seemed to nibble at his sex, the tongue swift as lightning.

'You are mad!' Mr. Broadhurst cried. He made to snatch at the viper, and the black girl prevented him.

'He is telling if he is truly a friend,' she said. Hester drew her father away. Behind them the girl's voice grew louder. Léonie came to the door of her room. 'What are you doing, why do you not come to me?'

'You know what I am doing,' the Negress said. 'I am with Samedi.'

Léonie met Hester's eyes, tried to look as if she did not know what the girl meant, and looked away. 'It is all wicked foolishness,' she said, her voice low and uncertain.

'Come and look, matelotte. Come.'

And Léonie went, slowly, but obediently.

'Come, Madame Estaire. Come, monsieur. Samedi is healing.'

They stood behind the kneeling black girl. The snake had coiled itself on the bandage above the wound. It stretched out its head and throat exactly where the musket ball had entered. Blood had begun to stain the linen. They could see the pale yellow of the viper's throat pulsing slowly, as if in the same rhythm as the blood beneath its head.

'He must be admired,' Euphemia said. 'He is a king of serpents. He conquers Death. Stroke him, matelotte, touch him, madame, monsieur. Gently.'

Léonie put out a finger-tip, stroked the flat diamond head. Her whole body shivered as if she was chilled to the bone.

'Madame Estaire. Touch him, show you are his friend.'

'I will not!'

'Please,' Léonie said, 'please Hester, I beg you, do what she says. And you, Uncle, you must.' Her voice so urgent, so unlike its usual languid petulance or honeyed caressing that Hester did as she asked. Cold scaliness. She found herself shivering.

'Uncle, please.'

'You are all gone mad. I would not touch that thing for a hundred guineas. It should be destroyed. And the girl should be——'

The snake seemed to look at him. It was not possible but it seemed also to grow larger. For a moment it was as large as the man's thigh, as his whole body, covered him. Mr. Broadhurst's hand went out towards it, his fingers shaking. He touched the huge, quivering, armoured throat. The snake was quite small, lay as it had been lying, drowsing, motionless. Mr. Broadhurst was stamping away to the door.

'I know what I would do with her,' he said. 'And with that thing.' He made a strange sound, went hurriedly out and to his own room. Hester heard him vomiting into a basin. When she went to him he was sitting on his bed, the basin held between his knees, his face green-ghastly.

'That damned chocolate you gave me for breakfast, such wretched sickly stuff, I never could stomach it. And all that blood! I don't know what the devil that black witch is up to but she seems to have stopped the bleeding all right. We must get a doctor.'

'That snake——' Hester said. She wanted to be sick herself.

'Snake? What snake? What are you talking about?'

She stared at him, felt the sickness like a tide rising and had to run out of his room and find a basin for herself. After a few minutes she felt better, but as drained of strength, as limp as if it was she who had lost half her blood. She had to drag herself back to Léonie and the black girl beside the wounded man. They had covered him with the bedclothes and he lay looking more as if he was quietly asleep than shocked unconscious. His face still wax pale but no longer with that look of death about it. The Red Indian nose curved and powerful, the mouth clamped shut as if to keep life in.

'The snake——?' Hester said, and found she was whispering.

Léonie looked at her in astonishment. Real? Pretended? Euphemia simply looked at her and then away. She began sponging the man's forehead, and said almost indifferently, 'He will get better. Ten, twelve days, then he can walk a little. Do not send for anyone to heal him. They will tell the police and you will be put in prison.'

'We must wash away all the blood,' Hester said, trying to take control. 'Why do you say that about the police? What can you possibly know about it?' But it was so obviously true that she felt a worse fool than before. And it was impossible to take the bloodied sheet from under the man, at least for the present. There *was* a snake, she told herself. There was! She felt the vomit coming and ran. The snake seemed to look up at her from the bottom of the china basin on the washstand as she leaned over it. A green snake. It *had* been there. It had! And then the certainty was gone in a new spasm of retching, and there was room for nothing in her mind but the blood. That dark red flood from inside his thigh. And the man who had knelt down in the road and looked towards them, his face gone, smashed away, the blood pouring. Like a red scarf. And the woman with the axe. She had thought that nothing could have shocked her, nothing could have frightened her. She had dreamed of battles since she was a child. Of heroic actions. Of what she would have done if she had been a man. And now she was worse than a kitchen maid, worse than Léonie. I will not be sick, she commanded herself. I *will* not! And spewed up what felt like her heart.

Chapter 4

The old servant Anne found a doctor for them the next day. Their own servants had come back at six o'clock in the morning, quarrelsome drunk, the valet in someone else's coat and hat and with a gold watch that fell out of his coat cuff as he staggered into the apartment at Mr. Broadhurst's furious summons. He and the maid were dismissed on the spot, shouting threats against spies and foreigners, and they were left without servants, except for Euphemia.

'It does not matter,' Mr. Broadhurst cried. 'Good riddance to 'em, damned thieving villains. I'll have you arrested!' he shouted after them from Hester's window. 'I'll have you hanged!'

The valet turned and shook his fist and fell over. The maid picked him up and they went staggering away down the street towards the river, quarrelling between themselves. 'Villains!' yelled Mr. Broadhurst, in case they had not already discovered his opinion of them. 'Damned looting drunkards. Upon my soul, let them ask me for a character for their next employment and they shall see what I shall give them.'

'Hush, Papa, you will wake him.'

But the man was already awake, tossing in fever, and muttering sentences that were intelligible in themselves, and yet had no meaning for Hester or her father. Speaking of a Colonel Armand. Of men waiting at Compiégne. Of its being too late. Too late. Curse the cowards! And then 'No, you devils, *No*! No!' He started fully awake at that and stared at them as if he did not know who they were or where he was or anything of how he had got there.

'You are safe,' Hester told him, 'we have sent for a doctor for you, you are quite safe.'

He still lay in her bed because there was no other, and she had slept in the ante-room on a mattress provided by Madame de Richeteau's servant. His beard had grown, soot-black, and his skin, already dark with sun tan and weather, was grimed darker still with gunsmoke and dried blood and dust from whatever fighting he had been in.

'We must wash you before the doctor comes,' Hester said. The fears of the day and night before, of being reported to the authorities, Euphemia's warnings, seemed the absurdities they were this morning. Who could object to their caring for a wounded man? And although by a miracle the man had not died of Euphemia's witch-doctoring, it was a miracle, and not one that could be trusted to continue much longer. They had sent Anne to find someone even before their own servants came back to be dismissed. 'We must have you clean at least,' Hester said, 'even if we cannot shave you.'

It gave her a feeling of strength to prepare to wash him. She knew he hated it, and would have prevented her if he could, and it was like taking a small and charitable revenge on him for her own fearsome sickness and horrors of yesterday. And at the same time she could prove to herself that she would not be sick again.

'Euphemia will do it,' Mr. Broadhurst said. 'Euphemia! *Euphemia*!'

'She may hold the basin and the towels. And tell her to bring clean sheets. There are some in a cupboard in the box-room at the end of the corridor, I saw them there. Now, are you ready? I shall not hurt you.'

She had to lift him bodily for Euphemia to put the clean sheet and blanket and towels under him, and she held him, if not easily, at least not staggering under the burden, although he was a tall and strong-made man. As if with all the blood he had lost he had lost half his weight. And she felt her self-confidence coming back like a tide as she lifted and supported him, one arm behind his knees, one under his shoulders. She laid him down again and between them they stripped him naked, ignoring his shivering, sweating protests. After a moment or two he said nothing, looking at them with eyes at once dulled and feverish, as if he no longer cared what they did, or scarcely knew what it was.

He had a fine body, broad and deep-chested, and wide-shouldered, with a narrow waist and long, horseman's legs, the muscles lean and long and hard. When his stomach contracted with the cold of their sponging she could see the ridges of muscle. His arms were tanned to the elbow and his legs from ankle to knee, as if he went mostly in shirt-sleeves and without stockings, and there was a deep vee-shape of red-brown skin on his chest where his shirt collar must usually lie open. The rest of his body was white as paper from the loss of blood.

'You have sent for your own people's doctor?' Euphemia said. She did not look at Hester as she said it. She was lifting the man's sex with her black fingers as if she was a cook in a kitchen handling meat, and sponged under it. 'He is strong,' she said, 'but he will die. I have told you.'

For a moment Hester felt so angry she was astonished at herself. 'Of course he must have a real doctor. He will die without one.' The bandage the girl had put on last night was blood-stained, but not frighteningly so. He had begun to bleed again with their handling him, and it crossed Hester's mind that they might have been wiser, she might have been wiser, to leave him alone. But cleanliness was essential, it was the worst thing in hospitals that they were always so filthy, she had heard a dozen people say it. She put out her hand to lift the wounded leg and clean it. Euphemia took hold of her wrist and held it still.

'No, madame, no.'

'How dare you!'

Euphemia looked at her, without insolence, or defiance, or fear, or any discoverable emotion. Simply looked.

'Cover him up,' Hester said. 'We must keep him warm.' She felt herself shaking. 'Your mistress spoils you, but that does not mean that you can be insolent to me.'

'Yes, madame.'

And the girl was so quiet, so submissive, so—there was no word for it but courteous—so courteous in her slavery—that Hester felt bitterly ashamed, and then still more angry, as though somehow the girl had triumphed over her, made her an utter fool in her own eyes. She began to say something, anything that would restore and establish their proper relationship. And the girl still looked at her as if she knew what Hester was thinking, knew what she was going to think, knew everything there was to know about her, and felt it to be of very small consequence.

'I can imagine beating her,' Hester thought, horror at her own

[43]

feelings and anger at the girl's calmness seeming to twist round and round one another like the strands of a rope, the one strengthening the other. 'I can understand why they beat their slaves.' She had to shut her eyes.

When she opened them again the moment was gone and common sense had come back. Daylight and cleanliness and a sick man and a servant who happened to be black. She was still not well from yesterday, that was all.

'Fetch him some broth and I shall feed him.' And the girl went, obedient and meek, leaving her in command of herself as well as of their patient. Or almost. She had only to glance down at where the covers hid his leg to remember. And when she shut her eyes she could see the kneeling man, the axe. Had that woman dreamed of heroics as a child?

Hester laid her forehead against the cold surface of the bedside table and clenched her teeth. When the doctor comes, she determined, I shall stay and watch. Everything.

He came soon after nine o'clock, when the sick man was asleep again, his fever seeming to have gone down, and something like the beginnings of recovery to show in the colour of his skin, his easier breathing. Or so Hester thought. But the doctor was horrified at his appearance and at what Hester told him had already been done.

'You might have killed him!' he cried, Mr. Broadhurst nodding sombre agreement, with his tone if not with his words. 'Quackery! To let that black creature touch him! Touch such a wound with who knows what savage devilments! Adolphe, Adolphe, the bleeding bowl, quickly, boy.' He had an apprentice with him, lantern-jawed and squint-eyed, wearing a dirty brown Holland coat with bloodstains on the sleeves and skirts of it, and with his finger nails in mourning, presumably for the patients he had helped to kill. He unwrapped a white china bowl from a filthy neckcloth, and took a worn red morocco case of scalpels from his sagging coat pocket, thumbing among the contents for one that was sharp enough for his master's needs.

The doctor had meanwhile woken their patient with a hearty jerk at his shoulder. 'Well, well, citizen? What have you been doing eh? Let us have a look.' He pulled back the sheets and clicked his tongue at the sight of the bandage. 'You are lucky gangrene has not set in already,' he said. And before Hester could even guess what he meant to do, let alone prevent him, he had begun to pull off the bloodstained linen as if he was unwrapping a parcel whose contents were guaranteed indestructible. The wounded man screamed with the pain, and jerked his knee, sending the doctor staggering. 'Hold him, Adolphe, hold him, my boy, he's delirious and no wonder.'

'What are you doing?' Hester shouted. 'You have hurt him terribly!' The blood was pumping out. 'Are you mad?'

'That is a doctor's business, madame. Stand away. Stand aside. We hurt to cure. You have near killed him, now I must make good the damage. Look how well he is bleeding already! Catch it in the bowl, Adolphe, it will save cutting him. Draw two pints and then we can staunch him for today. I will make the tourniquet.'

Hester caught him by the shoulders and spun him round to face her. 'Are you a doctor or a butcher? To draw two more pints of blood from him? He was nearly dead yesterday from loss of blood. Stop it now, now, I tell you. He was almost recovered and now he is——'

'Hester, Hester, what are you saying, what is the matter?'

'Leave me alone, Papa, this man is an imbecile.' She began to shake the doctor in her fury. He was small and plump, with eyes like spoiled grapes, grey-pouched and watery, and as she shook him his head rolled back and forward like the bladder on a Fool's stick. His tricorn hat fell off and his wig threatened to follow it. She pushed him to one side. 'Euphemia! *Euphemia!* For mercy's sake come.'

But Euphemia merely stood in the doorway of her mistress's room, looking impassively at Hester, at the furious doctor, at the apprentice Adolphe bent down by the bedside with his white bowl already half filled with blood, his stupid mouth gaping first at Hester and then across the bed towards the Negress. Hester pushed her thumb into the wounded man's inner thigh, where Euphemia had told her to do it yesterday. The bleeding slackened, almost stopped. Only a slow, crimson welling up of blood. 'Euphemia!' Torn between anger and terror, wanting to shout at the girl, to threaten her, and knowing that it would achieve nothing, that the only course was to humiliate herself, to beg for help. And even then it might not be granted. 'He will die,' she said. The doctor was calling her names and crying that never in his professional life, never in the history of medicine had any doctor, had any French doctor, had any Parisian doctor been so insulted, nor any patient so endangered. That he would report her to the police, the Section, the Commune. Crying, 'Murderess! Murderess!' While keeping well away from her, and any possible reach of her hands.

'Send him away, Papa, before I strike him,' Hester said. 'Euphemia, I beg you, you were right, we should have obeyed you, please, you cannot watch him die like this.'

The Negress vanished, and a moment later came back carrying her bundle.

'I shall not stay to watch this blasphemy!' the doctor shouted. 'If that man dies—*when* that man dies—you shall answer for it, it is murder, I shall report this to the Section, murder is being done.'

'Shut the creature up,' Hester cried, 'or I shall not answer for my temper. Monsieur, you have one minute to be out of this room, I would not let you worm my dog. *Get out!*'

Mr. Broadhurst led the doctor away. A door slammed. A few moments later the street door slammed also. Mr. Broadhurst came back. 'French jackanapes,' he said. 'They do not know the meaning of the word doctor, I always thought so.'

'Give me patience! It was you who insisted that he be called—I am going to be sick again. A basin, for pity's sake, give me a basin, anything. I must keep my thumb in place.'

They had him rebandaged and covered at last. He looked as ghastly as if he had been wounded a second time, as indeed he had. Euphemia put away her bundle of remedies. It seemed distantly to Hester in her faintness and nausea that there was something missing. But she felt too ill to try very hard to remember what it was. 'You are a good girl,' she said. Léonie was watching them, leaning in the doorway of her room. She said something in Créole.

'No,' Euphemia said in proper French. 'Once is enough, madame. You do not listen to me, I do not do that again. He will live or he will die.' She looked at Hester out of the ivory corners of her eyes as she said it, saying it, Hester knew, for her benefit and not for Léonie's. Léonie came into the room, with her cat's slow languor and indifference.

'*I* do not care,' she said, also in proper French. 'But he is a fine

[46]

large man to be allowed to die so soon. Lalitté, my cocotte, please, give him a little proper medicine? He would give some woman a lot of joy if he was well again. Maybe even you, eh, ma chère?'

The Negress smiled contemptuously. 'I have my loa,' she said, 'I have the Legba. I do not need that.' They fell into Créole then, as if Hester and her father did not exist, until after a few moments more Léonie said to Hester, 'Leave us alone for a little while. She will make him well. Won't you, matelotte? You see, I do call you matelotte, you are my dear, dearest friend, I am not ashamed to tell everyone, to say it in French. Matelotte, matelotte, you shall sleep beside me tonight in the same room, like at home, I promise.' And turning back to Hester, and her father, 'Now go, cousine, please, monsieur, there is something more to do. She says she will not do it if you are here.'

They left them to whatever it was that needed doing, and again for a moment Hester thought that she remembered, even remembered the snake, and knew that she was dreaming. 'I dreamed last night that there was a snake lying on his chest,' she said to her father as they went into his bedroom for lack of anywhere else to go. By unspoken agreement they seemed both to decide they could not use the ante-chamber, in Hester's case for fear that the Negress might think that they were listening.

'That doctor!' she said, staring into the empty fireplace as though her dream was enacting itself there.

Her father sat on the bed and picked up one of his boots and considered it sombrely. 'I told you you should not have brought this fellow in. That doctor creature will go to the police, I am sure of it, and we shall have untold trouble. Why could you not leave him to do his business as any ordinary girl would do?' But the question was purely rhetorical and he said after a moment, scratching at his head with the pointed end of the dog bone he had picked up with his boot. 'It is an extraordinary thing, Hester, but the moment my sister Jane and her poor wretched husband, and that girl and that black creature stepped out of the coach at home, I knew that nothing but disaster would come of it. I said to myself——'

'Papa, do you really think he will go to the police?' She stood up and began to walk up and down the room. It was too small for the length of her stride and she had to step over her father's outstretched feet. She stopped with her back to the still drawn curtains. 'Such a monstrous fool. And to call us murderers! They could not take any notice of him. I doubt if any patient has ever survived him.'

'For my fellow to call himself a valet!' her father said. 'Look at this boot! For heaven's sake sit down, child, you are making me giddy looming over me like that. If you had not brought him in in the first place——'

'But I did bring him in. And if I had not he would be dead. Oh Papa, think, we must both try and think what we should do.'

'I tell you, I should never have agreed to come here if I had known what it was like. I can scarcely bring myself to say it, and I would not admit it to his face for a thousand pounds, but your Uncle George was quite right, this is a dreadful hell's kitchen of a city and I was quite mad to let you persuade me to bring you here.'

'Papa!'

'I thought of it as it was when I saw it with your mother when—when you were born. Only improved. No one told me they would be killing each other in the streets, and chasing their Sovereign out of his palace like a chimney-boy out of a chimney. And I would not have believed them if they had told me. These damnable estates of your cousin Léonie's! Why could not my brother-in-law look to his own family's affairs instead of leaving them to me, and lying about in a dressing robe all day saying he is dying? He cannot even speak decent English! And as for your aunt Jane!'

'Papa, you know you wanted to come. And you wanted me to come with you. And now we are here——'

'You would not let me rest or sleep till I brought you, and instead of being a help to me——'

'Oh Papa, Papa! What does it matter now who persuaded whom? We are here, and that man is in there. If the police find him they will want to take him away as—I don't know as what, but they will do it, I know, and he will certainly die. And they will probably want to arrest us as well. What shall we do? Euphemia said last night—I don't know how she could guess it, but she said last night that if we——'

'Your cousin spoils that girl until she is useful for nothing. She cannot even make tea. I asked her this morning——'

'Papa, put down that boot, you are ruining it, and listen to me. What are we going to do with him?' She had begun striding up and down again, kicking her father's other boot under the bed in order to clear a path for herself. 'You say it is not like *you* thought it would be! That woman with the axe! I shall not sleep again all my life without dreaming of her. And the man she killed!' She put her hands to her face as she stood against the window.

'We must hide him!' she said, swinging round. 'If—when the police come he must not be here. We can say—we can say that men—that some friends of his came and took him away, we do not know who they were, or anything about them. We will hide him upstairs, in one of the servants' rooms—no! There is an attic above those again! If we can—quick, quick, Papa, we can carry him up in a sheet, each of us taking a corner, it is the only way to save him.' She felt almost as if a hand was pulling her towards the door, a voice was shouting to her, 'It will be too late! Too late in another moment!'

'Hide him from the police? Are you mad?'

'Papa, do you want him to die? And do you want us to be arrested for sheltering him? They may come here at any moment, quick, hurry, we have been wasting time as it is. Papa!'

'Where is my boot? What have you done with my other boot?'

'What do your boots matter? Papa, come with me now, now!' She dragged him up from the bed by the arm, and brought him still protesting that she was mad into the other room. 'Quick, Léonie, Euphemia, we must hide him, we must take him up to the attics. And a mattress, and blankets and——'

The man lay unconscious, looking as if he was already dead. Léonie was at Hester's dressing-table, playing with a hare's-foot and gazing at herself in the mirror. The black girl was putting away her medicines. The idea of their managing to carry the man up several flights of stairs, and then up a ladder into hiding in the attics seemed the madness her father said it was. And if they could do it he would probably die of being moved. Euphemia looked at her and looked away, as if not wishing to let Hester read the mockery in her eyes.

'What else can we do?' Hester cried. She went to the window and opened it and leaned over the balcony. The street was busy with traffic again, people hurrying, not with yesterday's singleness of purpose, but as if they were frightened, and were scurrying to shelter. A coach, loaded with trunks. A cart, a *fiacre*. The *fiacre* stopping under the balcony, a man jumping down before the driver had pulled up the horse. A short, thickset man in a long blue coat and a tricolour sash, a great red and white and blue cockade in his hat. Two ragged guardsmen with muskets and bayonets tumbling out behind him. The first man was already hammering at the street door, shouting, 'Open up! The Section, we are from the Section, open up I say!'

'They are here!' Hester whispered, 'For pity's sake, what shall we do? Under the bed with him, Euphemia, help me lift him, quick, Papa, Léonie, they are outside, hurry, take his feet, gently, now Léonie fetch your own eiderdown, your pillows, lie down here.' Pushing the man under the bed as if he were a trunk, a roll of carpet, wrenching off the bloody sheets, bundling them after him. She had to run into Léonie's room herself, and fetch an armful of bedclothes and pillows, spread them out, push Léonie down onto the bed and cover her. 'Look ill, look as if you have fainted. Papa, the door, answer it when they come. Listen to me. The man was taken away an hour ago, immediately after the doctor left, you understand? Two men came. He was not really badly hurt, he could walk when they helped him. Two men in black. We knew nothing about him. Leave it to me to talk to them. Lie *down*! You are always wanting to lie down, now *do* it.'

She could hear the sounds of the men on the stairs, knocking, kicking at the door. Her father's voice. A man shouting, 'You are hiding a Royalist assassin here, I know it, deliver him to me, I am the Commissary Lenôtre and I have an order from the Section to bring him to the Committee for questioning. And you, who are you? What is your name, citizen?'

Her father shouting in answer, or rather in competition, 'Damn you, sir, take your hands off me, tell those ruffians to stay outside, what the devil do you mean by pushing your way in like a gang of cut-throats, take your hands off me, I tell you, before I knock you down.'

'Papa, Papa! Monsieur, citizen, what is it you want?'

'We have come for the suspect Michel Vernet. I am to bring him before the Committee of the Section. Stand aside, citizeness, it is useless to protest.' A stout, red-faced man who looked as if he might be a butcher in private life.

[50]

'Protest?' Hester cried. 'I do indeed protest, monsieur. We are English visitors, friends of France, of your revolution, and we have been treated shamefully, shamefully I say and I mean to protest to the Commune, to the Mayor.' She was barring his way into the bedroom by simply standing in front of him and towering above him. He stared up at her in astonishment, one fat and hairy hand raised to put her aside.

'Citizeness——'

'A wounded man, one of the brave *sans-culottes* who attacked the tyrant's palace yesterday, came here to be succoured, and he has been kidnapped, monsieur. I fear he may be already dead, murdered. Heaven knows. Is there no law in France?'

'What, madame? Citizeness? Kidnapped? The man——'

'Kidnapped! Abducted!' She struck an attitude that had had a great success in the Christmas charades when she was Boadicea before the Romans. 'That poor brave man! Two villains armed with pistols took him an hour ago, my brave Papa risked his life to defend him but was struck down.'

'Kidnapped?' the butcher shouted. 'He was a Royalist agent, where has he gone, who has taken him away? You monsieur, citizen, where has he gone, I demand to know! I do not believe you, search, search this house!' Shouting contradictions at Mr. Broadhurst, at Hester, at his two helpers who had grounded their muskets and were staring about them as if they were expecting to loot the apartment and were making up their minds where to begin. 'I know he is here! Stand aside, madame, I order you.'

He pushed by her into her bedroom. Euphemia was kneeling by the bed, sponging Léonie's forehead with scented vinegar. Léonie was crying, genuine terror helping artifice. The butcher stopped short, taken aback by the sight of a woman in the bed where he had expected to find a wounded man, or else by Euphemia's blackness or the feeling that he had already lost his prey. He turned fiercely on Hester.

'Where is he? What have you done with him?'

'What is he saying, Hester? Damn this French jabbering, tell me what is he saying? How dare you force your way into a lady's bedroom, you scoundrel? And these ruffians! Out, out of here! They stink like ferrets! Out, I say!' Mr. Broadhurst waved his arms in front of them and they retreated, clasping their muskets to their chests.

[51]

'Search the house!' the butcher roared. 'Stand back, monsieur, we have a warrant from the Section, you interfere with us at your peril, search, you imbeciles, that room there, in there. And there! He cannot be gone, Doctor Robineau said——'

Hester sat down on her dressing-stool, not sure she could trust herself to stand upright much longer. Léonie wept. Only Euphemia seemed unconcerned. The two men with muskets searched Léonie's bedroom, and the small powder closet beyond it where Euphemia had her bed. They pushed Mr. Broadhurst out of their way and searched his bedroom, Mr. Broadhurst threatening them with the English ambassador, with Mr. Pitt, the King. The butcher stood over Léonie and stared down at her as if he wanted to tear back the bedclothes. She opened her drowned blue eyes to look at him and whimpered with fright. The butcher's left foot was actually pushed under the spilled corner of the eiderdown. It could not have been a hand's-breadth from the hidden man. If the man moved, groaned in his unconscious-ness—he had only to cough from the dust under the bed.

I have to say something, get him out of this room, Hester thought. But the butcher was riveted where he stood by the sight of Léonie. She was in a negligée of rose chiffon and satin, her shoulders and bust and throat almost bare. Like cream moulded in a woman's shape. Hester could see the man swallowing. One fat, thick hand moved as if it had a life of its own, like a black and white spider, hovered in the air above the bed, before he brought it under control.

'What is the matter, madame? Mademoiselle?'

'I am frightened,' Léonie whispered. 'What is happening?'

'The men who came to take him away,' Euphemia said. 'They frightened my poor mistress into hysterics. Will they murder him, monsieur?'

The butcher swallowed again, seeming to be returning slowly to reality after looking into Léonie's eyes. 'There were really two men? Someone came——?'

'But have I not told you?' Hester cried. 'Monsieur, if you want to search the entire house! There are garrets, attics, no doubt there are cellars. Why not look on top of the roof?'

'Citizeness, I order you to be silent! You are trying to prevent this poor creature from telling me the truth.' He looked down at the kneeling black girl as if he meant to lift her up and free her from slavery then and there. 'What happened? Tell me the whole truth. Have no fear, the Committee of the Section will protect you as it protects all patriots. You have been a slave, have you not?'

'I am a slave still,' Euphemia said. She seemed able to make her eyes enormous at will, and to fill her expression with pathos.

'A slave still? You are free!' the butcher cried. 'Have they not told you?' He swung his thick body towards Hester as if he held her responsible. 'There is no more slavery, citizeness! How dare you keep this poor benighted girl in ignorance of her rights? Stand up, child, do not kneel to me.' He grasped his tricolour sash and pushed the end of it towards her. 'Here is your warranty of Freedom! If you are ill-treated, come to me, the Commissary Lenôtre, and I shall protect you. Now, tell me what happened.'

'There were two men, monsieur, two men in black, with pistols, we were so frightened of them. They carried him away, he could scarcely walk. Is he dead, monsieur?'

'I hope so. And you let him be taken away! That murderer! That spy!' He had turned himself round again, standing on tiptoe to thrust his face as close as possible up into Mr. Broadhurst's. 'You shall answer for it, you shall answer to the Section, to the Commune. This is not the end of this business, monsieur, it is only the beginning.' He pointed his stubby finger at Hester. 'And you, citizeness, have a care. If you ill-treat that poor girl for telling us the truth you shall answer for it:'

'But she is telling you what I told you,' Hester cried. 'How could we know that he was a Royalist, how could we turn away a wounded man?'

Out of the corner of her eye she could see a hand pushed out from under the hanging eiderdown. The man in the sash had only to look down. Euphemia moved, still on her knees, covered the exposed hand with her crimson satin skirts, and came with a slow suppleness to her feet, like a graceful black snake uncoiling itself.

'Oh monsieur,' she said, grasping the Commissary's hand. 'How can a poor slave thank you?' Lifting the hairy pudginess towards her lips but allowing it to stay a good inch or two away from them. The Commissary flushed even darker red and freed himself as if he too was not anxious for actual contact between black and white.

He shouted at Mr. Broadhurst again. 'I shall make a report of this. Aristocrats! Foreigners! If you touch one hair of that girl's head, I warn you, citizen!' And turning towards Euphemia. 'You are free, free as I am, remember it, citizeness. Be a good patriot, denounce our enemies, no matter who they may be.' Giving a look full of threatening and meaning towards Hester and her father. 'Come, come, citizens.' His men followed him. The door banged. A smell of stale wine and garlic and sweat and unwashed rags hung in the room.

Euphemia took the Vinaigre de Quatre Voleurs and shook it on the bedclothes, into the air. Hester stayed sitting on the stool, unable to stand up. They must fetch the man out from under the bed, he would stifle there. But she could not move for a moment. Euphemia went to the outside door and listened. Léonie cried in a weak voice, 'That man! How he smelt! Are they gone?'

'I have never been so angry in my life!' Mr. Broadhurst shouted. 'To come bursting in on us!' He had to struggle for breath. 'And to call us foreigners! To insult me in my own house!'

'Papa, we are foreigners to them, and it is not our house.' She felt so tired it was difficult to think.

'We are English, damn them,' Mr. Broadhurst said. He went to the window as if he meant to shout it after the three men.

'Help us to draw him out from under the bed, Papa. He cannot breathe.'

Euphemia was already there, and between them they brought him out into the air. He looked dreadful, his mouth open, his breath rasping. The bleeding had begun again.

'Get up!' Hester said to Léonie.

'You wanted me to lie down.'

'And now I want you to get up! Cannot you see the man is dying, can you see nothing but yourself, ever?'

Léonie gave a wail of wretchedness at being so attacked. Euphemia took hold of her hands, gently raised her up in the bed. 'Ma pauvre petite, ma poupée, come, Lalitté will put you to bed in your own room, she will make you a tisane, come, take no notice of her.' Whispering then in Créole, putting her arm round Léonie's yielding waist, lifting her out of the bed like a great white and gold Persian kitten.

'I shall kill her,' Hester said between her teeth. 'I swear before Heaven. Lift his legs gently, Papa.'

'We shall leave here tomorrow,' Mr. Broadhurst said. 'Tonight. I would not spend another hour in this ruffian town, not for a pension, the place smells like a tavern. Your cousin's damnable scents are bad enough, but——'

'Gently, Papa! Euphemia, please, come quick! He is bleeding again. Quickly!'

Euphemia came, slowly, looking at Hester, at Mr. Broadhurst, not quite smiling, but the hint of it there, in the way the dark, purplish lips parted over the white blaze of her teeth, her flattened nostrils seeming to flare slightly outwards, her great eyes widening still more under the round black forehead. It was impossible to tell what she was thinking. An absurd temptation came to Hester to ask her what would happen now, whether the men would come back. And she felt for a moment as if Euphemia knew what she wanted to ask her, and could answer if she wished.

'How can we leave here?' she said impatiently. 'He cannot be moved for days.' She went to the window so as not to look at what Euphemia was doing, and stared down into the street. The *fiacre* was gone. People were hurrying. It was only imagination that there was fear in their hurrying. Imagination. A fat, absurd creature in a stupid sash who should be behind his butcher's counter. What was there to be afraid of? At the worst they might have to make explanations, find an intelligent man in authority to whom they could explain exactly what had happened. But she could see nothing but the woman with the axe. The kneeling man. And this man lying on the bed. As if Sussex was another world, as if everything she had ever learned or thought was meaningless. Surely this could not be the reality of what was happening here?

Those men in the Assembly, the crowd outside the Palace, the rags, the shouting, the filthy insults, the woman with her basket of rotting fish? The killing? Was that what revolution really meant? It was not possible. She put her hands over her face.

'Madame Estairre! Hold him down, I must hurt him, hold him tight.'

She held his wrists, and he jerked his whole body upwards, such a burst of strength that she needed to bear down with all her force to hold him. He lay limp, shuddering, staring at her with uncomprehending eyes. Euphemia bandaged him.

'Will they—come back?' Hester whispered. Could not prevent herself.

'Not for a time,' Euphemia said.

Chapter 5

The nursing fell to Hester, or almost all of it. Euphemia helped her to wash him and do such things as needed two women, or she sat with him while Hester dined downstairs with her father and Léonie and old Madame de Richeteau, listening to stories of Louis XV, and of Léonie's great-grandmother, and of the grandeur of the de Richeteau lineage and their connections with the Trémouilles and the Rohans and the de Luynes. And once or twice Léonie would come and sit beside the bed, holding the man's hand and contriving to look as though it was she who had saved his life. But for most of the hours of the day and night it was Hester who sat with him, or slept on the pallet laid in front of the fireplace, ready to give him water, or dry the sweat from his face, or cover him when he threw off the bedclothes and then lay shivering with fever.

The men from the Section did not come back and the streets were quieter. Or at least there was no fighting. They heard of arrests. Old Anne brought them news, and Hester herself, when she walked out to take the air with her father, could sense that things of great significance were happening. There were soldiers everywhere, columns of men marching towards the eastern barriers. The people in the streets had become more insolent towards anyone who seemed rich, or even well-dressed. Once they saw a priest being arrested and taken to the Section. A mob gathered round the small squad of tatterdermalion soldiers taking him from his house, and shrieked abuse. 'A bas les calotins! Voilà un jean-foutre! À la lanterne!' But they did not go beyond abusing him. And it was not easy for foreigners, or indeed for anyone, to tell what lay behind the arrests, and what the authorities intended. Or even who the real authorities were. Only a sense

[56]

that with the King's imprisonment there had come a great change in affairs, that something decisive had happened, new men had taken control.

Mr. Broadhurst still spoke of leaving for Nantes at once, or at least tomorrow or the next day, and but for the wounded man Hester would have agreed with him. If they could get passports. And horses. But until he was well enough to be moved and could tell them of a safe place to take him to, it was out of the question even to think of it. And for days he was too feverish to tell them anything. It began to seem to Hester that she had been nursing him for ever. That it was the most natural thing in the world to lift his naked body, wash and dry it, change his linen, hold up his head on the crook of her arm to feed him with broth. Sit watching him as he slept. She began to feel that she knew him better than she knew anyone else on earth. And yet she knew almost nothing about him beyond his name. Michel Vernet. And that he was in some way connected with the Count de Richeteau, Léonie's great-uncle. Here and there, as he talked in his fever, she gathered or guessed a few more details. That he had been a soldier and had fought in America. He talked again of the Colonel, Colonel Armand. Of a man called Patrick. Of Indians. He seemed to think that he was with the Indians now, hunting in a forest. The second night as he muttered and twisted and tried to crawl out of the bed she realized that in his delirium it was men that he was hunting. Redcoats. Tories.

She would have to hold him down while he cursed her in French, in English, in a guttural language of which she could not recognize a syllable. His eyes burning in the candlelight, mad with fever and then like grey glass, blind with weakness, spent and dying, so that she thought he would not live until morning. She still did not like him, there was nothing likeable about him except his helplessness. A man does not change his character for being ill. And yet there was a sense of more than pleasure in nursing him. A kind of triumph in having such control over him, over a man who had so clearly disliked her at first sight. He had seemed like a man who had had small respect for any women except to make use of them. She wondered how he would feel when he was well enough to realize what had happened to him and how weak he was.

The moment came in the early hours of the fourth day, about

two o'clock. She heard him moving, woke out of her own light sleep and lifted the candelstick to see what he was doing. He was looking at her, his eyes bewildered, and yet clear of fever.

'Where the devil am I?' he said. Trying to get up and having to clench his teeth against the pain of his leg as he moved. And then 'Madame! What are you—where is this?' Staring round, staring at her again. She had lain down in her shift and her hair was loose on her shoulders. She had an impulse to tell him not to look at her, to shut his eyes or turn his head away. She felt for her nightgown and pulled it round her. 'Lie down,' she said. 'You must not try to move.'

'How long have I been here?'

'Three days. Almost four now.'

He lay back on the pillow. 'And the King?'

'You must not talk.'

He sat up again at that, grunted with pain and propped himself on one arm. 'Tell me!'

'They have taken him to another palace, called the Temple. He is no longer King, at least that's what I have heard. Lie down or your wound will break open. You have almost died. You must do what I say or you will die.' His face was sheathed in sweat already, silvery in the candlelight. He had to lie back for weakness. He began cursing under his breath. The fever seemed to be coming back.

'Don't tire yourself.'

'And you've been nursing me?'

'All of us.'

'How did I come here? This is your lodging? Madame de Richeteau's house?'

'Yes. You just came here. You had been in the fighting and you were shot.'

'I know.'

She began to sponge his face. He was sodden with sweat, and she lifted the covers away to sponge and dry his chest and stomach. He tried to prevent her. 'Stop it, girl! What are you doing? I——'

'You have to be kept clean,' she said, 'do you think I haven't done this already?'

He turned his head away from her.

'I must lift you up.' She put her arm under his shoulders. It was an extraordinary thing. She had done it a dozen, twenty times while he was unconscious. And now she found herself flushing, her face burning. She almost dropped him. His naked body against her arm, her own arm bare to the elbow. His head fallen back, something between horror and despair in his eyes. And then something else. As if he had never seen her before. Astonishment. And she knelt by the bed holding him, her hair fallen forward onto his chest, copper bronze against white, the candlelight throwing shadows, brightness, the glisten of his eyes, of her hair, the gold bracelet on her wrist, her grandmother's emerald ring. The whiteness of his body, and then the dark skin where he was sun burned. Her own arm as though it had been dusted with gold, like pollen. His hair like midnight, the darkest of shadows. As if he was her child. Her—lover. Like a shock. Like touching fire. A word she had never dreamed of, that had never entered her mind. Her lover! And that sense of burning, her face burning, flowed through her as if her entire body was flushing scarlet.

She must move, do something, go on with drying him, lay him down again, cover him. And she could not move. She wanted—imagined putting down her head until her hair covered both of them like a curtain. She did lower her head a little, until her hair lay spread out on his chest, a heavy mass of it. It spilled down his side. I am mad, she thought, and could not do anything. Could not draw back, control her mind. Her mouth so close to his that she could feel his breath.

She heard him moving, his hand moving. His arm behind her neck. Pulling her down until their mouths were touching. His dry with fever, parched, dry and burning. What are you doing? What is happening? Her questions made no sound, made no sense. Held him against her as if by her own strength she could heal him. And the sense of burning.

She was no longer kissing him, he was whispering against her mouth. 'Lie down beside me. I'll die of it, but lie down with me, now, now.' His hands at her shift, she did not know what he was doing, and then his body shivered, grew rigid, he made a furious sound of agony between his clenched teeth and lay slack and barely conscious in her arms, his head fallen sideways away from her, sweat running like water on his throat, his back, so that her shift was soaked with it, her arms wet. She looked at him for a moment of bewilderment. And very slowly put down her mouth against the brown skin of his neck. The taste of salt. Cold damp.

And she thought on the instant, 'He is dying, dying! What have I done, what has happened?' She began to cry out for Euphemia, checked herself for a second as if no one must see this, know of this. But of what? Know what? '*Euphemia*!' She let go of him to run for help, held him close again, laid him down on the pillows. And the black girl was in the doorway, yawning, naked as she had rolled out of her bed, or Léonie's. 'Help me, he is dying, I have killed him!'

The black girl came and knelt beside her and peeled back the last of the covering from his legs. Blood. The black hands on the white skin, touching, feeling, lying still.

'What have you done, madame?' The eyes huge, knowing.

'Nothing! I lifted him up and—and—nothing! What do you mean?'

Euphemia made a clicking sound with her tongue. 'If you do that again he will die, he will die for certain.' She laughed, a low whispering of laughter full of malice.

'Do what? What do you mean?'

'Make love to him. Oh, madame!'

'Make—love?' Staring at the black girl as if she did not know what the word was. 'Are you—are you gone mad?' They knelt looking at one another, Hester too astonished, too frightened at what had happened, to be angry. Euphemia's expression changing from a cruel amusement to a slow incredulity.

'You don't know?' Euphemia said at last. 'You don't know anything.' Astonishment, something close to pity, contempt and again pity in her eyes. Kneeling naked, and yet dressed in her black velvet skin. Black velvet lap. The unconscious man naked in the bed. Only Hester covered, half-covered, in her damp muslin shift. And she felt that of the three of them it was she who was indecent. Even her breast burned crimson.

'I—I know everything,' she whispered. 'Everything.' She did not know why she said it. Thought suddenly of the hens and the cock in the stable yard at home. Of the bull covering a cow in the field beyond the orchard. Two farm boys with one of the dairymaids, in the dairy, breathless with laughter, and then running away when they realized that she was there. 'I know everything,' she said again. 'But——' What had that to do with

[60]

this, with—with holding up his head to—she felt the taste of the salt sweat on her mouth, tried to remember what had happened. Nothing! Love? Making love? 'You are mad! Wicked! How can you be so evil?'

Euphemia reached out and took her wrist. The black fingers cold. Drawing her hand forward, laying it palm upwards in Euphemia's lap. Coldness of fingers, warmth of lap. Bending her head down. 'Hold the candle nearer,' she said. And without knowing that she was doing it Hester obeyed her, held it so that the candlelight fell on black skin and white, on Euphemia's sea-coal hair, smooth, brown gleaming back.

'Loh! Loh! Here is so much love, to burn a man to ashes. Oh madame! And killing! You will kill more men than this one. You won't kill him, he is too strong, but others! Oh, oh, here is the path of the Grand Bois. So much death! Oh madame!'

Lifting her eyes to Hester's, for the first time something near to respect in them. 'Now I will bring him back to you.' She held Hester's knuckles against her breast for a moment, against the ribs over her heart. Hester could feel the beating of it and it seemed to stay with her when the Negress let go of her hand. Stayed in her knuckles, in her arm, seemed to become part of her own heart-beat.

She wanted to ask what the girl meant, but she could not make herself say anything. Euphemia went into Léonie's bedroom, and Hester knelt up and looked at the man. The girl was mad, evil mad. Making—preventing herself from looking at his groin, at his sex. But she did not cover it. Looked instead at his face. They had managed to shave him, Euphemia shaving him with Mr. Broadhurst's razors, while Hester held him still and turned his head this way and that. They had cut his cheek just below his left ear, and his chin. And now the stubble was already growing again.

I do not even like him. Making love? As if the girl had emptied filth on her. Why? She no longer wanted to touch him. If she had to lift him again she would not be able to look at him as she did it. What had he said to her? She could not remember, he had only been whispering in fever. She put her hand against his forehead. He was burning. His hands burning. His chest. Every part of him. She must cover him up. She touched his leg. Below the wound. Above it. So much love. To burn a man to ashes. The girl should be whipped. Suddenly she put her hands over her eyes. To ashes. What is in me? I must be mad myself. The two farm boys in the dairy. They had had the girl bent over the milk tub and—no, no! Boys playing a brutal game. Animals. And I? The cock jumping on the clucking hen, treading her down, beating his coloured wings in triumph. No! I lifted him up, nothing else! Love is—what was love?

'I love you,' cousin Henry had said once. When they were ten years old, before she had begun to grow so tall, to tower over him and over most boys. Most men. Love was—to be married, to be a mother, to nurse children, to—she had put all thought of it away long ago, years ago. She was too tall, too strong. And too intelligent. To submit herself to someone like cousin Henry! Or any of his Oxford friends. Or the young men in London, or the neighbours' sons. It had never been thinkable. They wanted wives like Léonie. And she wanted——

She had wanted to be a man. She touched the place where they had cut his chin. The bristles rasped her finger-tip. How had he looked at her just now? She turned his head towards her, opened his eyelid with her finger. 'Lie down beside me,' he had said. And then? She had a savage temptation to do it, to see how it might feel. To lie beside a man, naked. I am gone total mad. So mad that it no longer mattered, like a dream, like something for which one has no responsibility at all. She laid her head on his chest, felt his heart. The girl's heart. Now his. She held her hand against her own side. How hard it beat! Like knocking at a door, thudding. His was beating so feebly that she could scarcely hear it. 'You won't kill him, he is too strong.' But I have nearly killed him, she thought, and instead of terror there was something like astonished pride in thinking it. She had a momentary remembrance of that woman lifting her axe. The woman had been young, her arms bare to the shoulders, already stained with blood. And it was as though she herself was the woman, she knew how she felt, her teeth bared in a shriek of triumph, the strength of her arms as she swung the axe, the crunch of steel into bone. 'So much death.'

Her eyes shut. Looking into the dark.

Euphemia came back with a tumbler filled with a smoky, milky, acrid-smelling liquid. 'Hold up his head, madame.'

They gave him the drink, and it was as though he belonged to her. Completely hers. To heal. To—he lay against her shoulder, swallowed, muttered something, his eyes shut, some of the liquid spilled down his chin. She held him like a possession, as if someone was threatening to take him from her. Still in that curious, suspended state of mind in which she was not responsible for her thoughts, could let them take their own path, drift like clouds, like the wind. The fact that she knew nothing about him, that he had not seemed to like her when they met, had seemed even to dislike her, made no difference, or rather, added to the sense of possession, conquest. Like catching a wild animal in a trap, and it twists this way and that and only binds the wire noose tighter, strangles itself in trying to escape.

Euphemia looked at her and nodded, her eyes saying, 'Yes, yes, madame, he is yours.' She drew up the covers over him while Hester still knelt supporting his head.

'You must let him rest,' Euphemia said. Smiled with her white magnificence of teeth. Hester laid him down, reluctantly, and went to her own mattress by the fire. Euphemia knelt, and covered her up, as though she had decided to become her servant as well as Léonie's and wished the decision to be known. She went back into Léonie's room, and Hester lay awake, listening to his shallow breathing, his occasional whispering and stirring. In the morning, she thought, all this will have gone away, I shall be—I shall be myself again. She shivered, a long shivering from shoulders to feet, a trembling in the muscles of her legs. 'So much love.' What did she mean? It was not possible, it had no meaning. Cousin Henry listening to Miss Fairfax playing the spinet, and swearing that she played like an angel. That was love, God knew, or else he was tone deaf. She laid her hand flat against her heart, under her breast. Love? The way the bull had roared, the cock flapped his wings? It is I who should be whipped, whipped at a cart's-tail. She put her hands over her eyes and the palms were burning.

[63]

Chapter 6

He began to be able to sit up, to talk. It tired him to talk much for the first day or so, but he wanted her to talk to him, and he listened, watching her, a complex of interests behind his eyes, in his expression, the beginnings of a smile that he kept holding back. Neither of them spoke about what had happened. She made herself believe at times that nothing at all had happened. He had had a crisis in the illness and she had brought him through it and now he was mending at last. That was all. She told him so, and he looked at her without answering. And asked her the exact question the young officer had asked her at the Tuileries, the day of the fighting.

'Are all the women in your countryside as tall as you?'

'Of course not.'

'Are you a horsewoman?'

'Yes.' She began to tell him about Bayard, her hunter, who was descended from the Godolphin on his dam's side. About the stables, and the dogs, and the Sussex Downs and fencing with cousin Henry. 'He isn't much good at it, he is going to be a clergyman, but at least he is someone. And there's Samuel the coachman. He was in the Life Guards, but he can only fence with a sabre.' She held out her fist and turned it for a cut.

'You can use a sabre?'

'Oh yes, I am better with it really than with a foil, because poor Henry is almost useless. He doesn't like to fence with me at all now, he says it's immoral for a woman to fence. But that's because he always loses.'

She got up and found a poker and held it *en garde*. Slowly extended her arm until the point of the iron was aimed at his chest. Slid her right foot forward, still very slowly, right knee bent, until she was at full lunge and the tip of the poker touched his shirt. Altered her fist to a sabre grip and cut to his right cheek and then to his left, touching each time. He did not move, his eyes watching hers, amusement, admiration, something else in them.

He took hold of the poker and drew it, and her, towards him. 'Do you want to kill your patient?'

She did not answer. She let go of the brass handle and knelt down beside the bed. 'I must make you comfortable,' she said. But she did not do anything to alter his pillows. He laid down the brass and iron poker on the bed, like a sword between them.

'I must thank your father for letting you nurse me. I owe him a debt. And you a greater one.'

'It is Euphemia who saved you.'

'I must go as soon as it's possible. I've brought you all into danger.'

'The danger is gone. If there was any. You must let yourself get well.'

He looked at his hands, lying on the covers. They had grown pale with illness. Well-shaped hands. The bones long and straight. She wondered what and who he was, apart from having been a soldier, and whether Vernet was his real name. She wanted to touch him. In a moment she would lift him up from the pillows and rearrange them. Hold his head against her shoulder. It was the most natural thing in the world for a woman to find pleasure in nursing the sick. The wickedness of that girl to try and make out that it was—she found herself begin to burn.

He was looking at her, and the flush grew darker, scarlet, made her furious with him. 'What are you smiling at? Do you think it is amusing to have me kneel down to make a man's bed for him?'

He stopped smiling. 'Do you look like that at cousin Henry?'

'What do you mean?'

'No wonder he loses, poor devil.' He took her hand, and closed it into a fist. Touched the sinews on the inside of her wrist with his finger-tips. 'Maybe one day you and I'll fence together. Although I'm better with a gun than a sabre.'

'I must make your bed.'

She was making it when her father came in to bring her for a walk with him.

'That damn fellow,' Mr. Broadhurst said when they were out

of the house. 'How you can stomach puffing up his pillows and—and whatever you do for him. Why the deuce don't you leave it to the black girl? And sleeping in the same room! What would anyone say if they knew of it at home?'

'But they will not know of it, Papa. And suppose he should be taken ill in the night again? I told you, he almost died the other night. He is still so weak that——'

'Your mother would have a fit if she knew.'

'And then she would leave everything exactly as it is, you know it.'

'You ignore all she says, as you do with me, I know that. We shall have to get you married when we are home again, and then you may torment some other poor wretch and leave me to grow old in peace. You are twenty-three, Hester, it is high time you were settled in life, I have meant to say it to you before. Good heavens! Look at that villain over there, did you ever see such a face? And that one! The deuce, what ruffians, where do they come from? I haven't seen a clean shirt in the length of this street. No, we must get you settled, Hester, a nursery full of babes will give you better things to think of than all these books you read and politics and riding harum-scarum over the countryside. Farmer Trower was saying to me only the day before we left, he never saw anything like you, he was sure you would break your neck. Get away from me, curse you, tell her to be off with herself, Hester, ally-voo you damnable hag, ally-off!'

They had begun to be surrounded by a small crowd. 'We had best go back, Papa. Citizens, we are English visitors, we wish you every good fortune, let us by if you please.'

'Unwashed scoundrels.'

Something else distracted the crowd's attention, and it began running down the street after a loaded coach, shouting, 'Stop the horses, stop them, search inside!'

They turned back, Hester trying to make her father hurry. She was not afraid for herself, but she had a sudden fear that the men from the Section might come again, were already there. 'We must hide him in the loft,' she said. 'We could move him now, he can help us himself to get up the ladder. We cannot leave him where he is.'

'Damnation, you race along as if you were on horseback. I won't hurry for these devils. As for that fellow, surely he has some friends in Paris who could look after him? I should like to leave for Nantes as soon as we get word again from old de Richeteau. Even in these times he must have got my new letter by now. Telling us to go back to England! If he does not answer, we shall simply go to him and make him do what is necessary. As like as not he has his eye on his own advantage out of this business and would as soon see the devil arriving as your cousin Léonie and someone to protect her interests. We should have gone already but for this Vernet fellow of yours.'

'He is not mine, Papa. Oh please, hurry! Hurry! I should not have left him.'

But nothing had happened. Only the news that old Anne gave them at dinner was worse than ever. Of more arrests, of stories of a plot to burn the city, to murder the government, to murder everyone. Rumours full of old woman's terrors and nonsense, but behind them an atmosphere that Hester had felt herself in the street, of a new storm gathering, like the tocsin sounding the day of the fighting and the King's arrest. Old Madame de Richeteau trembled at every word her servant repeated, clinging to her rosary beads even while she was eating. She was eighty-seven, and sometimes her mind wandered, so that she was not quite sure who Mr. Broadhurst was, or any of them. She had got worse in the past days, as if the rumours had driven away the remains of her wits, and she thought that she was still living in the de Richeteau mansion, with a staff of servants, and her coach waiting below in the courtyard. She would tell Anne to summon this or that manservant who was probably dead for the past forty years, so that they might go out into the streets and gather more news. It made for an uncomfortable meal, and Hester was on tenterhooks throughout it, waiting for the moment she could carry out her plan for bringing Monsieur Vernet up to the loft.

It took a good hour to manage it, and when it was done he lay on his pallet bed so spent with the effort that she was afraid again that she had killed him. While her father was not there she brought a mattress up for herself and laid it with pillows and covers in a corner of the loft, trying to ignore Euphemia as she did it. Until at last she was alone with him. Supper finished, her father gone to bed, the house quiet, the candlelight throwing unfamiliar shadows. Roof beams. A black leather trunk with a velvet mantle of grey dust. The stool they had brought up, the white china wash-basin and ewer that had been in one of the servants' rooms, set on the floor.

The man lay asleep. She made herself comfortable on her mattress, watching him. The rise and fall of his chest. The shadows moving slightly on his face, round his mouth, as he breathed in and out, as the candle-flame bent forwards in a stirring of the dusty, stifling air under the roof. High time you were settled in life. A nursery full of babes. Oh no, oh no. I have not come so far as this, she thought, to go home and marry cousin Henry, which was what her father meant. Had meant for the past five years.

'You are a handsome girl, Hester,' he had said long ago. 'I am your father, but even I can see that. You will make a splendid mother for your children. But I have to be frank with you, my dear, your mother cannot say it to you, so I must. You frighten men out of their wits. I thought you might make a hit of it with Tom Fairfax, but he took off like a hare at the very hint of it. It is bad enough that you are very near six foot tall, and you are scarce eighteen, and not yet finished growing. But the way you behave!'

'But you are six foot, Papa, why should I not be?'

'Because you are a girl, of course! A man does not want a wife like a grenadier! You must make them think you are smaller than you are, damnation, that you are tender and weak like every other woman. And you go and lift Tom up in your arms to show him how strong you are, and offer to wrestle him for a guinea! Good grief, child, I doubt he is stopped running yet.'

'I do not mean to marry anyone and certainly not Tom.'

'You do not know what you are saying, Hester. Of course you will marry. If you were to marry Henry——'

'Cousin Henry! Papa! Are you mad?'

'It would keep the estate together and he has a great admiration for you. So has your uncle George.'

'Papa!' And she had known that it was her mother's wish, and not her father's. So that she would be out of the house, out of the way. She tried to stifle the thought before it took full shape, but it was impossible. Her mother had never liked her, and these last years she had known it more and more. And but for Papa she would have been glad enough herself to leave, and be free of that cold and irritable dislike that always seemed to lie below the surface of all the conventional shows of affection between her mother and herself. It was a thought that had come back to her again and again since that converstaion of five years ago. Of how pleasant it might be to become her own mistress. Except that the price seemed very high. To marry Henry! Or someone like him. To watch him as—as he lay in bed like—like this? Naked? To—hold him? She went and knelt close to the other bed, lifted the candle, and then shielded the flame with her hand. In all their lives together, in all their childhood, she had never seen cousin Henry naked. What did he look like without clothes? Not like this man. He would be thin and flat-chested, with bony knees and spindly legs. Did that matter? Was love anything to do with—the way flesh is shaped? A body?

For men, yes. A woman must be—her face—and—— But for the woman? Papa was handsome. Had that mattered to Mama? How could one know? Who could one ask? And she thought of Euphemia. Saw her face. Her smile. Knew the answer to what she had been thinking as if Euphemia was there, speaking. She wanted to pull back the covers, touch him. How beautiful his body was. She had not thought of it before. Not thought of the word as having anything to do with men. The depth and breadth of his chest, the long, flat curving muscles of his legs. His feet. Long, narrow feet. She would not touch the covers. Would not touch him. Only like thinking of a statue, of a picture. His face? That was not beautiful at all, except in the way that a savage, a weapon might be. The blade of a sabre, the way the hilt fits to the hand. She closed her fist. Cut to the left. Cut to the right. Parry. Cut low. Dear Samuel.

What is in me? What is it? Felt the trembling, the shivering of her body, her hand with its own life, taking hold of the covers. Had Mama felt this? Ever? For Papa? She buried her forehead in the quilt, clenched the silk between her teeth until her jaws hurt. I will not touch him, I will not. I will not look at him. Downstairs there were sounds, a brutality of noise, far down in the house, by the street door. She heard it for a second without moving, without knowing what she had heard. And was on her feet, knocking her head against the roof-beam. They had come back! She was right, they had come back for him, were going to search. She stood with her hands flat against her body, under her breast, listening. She must go down, be there, be in bed, seem to have been—Papa—

the ladder, the ladder up here to the loft. All in the second of listening.

She knelt again and shook him, whispering. 'Wake up, wake up, you must help me to help you, there are men come to search.'

His eyes open, clouded with the drug Euphemia had given him an hour ago. Trying to clear his head. Trying to sit up.

'I must go down to them. And you must take the ladder up, you must try and lift it in here. I shall push it up to you. And then you must reset the trap-door. Can you understand me?'

'Yes.'

Climb down. Push the loose wooden ladder up into the dark throat of the loft. His face beside it, candlelight behind him, shadowing him. 'Put out the candle.'

Downstairs, the crash of musket butts, the sounds of a troop of men, how many? Already crowding, pushing, hammering their way into the apartment. Ten, twenty men, Euphemia opening the door to them, Mr. Broadhurst shouting, protesting, holding his night candlestick. The Commissary, three other men in sashes, cockades in their hats. The sour smell of dirty wool, dirtier boots and sabots, the soldiers filling the landing, more on the stairs. Their eyes wide as they saw her.

'Where have you been, citizeness?'

'How can you ask such a question of a woman, monsieur, in the middle of the night?' Heaven's mercy, her bed, there would be no sign of its being slept in. She forced her way past the Commissary and his three colleagues, half a dozen of the soldiers. 'What is it you want, messieurs? Citizens? I told you, we knew nothing of that man.' In her room. And the bed was tossed, the covers thrown aside, the pillow dented. She saw Euphemia looking at her through the doorway. Behind her the Commissary was shouting, 'Search the apartment. All papers, all books. Citizeness, do not attempt to hide anything. Monsieur, you will make a statement to me, you will answer every question truthfully or it will be the worse for you.'

'What statement? What questions? My father does not speak any French, he cannot answer you.' Two soldiers dragging her bed aside, another soldier pulling out the drawers of her dressing-table, scattering contents, finding two letters, seizing them, holding them up.

'Papers, citizen Commissary! Papers!'

'Give them to me!'

'They are from my cousin. What do you want here, are you mad?'

Léonie screaming in Créole and then in French, 'You are ruining my gowns, don't touch them, you filthy wretches, get out of my bedroom, *Euphemia! Hester! Help!*'

'In the name of the Section I order you to allow the search, citizeness. We do not want to use violence.'

A dozen voices shouting, as Mr. Broadhurst tried to defend his mahogany travelling chest. 'The keys, monsieur, the keys! Your only hope is to confess everything. Sergeant, break open that box.' The splintering of wood, a scream of fury from Mr. Broadhurst, a man staggering back as Mr. Broadhurst flung him away from his beloved treasures of silver brushes and pomades and writing case and men's jewellery and whatever else he kept there. Hands grasping the papers from the writing case in triumph.

'Citizen, you must come with us to the Section, bring those papers, sergeant, and those books, there will be a code in them. I warn you to come come with us of your own accord, citizen, or you will be brought by force.'

'You cannot! Papa, Papa, they want to take you away. No!' Standing between her father and the soldiers, her hand lifted to strike the first man that touched him.

'Citizeness, stand aside. I warn you!'

A soldier stepped forward to put her out of the way and she hit him with all her strength. He fell as if he had been hit with a musket butt, his face astonished, blood streaming from his nose and mouth. Four men grasped her by the arms, forced her against the wall.

'Come, citizen, we do not want to do violence to women. Tell the citizeness to control herself or we must bring her as well.'

'He cannot speak French, I tell you, what do you want with him?'

'We suspect Monsieur Broadhurst of being an enemy of the people, an agent of the English government, and the *émigré* army. Your coat, monsieur, and your hat, unless you wish to go bareheaded.'

Nightmare. It could not happen. A flood of men pouring down the marble stairs, into the hall, her father almost carried by them.

[71]

Still in his shirt-sleeves, dishevelled and unbuttoned, just as he had dragged on his clothes when the soldiers came. Into the street. A crowd had gathered, even at this hour of the night. What time was it? One in the morning? Two? Men, women, pushing, shouting.

'A plotter, they've caught a plotter! One of the murderers!'

'It's a priest, a *calotin*! Filthy *jean-foutre*!'

'A plotter, one of the assassins.'

She was still in her shift and nightgown, her slippers, running after the soldiers as if she was a madwoman, her hair loose, crying out, 'Papa, Papa!' Without knowing it, her own voice coming to her like echoes, like the shouted insults of the crowd. The soldiers themselves were shouting, 'Make way, he's dangerous, look at the animal, he was going to murder us all, he was going to murder the Patriot Pétion, the Patriot Marat, we've caught one of the nest of rats, make way.'

A building. Stairs. Office. Men shouting. She had to translate, without knowing what she was saying, what was happening. They wanted her father to sign a paper.

'I'll sign nothing, damn their eyes! Monsters! Rights of Man! They should be hanged! Go home, Hester, go to the Embassy tomorrow and we shall have these villains set to their rightabouts, I shall have you hanged for the damned murderous ruffian that you are, sir. They broke open my box! My private papers! The thieving brutes. My ambassador, sir, Lord Gower, that is who will deal with you, the ambassador of His Majesty King George the Third, damn your French soul. Go back to bed, Hester. Heaven above, you are in your nightgown, you have no bonnet, what will people think? Don't speak to these ruffians, cover your chest girl!'

Looking down at himself, the knees of his breeches undone, his stockings round his ankles. 'What do they mean to do with me? By heaven, I shall have satisfaction for this!'

A man with a sneering face behind the long table, shuffling up his papers. Other men, grey-faced with exhaustion. Unshaven, red-rimmed eyes. 'Take him to the Commune, the Comité de Surveillance, citizen Commissary. Guard him well.'

More nightmare of streets. Crossing the river. The Place de Grève. A courtyard. The Hôtel de Ville, echoes in stone corridors, cold damp of the river, of winters caught in stone. A small room crammed with men shouting. Her father's box of papers handed through, tossed about like an ark on the waves. Men in tricolour sashes, rags, hoarse with shouting, stinking of stale sweat, an air of sleeplessness, dirty clothes.

Downstairs again. Another building. Someone saying, 'The Mairie, the Dépôt, the Citizen Marat will question him.'

Sudden quiet. Five men behind a table. Better dressed. But the same stale air of sleeplessness, exhausted hatred. The man in the centre of the five with a black fringe of hair above drooping, bloodshot eyes and a thick, clumsy mouth and nose. Savagery and madness in the way his mouth clenched and unclenched. Thick fingers scratching under his shirt, his body twitching.

'This is the Englishman?' he said in a heavily accented English. 'We know all about you. You had better confess at once, there is the guillotine for recalcitrants.'

'The guillotine? Are you mad, sir? Upon my soul, you look it. I demand that you send word to my ambassador. I am an English gentleman, a visitor here, damn my stupidity for coming into your vile country. My daughter has been brutally handled by your ruffians, my box has been broken open——'

A soldier emptied an armful of papers onto the table. Most of them about Léonie's estates, that were to come to her from her father's mother's family. Letters from her father when they were in Saint-Domingue. From the Comte de Richeteau, her great-uncle. From lawyers. Tenants. Notaries. The five men behind the table reached and looked, scattered the papers broadcast as if they knew the look of the documents they wanted.

The man in the centre read in French from a list that had been fastened to the bundle: 'Papers concerning the Limousinière estate near to Saint Fulgent, and the St. André estate in the district of Mervent. Item, maps of the farmlands, of the *manoirs* and their——'

'Maps!' One of the other men sprang to his feet. 'Who sent you here? Who has been giving you your orders? Citizen doctor, I demand that the woman he calls his daughter be arrested also. And the whole nest of *ci-devants* in that house. The woman de Richeteau, why was she not brought here?'

'Patience, patience, citizen. We shall have them all in good time. Sign this.' He pushed a document across the littered table, with a pen and ink. 'Do you claim you cannot understand

[73]

French? This is the *procès-verbal*, saying that you have been arrested and why, and your documents seized, and that you understand.'

'He does not understand!'

'Be quiet, citizeness.' His eyes not meeting hers, and then, when they did, seeming quite mad. And yet he was quieter than the others, almost polite.

Her father was brought away, down corridors, through a stable yard, up flights of stairs to a second storey, to what looked like stable lofts. Six men bringing him. He had stopped protesting, and seemed stunned. It must have been six in the morning, already light. Jailers, ragged soldiers. A woman with a covered basket was crying, 'They won't let me speak to him, messieurs, citizens, my master has had nothing to eat since before yesterday.' An old woman in an apron and wooden sabots, a cotton scarf over white hair.

The door grinding. A sudden stench from beyond it. Darkness, voices of men waking from sleep, growling, alarmed. Her father going in. Not even turning to look towards her until she cried out in terror, 'Papa! Papa!'

He turned then, his hat knocked from his head by the low lintel. He opened his mouth to say something, and the soldiers pushed him into the darkness of the room. She could not hear what he had said. 'Papa! Papa!'

The old woman was at her elbow, tugging the sleeve of her nightgown. 'Speak to them for me, madame, tell them he has had nothing to eat, he will starve, they give them nothing in there.'

She scarcely knew what the old woman had said. A soldier ordered them both down the stairs and when they did not obey other men came and hustled and threatened them away from the door, down the flights of stairs into the stable yard, shouting at them for aristocrats. When they were out in the street the old woman screamed suddenly, 'Yes, I am an aristocrat, imprison me too! I have been a servant all my life, the servant of aristocrats, of good, good people. Kill me for it but I shall not deny it.' She sat down with her basket and wept by the gates of the yard.

I should comfort her, Hester thought. I should ask her what one must do. But she could not bear to talk to anyone, to hear the words prison, arrest, tomorrow. She began walking, automatically walking the way they had come, towards the rue du

Bac. People stared at her, called after her, jeered her appearance, her nightgown torn, her hair falling round her shoulders, her slippers, her great height, her despair.

And in all the time she had not thought of telling them where the man was, that he was hidden under the roof. It would not have helped them to betray him, her father would have died rather than let that be done for him. But she had not so much as thought of it, thought of the man at all. She wondered if she should have. It was as if she was walking in her sleep.

Chapter 7

She did not know whether it was the days or the nights that were the worst. At night lying sleepless, trying to think, to plan. Plan what? Think of what? By day haunting the courtyard, the street outside where he was held, bringing him food, clean shirts, talking to him for a moment through the thickness of the timber door until she was forced away by the guards, or must give way to some other frantic woman calling her husband, her master, her father, her lover, also with her covered basket, her bundle of clean shirt and stockings. Bribing the guards to let her talk longer, come back, make sure his food at least had reached him.

Then the search for help, for someone, someone who could help. In a *fiacre*. On foot. Knocking at doors, sitting in waiting-rooms, starting up in hope each time a door opened, a face appeared, to find it indifferent, or full of malice, or fanatic's hatred, or vile suggestions. That she knew would serve nothing if she should have been able to give in to them. Or simply waiting, in halls, ante-rooms, in the street, for this Citizen, that Deputy, the Patriot such-and-such to come back, to come out, to wake up, to have time to receive petitions.

To the Embassy again. And again. His Excellency engaged, out, in the countryside, busy with affairs, one of the affairs being to play with a puppy-dog in the garden. She saw him from the window, and ran down calling, 'My Lord! My Lord!' but he was gone. The Chief Secretary passing her on to a junior who passed her on to an assistant, a young man with a stammer who passed her on to an elderly clerk, until in the end no one would receive her.

'My dear ma'am,' the Secretary had said at that first interview, eyeing her from the calmness of his safety, his diplomat's splendour, his consciousness that nothing dreadful ever happens to anyone unless it is grossly their fault. 'My dear ma'am, was it not a twifle ill-advised for you to come to Pawis at such a time? But I do assure you, if your farver is innocent, as I am sure he is, he will weceive the fairwest of hearwings. We are in constant touch with the authowities and His Excellency will make evewy wepwesentation.' While his cold, handsome eyes said clearer than his drawl, 'Your farver must be a weal Tom Paine sort of wascal to have come here at all, and jolly well serve him wight.'

'We did not know what it would be like!' she cried in fury, answering his accusing look rather than his words. 'We thought—I thought——'

'Pway, ma'am, don't upset yourself. Thomas! Thomas! Pway conduct Miss Bwoadhurst somewhere where she may compose herself, call one of the maids.'

Until by the fifth or sixth visit no one would see her except the usher, telling her that Lord Gower sent word that 'everything possible was being done, and that he begged her not to inconvenience herself by coming again to the Embassy, that everything was being done that was possible.'

Haunting the Palais-Royal, the Hôtel de Ville, crying out after members of the Commune when she could recognize one of them, 'Monsieur, Citizen! Citizen Manuel! Citizen Pétion! Listen to me, please, I have a petition!' Forcing her way through the crowds towards them, while they looked round in astonished anger, in fear, at the sight of the tall, the almost giant, girl breasting her way towards them like a swimmer in a flood. Until she too was threatened with arrest as a madwoman, a disturber of the peace. It was Doctor Marat who had her released, finding her in the centre of an uproar in one of the stone corridors of the Palais Royal, throwing off a soldier attempting to lead her away.

'I know her,' Doctor Marat said. 'Leave her alone. Go home, citizeness, your father's case is receiving attention. Look after yourself. Come and see me tomorrow.' His eyes on her body. She backed away from him, from the soldiers who had been arresting her, the crowd of onlookers, and ran.

And yet the next day she did go to the Mairie to look for him, but he was not there. An old usher to whom she told her case took pity on her. 'Mademoiselle,' he whispered, having glanced round to see that no one overheard them, 'Do not come back here. He will not help you. He may promise you everything, but he will do nothing. Pray to God for your father. There is nothing else to do.'

The days spent like that. At night lying sleepless. She no longer needed to sleep in the loft where the man was still hidden, and Léonie threatened hysterics if Hester was not there in the room next door to her at night. And she would lie trying to think, trying to plan. But all she could really do was ask herself how it had happened, why had they come, why had they stayed? She had been mad, mad. She saw herself of two, three months ago as if she was looking through a telescope at the moon and seeing a strange, a lunatic figure mouthing and posturing. The Rights of Man! Liberty, Equality, Fraternity! The Fall of the Bastille, Down with Tyranny! Striding about the garden at home in Sussex quoting Voltaire to the pigeons and Mirabeau to her tame rabbits. Trying to tell the head gardener's son about Rousseau, and Émile, and the sanctity of growing vegetables. No wonder he had looked at her as if she was wrong in her head.

Arguing with Uncle George and Cousin Henry at dinner, proving to Henry that God did not exist, and that he was an imbecile to want to become a clergyman. Telling Papa that if they were to come to France they must stay in Paris at least long enough to learn what Freedom truly meant. They would meet Thomas Paine, General Lafayette, listen to a free people deciding their own future, creating a new world. Oh Papa, my poor dear stupid, patient, kind Papa. Why did you listen to me? Why did we come at all? For that stupid, weeping bitch and her damnable estates. And to get away from Mama. And if we must have come why did we not go straight there, to Nantes, and wherever else it was, and do Léonie's business for her at once? Why, why, why? And Papa was probably lying awake in that stinking darkness asking himself the same questions.

Oh my dear, my dear, if—when—you are free again I will never, never contradict you so long as I live. I will never argue with you, or try to tell you what to do. I will look after you, I will see to your breakfast, I shall never marry, never never never! No matter how unpleasant Mama is. I shall devote my life to making you comfortable. I shall never let her torment you again, I shall kill her if she makes one complaint about you. Oh dear God, please let him be safe. I believe in You, I swear it, I believe in You now. Let him go free and I shall believe in You for ever. I shall go to church, I shall never make fun of clergymen, I shall make Cousin Henry take Holy Orders, I shall make him do it, I swear.

Why did we come here, I was mad, I was raving mad.

What will happen? They cannot punish him. For what?

And the rumours. The women who said, whispering, 'They mean to kill them, I heard it, I heard it in the Section, I heard it from someone who knows someone in the Commune, an usher, he said——'

The news of the war, the men going to the frontier. 'They're afraid of the prisoners breaking out of the jails, with all the men gone to fight. They're going to kill them before they can escape and kill all the deputies, that's what I heard.'

Mad women talking, whispering, demented for their imprisoned men. A haunted comradeship of terror, the same faces every day, the same baskets. Only the rumours new. The Austrians, the Princes, the Prince of Condé, the Duke of Brunswick, they were coming, they would save us, they would murder us, they would burn Paris, they were coming to save the King, the Queen. There was no more King, there was a Republic. They were going to try the King. They were going to send him out of the country. Tomorrow all the prisoners would be freed, there would be an amnesty. The Duke of Brunswick demanded everyone be freed or he would destroy Paris. His army was advancing, he would be here soon, next week, tomorrow. All the prisoners would be killed if he came too close.

Her father's voice through the door grown hoarse and unfamiliar with the bad air. As if he was too ill to be angry. If he would shout at her! If only he would blame her!

'Papa, it is all my fault, my wickedness, oh Papa, can you forgive me?'

'The people in here, they are—they are all gentlemen,' he said in that lost, wondering voice that had become his. 'Some of them speak English. I don't understand anything that has happened. There is a priest here who is eighty-four years old.'

'I have brought you some wine, Papa. And roast meat, and some peaches, they are very fine ones.' She could not stop herself from crying. 'I am meeting someone this afternoon who promises me he can bring a petition in front of the Citizen Manuel, they say he has a great deal of power.'

'The Citizen Manuel? Have you not seen Lord Gower yet, the ambassador?'

'I have tried, Papa, I swear it. I'll try again tomorrow, but this man, he says that he knows an old servant in Citizen Manuel's house, she will give him a letter I have written.'

'If only you could manage to see Lord Gower. I cannot understand it. I met his cousin once, at Lady Ashbury's house in Town. I cannot understand why you have not——'

'They say they are doing everything. But this old servant of the Citizen Manuel, she is supposed to be very kind and to have helped——'

Another woman forcing her away from the door, crying out, 'Monsieur l'abbé, it is Blanchet! I have brought you your dinner!'

At night, when she could not bear it any longer, to be alone, thinking, she would go up again to the loft, to talk to Captain Vernet, to ask him questions that he could not answer, talk to him before she went mad of her own thoughts. The first day he had offered to surrender himself for her father's release, but they both knew that that would be insanity. It would make things worse instead of better, would only be proof of whatever the authorities wanted to believe. Then he had wanted to leave the house for fear of bringing more danger on them, and she had had to make him swear that he would not.

'Your wound would open again and you would die in the streets, or be arrested and they would know that you had been hidden here. They will not come back to look for you. I know it. Only tell me what I can do.'

'Curse this leg. What have I brought on you all? They cannot do anything to him, even these people, not to a foreigner, an Englishman. Your ambassador——'

'Our ambassador! He thinks more of his puppy-dog than of—they think we are radicals to have come here, democrats, I can see it in their eyes, they think it is Divine Punishment on us.'

'I thought you were a democrat?'

She looked at him with such self-torture in her face that he said quickly, 'I'm not trying to be cruel. For pity's sake, how could I want to be? I was a democrat once, a Republican, I believed in the Sacred People. I still do, I still do believe in the real people, but not in these swine. If only I could walk, if I could get out and try and help him.'

'How? Tell me what to do! I'll go anywhere, see anyone, only tell me!' The candlelight, the shadows of the beams, the spiders' webs, the mice scurrying, no longer frightened of them, the stale remains of yesterday's stifling heat. She should bring him downstairs again, she had the certainty that she could, it would be safe, the men would not come back. But something held her, she did not know what. A sense that she did not want to trust him to Léonie, to Euphemia. Euphemia came up to him during the days, fed him, changed his bandages, gave him medicines. Perhaps Léonie came, she said she did. She languished about it, the heat, and the trials of nursing, between bouts of hysterics at their dangers, at Mr. Broadhurst in prison, at what would happen to them all. But that was different to having him downstairs, in the next room to Léonie. Although why she thought about it, why such a thing weighed with her in deciding where he should stay, she did not know. Except that he was hers.

Not in that way that—that she had thought of him before. Nothing of that. Not to touch him, look at him. Only someone to talk to, to tell him what had happened, to ask, 'Will it be all right? They cannot, surely they cannot——?' And hear him say, 'No, of course they can't, of course not. They'll have to let him go as soon as——'

And then for a few minutes to try to forget what was happening. To think of something else, tell him about Sussex, cousin Henry, uncle George—get him to talk about himself, about America.

He did not talk very much. Only a sentence here and there, broken off with a sharp impatience as if the past was done, and best not remembered. But gradually, over the days and nights, she began to learn something of his past, of what had brought him here. The war in America; not the war that uncle George and her father and their friends talked of at the supper-table in England, of sieges and strategies, and generals; but of swift night marches; of Indian tribes; of scouting through mountain passes and immense forests; of crossing vast rivers that no white man had seen before; travelling through an empty continent like the Garden of Eden soon after the Devil had entered it.

'If only I was a man!' she whispered. Imagined riding through those forests. Imagined him for a companion. Thought, 'If I had found such a country I should never have come back.'

He told her of that too, of coming back to a France on the edge of revolution; of the time when everything had seemed as if it was going to be made new; that General Lafayette would be the Washington of France and lead her to life and liberty and happiness.

'Instead of that,' he said, 'the damned lawyers' clerks and the money men have got hold of it. We tried to warn the King. We tried to tell him what was happening. Tried to save him. And now——' Opening his closed fist as if it held something that he was letting fall, to smash itself on the floor. 'Now no one can save him.'

And the thought of the King in prison brought them full circle, back to the present, and tomorrow. And she'd catch her breath, unable to manage her voice properly, wanting to cry out, shout at him: 'Tell me again! They cannot do anything to him? They talked of the guillotine! Why should they even say that? To frighten him? Frighten me?'

His hands had grown stronger, health was coming back into the feel of his skin. A restlessness. His voice grating with impatience to be up, to be out, to—to see to his own affairs? He had spoken once, a long time, days and days and weeks and years ago, of sending a message to someone, to tell them that he was safe, was being cared for. And then he had said, 'No. Better not. You can't know who's still to be trusted.' That had been when he still had the fever, before Papa——

'Is there no one who could help? That I could go to?'

'No one who might not make things worse. It's not a question of sending a message, I'd have to talk to them, sound them out, know what's been happening since I've been here.' He freed his hands and pushed his fingers through his hair. He could shave himself now, and his cheeks shone like ivory, all his tan gone, his eyes glittering, dark blue, almost black.

'I am so frightened for him. He can't understand anything, he can't talk to anyone. I don't know if he's even eating the food I bring him, he's probably giving it away. You can't guess how kind he is, behind all that noise he makes, and shouting at people.'

'I'll get up tomorrow and go out. I'll find someone. I walked the breadth of the room today.'

'You can't.' She caught his hands again. 'Lie down. Lie quiet. I should be letting you sleep instead of——'

'You should be asleep yourself. *You*'ll get ill.'

She pressed him down against the pillows. The covers had fallen away from his chest, and her hair spilled down to touch him, lay against his arm and shoulder. He had begun to breathe faster, his eyes staring into hers. 'Go away, now! You don't know what you're doing.'

She did not move.

'I'm warning you, go! Leave me alone!'

She shut her eyes. She wanted to put down her forehead against his chest. His hands were gripping her wrists, tighter and tighter. Making her feel that she was captured, that she could not move. He was trying to push her up, away from him, but he could not. Could only spread her wrists apart. She laid her head down on him. Like surrendering. His heart beating, heavy, against her mouth.

He put his arms round her, and she stretched herself down beside him, the covers half between them, her breast against him, their mouths close.

'You don't know what you're doing!'

She did not answer him. Kissed him without thinking that she was going to. As if it was only for reassurance, forgetfulness. 'Hold me.'

'No!'

She was shivering, long tremors running from her shoulders down to her feet. His hands on her skin, under her shift and night-gown. His hands also shivering, gripping suddenly, gripping her buttocks, the insides of her legs, as if he wanted to hurt her. 'For the last time, go away!'

She had her arms round him, held him. 'Let me lie beside you,' she whispered. 'Just for a little while.' She did not know what she was whispering. Fastened against him. He was pulling the blankets away from between them, pushing her legs apart.

Like being stabbed, like a thick knife forced into her body. Lying on top of him, her face against his neck, in the hollow between head and shoulders. The muscles of his shoulder between her teeth. His hands pulling her down, his fingers digging into flesh. Crying with pain, hearing his breath gasping, shuddering, his body under hers. Like riding bareback, naked, the horse gathering its strength, its muscles, stretching, heaving. Until he went slack. Lay still. The pain died away.

'I have killed him,' she thought. And could not move. She lay on top of his dead body, holding it, tasting blood and salt sweat. Her hands behind his shoulders. His heart was still beating against hers. They lay like that for a long time. Until he began to stroke her back, under her shift. His fingers running down the valley of her spine, to her waist, over her hips, down as far as he could reach.

'I've lain here thinking of doing this,' he whispered. 'I swore I wouldn't.'

'What have we—what did you——?' They had made love. Made love, she thought wonderingly, like dreaming, everything far away, infinitely far off. That was what the pain had been.

He held her by her hair, lifted up her head until he could look at her and she must look down at him. He is my lover, she thought. Mine. She wanted to touch his face, stroke the lines of his mouth. She wanted to say, 'You're mine, you belong to me.' She wanted to kneel up and look at every part of him, at what had hurt her so much, at where she had bitten him. She could see that. The mark of her teeth, a dull purple wound, the ooze of blood. Her hair falling forward, the candle-flame catching its red and golden lights, like molten copper.

'Lie down beside me.'

She lay down. His hands touching her as if they were exploring, finding, wanting to remember. Pulling the covers over her, holding her close against him.

'What have we done?'

'Your father——'

'Not now. Tomorrow. Hold me closer.' And then, 'Nothing will happen to him? Promise me?'

'Nothing. I swear it. Let me—and I'm the first? You've never——?' Touching her hair, her throat. Kissing. 'I've lain day after day, night after night. Imagining—how has no one ever—what are Englishmen made of?' stroking the length of her side, from armpit to hip bone, round to her groin, her lap.

'Papa says I frighten men away.'

He began to laugh, choked with coughing, lay spent.

She turned on her side towards him, and laid her arm over his chest. 'And you? You've had a lot of—lovers?'

He looked at her. The candlelight striking glistens of laughter from the black depths of his eyes. 'Are you jealous already?'

And suddenly she was. Such a shock of jealousy as was like the pain coming back. 'Don't laugh! Don't tell me!' She laid her palm over his mouth, raised herself on her elbow, stared down at him. Like a lioness over her kill, over her mate.

He held her away from him for a second or two, and then drew her down until only her hand separated their mouths. 'Lie on me,' he whispered, his voice thick. She felt his heart beating against her breast, his body damp cold with sweat as if the fever had come back. He is mine, she thought. If he has had a thousand lovers he is mine now.

Chapter 8

She woke up without being sure of where she was, or what had happened. Felt the emptiness of the bed beside her. A dream? She sat up. In the greyness of light from the small, dust-covered skylight, he was walking about. He had to bend his head, as she did, to avoid the roof-beams and the joists and the matted cobwebs, even where the roof was highest. He limped as he walked, cursing under his breath, holding his wounded leg with both hands clasped against the bandage, and she knew what he had in mind to do. She sat up violently, furiously.

'No! You're not going!' She reached out and caught hold of him, and dragged him back and down, onto the mattress.

'I can walk,' he said.

'No!' She held him to her, found his mouth. She could feel her nerves quivering, every nerve in her body. It seemed to her as if she had never been alive before, never known what life was, what her body was. Her hair part of her, alive, burning. Her hands. Her skin. She could feel the beat of her own heart. She felt that she needed to do some tremendous thing, break, smash, crush something, use all her strength. She felt it like a pressure bursting inside her, for the first time in her life thanked God utterly and without reserve for her height, her power of body, her muscles, that feeling of being set apart from other women, not like them, not like anyone, only herself. As if she belonged to a new race, had nothing in common with the Léonies, the Jane Fairfaxes. Come from the moon, or the forests of America.

She kissed him gently, brushed her mouth against his forehead, his cheekbone. He began to kiss her, her shoulder, her breast, slide his arm behind her back. She whispered, 'No, no, it will kill

[86]

you, wait, wait for a time, until tonight, until you're strong again. I'll fetch you broth, Euphemia will make you more medicine.'

It seemed like an immense sacrifice, and the pleasure of making it had its own sensuality, its own joy. She began to lay him down, cover him. She would have liked to be able to fasten his hands, imprison him. But he did not need imprisoning. He lay as weak as a drowned man, only his eyes alive, still independent, full of that amusement that angered her whenever she saw it. She closed his eyes with her finger-tips. What made him laugh? What could he find to laugh at in making love?

She forced herself up. Her shift that she had torn off during the night, during their love-making, was still damp, clammy with sweat, and she threw it away into a dark corner where it lay like the ghost of their darkness, of the night. She pulled on her nightgown and fastened it. Something different about her waist, her body, the feel of her own flesh as she tightened the girdle. She felt such strength in her hands, her body, that the girdle would burst if she drew it tighter.

'Lie still,' she said. She went down the ladder, down the stairs to the apartment. Her bedroom seemed strange and cold, as though it belonged to someone else. She opened the curtains and the window, breathed in the morning. She had not forgotten her ather. Forgotten? She had not stopped from thinking of him all night, during—everything. He had been there. But they would get him out of prison, she knew it, as she knew her own strength. As if she would need only to burst down the door to free him. There was nothing in the world that was not possible. She wanted to shout at the curtained windows across the street, to those other bourgeois houses, safe and shuttered, to the people who lived in them, 'This is another kind of morning. Look at it! Look at the sun!'

There was a sound behind her and when she turned Euphemia was there, sleepy, fastening her gown, yawning, stretching, stretching her black velvet body, her eyes sly, malicious, admiring, fondling. 'Madame Estairre!' Looking at the un-touched bed, the smooth pillow. 'Madame is early.'

'Make us some broth. And medicine. And—food.'

'I will bring it upstairs to you.'

She went to the black girl and caught hold of her, gripping her by the shoulders. The shoulders smooth and rounded as ebony, and then soft and yielding, under the white muslin, the satin ribbons. Warmth of bed from her, muslin and silk and satin, and ebony skin. A smell of musk, of sex.

'Why does he laugh at me?' She wanted to shake her until the black round head would roll on her shoulders, the eyes would be frightened. But they would never be frightened.

'Men have to laugh at what makes them afraid.'

She did not understand it, but she let go of Euphemia. She wanted to say, 'Medicine to make him strong,' and was ashamed. But she did not have to say it aloud.

Later, upstairs, as they ate the food and drank the wine and the broth, she said, 'Why do you laugh at me?'

'I don't laugh,' he said. And laughed aloud. But it no longer made her angry.

He truly is afraid of me, she thought gently, considering him over the rim of her cup.

'Because I'm so big, so tall? I'm not like—other women?'

'It's wonderful,' he said. 'I swear it. You're wonderful.' But his eyes still laughed.

'I must get dressed and go,' she said. 'Don't move. Don't——' But there was no need to say it. He lay very still, trying to smile. 'Euphemia will come to you.'

He whispered blasphemies under his breath. She knew they were at himself, his condition, not at her, but the knowledge gave her no comfort. The night had gone. The terror had never left her, had only withdrawn into the shadows. Everything else was charade. She went downstairs and gave her orders to Euphemia, looked into Léonie's darkened, scented, orchid-house of a bedroom, tried to say something courteous.

'Are you leaving us again?' Léonie said, plaintive voice out of the dark. 'I'm so afraid. And that man up in the loft. Oh Hester! How can you be so cruel to me?'

She hesitated, closing her eyes. Imagined lifting her out of the satin nest of her bed and beating her senseless.

'I shall be back before dark,' she said.

She did not bother looking for a *fiacre*. The air cleared her head as she walked. The basket weighed nothing on her arm, and to ride in a *fiacre*, even the broken-springed *coucous* from the stands, drew attention, could draw a hostile crowd wanting to see who was inside, wanting to know where they were going, why. As it was, except for her height, she had contrived as the days went by to look more and more like a market girl with a basket of eggs for sale. Had found an apron, and long blue cotton skirts, the right red kerchief. And if when she spoke her French was still the school French she had learned from Madame Dumesnil in the Young Ladies' Academy, she had already begun to understand the street argot of the jailers and the gatekeepers, of the guardsmen and the crowds.

She strode in the sunshine, carrying her basket of wine and chicken and peaches and hard-boiled eggs and fresh bread and the jar of broth, and the packet of coins wrapped in a clean handkerchief; the clean shirt and stockings and drawers and cravat; and tried to recover her certainty of an hour or two ago, that she would free him today, that she had only to force open the door and he would be free. It must happen, it must! She would go to the Embassy again, Lord Gower would see her at last, perhaps he had already done something, had only refused to see her not to raise her hopes too high, too soon. But now—or the Citizen Manuel's old serving-woman—or Doctor Marat—he had not a wicked face. Mad but not wicked. A lot of people said that he was the only one who cared anything for the real people, the poor and wretched, the workmen and the beggars. The others were what you liked, they were in it for themselves, as Michel said they were. Lawyers and shopkeepers who wanted nothing out of the Revolution except what the aristocrats used to have. A revolution to pull down the dukes and set up money-lenders in their places. But Marat was surely different, he was what she had always thought of ever since it had begun. Of men who burned with love of men and not with hatred. She would go to the Hôtel de Ville again, go to his office, wait for him, no matter what the old usher had said about him. She saw the thick, broken nose, the wet mouth, the mad, searching eyes, the twitching of his body, the thick hand scratching.

The world is mad, she thought, and looked at the street round her, the people, the river, the bridge, as if it was made of nightmares and at any second would turn to blood and shrieking. Doctor Marat its image. The Citizen Pétion, with his pretty round face and his fresh, scented cravat. 'No, no, citizeness, leave your petition with the usher. It shall be attended to, I promise you.' Like a plump little dancing master. And that stink-

[89]

ing room where Papa and all the others, eighty, ninety of them, were crammed in without air to breathe, water to clean themselves, a closet to go to in decency. Only buckets overflowing vileness.

The Mairie's courtyard. Crowded as always, guards, ushers, messengers, idlers, but a difference about it, different faces, a hurrying, tension. She felt it like turning a corner into a biting wind. She began to hurry, to push her way through to the doorway, the stairs.

'You, citizeness, you tall one, where are you going?'

'To my father, he is——'

A guard she knew taking his pipe out of his mouth, spitting, looking at her almost pityingly, almost kind. 'He's gone, they're all gone, the ones as was upstairs, we're getting a new lot soon.' Old moustache. Old eyes. Spitting again.

'Gone?' Like a shriek, like a wound. Grasping his arm. 'He cannot be gone, tell me, where have you——?'

'Get off with you, find him for yourself, bitch of an aristocrat.' Pushing her roughly from him, and his eyelid dropping as he pushed. Winking. She hesitated. His eyes looking towards the gate, nodding slightly. She forced herself to turn away, push through the crowd of indifferent people, back to the gateway. People going by. The woman, the abbé's servant, coming breathless, late, hurrying, her basket dragging her down sideways.

'They are gone,' Hester said. 'They've taken them away.'

'Gone? My master?' Trying to run into the courtyard, trying to shake off Hester's grasp.

'Wait.'

They waited for a quarter-hour, the woman, Madame Blanchet, trembling, not believing.

'Wait.' As if in these twelve days she had learned an infinity of waiting, learned the patience of stones. She leaned against the gate pillar, staring at nothing. The woman sat down on the *pavé*, crying. Her head bent over her knees. An old, grey-haired woman with a black cotton bonnet and a black shawl.

The guard came out, spat, wiped his moustache. 'The Abbaye,' he said, looking at neither of them, at the sky, at the rooftops.

'My master——'

'Get away from here, you old hag. You should be in jail with him. Clear off with you.' He went inside. Hester dragged the old woman to her feet, pulled her away.

'Be quiet. Come with me. Where is the Abbaye prison? Which one could he mean?'

'The rue Sainte-Marguerite,' the woman said, her voice stupefied and lost. 'Why have they——?'

Across the river again. Rue Sainte-Marguerite. Stone walls. Locked timber gates in a vast archway. Wicket gate. Knocking. Waiting. Let in at last. The Chief Gatekeeper. Red bonnet on round, sweating, cannon-ball of head. Gross, unshaven, belly half naked through his open shirt, black hairs on greyish-white skin. She could see his navel. Thick finger slowly tracing name after name in a heavy book.

'Abbé Montbeliard, *réfractaire*. Yes, we've got him, old woman. And we'll keep him, don't you worry. He'll not get lost.' Gross laugh, stink of garlic, stale tobacco, brandy. The Under-Gatekeeper laughing, an apprentice sycophant.

'Be-ro-de-hut—huss—the devil take his wretched tongue twister of a name. What do you call your old imbecile of a father?'

'Broadhurst. Monsieur Henry Broadhurst. Is he here? Is he?' Thinking of money. Finding the packet of money in the basket, sliding it across the table into the gross spider hand.

'Aye. He's here, if that's how you say it. It's like puking up, your filthy language. Be ro de snot, foreign agent. Spy. Let's see your baskets, you don't fool me with your foreign tricks. No weapons in the bread, eh?'

Filthy hands, digging under the white cloths, breaking open the white loaves, the fresh crust.

'Good white bread for these whore's droppings, and we get stuff that'd plug up your guts. All right, let 'em through.'

Iron grinding. Having to bend double to go through the *guichet*. Stone corridors, stench of urine. Echoes of iron crashing, nailed boots, echoes. Gates clanging, doors slamming, voices calling. Despair. Stone steps. Bits of straw. Arrow slits of sunlight. A guard leading them, going slower and slower, looking thoughtful. She gave him the last of the money she had brought, a few sous from the pocket in her apron. Going quicker, whistling.

'In here. Shout through that door. I'll put your baskets in when you're going.'

[91]

'Papa! *Papa! Are you there?*'
'*Monsieur l'abbé? It's me! Blanchet! Oh my master!*'

Voices, shuffling feet. Papa calling to her, 'Hester! My dear! My dear!'

'I've—I've brought your—your dinner.' Leaning her forehead against the timber, the tears running. Hearing the sound of his voice, imagining his face. The old woman crying beside her, whispering to her abbé. 'They cannot do anything to you, you who are so good.'

Another woman behind them, crying out, 'Monsieur, Monsieur Georges, Monsieur Charles, my children, are you there?' Nurse woman, her basket so big she staggered lifting it. And an old priest, how he did dare to walk through the streets now, dressed as a priest?

'I have come to find my brother.' The guard laughing at him.

'He's in there all right. We'll put you in with him now you've come.'

'Put me——?'

The door opening, their guard taking their baskets, throwing them inside. Another guard, who had brought the nurse woman and the priest, putting his hand in the old priest's back, giving him a great shove that sent him staggering into the room.

'Get in with the rest of them.'

A glimpse, her father beside the half-opened door. A long, crowded room, so high it vanished into shadows far above the prisoners' heads. On the littered floor she saw mattresses, straw, greyness, men lying down, sitting with hunched knees, those staring faces that prisoners have, staring towards any door that opens, any breath from the world outside. The door slammed, the old priest cried out, 'What are you doing, I only came——'

The guards laughed, slapping their thighs. 'The old fool can talk his head off now, *say Mass with 'em.*' Catching Hester, and Madame Blanchet, and the nurse woman, by their elbows, the familiar grasp of prison comradeship, of blunted senses, blunted to suffering. 'Come along with you now or we might throw you in with 'em as well. Or how'd you like to stay with us, eh? You're a fine handsome girl, big enough for the pair of us.'

Down the echoing, urine-smelling stairs. Outside into the air. The walls heavy above them. The day stretching, empty and hopeless. Go to the Embassy? Look for Doctor Marat? Go home?

[92]

The old woman Blanchet, the nurse woman, hurried away, each in a different direction, not looking back. As if they had somewhere to hurry to. She herself began to walk, found herself walking fast. Why? Where? Where was there to go? But go somewhere, walk fast, as if there were a purpose.

The Embassy. The Mairie. The Hôtel de Ville. Doctor Marat. Mayor Pétion. Crowded corridors. Petitioners. Bribes. But she had spent all the money she had brought out with her and the ushers would not so much as listen. She saw the Citizen Manuel and ran after him, and was pushed away. The Citizen Creuzot whom she had seen outside the Tuileries, and twice since. 'Citizen, please, listen to me, let me speak to you, only a moment!'

But he went hurrying on, surrounded by men with papers, tatterdermalion followers with scraps of uniform and tricolour sashes, cockades in their hats. Two or three men dressed *à la bourgeois*, like himself. Grey, unslept faces, red-rimmed eyes. As if anarchy needed more hours of the day than order, gave less time for sleep. Gone. Only the women, the rumours, the crowded corridors, the whispers running like wind in grass. The Duke of Brunswick. Paris'll be destroyed. They'll kill us all!

'Citizen, listen to me, let me speak with you, only a moment, it is life and death!'

'No, me, listen to me, I knew your mother, God rest her soul!'

'Citizen, I submitted a petition, did you get it, don't you remember me?'

'The men from the *ateliers*, the workmen, they're coming, it'll be the tenth of August over again. But this time——'

'Sssh, you look like someone with a bit of trouble. D'you want to buy gold? Real money? And a passport maybe?'

Out into the streets again. A crowd at a street corner, looking at something, a poster, an announcement fastened to the wall. She stood at the back of the crowd for lack of will to go by, for anything else to do. A man was reading slowly, at the top of his voice. 'Citizens, this is to warn you of the day's General Order for all the inhabitants of Paris. At 8 hours of the evening all active citizens are to report to the headquarters of their Section for important instructions. Every other person, male and female, is to be indoors in their own house by eleven o'clock. Each house must be lit, and the door left open, whether the street door or into

[93]

the courtyards. Obey without fail, on the order of the Commune, this Wednesday, the 29th August 1792.'

'What does it mean?'

'They're looking for spies.'

'No, priests! *Réfractaires*. They're going to search every house. I heard it from my brother, he's a cook in the Palais-Royal.'

'They're going to search for arms, you fool, they're looking for Royalists. There's ten thousand of 'em hidden in attics all over Paris, they've got guns and they're going to start a rising on Sunday, I heard it from——'

'I'm going home now. I've got a bit of cash put away that I don't want those thieves laying hands on.'

'What's that you said? What did that man just say? Stop him, the man with a blue coat, stop him! Bring him to the Mairie, I heard him. Calling good patriots thieves! Hoarding gold! He's one of them, bring him along, and you, citizen, you must have heard him, we'll need you for a witness.'

The crowd melting, vanishing. The man in the blue coat shouting protests, led away by three ruffians and the denouncer. 'I never said anything, it wasn't me, citizens, do I look like a man who would——?' The witness following slowly, unwillingly, looking round for escape.

Hidden in attics all over Paris? Attics? Every house to be left open? Eleven tonight? Searched—running, afraid to run, to be seen running. Walking fast. Not till eleven? What time was it now? Four of the afternoon. Quarter past. Running again. Making herself walk quietly. What would she do? Where would she hide him? How? A cupboard, a chest, the cellars, in bed disguised—disguised as what? An old woman, a servant? They would see his wound, his limp. Running again. The rue du Bac. The house. Upstairs. Not even stopping to speak to Léonie, Euphemia. Up to the loft.

He was asleep, waking as she came through the open trap-door. Dear heaven, how could she have left it open, the ladder there, as if there was no more danger? Panting so that it was hard to tell him. He waited, watching her. His eyes serious, his expression changing. Concentrated, swift.

'Give me my clothes.'

'No!'

'Do you think I'm going to stay here and let you be——'

[94]

'No!'

He sat quietly, looking down at his wounded leg. 'Get me a *coucous*. It'll bring me where I need to go. There's a man——'

'No!'

'Listen to me. I should have gone before. I'm going if I have to get up through that skylight and crawl from roof to roof. Get a *fiacre*, now! I know what I'm doing.'

She began to argue and he gripped her wrist. 'Do what I tell you,' he said. As if he was talking to a man, a soldier under command.

'Michel.' She had never said his name. Never so much as 'Monsieur Vernet.'

'Do what I tell you,' he said again. He caught her with his other hand at the nape of her neck, pulled her roughly towards him. 'I'll not laugh at you again.' Kissed her mouth. 'Now go.'

When she came back with the *coucous*, tilting and swaying on its ancient springs, its horse spavined and starving, its driver complaining of the heat, his nose like a ripe plum, Michel was already waiting for her in the hall, Euphemia supporting him.

'Not dressed like that!' Hester whispered. She ran upstairs, found her deepest-brimmed bonnet and a cloak and a scarf, and came running down again, put them on him. 'You are my grandmother, very ill, I thought of it as I looked for the cab. Come, I'll help you, I'm coming with you to where you're going, to see you safe. Don't argue!'

He was not strong enough to argue. Even the effort of dressing had brought on a fever sweat, the look of wet silver on his face. She took him outside. 'Not you,' she said to Euphemia. The driver would remember a black servant-girl, remember the address.

'This is my grandmother,' she said to the driver. 'We must go very gently, don't drive too fast, she shouldn't have come visiting today, she's not well enough.'

'Rue de la Sainte Vierge,' Michel whispered, his voice an old woman's whisper, as if all his life he had play-acted. 'Just by the church, number fourteen.'

In the cab they held hands. Like lovers. Except that she sweated fear. They were lovers. One night! And now—— 'How will I know you are safe?' she breathed. 'Where are you going?'

He rested his head on her shoulder, an old woman's head on

strong granddaughter's shoulder if anyone was looking. 'A man called Creuzot,' he said. 'A swine, one of the patriots, but he owes me a great favour, and he can't refuse me.'

'Creuzot? Isn't he——?'

'We were in school together. He's probably a great man by now. But he likes to keep in touch with both sides, just in case. What do you know about him?'

'Nothing. I've only seen him. He's in the Commune, on the Committee of something, I'm not sure.'

'Maybe he can help your father. I'll try. Sssh, we're near. Get out with me, let the driver go.'

They got down in a narrow street. Meaner houses, filth in the gutter that ran down the centre of the cobbled roadway. A stray cat, children, a knot of people reading the same announcement, fixed to the wall at the street corner.

'Oh, my rheumatism!' Michel whispered, 'be careful of me, girl, you're so big and clumsy!'

'You're not so small yourself, old grandmother,' the driver said. 'She's a good girl to mind you so well.'

Michel fumbling under his woman's cloak for sous. The cloak and bonnet were too smart for the street, too foreign. Please heaven the driver had no eye for details.

'Here,' she said to the driver, paying him, 'we are all right now.'

He drove away. Michel hobbled, leaned on Hester's arm. 'Not fourteen,' Michel said. 'That was for him. Eighteen, over there.'

She felt him weighing on her arm. Footsteps beyond the door, brisk, a man's tread. Somehow she had expected a woman to answer them. And it was the Citizen Creuzot himself. The tall, thin, stooped figure, the small, muddy eyes, the long, upturned nose, the crooked teeth. The habitual sneer. As if she had known him a long time, his face was so instantly familiar. And he did not seem surprised to see her. Only angry. Remembering her calling after him at the Palais Royal? Thinking she had traced him here?

'Citizeness!' He looked at her companion.

'René!' Michel said. 'Let us in quick.'

Monsieur Creuzot stook back, to make way for them. He did not ask any questions. When the door was shut he led the way at a quick pace down the hall, past a dark stairway, and opened a door into a courtyard. Hester supported Michel, almost carrying him. Monsieur Creuzot seemed to know without asking what they wanted. The courtyard was occupied with a carpenter's affairs. Stacks of fresh-cut timber, work benches, a lathe, some chairs half made. Rough, kitchen chairs with straw seats. Timber steps led up to a loft. Monsieur Creuzot climbed them without looking back and she followed him, Michel hanging so heavily against her that she almost fell with him before they reached the top.

In the loft there was a smell of sawdust, of wood and resin. Stacks of the same rough-made chairs. Piles of timber. Bales of seating straw. She eased Michel down on one of the bales. He had shut his eyes and the sweat poured down his face.

'Come,' the Citizen Creuzot said. He beckoned her out onto the wooden stairs again and led the way down and into the house. He still did not ask anything. In a small room there was a mattress on a truckle bed and he gave it to her to carry. Then blankets and a pillow. Nodded for her to take them to the loft. While she was still arranging them in a corner for Michel to lie on he followed her with a basket. Wine and glasses and clean rags and a loaf of white bread.

'I warned you,' he said to Michel, pouring out wine. 'Give it to him,' he said to Hester. He poured wine for himself, but not for her.

'What is going to happen tonight?' Hester said, not able to keep back the questions any longer. 'Will he be safe with you?' Looking at him, at his sneering mouth, his eyes, trying to believe that he would help, that he was not what he seemed. Or was something else besides.

'We're searching for arms,' he said. 'And suspects.' The sneer became deeper, more mocking. 'He'll be safe.' Looking at her, seeming not to need to ask anything. 'You can go now.'

'But——'

'Do as he says,' Michel whispered. 'I'll be all right here.'

She stood up. Monsieur Creuzot did not stand. He had pulled forward one of the kitchen chairs and was sitting quite elegantly, legs crossed. Black bourgeois breeches, stockings, buckled shoes. Sipping his wine.

'Wait down there,' he said, nodding to the doorway, the sun-light beyond. She went slowly, looking back, Michel lost in the shadows, lying on his mattress. As if he had never belonged to her, she would never see him again. She wanted to go back, touch him. And Monsieur Creuzot's eyes were on her. She went down the steps and stood in the courtyard.

It was ten minutes before he followed her down.

'Go out this way,' he said, nodding towards the gates. 'And walk home. Make sure there's not a trace of him where you've been keeping him. Nothing.'

'Will he——'

'I've told you.' He gripped her by the elbow, making to push her out of the courtyard.

'If he's not—if you——'

The sneer deepened. 'You'll do what? Mind yourself, and I'll mind him. Now go.'

It was only then that she thought of her father. She turned and caught hold of his black coat-sleeve. 'My father is in prison!'

He tried to push her outside but she was too strong for him. She caught hold of him with both hands. 'You must listen! What is going to happen to him?'

'How do I know? Let go of me!' His voice was savage with dislike. 'Why did you come to Paris?'

'We—I *believed* in you! In what you're doing! I'm still willing to—I know it's a mistake, someone thought——'

The contempt in his face was like a whip. 'You believed! You English imbecile! What do you know about anything? You— *woman*! Get out, don't dare lay your hands on me.'

'I won't go till you tell me! He has done nothing, he is more innocent than Michel. Ten thousand times more.' She would not let go of his wrists, and after a brief attempt to free himself he gave up.

'What do you want?'

'I want him to be free, of course!'

'Let go of me. You don't know what you are asking. Let me think.' She did let go then, and he turned and walked the length of the courtyard. After a moment he beckoned her. In the house he took a sheet of paper and pen and ink and rested them on a bookcase. 'Take this to Pétion,' he said. He scribbled for a moment, sanded and folded the sheet. 'Now go before I have you arrested too.'

'And Michel, how will I know—when will I——'

'Get out of my sight!'

[98]

'But I must know!'

'Why did God make woman? Get out! He'll send word to you. Someone will tell you the American is safe. Now go, damn your soul.'

He pushed her out into an empty laneway. She opened the folded paper. 'I know nothing against the foreigner she will speak of. Help her if you think fit. Creuzot.' On the outside of the fold he had written, 'To Mayor Pétion, by hand, urgently.' Behind her the wicket gate was shut, his footsteps hurrying away. 'Monsieur!'

No answer. 'I know nothing against——' She tried to think. Could that be enough? Had he tricked her, fobbed her off? Urgently. By hand, urgently. She began to run. A clock chimed seven, and then a quarter. Quarter past seven! Where would he be now? Where? The Mairie? The Hôtel de Ville? At his house? Where was his house?

It was ten o'clock before she saw him. She had sat in his ante-room for two hours, she had been told a dozen times he would not come, to leave her paper, surrender it, come back tomorrow. He would see no one, tonight of all nights. He was still at the Hôtel de Ville.

'He is not! I have been, they told me!'

'He will not come here, go home, everyone must be indoors by eleven, there is a curfew.'

But she would not move, and at ten, five minutes past ten, he came, with his quick bustle, his dancing master's light, pretty step. He looked exhausted and yet still pretty and neat and with a breath of scent from his cravat, his handkerchief in his sleeve, like a flower in a bunch of nettles among his ragamuffin entourage, with their red bonnets and *carmagnoles*, and sagging, dirty pantaloons, sabots, filthy stockings, ragged shirts, greasy scarves and sashes. Only the cockades in their shabby, broken hats blazing with clean colour, red, white and blue.

'Citizen Pétion, here's a message from the Citizen Creuzot, let me give it to you, please, it's urgent, it's marked urgent!'

He recognized her, a look of tired exasperation came over his face like a grey veil. 'Citizeness!' And then, as if it had taken moments for what she said to penetrate through his tiredness, his preoccupations, he clicked his fingers and said, 'Give it to me.' One of the ragged patriots surrounding him made to take the paper from her, but she forced her way past him until she could lay it in the manicured fingers of the Citizen Pétion himself, as if no other hand must touch it. He read it, raised his delicate eyebrows, pursed his baby lips. And with a sweet, exhausted smile folded the sheet again and offered it back to her.

'Have no fears, citizeness. All will be well with him.'

'But I've not told you yet! My father, Monsieur Broadhurst, the Englishman, he's in the Abbaye prison, he was transferred there today, last night, they are saying——' She dared not say the words, 'Murder, executions', dared not say anything. The sweet smile fixed on her.

'All will be well by the weekend. By Sunday night. He will be released by then, I promise you.'

'But—not until Sunday? It is Wednesday, only Wednesday, he has done nothing!'

A *sans-culotte* pushed her away. She fended him off like a child annoying her and the man staggered and shouted. 'Whore's bitch!'

'Sunday, I tell you. Now, citizeness——'

'Then at least write it here. Write an order, put your name here that you approve, I beg you, in the name of everything you believe in, I beg you, he's totally innocent, he loves France, we're Republicans, we hate tyranny as you do. Please!' She would have gone down on her knees.

Mayor Pétion clicked his fingers again. 'Pen and ink. A daughter's prayers.' So sweet a smile. Like a saint. Men brought what was needed, a man bent his back for the mayor to write on his bowed shoulders. Waving the paper delicately in the air to dry the ink. 'There, citizeness. Do your duty. Love Liberty. Have no fears.'

He had written, 'An order will arrive for Monsieur Broadhurst at three o'clock of the afternoon, Sunday, 2nd September, signed, Pétion, Maire de Paris.'

Thank God, thank God. She wanted to kneel down to thank him. But he was gone, his patriots following, his flower scent lost in the stench of sweat and garlic and dirty clothes. The dusty, empty room. The paper in her hand. Sunday. Not till Sunday! But then! Then!

Half past ten. The streets already empty, except for soldiers. Looking after her as she ran. A patrol beginning to stop her until someone cried, 'It's not time yet.'

The streets quiet, silent, her lone footsteps echoing like shots in an empty city. Windows lit. Doors open. A face at a window, drawing back as she went by. The patrols closing the entries to the streets, four and five guards and a barrier of trestles, of tables commandeered from somewhere.

'Why are you not at home, citizeness? Didn't you hear the Retreat?'

'I've been to Mayor Pétion. I'm going home now.'

'Hurry. It's almost eleven.'

The rue du Bac. Old Anne at the door, looking out for her. 'Madame! Madame!'

Inside. All safe! Thank God, thank God, all safe!

Chapter 9

They did not come until four o'clock in the morning. All night the silence. The silence of a dead town. Dead streets. Such quiet. Waiting. Now and then the tread of a patrol. Once there was shouting far down the street, a woman shouting, 'No no no no! He is not a priest!' Then silence.

Waiting. She did not undress. At one o'clock Léonie fell asleep. She had dressed herself in her most beautiful négligée and spent a long time doing her hair. Once she knew that Michel was gone she was no longer really frightened, only pleasantly afraid, allowing herself sensual *frissons* of terror and begging Hester to comfort her, to hold her. In the absence of any man she treated Hester like a substitute, stroking her arm and saying how strong she must be, how dreadful it must be to be so strong, and how wonderful, and asking again and again what would happen, who would come to search, what would they say, what would they do?

'How do I know, you imbecile?'

'Oh Hester, you are so cruel to me!' As if she longed for the right kind of cruelty. Then she would rearrange her hair and want Euphemia to massage her feet.

'She cannot, not now. She must help me.' She and Euphemia scouring the loft, and then the apartment, for any trace of Michel, any sign that anyone had been hidden there. And next for any papers of Mr. Broadhurst's that might have been overlooked before, and could still be taken. When they had done everything that could be done they went down to Madame de Richeteau and Anne to see if they needed anything. But the two old women had already stupefied themselves with brandy and laudanum, and sat holding hands, mistress and maid, crying over the death of

General de Richeteau, who had died twenty-two years ago.

Then there was nothing to do but wait. Léonie asleep, Euphemia silent. Hester wanted to ask her, will he be all right, will he be safe? And would not. Could not. Now and then Euphemia looked at her, those jet and ivory eyes seeming to be able to look at her no matter how much the black round head was turned away. Ask me, her eyes said, mocking. Ask me, white madame, big woman, stupid lover who knows nothing. Get down on your knees to me and ask me and maybe I shall tell you something, and maybe not.

Silence.

Three o'clock. Half past. Four striking. In the silence of the house the mantel clock in the ante-room striking a warning. Silvery and soft and far away. Euphemia lifting her head, listening, coming to her feet slowly, her eyes narrowing. Like a black snake lifting itself, supple and handsome.

'They are coming.'

It was another minute before Hester could hear their footsteps. No shouting, no banging of musket butts against doors. Into the hall below. A man reading from a paper. The Citizeness de Richeteau, a *ci-devant*. The Citizeness Anne Delon. Three foreigners. You two remain here, the rest, upstairs, begin with the attics.

The search was quiet, polite, methodical. She had left the ladder on the landing below the loft.

'What is up there, madame?'

'I don't know. We are only visitors here, Madame de Richeteau is a distant relative of my cousin's.'

'Nothing up here.'

Two men climbing down, cobwebs draping their shoulders, their hats.

'The two old women below are drunk, citizen, nothing down there.'

'What are you looking for, citizens?'

They did not answer. Léonie was awake, beautiful in terror. The officer, if he was an officer, took off his hat to pay his respects to her, gave her 'Mademoiselle', as if there were no such things as *ci-devants*, his eyes admiring. He had the manners and bearing of a *ci-devant* himself, salon grace. Even his men were cleaner than the ordinary. But very thorough. They did not smash locks, or throw things about, but if there had been a mouse hidden they would have found it. Hester felt her heart beating as if Michel was still there.

'The roof,' the officer said to the men who had searched the loft. 'Did you look on top? There is a skylight?'

'Yes, citizen. Nothing out there.'

It was quarter past five before they left, the officer saluting Léonie again, Hester. Ordering one of his men to replace a carpet that had been turned back to look under it.

She sat on one of the chairs in the ante-room, her eyes shut. Euphemia was putting Léonie to bed. I must go to bed myself. For an hour. It was too early to go to the prison, to tell her father that he would be released, that it was only until Sunday. Too early to hope for word from Michel. How would word come to her?

And like a knife in her breast, fear. That he had been found, that that man had betrayed him, had not been able to—she sat still and rigid. She had to hold herself back from running down the stairs, into the deserted, guarded streets, from running to the street of the Holy Virgin to find him, beat on that courtyard door and force her way in.

Euphemia was at her side. 'Stay quiet, madame,' she said, although Hester had said nothing, had not moved. 'He is safe enough.'

'How do you know?' She caught Euphemia's hand and held it in both hers, beseeching.

Euphemia looked down at her as she sat, the malice gone from her eyes, or at least hidden. She looked almost sad, as if she did not want to know the things she knew. 'He is safe.'

'And my father?'

'He too.'

'Thank God!' She buried her face against Euphemia's body. The smell of musk, and Léonie's scent, and that other scent of—blackness. 'How do you know things?' Almost like a child's body, small breast, hard, narrow waist, narrow hips. But not a child. Far from that.'How?' She was so tired she could rest her head there, against Euphemia's breast. She could understand how Léonie got such comfort from her, depended on her. She felt as if she was surrounded by safety, by strength. Like being held by one's mother, an ideal mother who knew everything and was so strong and wise that nothing could ever harm one. As unlike her own mother as——

'Are you good?' she whispered. Euphemia touched her hair, slowly closed her fingers in it, wound the hair round until it was tight on her clenched fist, lifted Hester's head away from her, forced it back until Hester must look up into her eyes. Like looking at a snake. The eyes narrow, the head no longer round, but flattened, triangular.

Then nothing. Crimson. As if blood was running down the wall, a curtain, a cataract of blood. But it was only Euphemia's gown, her tight crimson bodice, her silk skirts. She felt sick and dizzy and frightened, sick with fear.

'Go and sleep,' Euphemia said.

She did sleep, and dreamed of blood.

At the prison her father seemed scarcely to believe her, that he would be freed on Sunday. And then he pretended to believe her, and she knew that it was pretence. She showed her paper to the gatekeeper at the Abbaye, the under-gatekeepers, the guards, holding it all the time in terror that they might snatch it from her and destroy it, and yet needing to show it.

'Oh aye,' they said, 'Sunday, is it, three o'clock? Oh aye, like enough.'

Thursday. Friday. Saturday. To the prison every day with his food, his linen. Home to the rue du Bac. Going towards the rue de la Sainte Vierge. Nearer each morning, each afternoon. On foot, cautious, going by the entrance. Talking to no one. Not looking at the house. The streets were full of rumours. The army. Every one must report. Every one between sixteen and fifty-five, no sixty, no, fifty-five. They cannot take the old men? My husband is ill, they cannot take him? They cannot! Women talking. Posters on the street corners. Every propriétaire, every head locataire of every house must take the new oath of loyalty. Report to your Section, you must answer for every tenant, every occupant of the house. Every man must be prepared to volunteer. To arms, citizens! The Revolution is in danger! The enemy means to destroy your lives, your liberty. Report to your Section. Report what arms you have.

Every horse, carriage or saddle-horse is to be reported.

To arms!

Defend your lives! Defend the Revolution!

[105]

Sunday. Waking. Touching the paper on her bedside table. An order will arrive—at three o'clock. Three o'clock. Eight more hours. Eight! Make herself eat. He would need food like every other day. Clean linen. Money. Money for the gatekeepers and the guards. Money to leave behind with the poor men who would not be freed today. Or would they all be freed, now that the search was over?

She made up the basket, forced herself to drink coffee, forced herself to wait until nine o'clock. Yet she could not stay in the house, listening to Léonie gossiping in Créole with Euphemia, sipping her chocolate as if she was making love to the cup, chattering about clothes.

Hester went down into the street and began to walk. Men leading horses out of the courtyards, the horses fretful at being taken away by strangers. Old grooms protesting, complaining, being forced away from their beloved horses, cursed for aristocrats and lickspittles. The hours going by like snails. Eleven. Twelve. One o'clock. Crowds gathering everywhere, men haranguing them. 'La Patrie est en danger! Aux prisons, citoyens, they will try and break out and kill us all. Aux prisons!'

Some of the onlookers with cards pushed into the ribbons of their hats. 'Pétion or Death.'

I have his paper, she thought, I have his promise. Found it hard to breathe as she walked, began to run. To the prisons? What were they going to do there? More crowds. So that she could no longer run, must force her way through, be shouted at for an ignorant great whore.

'The Prussians have taken Verdun! Everything is lost, the army is destroyed!'

'To the prisons, kill the bastards, kill the aristocrats, kill the priests! Burn them out!'

Crowds running.

She could not breathe, could not think. Wedged into a doorway while a man made a speech, screamed for death for the traitors. Two o'clock. 'To the prisons!'

The crowd like a river, like a flood. Hatred and fear like stenches coming up from mud, boiling, bursting. The rue Sainte Marguerite, not the great door, the little one. She could not get out of the crowd, only see over the heads in front of her, see the stone wall. A man was there giving orders. The Citizen Creuzot.

Black-coated, stooped. She began to fight her way towards him, kicking and pushing. The Citizen Creuzot giving orders to half a dozen men in shirt-sleeves. 'Let me through! I have a message for the Citizen Creuzot.'

They let her through. The men in shirt-sleeves held axes, clubs. They looked like porters from the meat market. Cockades in their hats, savage faces looking at her, as if she was a beast for killing.

'Monsieur—Citizen, I have seen Mayor Pétion. He has given me a promise, a paper——'

At the name Pétion the crowd had drawn back, giving her room. The Citizen Creuzot looked at her with hatred. 'What the hell are you doing here?' he whispered. And then in a louder voice, 'Mayor Pétion? Why of course, citizeness. Show me the paper.'

He read it, his mouth sneering, but only from habit. Almost laughing, as if he was pleased now that he had helped her. 'What do you want?'

The butchers' men craning their heads, staring at the paper that was from the Mayor, from the Blessed Pétion.

'To go in to him, to wait with him until he is released.'

He hesitated, smiled wider, an ugly, crooked smile, showing all his bad teeth. 'That might be best,' he said. 'But you'll have to go in here, they won't let you in anywhere else.' He took one of the men's clubs and rapped on the heavy timber with the butt of it.

'Hulloa! Inside there! Citizens! Open up! It is I, Creuzot, the Citizen Creuzot waiting out here. I've a woman with an order for release for a prisoner. Let her in.'

The crowd murmuring, 'Release? Release?'

Bolts, locks. Darkness inside, a narrow passage, men. 'Take her where she wants to go.'

A hand pushing her inside. The door slammed, was bolted behind her. A long passage. Steps at the far end. As she came to them a man was coming down towards her, driven along by two warders. In his shirt-sleeves, and hatless. Grey hair, a bewildered face. An old man. 'I am being released,' he said, as if he could not believe it.

He was shoved past her. 'Get on with you, old mummery man. Out into the sunshine with you.'

Up the steps into a small room, stifling hot. A table, five men like judges, a crowd of guards, prisoners. The judges looking at her in astonishment.

'An order from Mayor Pétion. The prisoner Broad——' the guard could not pronounce the name and showed the paper. The judge waved it away.

'Not here, take her to the *greffe*. Next prisoner. Have you taken the oath?'

'No, monsieur. I cannot.'

'Ah well, release him.'

'Release me?'

She did not hear any more. Outside she heard a muffled shouting, a roar of hatred. Through corridors, courtyards. To the gatekeeper's room where normally she was let in. One of the gate-keepers whom she knew was behind the table, sweating with fear. She could see it in him. Smell it.

She gave him her paper, and he shook his head over it as if he had forgotten how to read. Outside, that mufled roar again. As if the whole prison was surrounded.

'What is happening, are they releasing people already?'

'They're killing them,' he said. 'Christ save us.' He crossed himself, and then looked fearfully round to see if the guard was gone. He leaned towards her across the table, his stomach creased in half, the sweat like lard on his fat throat. 'They're going to kill them all.'

'But my father! I have an order—Mayor Pétion! The mayor himself, you've got to release him, where is he? The order will come at three o'clock, it says it here, in his own writing. I've just seen two men released!'

He stared at her. 'God can't permit it,' he whispered. 'I've been a jailer thirty years. I——'

She realized he was drunk as well as terrified. She went round the table and lifted him up from his chair. 'Please,' she said. 'Take me to him. Where are the guards?'

He waved his arms helplessly. She took the keys from a numbered hook. 'Take me to him yourself.'

'I can't. I can't leave here.'

The roar lifting, like the sea beating against cliffs. She thought she could hear 'Death, death, à mort!' The crowd angry that prisoners were being set free?

'Take me to him!'

He led the way up the stone stairs, trembling. 'They are

eating,' he said, 'they don't know yet. Oh God, oh God.'

A man was hurrying down the stairs. 'They've paid me,' he shouted. 'Now they can go to Hell with easy consciences.' He laughed like a madman and went running past them.

The door that was as familiar as her hand. 'You'll have to shout loud——'

'But you are going to release him! You've seen the promise! Let me bring him down to your gate. The order will come any minute.'

'No no. Shout to him. Give him a bit of hope. Oh God forgive us.'

She snatched the keys from his hand, fumbled for the biggest, tried it. The next. The next. The lock turning, giving. 'Papa! Papa!'

Men's faces, staring at her, greenish-grey with fear. A long table set with the remains of a meal. Slants of light from high windows.

'Papa!'

Down the stairs behind her a door crashed, there were shouts, screams of rage, of triumph. Stone echoing.

'Get inside!' the old gatekeeper shouted. 'They've broken in! Christ have mercy on us.' He pushed her into the room. 'Keep quiet,' he shouted, then hissed, 'Quiet for your lives. They may not come up here.' The door slammed shut. She was inside the room, her promise of her father's freedom still in her hand. Papa coming towards her.

'They are going to release you,' she said. 'Mayor Pétion——'

Men were looking at her, most of them old men. But two of them young, so alike they might be twin brothers. Beautiful.

'They have just given us a meal,' her father said, as if that was an important thing. He had grown strange in these past weeks. She had put down her basket and flung her arms round him. They could hear the noise of the mob through the thickness of the door behind her, through the high windows. One of the prisoners had climbed up to the window-sill and was trying to look out.

'I can't see anything,' he shouted.

'Be quiet!' another man said, 'you heard what the gatekeeper told us.'

The two boys had approached her. One of them said, 'What is happening outside, mademoiselle? Have they begun the massacre?' He said it as if he was asking for news of dear, dear friends, his face alight with something past comprehension. He could have stepped out of a painting, his hair angel-gold.

A crash of musket butts, of clubs, battered against the door, the timber shuddered, the air echoing. In the middle of the room a half-dozen men were kneeling, surrounding another man, very tall, very old, his hands held out above them.

'They are priests,' her father said. 'They have been very kind to me.'

'I confess before Almighty God——'

The two boys had joined the kneeling men, knelt with them.

There was a thundering against the door, shouting, cursing, beating of clubs. 'Cursed traitors, assassins, priests, the Justice of the People is here for you. Death, death to them!'

It was not possible to think. Holding her father against her, looking at the kneeling priests, the two boys. Other men running from one end of the long room to the other, trying to climb up to the windows twelve and fifteen feet above their heads, making the trestle tables into a useless barricade.

'Go forth, O Christian souls, from this world, in the name of God, the Father Almighty——'

Men were getting out through a window, vanishing. There were shouts from outside, from an invisible courtyard: 'The bastards are escaping, pike them down, give me an axe, hack at them. Murderers, murderers!'

'Christ have mercy on us. God have mercy on us. Christ have mercy.'

'I love you.'

The door at the far end smashing open.

'Now in the hour of our death——'

The old, tall priest spread out his arms like the Crucifixion above his kneeling brothers. Men were running towards him, towards the kneeling group. Axes lifted, sabres. She could not move, could not shut her eyes, not speak, not think. A sabre swung. The old priest bent his head under the blow. There was blood. His lips still opened and shut but she could not hear what he said. The room was full of men, shouting, cursing, clubs swinging, axes. Blood and blood, and the screams of wounded men. The old priest falling like a grey tree, and a scream of triumph.

[110]

'Kill the bastards, kill the murderers!'

A stench of blood, of terror. She wanted to faint. She had dragged her father into a corner, by the far door that still held against other axes, the battering of men held out, prevented from joining in the massacre. She knelt with him behind the half-made barricade of tables, fallen trestles, benches. Almost hidden. The priests still kneeling as they were being killed. A patriot dragged one of the young brothers by his hair, lifted his axe.

'Not him, he's too young, he's not a priest, hold hard, citizen.'

'Are you a priest, little rat? Confess it!'

'Kill me, kill me!'

'And me, I am with my brother, blessed be God!'

The knife in the white throat. She shut her eyes, half-fainted, hung against the wall, one arm still round her father. The voice of a leader, shouting, *'Stop! In the name of the Revolution stop. All is to be done by law.'*

Silence. Men groaning as they died, as they lay in agony. The old, tall priest was already dead, and one of the two brothers. He was lying on his back, his throat cut, blood pouring, the other kneeling beside him, praying. How many others dead? She could not look, could not trust herself to move. And then found herself moving, kneeling beside one of the dying priests.

'God forgive them,' he whispered. She held up his head. One of the patriots made to kick her aside and the leader prevented him.

'Let her be,' the leader said. 'Her turn'll come. Why is there a woman here?'

'My father is to be released.'

He was not listening to her. Quite calmly, stepping over the dead, the dying, the pools of blood, he was ordering the barricade of tables to be dismantled and rearranged down one side of the room, under the windows. Calling for ink, pens, paper, sand, for some colleagues to be sent for, told that everything was ready.

She had carried the wounded priest to a corner and made a sort of bed from the discarded tablecloths. She found wine in a fallen wine-bottle, a glass of it, and held it to his mouth. But he could not drink.

'Now I am content,' he whispered. 'I have shared my Lord's pain.' His eyes looked a long way off and grew veiled.

There were other wounded men. Her father helped her, the brother who had not been killed, other priests. The men who had tried to escape into a courtyard below the windows were brought back, their hands roped, driven like cattle with pikes jabbing at their shoulders. A sort of order began to be established, the prisoners who had not been wounded were made to stand in a line, a queue, before the long table. Behind the table, five men, sashes and cockades, their faces with that mark she had begun to recognize, of exhaustion and hatred, violence and brutality like stains, like a grey hand-print left there by a plague. The leader who had shouted '*Stop*' placed at the centre of them. Younger, better dressed, a fanatic's handsomeness, white-faced and burning, and yet full of joy. He made the others look like simple murderers.

Along the far wall Hester and her father and the others helping them had laid the dead and the wounded, and for ten minutes, without being conscious of time, or even of horror, she worked and tried to comfort, tearing her shift and underskirts into rough bandages while behind her back what sounded like the preparations of a trial began, and outside the windows, outside the still locked door, in distant courtyards, corridors, other cells, shouting rose and fell, yells of rage, screaming, now and again a roar of triumph.

Four dead. Seven wounded and bound up.

'Take him away,' the head judge was saying. One of the unwounded priests, his hands bound behind his back, was led out. At the door one of the patriots knocked his hat from his head and kicked it across the floor.

'You won't need that, old God-maker.'

'Next. Have you taken the oath?'

'No, monsieur. I cannot.'

'Take him away.' The hat knocked from his head. Outside guards laughing. And then, from far away, down steps, a long, old man's cry of terror, of agony. 'Oh my God, oh my God, my Lord and my God.'

The boy, the surviving brother, crying, 'Take me! Take me! Let me be with my brother. Let me die for my Lord!'

They took him. He had no hat to be knocked away and went like a bridegroom out of the far door.

She knelt where she was, by the line of wounded men, holding her father's hand. They are going to release him, she told herself, over and over. The order will come. She knew it would not, that she had been tricked, that they would both die here. She recognized the priest, the old man who had come there only to see his brother. He went out of the same door as all the rest, his hat knocked away.

They are killing them outside, she thought. It could not be true, but they were doing it. One after the other, these old men, and the young man, and the others. A man was arguing. Almost the first to argue.

'Ask about me in the Cordeliers, citizens! They will tell you! I swear by the name of Liberty that I am as good a patriot as you are. Ask the Marseillais where I was on August the tenth! I was with them!'

'He was only brought in this morning,' her father whispered. 'He kept shouting at everyone.'

The man was put to one side. A messenger was sent off for witnesses. The trials went on. 'Have you taken the oath?' Most of the prisoners seemed to be priests who had refused the oath binding them to the state. One of the wounded men died. The bodies lay. The line grew shorter. Outside the storm rose and fell, a burst of screaming, as if someone was being hunted. Dying away. She knelt, her mind grown numb.

Until only the man who had argued, and she and her father were left, and the wounded men. As if they had been forgotten in their dark part of the long toom. The guards came for one of the wounded. She saw him lifted up, made to stand.

'Have you taken the oath?'

She was on her feet, staggering, her legs gone to sleep from too long kneeling.

'You cannot! You cannot try a wounded man!' She did not know why she said it. Said anything. She had even shouted in English, not in French. They stared at her like an apparition. Tall, lurching, blood to her elbows, her skirts in rags where she had torn even the hems for bandages. Blood on her face, her hair fallen, burning in the last of daylight. Perhaps for a second in their exhaustion they thought that she was one of their own, burst in from the courtyards.

'You can't touch him! Lay him down again!'

'He is a guilty man,' the leader of the judges said, his voice almost polite, hoarse with tiredness. 'Guilt does not come to an end with being wounded. What is your answer, priest?'

[113]

But the old man could not answer. He stared round him as if he did not know where he was.

'You cannot try him if he does not answer. Lay him down!'

The door opening, tread of men. Doctor Marat, the Citizen Creuzot, four others. The judges getting to their feet, crying, 'Welcome to the Citizens from the Union of the Cordeliers! Welcome to the Citizen Marat, to the Citizen Creuzot and their colleagues. We invite your aid in dealing out Revolutionary Justice.'

'I see that Justice is being done, citizens,' Marat said. His hand under his shirt, raking and raking as if his flesh tormented him. Twitching, staring about with his mad, visionary's eyes. He saw Hester. The Citizen Creuzot had already seen her and seemed ill-pleased.

'Let the Patriots of the Cordeliers judge this case,' the leader of the judges said. He told Marat of the argument over the wounded man, as if he was telling a joke at which he himself was too tired to laugh. The embers of fanaticism in his smile, a holy idealism that gave him inner joy, if not peace.

'What has been begun must be ended,' Doctor Marat said. 'The Delegation of the Cordeliers votes for Death. If my colleagues agree?' He looked round him. One of his companions struck himself a blow on the chest. 'Death for all suspects, all *calotins*, all traitors! I move that we resolve on cruelty! Only the axe can save us!'

They carried the wounded man away. It took four other men to hold Hester still.

'Who is this woman?' the leader of the judges said, wonderingly. 'Is she mad? Why is she in here?'

'I know her,' Doctor Marat said. 'An Englishwoman. She has a father, I think.'

'I have an order from Mayor Pétion for his release! Look at it, look!' Searching her inner pocket for the sheet of paper, holding it out, blood on it like a seal. 'The Citizen Creuzot——'

'I know her too,' Creuzot said. 'She is stark mad. She should be locked away.' His eyes caught hers, threatening death.

'You are monsters,' she whispered. 'Monsters! Give me my father, he has done nothing, we came here as friends, as lovers of Liberty!' She shook herself free, and came to the table as if it was she who was on trial.

'Let her go free,' Doctor Marat said. 'I never saw so tall a woman, she is like a giantess, she will have splendid children.'

'Give me my father!' She held the paper out in front of the judges, in front of Doctor Marat. 'You sent me to Mayor Pétion,' she shouted at the Citizen Creuzot. 'He promised me an order of release by three o'clock.'

'Ah, Pétion,' Doctor Marat said. 'He is a humorist. But why not? Give her her father. He must be a strong man to produce such a daughter. I move to free this young woman and her father.'

They were being led out of the door. She tried to struggle, wanted to say more, about the wounded men, but they forced her out of the door as if she was one of the condemned and in a distant part of her mind she thought again, 'It is a trick, another trick, they will kill us both.'

'Give the citizen his hat. Any hat. Put it on, citizen.' Cramming a hat on her father's head. Down steps. Through a courtyard. Bodies lying. Blood. Through corridors, into a stone passage she remembered. A door. The guards with them shouting, 'Two prisoners released, by order of the Citizen Marat.'

Outside men with clubs raised, axes, a bloody sabre, as if they had raised them at a signal, at the opening of the door. A crowd staring, murmuring, shoving forward to see, blocking the rue Sainte Marguerite. Her shoes slipped and she looked down. Like a river of blood. She swayed. Hands held her, supported her, voices shouted, 'They are released, released! The Citizen Marat has released them.'

'See his hat, he is wearing a hat! To go free!'

The crowd surging, hands pushing them into the crowd, the men with axes and clubs making way for them.

They will hit us from behind. Felt it before it came. But the crowd was laughing, shouting, taking hold of them, lifting them up.

'The friends of the Citizen Marat! Released, released! Where to, where do you live? We'll bring you home!' Like a flood. Like a Roman triumph. Half the crowd abandoning death for life, for freedom, for the joy of difference, chanting the *Ça ira*, dancing.

'The rue du Bac, the rue du Bac! They live in the rue du Bac!'

They brought them home like captives, like heroes, like a sacrifice, set them down in the hall, invaded the house.

[115]

'We must give them drink,' Hester said. She wanted to lie down and vomit until her soul was empty, but somewhere in her mind there was still a corner of reason. She found Anne trembling in the kitchen, got wine from her, bottles and bottles, God knew if it was good or bad, kitchen wine or valuable. Filled a great basket, filled another with glasses, jugs, cups, anything that would serve to drink from, and went down to the hall again.

Men shouting, 'Long live the Citizen Marat, long live the Jacobins, long live the Cordeliers. Here's to you and your father, citizeness.' Wiping dirty mouths with dirty hands, embarrassed in a gentlewoman's house and presence. Remembering themselves and crying again, 'Long live the Revolution. Death to the traitors!' Emptying their wine, thanking her, wishing her joy of freedom, her father's joy. Going at last. The door shutting.

She sank down on the floor of the hall, the black and white marble, and began crying, as if she was weeping blood.

Chapter 10

She could not sleep, or rest, or even keep in the house. That first night she had slept. Euphemia had given her a drug, and she had slept for twelve hours and each of them had been a century of nightmares. She woke ill and feverish, and had to go out into the streets to breathe. In the streets she heard that the killings were still going on. Had to go to the Abbaye as if she was drawn there by a lodestone. The same crowd outside the door, coldly watching. Coldly. Not shouting now, not roaring in triumph. But like onlookers at a bloody play in endless, endless scenes. The door would open, a man would stagger out into the daylight, hatless, wondering. Old, young, joyous, frightened. And the axes and the clubs would lift and strike, the man would scream and fall, vanish among the legs of his executioners. Writhe like an animal under the heavy sounds of blows. Die.

The crowd would make a silent passage-way for his body to be dragged to a waiting cart, added to the corpses there. When the cart was full it would drive off. Every few minutes the door would open. She stayed for she did not know how long. Heard talk of the other prisons where they were also killing. The Carmes, the Salpêtrière, the Bicêtre, every prison in Paris turned to a pool of blood. As if they were comparing theatres.

She went away from them, not knowing where. Not even thinking of Michel, of her father. Like a sleepwalker. Still half-drugged with Euphemia's medicine. Crowds everywhere. A sudden rush of men and women, more women than men. A column of recruits, marching, singing. They too going towards death. She wrung her hands in a fury of despair, not knowing where she had got to, not caring. Crossed the river, went on.

There was a thickening of the crowds, another prison, the Temple. A garden round it, the crowd broken into the enclosure, surging against the tower.

'There they are, the tyrants, the Austrian. Inside there. Guillotine the bitch, the Austrian whore. Kill her!'

'That window there! There she is! Austrian wolf bitch, you'll not live to see your brother.'

The crowd swaying, a column of men and women running, driving into the crowd, carrying something on a long pole. A head. A woman's head. Long hair and a bloody, battered face, unrecognizable as anything but a woman's head.

'The Lamballe! Here's your Lesbian, here's your paddler! Kiss her mouth now, you whore!'

The head pushed up towards the tower window.

A woman looking out. Vanishing. The crowd chanting, chanting, waving their bloody trophy like a flag of glory.

'I ate her heart!' a woman screamed, 'I ate it! Don't you envy me? That's all the food I ever got from you, curse your soul!' Demented woman, screaming, hair in grey serpents, tearing her clothes as she ran and screamed and danced in triumph.

Going away from that nightmare to another, outside another prison. Blind with horror.

I shall go mad, she thought.

Notre-Dame. The doors open. She went in, not truly knowing where it was, what it was, not caring. She wanted to sit down. I am so tired, she thought. My bones hurt. There was candlelight, in spite of the day outside. And people praying.

Praying? For what? Were they mad? If there is a God, she thought, He is not here, nor looking at any of this. It would not be possible, He would destroy everything.

She went home and collapsed, and Euphemia gave her another drug. But she could not sleep.

The killing went on for five days and she walked about and looked at it. Her father was ill, and somewhere in her mind she knew it. Even helped in a distant way to look after him, while Léonie reproached her for heartlessness. 'How can you go out and leave him? You don't have a woman's heart at all.' She did not want to hear about the massacres, and would put her lovely hands over her ears and cry, 'Stop! Stop! You are inventing it. Oh, how wicked you are to make me so frightened!'

She ate a little. She must have done, or she would have collapsed with hunger the fourth or fifth day. The fifth day she found herself without knowing it in the Street of the Holy Virgin, outside the Citizen Creuzot's house. She knocked and knocked, and at last a servant answered, a hunchback man, dragging a foot as he came to the door. The same ugly, sneering mouth as his master. Perhaps he was not a servant but a poor relation.

'He's not in.'

'Then I'll wait.' She pushed the door in, driving the hunchback against the wall. Not from intention but indifference, not thinking about her strength or his weakness. He snarled and cursed and shuffled backwards down the hallway. 'I'll wait in the courtyard,' she said. He tried to bar her way and she lifted him aside like a doll. Michel was sitting in a broken armchair beside the lathe, his leg stretched out on one of the new-made chairs. He had another chair beside him, and a board and paper on his knees and pen and ink.

She did not say anything to him and went and sat on a chair on the other side of the lathe. 'It's all right,' Michel said to the hunchback. 'She knows. She's safe.' And to Hester, 'You got my letter?'

She shook her head. She felt that if she could lie down now, even on the cobbles and the sawdust, she could sleep. The sun on her face. Quiet. She could imagine that none of it had happened. It seemed a thousand years since she had been here. She tried to remember what she had been like then, what she had thought and felt. But she could not. She was only tired.

He seemed to understand. He did not say anything, and after a time he began writing again. The sound of the quill. Sparrows chirping, fighting over crumbs in the sunlight. Flying up and out of the yard. Neighbours' voices, the sounds of a cart. More sounds far off, city murmuring.

'It will come to an end today,' he said, after an interval. 'Your father is all right?'

'Yes.'

And after another interval, more writing. 'I'm leaving for the West very soon. He's getting me a passport. You—you and your father could come with me. All of you.'

She was half asleep. It took time to think what he meant, what he had said. And it still seemed distant, to concern other people.

'It would be safer. And you've got business there, near where I'm going.'

'We have no passports,' she said. She did not want to talk, to think about doing anything.

'He'll get them for you. He'd be glad to see you out of Paris. He's not happy about my being here, and you knowing it.'

'He tried to get me killed,' she said, realizing it almost as she said it. 'Only for that? That I knew he had helped you?'

'This is the Age of Humanity,' Michel said. 'What more reason would he want? Come here.'

She made herself stand up and walk round the lathe to his chair. She pulled another of the new straw-seated chairs from a pile of them, and sat down, close at his side. But she still could not take his hand, or touch him. Or tell him what she had seen. She put her hands to her face.

After a minute or two he put out his hand and pulled hers away. 'Look at me.'

He was no longer laughing at her, not the shadow of laughter in his eyes. Their hands lay together on her lap, as if it was their hands that were lovers, and not their eyes, nor their minds.

There was nothing to say. Nothing that needed saying. 'We belong to one another,' their hands said. 'They do not know it yet, but we know.' She sat looking at the courtyard, driving away the nightmares.

'Yes,' she said at last. 'We'll come with you. And you'll need someone to look after you. Ask him to get four passports for us.'

The sparrows came back, still fighting.

Chapter 11

She rode a length behind him along the lane. Frost lay between the hedges like a mist, a living coldness. The snow itself hung in the branches of the thorn trees, dressed them with ice glitter; lay in a thin and shivering blanket on the fields; made a soft ermine carpet for their hoof-beats. Only the sky black, and their horses, and themselves.

February. Midnight. The road between Heaven knew where and nowhere. She had long stopped questioning where they rode, or why. Knew only that tonight, for this journey, the sea and the marshes lay behind them. That they had not eaten since midday, and there seemed no likelihood of their eating now. They had travelled a long time through a forest, and twice passed by lit houses without stopping. Houses? Huts. But there had been the signs of fires, and the promise of warmth and food, and they had not stopped.

That had been hours ago. He rode without turning his head, without speaking, his shoulders slightly hunched against the cold. They had an unspoken bargain between them, that she would never complain, and he would never ask if she was tired, or hungry, or treat her in any other way than if she was a man. Once he began that it would become impossible for her to ride with him on these journeys. She rode in men's clothes more to seal that bargain with him than from necessity, although often it made things easier. Easier for riding, for one thing, and in the rain or the snow a man's breeches and high boots were better protection than skirts. And if they were stopped or questioned by Republican troops a tall manservant who did not talk caused no comment, where a woman riding abroad with a man——

That bargain too, that she should ride with him, that where he went she would go, had been made without words. That she should not stay with her father, and Léonie, and Euphemia, in the *manoir* near Mervent. She had listened to her father's protests as if he was talking about someone else.

'Papa, I love him, I love Michel as my own self, as I love you.' Talking to him as if he was a child who must be comforted. And as for riding with him, 'He needs me.'

From the day of their marriage, that hurried, illicit ceremony, their blessing by a refractory priest disguised as a peasant in sabots and fustian, she had ridden with him. Had never shown by a look or a word that she was ready to fall from the saddle, that she was fainting with hunger. Although she learned very soon always to carry a loaf of bread and a lump of cheese in her saddle bag, and a goatskin of sour milk, and she dined as they rode, often enough.

Now, in the second half of February, after two months of it, she could ride for ten hours on end without thinking it extraordinary. There were many days they covered sixty miles. Up north into Brittany, across the Loire, once as far as the English Channel. They had seen sails that might be English men-of-war, and had waited all night on a beach. A longboat had come in at dawn, and two men had landed, and they brought them swiftly inland, without talk, received a set of documents from them, and handed them on to other guides who were to bring them east into Normandy. Or so she imagined. Michel told her none of that part of their business. Only to remember roads, remember people, remember houses.

Often they stayed all day without talking, as if she was really a man, a comrade, and there was nothing that needed saying. When they made love it was like the completion of comradeship, the completion of the day. Or sometimes they were too tired, and only held one another. At times like that he seemed to belong to her even more closely than when they were lovers in the ordinary sense, and she would smooth his mouth and his forehead with her fingers, smoothing away the day's exhaustion, resting her face against his. And she would wake first in the morning, and look at him, before he opened his own eyes. In that moment, his eyes still shut, still sleeping, he was completely hers, body and soul, and she felt sometimes that she could have wished him to sleep for ever, if only she could watch over him.

It was like an image of her love for him. She did not ask herself, 'Why do I love him?' Or 'Does he truly love me as I love him?' She said only, 'He is mine, and I am his, and we must be together so long as we both live.'

Her determination had borne down her father's sick man's objections, still lost in his fraily reconstructed sanity, those weeks in the prison, those hours of survival and death mercifully blotted out of his mind. He thought that he had fallen ill as a result of the Commissary's search and had had an apoplexy.

He had indeed had one, or something like it. Not that same day he was released from the prison, nor for four days afterwards. Only on the Thursday, the evening she had gone back to the rue du Bac from Michel's hiding-place, she had found him in bed. Quiet, and limp, not able to move properly, not really knowing who she was. It seemed to have happened ten minutes before she came. Euphemia was with him. She had heard him fall, and she and Léonie had got him into bed.

It was mid-October before he was anything like himself again, and could move about. One foot dragged a little, one eye seemed to stare, and to move slower than the other. And those weeks in the prison were blotted away, vanished. Michel had gone within three days of that Thursday afternoon in the courtyard, but she had scarcely minded. She would find him again, she knew it. Even though his letter sent to her by means of the Citizen Creuzot had not arrived, and never did arrive.

'Don't trust him,' Michel said, taking leave of her. 'I could. Just. This time. But not again.' He had not said 'I'll write to you' or 'I love you' or 'Do you love me?' Nothing. Had held her hand for a moment, and gone, hauling himself into the *fiacre*. And two days later the Citizen Creuzot had called to the rue du Bac to make inquiries that looked and sounded like sneers, as to the health of the esteemed friend of France, Monsieur Broadhurst.

As he left, he had said casually to Hester, 'Oh, our mutual friend, Monsieur Vernet, I shan't wrong him by calling him citizen, he left some papers behind. Can you tell me where I may forward them? Or——' His eyes fixed on hers not casually at all —'you will no doubt be seeing him soon yourself. Perhaps——?'

'I have no address for him, citizen. It was you who were his friend. No doubt he'll write to you.'

Afterwards, when she thought of what she hated most in the Revolution, he was its symbol. Not Marat, with his madman's eyes, and his twitching body, nor Pétion, nor even the mindless creatures who had done the killing. How had he ever become Michel's friend?

It was almost the first question that she had asked Michel when they were together again, in Mervent, towards the end of October. She had got their passports herself through Mayor Pétion, who had shown himself charmed, delighted, oh how relieved, citizeness, to see her still alive. And her good father? He had been ill? What a shame! But with such a daughter to nurse him. Smiling with his baby lips, his *petit-maître's* charm. But he had got them their passports, and they had found places in a creaking old Turgotin of a diligence, and at last had rolled and shuddered and jarred their way out of Paris, into a cleaner air. Chartres. Tours. Cholet. And at last in a hired carriage to the *manoir* south of Légé, where Léonie turned from guest to hostess, and became, for the peasants, their Countess and proprietor. Although both titles were in dispute.

That was why Mr. Broadhurst, as soon as he was stronger, had documents to look at, and lawyers to talk to, visits to Nantes to plan and carry out, the Count de Richeteau to call on, rent rolls to examine and have translated, accounts to verify. And there were business letters to write to Léonie's father, not to speak of dutiful ones to Mrs. Broadhurst, and his own steward, and Uncle George, telling them of progress, and giving instructions, and promises that within another month all must be completed and they would be on their way home. But for Hester there was nothing to do at all, except to remember, and think. And she wanted to do neither.

She was not even needed often as interpreter. In the matter of her own estates, and the farms, Léonie showed a side of her character that nothing had revealed before, and was willing to spend hours over documents, or interviewing tenants, or talking to lawyers and accountants. As if her brain only woke up at the clink of money, and she would sit to dinner after a long morning of business with the air of a cat that has fed on cream, or someone who has made love.

'How lucky we are to have such loyal peasants,' she said. 'Everywhere else they have burned the rent rolls and all the

[124]

feudal documents, and seized the best land. And here everything is as it always was.' She had spoken as if that was arranged by God for her benefit.

It was not completely true. The newly proclaimed Republic controlled the Vendée as it controlled everywhere else, and the goods and estates of the Church and the *émigrés* were for sale, and being bought. Only that often they were bought in by men who meant to hold them in trust for their real owners, and this was an open secret. Léonie's estates were safe because she herself was there to claim them. But the churches were not, and the priests who had not taken the Oath of Allegiance were not, and a dozen times a month there were ugly flares of trouble, like a bush fire that burns itself out in minutes, but leaves an ugly scar. Patriots hounding a priest out of his church, and his house, and setting an oath-priest in his place, only to have the oath-priest driven out by stones and hatred. A patrol of Republican troops coming in to right things, and weapons drawn, shots fired, someone dead, someone wounded, two, three, four arrested, taken to Cholet to jail, sent to the galleys.

There were rumours of a new conscription law, and men swearing they would not go. Young men gathering, threatening patriots with a ducking, a stoning, their house burned.

The priests who had been dispossessed came back into their churches in defiance of the Law, to baptize, to marry, to say Mass, to preach against the Republic, against the oath-priests, against anyone who gave support to the new order in Church or State. Missionaries came by night to houses. One came to the *manoir*, talking to the servants about the Sacred Heart of Jesus, that was bleeding for France, and for His Vendée. He gave Léonie a red velvet heart, surmounted by a cross and a crown of thorns, stitched onto a white silk flag, and begged her to keep it safely hidden.

'What a sweet thing,' Léonie said when he was gone, and made it into a cushion cover.

And then Michel came, in mid-November. He rode up at dark and it was as if they had left one another yesterday. His eyes amused as he took her two hands, his face lean and brown again, tanned with weather, his cloak shabby, his hat fit for a scarecrow, his boots and breeches thick with November mud. But his hands as familiar as her own. She knew then that she would marry him.

[125]

As if she had known before he came, and did not need to think about it.

Afterwards she could not be sure how they had arranged it. He claimed that it was she who had asked him to marry her, and perhaps that was even true. But it did not matter. It was arranged, and she bore down her poor, beloved, bewildered papa's objections, the pretence that her mother would object; swept aside Léonie's cries of incredulity, and prepared herself to battle with a country priest's bigotry against a Protestant, and what he might be pleased to call a mixed marriage.

But there was no bigotry, at least of that kind. Only a hunted man with his eyes on more distant battles, much greater arguments than how she said her Creed. She became Madame Vernet at three o'clock of a dark afternoon, they drank a glass of wine together, and the priest vanished like a shadow among shadows, a gaunt, bony peasant of a priest in peasant's clothes, no older than Michel.

Then the renewed arguments with her father that her place was with Michel. 'Where he goes, I shall go.'

Michel accepted that without question. And with that unspoken bargain that she should come as a comrade, should not complain of hardships, should not claim a woman's privileges, let alone a wife's. Should expect nothing but long journeys and cold nights and rough fare or none.

'I have work to do,' he said, 'and if you want to join me in it——' That was as near as they came to setting out terms. Now, after eight, nine weeks of it she rode as soldiers ride, without effort, and thought of the ancient times when she was admired for the way she rode, lady's side-saddle, Diana's hunting-skirts and velvet cap and feather, stirrup-cups and compliments, with an amazed pity for so much ignorance. Her hands were like a man's, brown and hard, and calloused from wet leather reins that soaked her gauntlets and made it preferable to ride bare-handed even in the snow. Her muscles were as lean as Michel's, and as strong as most men's, or stronger. Her face had grown lean as well, bronzed with the weather. She looked like a tall young man. The eyes of the maids and the younger women in the farm houses they stopped at overnight, or spent a day in, told Hester that she was still handsome, and when she let down the copper abundance of her hair to dry it by the fire, better than handsome, and sometimes she was pleased at the thought, and sometimes too tired to do more than accept it like a hunk of bread and a draught of milk.

She would sit in the darkest corner, eating, or resting, or sleeping on her stool, her back resting against the wall, or taking in the company through half-lowered lids. Faces. Voices. Tricks of movement.

'A time will come when all this'll matter,' Michel said. 'I'll need to send you where I can't be spared to go. And you'll have to know you're talking to the right man. The cowman last Tuesday, in Vallon's farm. Tell me how you'd recognize him.'

'Last Tuesday? Vallon's?'

'Tell me! Don't just repeat what I ask you! Tell me!'

'He had a slight squint in the left eye. And his lower lip drooped down. It was very red and wet.'

'Ah.'

Sometimes, where the farm women were inquisitive, she was recognized for a woman, and there would be gasps of astonishment, a few down-drawn eyebrows and tightened mouths. Then the girls would cluster and stare at her, wanting to ask questions and make sure. That happened once when there was a priest there, the same curé who had married them. He heard two of the older women with their heads together, whispering condemnation, and he lifted his oak staff and brought it down on the massive table, filling the kitchen with a crash of echoes.

'She is the man's wife. And they are riding on God's business. May God's wrath burn the tongue that speaks ill of her.' He had gone, leaving the echoes to settle. That had been a fortnight ago. She thought of it, swaying with the tired walk of her horse. God's business. She knew that they were helping to prepare a rising. And that it was close to beginning, in spite of the death of the 'Colonel Armand' who had long ago begun the planning. He had died during the winter, last month. Like his King. That fat, vacant-looking man she had seen leaving his palace for ever, and had seen again in that low-ceilinged room like a cage behind the president's tribune in the *Manège*.

He had been taken in a coach to the Place of the Revolution, that used to be the Place of his grandfather, Louis XV, and had been guillotined like a criminal.

'He deserved it,' was all Michel had said when they heard the news, at least all that he said to her. 'How many men died for him because he couldn't make up his mind to fight? I'll keep my tears for them.' But he spoke a different elegy to the peasants. Their King, killed like God's son by wicked men.

Reading the King's Testament to them, his voice hoarse with passion; 'I, Louis the Sixteenth, King of France, imprisoned these past four months with my family, in the Tower of the Temple, by those who were my subjects——'

Men weeping, who would not have wept if it had been their own father who had died.

'I recommend to God my wife, my children—I beg my son, if he has the unhappiness to become king, to devote himself heart and soul to all his fellow citizens; to forget all hatreds and resentments, above all against those who have had any share in my misfortunes.'

When the reading was over, a priest in the audience, usually a Mulotin, would begin to preach the Sacred Heart like a crusade.

'Our King has died for us, as Christ died. His blood lies on the soil of France! How can we sleep until he is avenged!'

Michel would draw her out of hearing, and they would be travelling again. Did he believe any of it? She thought that now she knew less of his true mind than when they began. But she did not care. It was enough to be with him. He is mine, her heart said. Mine, mine. She imagined being warm with him, lying down, by a fire, a blanket over them, together. The thought of warmth made her shiver, and remember how hungry she was. She had a crust left in her saddle-bag and she felt for it, and began to eat, very slowly, to make it last.

'We'll be there soon,' Michel said, without turning his head. There were trees ahead, the dark mass of a wood. They rode among them, into a hooded darkness. And outside it, the snow-light, a soft haze of whiteness filtering from the thick roof of snow-laden branches above their heads. They followed a narrow path, branches raking at her cloak and knees. And without warning they were in a clearing, the trees fallen back, snow on the bare ground. By the reflected light of the snow she could make out a house, a cottage. A head forester's, or a gamekeeper's. No lights. No dogs. Nothing. But Michel dismounted and rapped with his whip-handle on the door. Twice, and then three times quickly. A moment more and the door opened, there was candle-light. The dark shape of a man. Whispering.

Michel nodded to her and went in. She spread out the saddle-blankets over both horses, and led them round the cottage, looking for shelter for them. There were no stables, but a kind of lean-to shed promised something, and she felt her way into it, stumbling over a chopping-block. There seemed to be a stack of firewood and a trestle to hold logs for cutting. She looped the reins round an upright post that supported the roof, and comforted the horses for a moment, holding their hard, rough heads against her cheeks. 'When will you eat, poor creatures?' she said aloud.

Something there? A sense of—someone? She was not alone in the shed. She stood as she had been standing, still stroking the harsh, frosted manes. And heard the soft, frightened outletting of long-held breath.

'Who's there?'

No answer. But the stillness had a tension about it, the dark seemed to thicken there beyond the piled logs. She thought of calling Michel, and heard his voice, almost close to her, but muffled by a wall. The wall of the shed that was also the wall of the cottage.

'Michel! Here, quickly, there's someone here!'

There was a knife-flash in the dark, and she flung up her cloak for protection. Cloth ripping, tugging at her forearm, a rushing darkness. She stuck out her boot and the darkness lurched, went sprawling over her outstretched foot. She bent and caught hold of the man. A man writhing and kicking. He must have dropped the knife as he fell. She let go of him with one hand and struck where his head ought to be. She thought she had broken her wrist. The man hung slack and she let him fall to the ground. Michel was there with a hooded lantern, three other men. They turned the eye of the lantern on the heap of shadow on the ground. A dark unshaven face, staring eyes, crow hair cropped in ragged, dusty feathers, a mouth already begging for mercy.

'Don't hit me, I'm only a poor beggar, looking for shelter, please, monsieur, messieurs, citizens, I was——'

They hauled him upright and round to the door of the cottage.

'Show me your hands,' Michel said.

Earth stains under the broken finger-nails. Callouses on the palms.

'Those aren't beggar's hands.' Michel slipped his own knife out of his pocket and snapped the blade. 'They'd look worse still with a finger missing. Bring him inside and stick his hands on the table.'

Hester walked away into the dark. After a minute or so there was a high, wailing scream. She put her fists over her ears. 'Christ have mercy on us.' And thought of the prison, the old priests, the two boys with their angels' faces and their longing for martyrdom. A voice jabbering, falling over itself to confess. A few more minutes and Michel called her. The prisoner had his left hand wrapped in a bloody rag. Round the long table that occupied the room were six men besides the prisoner and Michel. She recognized three of them as Mulotins, she had seen them before. Missionaries who had already spent half a lifetime tramping the roads of Brittany and the Vendée, rooting out the last of Calvinism that still lay dormant in the West, winning souls for the Heart of Jesus, coaxing the Faith into flame. Now their journeys were more urgent still.

The other three she did not know. One was a miller from his dress and apron, as if he had come straight from work, a trace of flour dust on his hands, in his hair. Young, but already thickset, ruddy, dark yellow curls over a bull's forehead, and a short, thick, powerful nose, broad mouth, broad cheeks. The other two were older. Men with an air of long authority, the *métayers* of big farms, leaders of their parish, their district. In the few weeks she had been riding she had learned to recognize types and character, could pick out master from man at fifty yards in the twilight, without needing to think about clothes. The way a man walked and held himself. She could tell a villager from a farm labourer, a weaver from a carpenter, merely by seeing them walk away from her. She imagined she could almost tell their politics in the same way. Patriots from Royalists. Sometimes it was easy. The townsmen patriots and Republicans. The countrymen royalist almost to a soul.

But this man? A casual labourer, getting day work here and there, a weak, sickly face. A man who had never his life long had enough to eat. Nor his father nor his grandfather before him. He stared at her as she came in with a new terror. She forced herself not to look at his hand and the bloody rag.

'Look at him!' Michel said. 'Judas got thirty pieces of silver, but this rat did it for paper money! Ten livres in *assignats*! Ten livres to sell your God, your King, your people! It won't pay for the rope to hang you.'

The miller and one of the farmers had a length of cord and they roped him like a pig for slaughter, heels to wrists, and took him outside. She expected to hear him scream again but there was no sound. Michel pushed a bowl of soup towards her across the table. She shook her head, and Michel thumped his fist softly and angrily on the heavy timber.

'Eat! Do you think this is charades? What would he have done to us?'

'Are they——' She found she could not ask the question, but he understood it.

'No. He'll be tried. He'll have his chance. Now *eat*.'

And she was so hungry that she found after the first mouthful that she could not stop, and was astonished to find the bowl empty. There was a fire, and she took a three-legged stool and sat by it while the men talked.

She shook herself awake and went out into the cold dark. They had tied the man to a tree away from the cottage and she could hear his shivering and whimpering as soon as she closed the cottage door behind her. They had gagged him, and the whimpers came muffled through a twist of neckcloth. When she came close to him his eyes grew wide and white with terror, the whimpering stopped, cut off. She went behind him to look at his bandaged hand. Another neckcloth twisted round it. It was sodden with blood. She made herself undo his wrists, bring his hand round to the front. The small finger gone from the knuckle. In the fierce cold the bleeding had almost stopped, as if the blood had frozen.

When she let go of his wrist he put his hands together in prayer to her, his eyes begging. Mumbling and retching deep in his throat like a dumb man trying to talk. She loosened the gag.

'Monsieur, for God's love don't kill me! I have a wife, five children, look at my hand, look what they have done to me! What will my children do if I'm killed? Please, in the name of Jesus, in the name of Mary the Mother of God have mercy on me! You have a kind face, you're not like them, you're young. We hadn't had bread for three days and they tempted me! Ten livres and work. To feed my children! I'll say I couldn't find the way here, I saw no one, heard nothing, I swear it, on my mother's soul I swear it, please!'

In spite of his bound legs he had managed to go down onto his knees and clasp her boots with his hands.

'Stand up,' she said. 'They will give you a fair trial. Tell them what you have told me.'

'A fair trial?' He stank of terror. He must have soiled himself. There had been the same stench at the massacre, men emptying themselves in terror. It made her feel sick remembering. 'They'll shoot me in the back like a dog, they've no mercy in them. Look at my hand!'

Something about her face, the few words she had spoken, the way she stood, that woman scent that no man has, made him flare his nostrils like an animal. 'You're a woman!' He sank down onto his knees again. 'How can a woman see me murdered? I must feed my children! As you love someone pity me!' Bloody hand grasping for hers, wet mouth kissing, tears.

She could not touch him. 'Untie your legs,' she said. 'Can you? I'll walk to the trees and back again.'

She went slowly. When she turned back he was already gone. A moment later there was a shot among the trees. She stood still. Michel came out of the wood into the snow light of the clearing. He had a pistol in his hand and she imagined she could see a wisp of smoke still coiling out of the barrel. He came towards her, his face savage. 'If there were two barrels I'd empty the other into you. You great stupid bitch, what were you dreaming about?'

His hand lifted to hit her. If he hits me, she thought, that is the end of us. But already the other men, all six of them, were pouring out of the cottage, jostling in the narrow doorway before they could free themselves. 'What—what is it? Who——'

They saw Michel and Hester together. Michel turned towards them, putting his pistol into his belt. 'Our prisoner was escaping, that's all,' he said. 'We stopped him.' He jerked his head to where the body must be. The men went to look, and bring it back with them. Michel dug his fingers into her arm like hooks.

'I can guess why you did it,' he whispered. 'But I've told you, this isn't charades. If you ever do anything like that again, if I so much as think you're going to, I'll kill you.'

I'm looking at a stranger, she thought. She felt not anger but sadness, and then tragedy, as if this death would always lie between them. Perhaps he saw that in her eyes.

'Have you already forgotten the Abbaye?' he said. 'Those two boys? The priests?'

'No,' she whispered. 'But you owe me your life. If I'd asked you for his life in exchange, would you have refused me?'

'That—that Judas rat?' She thought again he would hit her, and shut her eyes in preparation. But he walked away. The men were coming back with the body, the two farmers carrying it, one of the Mulotins reciting a prayer for the dead.

'The ground's too hard to bury him easy,' one of the farmers said. 'But I know a safe place.'

The men went inside. The dead spy looked up from the ground with shocked eyes, at her, at the black sky. I have destroyed everything, she thought. To save this. And instead I killed him. If I had done nothing he would still be alive, he would have his chance of mercy. Now he is dead.

She did not feel anything but a tiredness like iron weights bound to her. Her bones hurt. Like an ill-shapen mass inside her body, hard and painful. Ten minutes later Michel came out alone.

'We're riding back,' he said. Nothing else. She followed him round the cottage to the shed, and the horses. They mounted without another word and she followed him, across the clearing, back the way they had come.

There is nothing left, she thought.

Half an hour. An hour. Asleep as she rode. She had forgotten hunger, forgotten cold, forgotten tiredness.

They came to a farmhouse they had passed an eternity ago. That she had sensed then rather than seen. Now the sky had cleared as the cold grew fiercer, there was starlight, and the farm buildings were a dark hummock of man's presence among trees and hedges. Michel turned his horse's head up the whiteness of what might be a track to the farm. And then round to stables. Dogs bayed. Hens in a poultry house woke and fluttered, fearing death. A shutter opened, and the muzzle of a gun caught the starlight, metal clinked against the metal of a latch.

'Who's there?'

'Two of the harvesters,' Michel said. 'We want to sleep in the stable loft.'

'Sleep well.' The shutter closed.

[133]

When she got down from the saddle she could hardly stand and had to support herself against her horse. Michel said nothing and began opening a stable door. She led the two horses in and made herself see to them. Water. Hay torn from a bale. Michel had lit a lantern with his flint and tinder and a spill of straw. He hung it on a nail and went up a ladder into a loft above, moving as if he had no need of a light to find his way. She made her business with the horses last longer than was necessary, until at last it became cowardice, and she must go up to him.

He was lying down under his cloak. She expected him to be asleep, or pretending to be. To have his back to her. But his eyes were watching her, bright points reflecting the lantern light. She set the lantern down, and began to undress. She had always hated sleeping in her clothes, no matter how cold it was, and she would not let herself change her habits now, because of their quarrel. Quarrel? What a stupid word for it. She felt sick and empty. Stripped off her shirt and boots. Her breeches. Stood naked. He watched her, not saying anything.

She knelt down to make herself a bed of the straw that was heaped about, and found that he had already done that. For her as well as for himself. She began to spread out her cloak to lie on, and then wrap round herself, her clothes rolled up for a pillow. But Michel was lifting the edge of his own cloak.

'Here,' he said. 'What a great fool you are.'

Chapter 12

The eleventh of March, riding south from Pornic towards Légé, and beyond it to the *manoir*. Riding through a countryside already in rebellion, through small towns where fear hung in the streets like fog. The news of the men to be conscripted, ordered by the Convention in Paris—the word of that had run through the countryside like a burning fuse to a barrel of gunpowder. Five thousand men to be torn from the farms and villages of the Vendée, because almost all the townsmen would escape the net. Five thousand families to be robbed of their strongest pairs of arms. Five thousand young men to be marched away from their fields, their woods, to defend a government they hated, that had wronged their faith, driven out their priests, killed their King.

In Cholet and St. Florent le Vieil and half a dozen other places they had already rioted against the drawing of lots and attacked the National Guard. The Republicans' hunting of the true priests became more savage. The coming revolt hung in the air like a gathering storm.

Michel and Hester had ridden west to the sea and north to Pornic to get and give news and arrange things there. And now south, and homeward, through Machecoul, to wait in Léonie's *manoir* for the final orders. They would have to come earlier than had been planned, because of the conscription. It would not be possible to hold things back.

Already dark. Ahead of them they could make out the huddled mass of the town. Lights. More than there should be, as if there were lanterns in the streets, windows lit by candles, movement. They stopped riding, and sat quiet to rest the horses. And as they sat looking, listening, they heard the sea. She thought nothing of it for a moment. Waves breaking, rushing, that indistinct, yet unmistakable sound of the tide rising, growling against the shore. Until she remembered that the sea was ten, twelve English miles behind them, beyond all possibility of hearing. And the sound was coming from the east, not the west.

Michel was also listening, lifting his hand to silence any question from her. Growling, rushing, rustling. She shut her eyes to listen, opened her mouth, turned her head slowly.

'The *moutons noirs*,' Michel whispered. 'Souchu is coming.'

She shivered as she sat. She had already seen them, in the marshes. Marsh men, dressed in the filthy, blackened sheepskins that gave them their nickname of black rams. Gaunt savages armed with scythes turned into weapons, promising one another loot and murder, rich townsmen to hang up by their heels while the gold fell out of their purses. Axes, billhooks, massive, iron-bound clubs, hunting guns. Ferocity. And Souchu, their leader, like a mad butcher. How many were there, to make such a sound?

As they sat listening the sound took shape. Shadows. A great arc of shadows ahead of them, between them and the restless town. Voices whispering, a thousand whispers joined together, like the sea. A thousand? Five thousand, ten. Like the marsh water rising, drowning the land. The lights in the town growing agitated, men running in the streets.

They sat for a half hour, unconscious of the wind, the cold. The horses stamped and shivered. The shadows reached the town. The first screams came within moments. Michel began riding away to their right.

'We'll ride round,' he said. The noise followed them for an hour until they were well to the south-east of the town. Volleys of musket fire. The louder crash of hunting guns, loaded with nails and heavy shot. Shrieking of women. She found herself praying as she rode. 'Our Father.' She would have liked to pray to the Virgin, if she had known how.

The next day they were resting in Léonie's *manoir*, log fires, meals that lasted for two hours, Papa. Papa unaware of anything. Full of documents, plans for the lawyers, a dispute over where a boundary line should run, and fishing and hunting rights in a marsh and some woods. A half dozen disputes with neighbours, and with *métayers*.

'But we'll have your rights, my dear. Depend on it. They shan't wear *me* down.' As if he had really been born to be a lawyer, his conversation full of French legal terms, feudal rights, antique dues owed to the estates since the time of the Capets. One document claimed twelve swans a year from Léonie every Christmas, by a grant given to the mistress of one of Charlemagne's sons. In her turn she had the right to take them from the marsh.

'A thousand years!' Mr. Broadhurst cried. 'I'll not let such a great tradition be broken!' As if the whole world was not breaking round him. He had begun to treat Léonie as his daughter and Hester—not as he had once treated Léonie, but with an unspoken reproach, for her marriage, her way of life, the way she looked and dressed. In the *manoir* she dressed as a woman, but she could not think like the woman her father wanted her to be, or that Léonie would have approved; concerned with fashions, recipes, children, talk of love. She sat at the table and in the drawing-room after dinner pretending to listen to Léonie's chatter, or to the talk of rents and dues and law cases when her father came in with Michel from the dining-room to take coffee with them. Sat pretending to listen while her mind was on Michel. On what they had done, would do.

She was not really thinking at such times. Only seeing. Seeing his face, the movement of his hands. A wood they had ridden through, a farmhouse where they had met others of the leaders, or couriers, or Mulotins. Saw the barns, the empty huts where they had slept a night. The sometimes comfort of a farmhouse bedroom, shown up to it by the farm wife, or a daughter, or a maid, her eyes round at Hester's appearance if she knew her to be a woman, or sly if she still thought her a handsome man. Lying with Michel in the luxury of a warm bed, a fire burning, candlelight. Making love by candle shadow, recovering that first ecstasy of the rue du Bac.

More than recovering it, building on it, their bodies growing used to one another, fitting together like two halves of one being. He still laughed, but with a difference in the laughter, a tremendous joy. Holding her as if he could not believe in his fortune, to have such a partner in love. He had never told her about other women, but she knew there had been many. Must have been by the way he made love. But she was not jealous of the past. And·

since that night of the spy's death they had grown closer. They had each accepted something about the other, respected something unbreakable. One must, she thought, bring to marriage something that cannot be broken even for the sake of the marriage. If one does not one is not a wife, nor a partner, only a slave to lie in the bed. And if the man cannot accept that he is not worthy of being loved.

The thought of slavery made her look at Euphemia. The black girl sat on a stool beside Léonie's chair, doing her embroidery for her, the black fingers and the coloured wools making patterns by the firelight. The patterns, the firelight, the black head bending over the embroidery frame, the scarlet bodice, the swell and fall of scarlet silk over her knees, skirts and petticoats, seemed to become something else, a sunset, a landscape lit by sunset, full of blood. For a second she saw herself, saw Michel, saw men fighting, falling. She had such a sense of disaster coming that she started forward, looked into the fire to break up the imaginary vision, and in the chimney a man was hanging, as if he was hanging by his throat above the fire.

It was gone, and she looked at Euphemia, head bent, fingers busy. The head turned, looked at her. Not with malice, and not tragically; not as if she had shared the vision and found it as terrible as Hester did. With hauteur rather, the black, delicate nostrils slightly flared in disdain for the things she saw, the people who took part in them.

What have you made me see? Hester wanted to shout at her. Why? What have I ever done to you?

There was an alteration in Euphemia's expression. Polite inquiry, a hint of mockery behind it. And then invitation. To go out of the room. Hester could not tell how it was done, but she knew that she was to go out, and wait. She made an excuse after another minute or two, and went outside. Euphemia joined her, a rustling of silks. Going ahead of her up the broad stairs, into a small room that Euphemia had adopted for her own. Her trunk there, and her clothes. The smell of musk, and herbs, now sweet, now slightly acrid, heavy, tropical, as if they were in a forest in Africa. The curtains drawn, a fire burning. She did not look at Hester, but into the fire.

'You are going away tomorrow,' she said.

'How do you know that?'

'Oh madame, Madame Estairre, we have only a minute, she will call me. Beg your father, order him, make him go to Nantes, and bring my mistress and myself with him. Tomorrow. The next day at the latest.'

'But I cannot order any such thing. Your mistress orders everything here. Tell her.'

'She will not listen. She used to listen to me, but since we have come here she can think of nothing except how great she is in this place, even greater than she could have been in Saint-Domingue. She is like a child with new dolls, I cannot make her listen without doing things I do not want to do. That I am afraid of doing.'

She turned, and with nothing careless or unthinking about the gesture, laid her hand on Hester's. Like a declaration of equality. She was no longer a slave, no longer even a servant.

'My mother gave her to me. She gave her to me as a charge when I was seven years old. You must help me. Now.'

'You don't understand,' Hester said. 'Even if I could give such orders, or persuade my father and your mistress, it would be dangerous to go. More dangerous still in Nantes. I cannot tell you about it——'

'I can tell *you*!' Euphemia gripped Hester's fingers, thrust her head forward so like a snake striking that Hester drew back, 'I *know*.'

'What do you know?'

Euphemia let go of her, turned back to the fire. She sat hunched over it like a witch, her face suddenly old. Like an old, old black woman, toothless, all bones and shrunken flesh and wrinkled blackness

'I know what must happen. What I am to make happen. But not how. Tell me!' She whispered to the fire. 'Tell me!' Her voice commanding, then pleading. She put down her hand into the fire and picked up a burning log, rearranged it. Slowly, not hurrying. Carefully.

'What are you?' Hester whispered. She thought she must see the hand burn, the flesh crack.

'I am a poor slave,' Euphemia cried in her pure French. 'I am Euphemia. How honoured I am that Madame Vernet comes to my room. So you will not do what I ask? Very well. Ride away tomorrow, and I will see you here again.'

She made to get up, and Hester caught her by the arms and held her. 'Tell me what you are!'

'Madame,' Euphemia said, as if she was talking to a child. 'Madame Estairre.'

Like trying to hold smoke. Euphemia was by the door, waiting for Hester to go out ahead of her.

In the drawing-room they were getting ready to go in to supper. Michel beckoned her. 'Come and see to the horses,' he said as she came in, and they went together, her father trying to conceal his disapproval, and saying in a loud voice long before they were out of earshot, 'What are they at now? They cannot sit still a moment.'

Léonie laughing, saying, 'But uncle, they are lovers, lovers must have excuses to be together, is it not so in England too?'

The next morning they rode away very early, towards Cholet. Overhead the sky was bright, the fields were green with spring.

They came to Maulévrier that night. A dozen leaders crowded into a small cottage, all shouting at once, as if the time for whispering was ended. The huntsman Stofflet at the head of the table, hard-featured and older than the others. She sat in a half-hidden corner as always, while Michel made his reports, recited lists, of men, weapons, supplies, horses, carts. When he was finished Stofflet laid his hand palm down on the table. 'That is good. Now go to sleep everyone, we ride to meet Jacques Cathelineau tomorrow. Early. Four o'clock.'

They started in the cold darkness as a column of two hundred men. By dawn they had become five hundred, like a river that gathers tributaries from every valley, every hillside. Men riding by twos and dozens to join them, out of a wood, a hamlet, a farm. Michel rode close to Stofflet, and Hester behind him. Men spoke to her and she answered with half a word or a nod. They were going to take Cholet. She felt her heart and muscles tighten, not with fear, but a kind of astonishment that she was there, that Michel was there, that their solitary riding had ended. They were part of an army.

They ate as they rode. Beside her a man was praying under his breath. When she looked sideways at him he was very young. He was not praying because he was afraid. She could see that in his eyes, the set of his half-childish mouth. Burning to serve, to fight for his cause.

'Holy Mary, Mother of God, pray for us sinners——' A man beyond him took up the prayer, and within moments twenty riders near her were saying the rosary in unison. A priest rode up and smiled. He rode like a soldier but he had no weapon. She thought suddenly, that priest and I are the only two who are unarmed. She expected at every moment that Michel would turn back to her and try to send her away, make a rendezvous with her for when the battle was over. But he did not.

They halted at midday and sent out messengers to find Cathelineau and his men. The priest said prayers and preached about the justice of their cause. He told them the story of Deborah and Barak, the son of Abinoam, and the ten thousand Israelites who threw down the might of Sisera, Canaan's general. 'As we shall throw down the wickedness that comes against us. A woman's hand, a weak woman's hand, was sufficient to slay great Sisera, to nail him to the ground where he slept. Shall not we who are men, and baptized in Christ's precious blood, do as greatly?'

The sound of men singing, far away and yet tremendous, five hundred, a thousand voices singing a hymn. She had already heard it, but only a few men singing it together. Now a thousand, and Stofflet's men began to answer.

'Vexilla Regis prodeunt.'

'The banners of the King.'

She felt tears coming without reason. The song rising, thundering. Birds flew up from a wood as if they meant to carry the words to Heaven. Men were crying. Unashamed, full of joy, lifting their weapons in promises of loyalty to their faith. Axes and billhooks, scythe blades turned and reset on wooden poles to make spears, curved and terrible. 'Fulget crucis mysterium,' the shining mystery of the Cross.

The men from the northern parishes, Cathelineau's army, came rushing towards them, crying, 'Welcome in God's name, welcome to our brothers!' Peasants. Wooden sabots and ragged clothes, their legs bound with strips of cloth. Long blue serge coats. Broad-brimmed hats. Muskets. Hunting guns. And as they ran forward, opening their ranks, a cannon. Drawn by six cart-horses, and a cart with ammunition following.

It became the centre of everything. A cannon! A cannon! Long, threatening muzzle, massive iron.

'The Missionary. Our Missionary! And here are the sermons for him to preach!' Hands smacking the iron cannon-balls heaped in the cart, the barrels of powder, the coil of slow match, the sack of wadding. They had captured the cannon in Jallais, on their march south.

'Form ranks! Form ranks! Order! One hour's halt.'

'They've got two prisoners,' someone said. 'They're sending them in to Cholet to tell them to surrender or else we'll burn it over their heads.'

'Give them warning? Are we mad? Why aren't we attacking now?' A field of men in the spring sunlight. Woods. Sky. Two thousand voices talking, laughing, praying. Men eating. Drinking. Squatting on their haunches, grouped by company and troop and commander. Only she had none. She sat slightly apart from the men she had ridden beside and finished her bread and wine. She must see to the horses. She was suddenly frightened that Michel would take her horse from her, want to give it to one of the men on foot.

It was still cold enough in spite of the sun. She led their two horses up and down the field so that their legs would not stiffen. As she passed near him Michel beckoned her from where he was standing with Stofflet and Cathelineau. A group of men on a small mound in the field, like a dais, or a grave-mound. He came towards her with long, impatient strides, his mind far away from her.

'I didn't think we would fight so soon,' he said. 'But it's going to be now. We're marching on Cholet in another quarter of an hour. You stay here. Give me your horse. I'll send back for you when it's over. It won't be long, but however long it is, don't move from here.'

She was going to protest, but she saw his face and stayed silent. He lifted down her saddle-bag and gave it to her. There was nothing in it beyond a clean shirt and stockings and a knife for her bread and cheese. He went away without saying another word, or even touching her shoulder, and she did not know if that was because he dare not for fear of showing emotion, or because he did not think of it, his mind full of other things.

My horse will be killed, she thought. And then, suppose—suppose Michel is—could not allow herself to think the word, and instead saw his body lying on the ground. She sat on the grass

[142]

and covered her face with her hands. The boy she had ridden beside came up to her and said, 'Courage, friend. You are not afraid?'

'He has taken my horse,' she said.

'Then you can hold my stirrup.' He sat down by her and clapped his hand on her knee. 'I'm longing for it to begin.' And as he said it, it was already begun. Shouting, men jumping to their feet, running, someone firing a shot, commanders shouting, roaring orders, to hold steady, '*Hold steady damn you!*'

She ran with the boy to where he had tethered his plough horse to a bush. He clambered onto its back as if he was more used to trudging behind it, and she gripped his stirrup-leather. She could not see why they were running, nor what was happening. The whole world shouting. Ranks forming, jostling, men stumbling against one another. And from the direction of the town other voices, shouting, hurrahing. Horsemen riding towards them, soldiers, blue uniforms, sabres glittering, shooting. Men trying to swing the Missionary with its muzzle forward, and then abandoning the cannon altogether as the peasant army, Stofflet's men and Jacques Cathelineau's together, rushed towards the Republicans, shouting, 'Christ and the King, Christ and the King!' Getting themselves between the cannon and the enemy so that it was useless to think of firing it.

But she saw that only with the tail of her eye, a fragment of her reason. The boy was riding, dragging her along, she was running with great strides, half-flying, horses everywhere, men running like herself with a left hand gripped to a stirrup leather and right hand swinging an axe. But her right hand held only her saddle-bag. She ought to let go, fall back, she would be ridden down, trampled into the ground. And then ahead of her she saw Michel, out far in front with Stofflet and Cathelineau and half a dozen others, carrying a sword he must have commandeered from someone, rushing towards the line of Republicans. And she no longer thought of anything but to follow, to reach him. 'Faster,' she cried to the boy. 'Gallop!'

'Christ and the King!' The two lines, two masses of men, the greater mass of peasants, the small, ordered troop of soldiers, more than fifty, a hundred horsemen, another hundred or two hundred infantry behind them; the two masses swept together, crashed like the sea on rocks. She saw men falling, jumped over a dead body. Blue uniform, white face staring up. Horses bolting, flying riderless. Horses screaming. A scythe blade going into a man like a sheaf of corn, and his arms wide in crucifixion.

'Christ and the King! Ride them down!' The Blues breaking, running, reeling away in panic. Men racing for their lives, stretched flat on the long necks of their horses, soldiers down on their knees for mercy, axe blows and shooting, the town ahead of them, houses, an old officer with white hair trying to stop the rout, trying to re-form his men. Falling beside a Calvary. Christ crucified. Flowers round the stones at the foot of the Cross. And as the first line of the peasant army reached the Calvary, and the old man's body, they threw themselves from their horses and knelt down. The men on foot joined them, pulling off broad-brimmed hats, kneeling, praying. The whole army kneeling, while the torn splinters of the Republicans found refuge in the town.

Re-forming, advancing. And out of the town three men coming with a white flag. Jacques Cathelineau went forward to meet them, half a dozen officers with him. The boy who had remounted gripped Hester's shoulder. 'We've won, comrade! Christ has given us victory.'

They entered Cholet as if they were going to Mass, marching in quietly, without shouting, without threats or triumph. Men going from house to house to arrest known Republicans and officials. To requisition arms. Requisition food. Giving receipts for everything. She found Michel in a house organizing that. He looked at her and said nothing. Only went on signing receipts, 'To be presented to the authorities of the Catholic Army for payment.'

She was afraid to meet his eyes and went to look out of the window at the market square. A man was being led across it and tied to the wheel of a cart. One of the cannoneers who were with the cannon, the Missionary, levelled his pistol and shot him in the back of the head.

'Tell him we're paying ten sous for a four-pound loaf. Does he think this is Paris? Ten sous, and I want a hundred loaves from him by morning. And you, go to every butcher and clear him out. Twelve sous a pound for everything. Pork, beef, mutton. If anyone argues, shoot him.'

There were no more executions in the square. Someone said

the man who had been shot was a priest-hunter, the worst in Cholet.

She lay down on a bench, and fell asleep listening to tallies of bread and meat and wine, and requisitioned horses, and captured weapons.

Michel woke her at midnight and brought her up the stairs, still half asleep. He pushed her down onto a bed and fitted his hand round her throat. 'Why did you disobey me?'

She said nothing, and he shook her head softly from side to side, tightening his fingers.

'You great fool,' he whispered, 'suppose you were killed?'

'And you?' she said.

He undid her coat and shirt, and put his hand on her breast. 'What shall I do with you?'

Outside there was still noise in the streets, men tramping, horses, carts, the glare of a bonfire in the square, throwing a red light on the white ceiling of the room. Michel pulled off her boots, and then his, and lay down beside her. 'What shall I do with you?'

She pressed her forehead against his. 'I shall stay with you. You can't make me leave you. I won't go.'

He held her. They were too tired to make love. And she had the fear that at any moment a messenger might come bursting into the room, or one of the commanders, or simply men looking for a place to sleep. They lay together in their clothes on the narrow, uncomfortable bed. He pulled a cloak over them and she kissed him gently, as if she had found him again after a long time. His hand under her shirt, warm and hard against the hollow of her back. We are one, she thought. More than if we were making love. Nothing shall ever separate us.

Chapter 13

Nothing shall ever separate us.

As if she had made a stupid challenge in the dark, and Providence had taken it up.

Michel behaving, speaking, as if it was already agreed that she should go, should leave him there, leave the town they had taken, leave the men, leave whatever was coming, and ride away into the quiet countryside. To safety. He did not say that, but it was what he meant.

'I will not go,' she said. She thought he would get angry, and wanted it. Remembered how casually he had taken away her horse, as if she was a child, something of no importance when great things were about to happen. To be made love to, and set aside, and laughed at. She stood at the table where he was writing, and banged her fist on it so that the ink-well danced, and splashed black on the scrubbed kitchen timber and a corner of parchment.

'You will do what you are ordered to do,' he said, as if he was too tired to get angry. They had been woken at half past four, and had not slept much before that. And then he shouted, even his shout exhausted, 'Give me patience! Someone must go, and at least I can trust you not to get lost or drunk, or go home to start haymaking or tousle your wife. Has everything got to take hours of argument?' He put his face in his hands, and then gripped her wrists, pulling her forward across the table and looking up into her face, his eyes red-rimmed, bloodshot, as they had been that day at the Tuileries, a thousand years ago. 'I want you to ride to Charette and Joly and the others, and Madame La Roche-foucauld, and tell them what has happened, and what we mean to do now. I want you to tell every parish, the right man in every parish that you pass through, the same things. And someone must get a messenger to England——'

'Not me!' she cried at that, 'I will not go to England, I will not leave here now!'

'I am not asking you to go! Be quiet! We are sending out messengers in every direction, and you are one of them, the one I trust most, and can spare least. For heaven's sake! You wanted to come with me, you wanted to be useful, now is the time. Don't argue with me about it or I'll lose my reason. You wanted to be a soldier. Do what you're told. And then come back to me.'

'Come back to you where?'

'Find out! How do I know where we shall be? We mean to take Montaigu in the next few days, and after that—with luck we should have the whole of the Vendée in our hands inside a week. But Charette must move, and that imbecile murderer Souchu must do more than kill prisoners if we're to hold what we win.'

They gave her back her own horse, and another as well, so that she could change horses as she rode. Her messages for the leaders down by the coast were sewn into the double brim of her hat. And at the last moment Michel gave her a pistol, an *espingole* like a short musket that one fires from the saddle and that can blow a man in half at twenty yards. 'You won't need it,' he said. 'You know the roads better than any fool who might give chase to you. Avoid Montaigu, that's all. Now go with God.' He squeezed her hand and went back inside the house he had commandeered. She had the feeling that the second his back was turned, she was gone from his mind.

She rode tired and sullen, trying to imagine that what she was doing had any meaning. Now and then she passed groups of peasants, hurrying towards Cholet to join the army there. Some already had white cockades in the crowns of their broad-brimmed hats, and the Sacred Heart in red cloth stitched onto a white square on their breasts. They stared at her suspiciously as she rode towards them, and once or twice men lifted their home-made weapons in threat, to stop her.

She had to open her cloak and show the same emblem of the Sacred Heart stitched on her own coat. When the peasants saw it they crowded round and clamoured for news.

'We have taken Cholet from the Blues,' she said, and felt her heart leap. 'We—we.' I was there, she thought. Not gloriously, but I was there! I have been in a battle, I have run with soldiers against an enemy, I have been at the taking of a town. The sun came out and shone with spring warmth as she rode. I have been in a battle! And now I am riding alone to bring news and orders, and fetch help to our cause! She lifted herself in her stirrups and set her horse to a faster trot, her second horse clattering behind her on its leading rein. Two horses! A pistol. God for Harry, England and St. George! It was not for any of those indeed, but the feeling was the same. The tiredness fell from her and she pulled out a hunk of bread and a corner of ham, and munched as she rode, feeling the spring in her blood and heart.

The feeling lasted most of the day. Riding into a village, finding a man she already knew by sight, giving him the news, the orders. Parish captains, who were to gather their men, if they had not already done that, and make for a rendezvous with other parishes. Bring stores. Food.

It was only as the afternoon darkened, and the tiredness came back like lead in her bones, that her exaltation drained away. No matter what colour he put on it, he had taken her horse from her, he had had no need for her when the real crisis came. As if she was a woman like Léonie whom one leaves at home.

I gave him everything, her mind cried. I gave him my soul, and he turned round and kicked me away.

Riding up the avenue at Fonteclose, the Chevalier Charette's *manoir*. He was gone.

'Gone north,' the old servant-woman said, grumbling, as if everything in the world was her master's fault. 'Gone with the peasants. They came and fetched him away. What do you want with him?'

Mademoiselle Charette came out at the sound of horses and their talk, but she could not add much to what her servant had told. Only that they were gone to join Souchu in Machecoul.

'And Madame de la Rochefoucauld?'

'Ah!' said Mademoiselle Charette. 'Madame! Wait till you see her! She is in Garnache, with a sword as big as me and giving orders like a general. But she can wait till morning, surely? Come in, come in and let me look after you.' She knew Hester already for who and what she was.

'I must find her tonight. And if I get down from this horse I won't be able to get up again.' She felt herself swaying as she sat. Since daybreak she had ridden the best part of fifty miles. And before Mademoiselle Marie-Anne could try again to prevent her she turned her horses' tired heads towards the road, and Garnache, and spurred and jerked them into a semblance of a canter.

But Madame de la Rochefoucauld had left Garnache for her *manoir* at Puy Buisson a few miles off, and Hester arrived there at last so exhausted that she staggered as she tried to stand and had to be held up by a groom.

'Bring him in,' Madame de la Rochefoucauld ordered, and then, recognizing Hester by the torchlight in the courtyard, cried, 'It's Madame Vernet! It is a woman, you fool, treat her gently. Here, Cécile, Céleste, Marguerite, come quick, there is someone to look after.'

'I need nothing,' Hester said furiously. 'Except—except a glass of wine—something to eat. I—if I could sleep for a few hours somewhere.'

'Be quiet! Outside, you oaf, leave her to me and the women. Upstairs with you, what have you been doing? You look like a corpse. Take her upstairs. What is Vernet thinking of to let you get into this state? Hurry, Cécile. Yes, yes, I will hear your news, I will read your letter. But upstairs with you! A bath before every-thing.'

She was too far gone to protest. Madame de la Rochefoucauld strode ahead of them down a wide, panelled corridor, swaggering in her wide green skirts *en amazone*, that parted to show long riding boots of soft brown leather. Her black hair fell in Créole splendour onto the green velvet shoulders of her riding jacket, and she still wore her gold and silver sword belt. Like a vision from the theatre, as if at any moment she was going to stop by the footlights and sing an aria.

Hester had seen Madame de la Rochefoucauld before, more than once, when they had first begun riding, helping to weave the network of the rising, and she had dismissed her as another Créole like Léonie; taller, stronger, more vital, darker, her hair coal-black instead of gold, but with that same supple, animal grace, the same golden-honey skin that set Hester's teeth on edge, as if there was something faintly obscene about it.

But now, in the face of such a splendour of health, of clean velvet and glistening skin, the maids themselves in their starched aprons and rustling skirts like a reproach to her filthiness, all that Hester could feel was an embarrassed shame, and a wish to be left alone.

'Please,' she began.

'Strip her. Burn those dreadful clothes. I am almost as tall as you and we shall find something decent to put on you.'

'Madame——'

'Stop arguing, get into that water. Look at you! There is nothing left of you! Is Vernet mad?' The maids had stripped her to the skin and suddenly, as she touched the water, sank into it, let her head that had begun to itch as she thought of it sink under the surface, she realized that she had not had a proper bath since she left England. She lay with her eyes shut, wishing they would all go away. But they continued filling the bath until it covered her knees, and one of the maids began soaping her as if she was a child and needed help. While Madame de la Rochefoucauld strode up and down the room like a cavalier in a play, reading Michel's letter, and asking about Cholet, and describing her own exploit in Garnache.

'Forty of us!' she cried triumphantly. 'We rode into Garnache and took the brutes prisoner before they knew what had happened. In a month we shall hold the Vendée from the coast to Saumur, from Sables to Nantes. And if the Bretons rise as they've promised, and Normandy, and Maine, nothing can stop us. We shall be in Paris by the summer!'

They were lifting her out of the bath. She would have liked to go on lying there but they pulled her upright and took her to a long couch covered with more towels.

'Now sleep,' Madame said. 'Then supper and we can talk.'

The maids woke her, bringing her some of Madame's clothes, and a fur cloak that fell almost to her feet, and when she was dressed they brought her to a small room bright with candlelight; armchairs and a table set for supper; silver dish covers, wine bottles in silver buckets. A smell of roast meat, and fresh-baked bread.

For no reason at all, for the luxury of everything, the warmth, the sense of cleanliness after weeks of hardship, she found that she was crying, hiding her face from the maids as they set chairs to the table, and attended to the fire. Madame came sweeping in, still in her riding clothes as if she could not bear to leave off her generalship.

'Now to supper!' she cried, rubbing her hands together. She shone with health and appetite, her hair raven black and gleaming, curls on thick curls swaying against her broad, full shoulders.

Hester began to feel again that she would have been happier left in the stables. Madame must be ten or twelve years the older and as Hester glanced at a mirror above the fire it seemed as if it should be the other way round, and it was Madame who was twenty-three, and she herself in her thirties. A gaunt, wolfish face looked at her from the mirror, grey and haggard, shadows under her eyes.

'You are going to stay with me for a time,' Madame said, as if she was reading Hester's mind. 'And I am going to turn you into a woman again. Your husband asks me in his letter to keep you here and it——'

'What?' She came out of her chair with the shock of it. 'He asks you to——?'

'I am glad to have you. I need someone I can trust, and who knows the roads. My people would be lost if they went ten miles from here. But I don't want a corpse. I'm going to put some flesh on you before I send you anywhere. Look at you! Look in the mirror!

'My husband asked you to—keep me here?' The feeling of betrayal made her choke. It was difficult to see for a moment. She got to her feet as if she meant to run out of the room and escape from this house, the threat of—of what? But it was not this woman's threat. Not her doing. She sat down slowly, wanting to get sick, as if what she had just eaten had poisoned her.

'It's the first sensible thing he has done with you,' Madame was saying. 'Of course you must stay with me! And I shall teach you how to be a woman. Did your mother never tell you what a woman is? And such a woman as you could be! You should be a goddess, and you run after your husband like a dog. Do you know what they call you? La Lévrière. Have you no pride? A man's greyhound bitch!'

'But I—to go riding with him, to dress as a man! Isn't that——?'

Madame threw up her hands in contempt. 'I could find you a

dozen girls on this estate who could do what you do, and not collapse at the end of it. That's not freedom, that's slavery. Ride with him, yes, but beside him, ahead of him! Don't follow him like a dog! How can you win respect like that? And dressed like a beggar! When I go hunting I go in lace and velvet, in honour of myself, and the things I kill. And now that I mean to hunt men I shall dress with twice the care because the prey is greater.' She caught Hester by the arm and led her to the mirror.

'Look! Do you think you'll keep him another six months, looking the way you do? The first woman with a breast and a clean shift that he comes across will take him away from you as easily as taking a toy from a child. No no, if you want to keep him, and God knows why you should, his grandfather was a miller and he looks like a Red Indian—but if you want him, there is only one way, and that is to make his knees tremble when he looks at you. Now go to bed, and sleep twelve hours, and I'll talk to you again.'

She slept not for twelve hours, but for fourteen, and woke with a headache, and a shock of alarm that something was terribly, irretrievably wrong. She sat up, unsure where she was. Firelight. The smell of coffee and hot bread. A woman laying out clothes on a couch.

'Where——?' The Countess. Garnache. Michel's betrayal. 'Where are my own clothes? I must go, I must ride in—in a quarter of an hour.'

'The Countess has sent these to you, madame. She says she will join you as soon as you are dressed.' She curtsied and went out. Hester got out of the bed and looked at the clothes.

A man's dark blue riding coat. The Count de la Roche-foucauld's? And white buckskin breeches. A silk shirt, a cambric and lace cravat. Stockings. Cordovan leather boots that must cover the knee, they were so long. Also the Count's? She had never felt such leather in her life.

She sat on the couch and pulled one of the boots onto her bare foot and smoothed it over her calf, her knee. Looked at her unfamiliar leg. Touched the leather. In a sudden passion of haste she pulled it off again, and began dressing in what the woman had brought her. Silk. Lace. Cambric. Fine, soft wool. Buckskin. As if she had been reborn.

When she went to the long cheval glass by the window it was difficult to recognize herself. Except for the grey, shadowed face, the eyes swollen with too much sleep after months of too little or none.

'I have been insane,' she thought, slowly touching her mouth with her finger-tips. Her eyes. Her throat that was like whipcord. 'I have been a madwoman.'

'The first woman with breasts, and a clean shift——' She touched the front of the blue coat. It fitted her as if she was indeed a man. Was that why he had sent her away? She knew that it was not, and still felt the chill of betrayal, imagined—imagined——

'Now!' Madame cried from the doorway. 'That is what I wanted to see! With your hair dressed, and a month's feeding, you can lay men before you like sugar plums, and make your choice of them. Come. Breakfast. I'll share it with you, and I shall tell you about men, and you shall tell me about Cholet.'

They spent the day eating, or so it seemed. That and talking. She could scarcely remember afterwards what they talked about, but it did not seem to matter. And the idea of riding back to Michel, and arriving as she had left him, sick, exhausted, half-starved, to quarrel with him over sending her away—that vanished as if it had followed her own wretched clothes into the fire, or the rubbish pit. To walk in the sunshine, to hear civilized talk. To feel silk against her skin. As though Madame de la Rochefoucauld was a wise, older sister whom she had been searching for all her life, and had now found.

'To be a man's equal, or his superior, does not mean we must give up being women. And to be women does not mean we must spend our lives sitting at home to embroider napkins for our babies. There is room for everything. For babies, and for love, for war and luxury. The way most women live is like eating only bread, and drinking only water, when the table is loaded with good things. Take life in both your hands, my dear, all of it.'

The Countess took a sugared almond from a silver dish, cracking it between her splendid teeth as if the almonds had defied her and were being punished for their temerity.

They were in the drawing-room, recovering from dinner, a fire blazing, and the lamps and candles already lit. Outside the tall doors there were raised voices, protests. The doors burst open and a dishevelled man came rushing in, sweeping off his broad-brimmed hat, a footman behind him still protesting at the invasion.

'The Republicans, Countess! They are coming! To retake Garnache!' So out of breath from running that it was hard to understand what he said. He put his hand to his heart to ease its pounding, and stood panting. 'The miller's boy——'

'How far away?' The Countess was already tugging the bell rope by the fire. The bell pealing somewhere in the house. 'Call everyone, Marcel!' The footman ran.

'Two hours at the most, madame. The miller's boy read the sails of the Mill of the Winds five minutes ago. Not more than two hours to the south of here, he thinks. Less.'

The *manoir* had already come alive. Servants running. Bringing Madame her riding clothes. Her sword. Pistols.

'Fetch a sabre for Madame Vernet. Send girls to the farms. Summon everyone. To meet in the square in Garnache in an hour. Under Monsieur Thomazeau here. Run like the wind.'

The man who had brought the news was given brandy, sent away to organize the men who would come to the *manoir*. 'Thomazeau,' Madame called after him, 'Madame Vernet and I will ride ahead of you to Garnache. Join us there as soon as you can. Bring every man who can handle a pitchfork. And every woman. Tell the women that I count on them.'

Five minutes more and they were riding for Garnache. Two men joined them as they rode, farmers on horseback, tenants of Madame's, one carrying a blunderbuss that might have seen service against Marlborough, and the other armed with an oak club bound round with iron and studded.

The village was already in turmoil, men gathering, sharpened pitchforks, axes, clubs, hunting guns with barrels four and five feet long, scythes with their blades turned, poles with iron tips like primitive spears. And not only men: the torchlight showed women, their skirts twisted to knee height, armed with meat cleavers and wood choppers or carving knives, or the long iron bars from the hearths that skillets stand on, and a priest with a crucifix, *soutane* swinging as he hurried, grey hair floating. Father Chuchotte. Hester knew him already, but he did not recognize her, and only bowed and put his hand on Madame's knee as she sat her horse.

'Thank God you are come, Countess. I shall speak to them, and then you can give your orders. I'll not be long-winded.' He turned and cried in a great voice, 'People! God's people! The enemy are coming, the enemies of God and His Holy Church. Children of Satan. Pray to Our Saviour for victory, and God will so strengthen us that their swords will fall from their hands, their bullets will fly uselessly. Let no man fear death this night for the Lord is with us, He goes by our side in the darkness. Now. Listen to the Countess, obey her as you would obey God Himself, for this night on this business she speaks with God's voice. Amen.'

'Amen' rang in answer, steel lifting. Hester drew her sword. As though she was drunk. Gloriously, fiercely drunk, her blood dancing, the hilt of the sword she had been given clenched in her hand. 'Amen!' she cried, her voice alone in the echoes of the crowd's amen. If he could see her now!

The Countess giving the orders for the battle. They were very simple. To follow the Countess and the other riders a mile down the road along which the enemy must be approaching. Then to hide themselves behind the hedges on either side of the road, and wait until the enemy troopers were caught between them like rats in a deep-throated trap. The riders, the Countess, Hester, the two tenant farmers, three more men with horses, were to go a quarter mile further, hide themselves, and let the enemy go by them. Then when the fighting started they would ride into the enemy's tangled rearguard and give the impression of a great force coming to Garnache's aid. While Thomazeau and the men from the *manoir* and the surroundings would come from Garnache and close up the other end of the road.

'We shall destroy them! They have horses, swords, guns, powder. When we have destroyed these wretches, those things are ours. If there is a coward here, let him go home and pray for us. I'll have no coward share our glory. God in our arms, Christ in our hearts. God and the King!'

The echoes clamouring. Then only the sound of marching, wooden sabots, like mallets beating the road. Whispering, laughing, praying. Father Chuchotte leading the prayers. 'God of battles——'

Dark. The dark of starlight. Iron shadows.

The armed men and women disappearing, vanishing. Only the hedges left, a rustling of grass, of branches. Silence.

The seven riders finding their own concealment. Waiting. She could hear her heart beat, feel her pulse. The fierce glow of excitement fading. It was cold. She was afraid of shivering in case the Countess should hear her, and think she was afraid. Clenching her teeth. Beside her a man was whispering his rosary. 'Hail Mary full of Grace, the Lord is with thee. Blessed art thou among women.'

The Countess gripped his arm in warning. A long way off there were hoofbeats, so faint it was difficult to be sure it was not her heart that she was hearing, the blood throbbing in her ears. Then clearer on the wind as it eddied towards them. Then monstrous, a regiment, an army riding, a ringing of brass, beating of iron-shod hooves, a power and majesty of force in discipline. Fifty, eighty men? There must be five hundred. Near, near. The Countess touching her sleeve. Brightness of steel. Great shadows riding on the far side of the hedge, two by two in the narrow roadway. Ten, twenty, thirty couples. Riding as if nothing but cannon-shot could dismount them. A minute more. And then a roar, of hatred, triumph, fury. Father Chuchotte's huge voice yelling, 'God and the King, God and the King!' and the peasant army with its own ferocious, ancient battle cry, '*Rembarre, rembarre*, kill kill kill!' Screaming of horses, screaming of men, shots, steel ringing on steel.

'Now Christ be with us,' the Countess screamed and cleared the hedge. '*Rembarre, rembarre!*' Hester riding behind her, head down, sword drawn and pointed, as long ago old Samuel had shown her that troopers ride in battle. Screaming. Not knowing what she screamed. Shadows in front of her, tangle of men and horses, the Countess striking. '*Rembarre, rembarre.*' Sword swinging at her; parrying, striking in her turn. Pitchforks and axes, men falling, horses rearing, shrieking in battle terror, screaming at the scent of blood. '*Rembarre, rembarre!*'

A trumpet blast ahead of them, trying to rally the Republicans. And then a crash, a shock through the tangle of men and horses as Thomazeau came hurling his reinforcements into the fighting. Strike and strike again. Men crashing, fighting their way past her on horseback, slashing, thrusting. Then only driving past, heads down in panic, flying for their lives.

'After them, after them! The rats are running!' The Countess screaming, pivoting, her horse fighting, striking out with its front hooves, battering. Crash of men through the hedges, yelling for quarter, or only yelling, the sullen heaviness of blows and the cries of wounded men. Until there was almost silence. Horses

[156]

shivering and whinnying, men groaning as they lay, men panting as they leaned on clubs and scythe shafts. Far away the sound of riding, hellbent for the sea and Sables d'Olonne and safety.

Twelve dead, all Republicans. Nineteen wounded and prisoner. More than twenty horses taken. A pile of captured muskets. Pistols. Sabres. Powder and cartridges and lead ball. Saddles and harness. Knapsacks and belts and bayonets. Everything loaded across the horses' backs, dead and wounded and booty. Of the Garnache army, only half a dozen wounded, and those not badly. A woman with a broken arm, another woman gashed on the shoulder by a sabre, a man who had lost an ear and two or three others with broken heads. Marching back, singing, as if they were a Roman Legion.

'Vexilla Regis prodeunt:
Fulget crucis mysterium.'

In the small market square, Father Chuchotte leading a prayer of thanksgiving. 'Now has God shown His mercy to His people, and His strength to their enemies. Let us kneel down before Him.'

The Countess like Joan of Arc, kissing her sabre hilt before the kneeling crowd, lit by torchlight, her hair black fire. 'May God so strengthen my woman's arm and heart that I may lead you to victory on victory, until we salute our King face to face. God save Louis the Seventeenth. God save the King!'

Hester erect in her stirrups, lifting her own sword. 'God save the King!' Echoing, echoing.

Chapter 14

She rode slowly as she came near to Montaigu.

'You have given me your oath,' Madame had said. 'Keep it. We have fought side by side. We are comrades. You have sworn me a comrade's oath to be as splendid as you can. If he does not like it then God rot his soul. What kind of man can want a dirty greyhound instead of a splendid woman? Look at you now! Joan of Arc grown tall. He should go on his knees to you. Go to him like a queen, like an Amazon. And when you are riding with him again keep yourself magnificent. The next time I see you I want to be dazzled. I want to see fresh lace and polished silver, your horse groomed like a black mirror. The way he is now. Even he is holding his head higher. He is a warhorse, he has smelled blood and powder. Look how he lifts his foot? God does not want His servants filthy, He wants them like bright stars.'

Even her father had noticed the change when she stopped at the *manoir*, before he so much as greeted her. And Léonie had clapped her hands together and called for Euphemia to come and look. Swinging down from the saddle, feeling selfconscious, longing to say to them, 'I have been in two battles! I have fought on horseback!' But she said nothing, and spent supper-time and the evening listening to her father talk of documents and rents and feudal rights, and the wretched stupidity of not being able to send letters home.

'I do not like you riding about the countryside with all the troubles one hears of. And alone! What can that husband of yours be thinking of?' Like an echo of the Countess. 'Suppose you were to meet—I don't like to think of it, let alone speak of it, but I must be blunt, Hester. Suppose you were to meet an unprincipled

ruffian, or worse still, two or three of them? These French——'
He cast an anxious look towards Léonie, who was playing
tric-trac with Euphemia, the clicking of their ivory pieces like
punctuation marks to the flow of Mr. Broadhurst's talk. Since his
illness he had grown both old and timid, as if somewhere in the
depths of his mind he kept a memory of the terror that was
banished from the surface of it. He was inclined to start at sounds
and go to the window to peer out into the darkness like an old
woman alone in a house.

'That is why I dress as I do, Papa. If I met such a rogue he
would take me for a soldier and leave me alone.'

Like an island of peace. The *manoir* with its moat long ago
drained to make a broad, sunken walk around the house. Green
lawns. A pond at the back with ducks and geese swimming. The
woods seeming to creep towards the house as if they wished to
recover their lost dominion. Pigeons circling about the dovecot
above the stables. The war ten thousand miles away, the
Revolution as far off as the moon.

Yet even there—— 'I don't know where all Léonie's people
have gone, these last days,' Mr. Broadhurst was saying. 'I was
looking for men yesterday to scythe the grass, it is already
growing quite ragged on the lawns, you must have noticed it as
you came in, and I could not lay hands on a single fellow except
one old man who said he had lent his scythe to a friend and so
could not do anything. And the steward here is as useless as the
peasants he is supposed to be controlling. Your uncle George
would take an apoplexy at half the troubles I have had. I do not
know what Léonie would have done if I had not been here with
her.'

Afterwards Hester had found herself alone for a moment with
Euphemia. 'I am glad you have told him nothing. And you see?
All your fears? If you had all gone to Nantes you would be among
the Republicans now and in the thick of the battle when we attack
them. While here you are as safe as——'

Euphemia looking at her with the strangest of expressions.
Almost, Hester thought, as she felt herself looking at her father,
pityingly, and a shadow of anger at such second-childhood inno-
cence and futility. She wanted to grasp hold of the Negress and
shake her but she knew without attempting it that it would be
impossible.

[159]

'How splendid you look, madame,' Euphemia said. Her eyes mocking, and knowing. What did they know?

She was glad to ride away from the *manoir* the next day. When she turned back to look at it from the edge of the wood, she thought that she saw Euphemia at a window, the top window of the square, main tower. Waving a red scarf. She did not want to answer the gesture, but her arm lifted almost against her will. She took off her plumed hat and waved in return. The trees fresh with spring, green buds, new leaves. Oak and chestnut and hornbeam and beech. Beechmast under the hooves of the horses, and a softly rustling carpet of old leaves. She had heard last night that they had taken Montaigu. He would be there, or else there would be news of him.

She found herself half hoping that he would not be there and she must ride further on, perhaps not find him until tomorrow. And then laughed at herself for madness, and despised herself for cowardice. Tried to remember Madame's tone of voice, her face. 'If you won't stay with me, at least make me a promise that you'll do as I say. Swear it to me. Be splendid. Be what you were born to be.' The sun grew warmer, and she rode with her head uncovered, shaking her hair loose onto her shoulders. The thought of Michel became the thought of a lover again. What has been wrong with me? He will love to see me fine! And she rode then lifting in her stirrups, remembering the battle.

She relived it as she rode, and had to catch her breath for excitement, hearing again the deep yelling of '*Rembarre, rembarre!*' and the crash of men through the hedgerows, and the ring of steel.

But in spite of that she found herself riding slower and slower, dismounting to eat on the pretence of resting the horses, instead of eating as she rode. And then, as she ate, feeling such a fury of contempt for herself, a hatred of what she had allowed herself to become, that she threw away the remains of her bread and meat and almost sprang into the saddle again, and forced the animals to a canter.

She rode into now-Royalist Montaigu as if she was riding at the charge, and shouted at the first man she saw, 'Where is Major Vernet?' Peasant soldiers staring at her in astonishment, and then doffing their broad-brimmed hats. One of them pointing up the street.

'Show me. Take me to him.'

The man trudged ahead of her, his home-made pike slanted across his shoulder, a Republican bayonet struck through the broad leather belt of his loose trousers like a hunting knife. There were not many people in the street, and fewer soldiers. She had expected the town to be aswarm with men. She leaned forward and said, 'Where is everyone? Has the army moved out already?'

'Gone home,' the man said, without turning his head.

'Gone home? I thought we should be attacking Nantes! Why are they gone home?' But the man only shrugged and looked stupid, as peasants do when they do not mean to be questioned or bullied by strange gentry. He brought her to a house with a court-yard, and here there was an air of soldiery, sentries to challenge her, men coming and going, horses, piled muskets with a man guarding them, barrels of powder, a man in shirtsleeves leaning out from a window to yell last-moment orders after a messenger. But to her astonishment the sentries who demanded her name and business were not peasants but officers, and so was the man guarding the captured muskets and the powder barrels. There was scarcely an ordinary soldier in the crowded courtyard. They let her through as soon as they heard the name 'Vernet' and that she was come from Garnache with news.

'He's on the first floor. You can tie up your horses over there.'

They did not know her, nor she them, and she had an irrational feeling of chill, as if instead of returning to her husband, to her lover, she was in a strange place, and homesick. Although home-sick for what other place?

She tied her horses to a pair of iron rings on the wall, beyond the powder barrels, and strode to the door the officer had shown her. Men hurrying in and out, scarcely noticing her. Up the stairs. Doors, men, voices, someone shouting. Trying one door, and another. He was in the third room she looked into. A small room, no more than a closet. Only one other man with him, the two of them one on either side of a long table covered with papers. An air of clerkdom. In the second before he looked up and saw her she sensed that he was wretched at such work, hated it. The way he held the paper in his hand, bit at the goose quill. His face still like the blade of an axe, but turned greyish, as if he had not slept since she left him in Cholet. And for that second, drawn out, seeming like minutes, she looked at him as if he was a stranger, or an acquaintance she scarcely knew, and thought with astonishment, 'He is my husband. I have given myself to that man sitting there. Given him my freedom, surrendered my judgement to his, become his creature.'

Then the familiar happiness of seeing him, seeing his face, seeing his hands. He had looked up, and still for another second seemed not to recognize her, and she waited with her throat tightened, as once she had waited for him to strike her. If he had struck her then, that would have been the end of everything, and now, if——

'My God, we are fine,' he said, almost echoing Euphemia. And she waited, her throat still closed, not breathing. Was he laughing? But she could not read his face. The other man had looked up and nodded and was continuing with his work, not as Michel had been working, but with a mole's intensity, his eyes close to his lists, his quill scratch scratching as if he had been born to make lists of things.

'I must leave you for a few minutes,' Michel said to him. He held the door for Hester and they went out onto the naked landing, the house stripped of everything that could be taken as the Republicans fled. Michel guided her not downstairs but up again to an attic bedroom, three or four truckle beds, a mattress on the floor in a corner, boots and equipment strewn here and there, an old trunk serving for a night table with a candlestick set on it, and flint and steel and a tinder-box. The smell of men.

She thought for a moment that he had brought her up there to make love to her, and did not know if she was pleased or angered at the thought. But he held her at arm's length and then led her to the skylight. 'What are you supposed to be? And why are you here, and not where I sent you? I gave orders to you. And for you.'

'I know,' she said. 'And I know what people have been calling me. Your greyhound bitch. That I will no longer accept. And that is—part of why I am here.' Wanting him to ask 'and what is the other part?'

But he only drew in a hard breath, and turned away, walking the length of the long narrow room, kicking at someone's boot in his path, so that it clattered against the leg of a truckle bed. He came back and faced her again. 'You wanted to ride with me.'

'With you. Not behind you. And you took my horse. When we

could have been truly together you took my horse and gave it to someone else.'

He had her gripped by the arms above the elbows, and began to shake her, slowly, but not gently. 'You fool! Who has been talking to you?'

'Do you think it must be that? That I have no mind of my own? I did not marry you to be your servant.' It was difficult to breathe. It was not that she was afraid of him, but of herself, of what she might say, or do. She freed her arms with a hard movement, and he stared at her as if they were opponents measuring one another's strength.

'Why did you marry me?' he said. His face so grey and drawn that she was almost sorry for him, and then impatient. If he could not so much as sleep without her to warm his bed, then what was he?

'I married you to be your friend.'

He laughed at that, sudden and harsh, like being hit. 'You're talking like a schoolgirl. My friend! In bed, yes. In a house with children, cooking meals, talking in the evening, yes, a thousand times. But this is a war, you imbecile. If you want to be my friend here, in all this, how much do you think you must learn first? You imagine it's just putting on a handsome coat and wearing a sword? I've begun to teach you something, as much as a woman can be taught, and now——'

'I think you know nothing about women,' she said contemptuously. 'I have been in a battle since I saw you.'

'You have been in a battle?' he interrupted her. 'Dressed like that I suppose? I have been in twenty, thirty battles. And——'

'I was not going to tell you about myself. Out of two hundred fighters on our side, forty were women. The Countess led them.'

'I can imagine the battle!'

She felt such anger that she could not speak, could not look at him. She began to walk towards the door. He would have to move aside to let her go by, between the ends of two of the beds. She hesitated for a second, and then lifted her hand to force him aside. He caught her wrist and held it.

'Let me go,' she said through her teeth. He reached for her other arm, and she thrust with her open hand at his chest. He staggered for a moment, and they were wrestling, his hands gripped round her wrists like handcuffs, breast to breast. She was stronger than he could have imagined, and she forced him back, lifted her two clenched fists in the air and jerked them downwards to break free. He let go and locked his arms round her waist, tightened them, his head buried hard between her neck and shoulder. Tightening, tightening his grip until her back seemed to be breaking. He put his heel behind her ankle, and they were falling, crashing across a bed. The bed gave under them, splintered. She caught his hair with both hands and lifted his head back and back until his throat was stretched tight as a drum, and then jerked his head sideways. He gasped with the pain of it and had to loosen his hold. She was on her knees beside him, lifting her fist to hit him when the door burst open and there were two men with drawn pistols peering into the room.

'What the deuce is happening here?'

'I tripped over some fool's boots,' Michel said, 'and brought my friend down with me. Who the devil did you mean to shoot with those things? Go away, damn you both.'

The two young officers drew back, bewildered more than apologetic. The door shut behind them. Michel sat on another bed, beside the one they had ruined, his expression so exhausted, so wretched, that it was as if they were in the rue du Bac again, he was still her patient, still belonged to her. She knelt in front of him.

'Lie down. You look as if you haven't slept for nights, days. Are you such a fool that you can't look after yourself when I am not here?'

When he did not move she took hold of him and forced him to lie back, lifted his feet onto the bed, drew off his boots. Pulled a blanket from the nearest bed and covered him. 'You are going to sleep for eight hours,' she said. 'I am going to stand outside that door and if anyone tries to come in and wake you I shall cut him down. And then I am going to go into that clerks' dungeon where you've been working and I'm going to burn every paper in it. That's not what you were born to do.'

'There's no one else can do it.' He was trying to sit up. She held him down.

'Then let it stay undone. Lie still or I shall throw your boots out into the street and your clothes after them.'

'Half an hour perhaps.' His eyes were closing as he said it. She waited until he was asleep and went softly to the door. There was a key, and she locked the door on the outside, pocketed the key and went down to see to her horses. Then went back up the stairs and composed herself on the landing, her sword drawn and lying across her knees, her shoulders against the door. She must have slept herself for an hour or so. A man woke her coming up the stairs, saying as he saw her half sitting, half lying there across the doorway, 'What—who the devil—get out of my way, sir.' Looked closer, saw the thickness of her hair fallen to her shoulders, her hat pushed forward and to one side by the door she was lying against. 'You are—who are you, I say?'

She lifted the point of her sabre towards his chest. 'Someone is asleep in there,' she said. 'Go down the stairs again and be quiet as you go.'

'But that's my room, curse it. I want something——'

'Do without it.' The point of the sabre touched his coat. 'If you make a noise I shall run you through.'

He went, and came back with the two officers who had earlier burst into the room. She stayed where she was, putting a finger to her lips. 'Major Vernet is asleep,' she said. 'I mean him to stay asleep till dark.'

They stared helplessly and went downstairs again. She went back to sleep. When she woke it was dark on the landing. The house itself was still full of the same hurry and clatter of movement, voices, spurs ringing, horses in the courtyard, footsteps running. But it was as though in her sleep she had become used to it, and the sounds had grown familiar, homely. She stood up and stretched, and went down to find food. There was a kitchen, and two women and a boy cooking. A smell of baking, and roasting, a huge black pot of soup on the fire, dirty plates everywhere, and broken crusts and cheese rinds, three men sitting at one end of the long table eating like wolves; a man who might be a house servant from a château laying a heavy silver tray with delicacies.

Hester found another tray and asked the women for meat and bread and soup, and a bottle of wine. They served her without question, and she took the tray upstairs and unlocked the door. He was still asleep, the room dark, the noise of the house muffled when she closed the door on it. She put down her tray on the floor and felt her way to the candlestick on the trunk, and the tinder-box.

He was awake when the candle-flame steadied, and watching

her. She came and sat on the edge of his bed, holding the tray on her knees.

'Wine first.'

He took his glass at a swallow and held it for her to refill.

'You haven't eaten since I left, nothing. What sort of fool are you? And you call me a fool! You're like a child!'

He began to laugh, and held out his hands to her. 'Put the tray down. It can wait.'

'No.' She sliced bread and meat for him, made him eat. But her body had begun to shiver as it had not done for weeks, for months. She had to make an effort not to touch him.

'Eat.'

'I think I like it after all,' he said. He wound the fingers of his left hand in the lace collar of her shirt, pulled her head towards him.

'No! Eat. Drink. And then we are going to talk about something.'

'It doesn't need talk.' He was unbuttoning her coat. She held his wrist and put it away. She felt so filled with strength that she could have lifted him like a child and carried him downstairs, could have fought ten men. She made him eat everything, finish the bottle of wine. He took the tray and slid it onto the floor, the dishes clattering, the glasses and the empty bottle rolling under a bed. Her jacket was undone and he began unfastening her shirt. She held his hands against her body, her hands themselves shaking. She could not breathe properly, her heart hammering, slamming against his hands.

'We are going to make everything different,' she said, finding the words hard to pronounce, her lips, her throat not obeying her. As if they had never made love before, this was the first time. He had her jacket half off her shoulders, her shirt open.

'I must lock the door.'

'Damn the door.'

But she freed herself, locked it, stood for a moment clear of him, out of his reach. Felt herself blaze with strength, as if she was fire and he was fuel for it. Was almost frightened, as if they must destroy the house if they touched one another. And then he was out of the bed, stripping her jacket down, shirt, breeches, cursing her boots. Kneeling in front of her, trying to pull off one and then the other. She made herself stand still, not helping him,

[166]

letting him lift her foot, pull and struggle. One. The other. Breeches, stockings. Standing naked. He drew back for a second as if he had not seen her before. Pulled off his own clothes slowly, still looking at her as she stood, statue-still. Reached out a hand, touched her with a finger-tip, drew a line down from her cheek, her throat, her shoulder, down her breast that was scarcely a woman's breast, down her side to her hip. Came closer, let his hands slide behind her, grasp under her buttocks, lift her.

She linked her arms round his neck and he carried her to the bed, carried her upright until the bed was behind her knees, and they fell onto it as if they were throwing themselves into water, into a river, the sea. The bed shuddered and cracked, a leg gave, tilting them onto the floor, onto the other pile of bedding. She lay on top of him, gripped his hair, his shoulders, shook her head from side to side with the ferocity of needing him.

She realized that there was someone hammering at the door, shouting, 'Open up, what are you doing in there? Let me in!'

It did not matter. Eventually the knocking stopped. Footsteps went reluctantly away.

'They'll come back,' she said, 'you're not going to stay here tonight. We'll find our own room.'

But it was too much effort to get dressed at once, and they lay looking at one another by the candlelight.

'You were going to tell me something.'

'I have told it.' She caught hold of him and drew him on top of her. 'And we are going to find a room with an enormous bed. What's the good of conquering a town if we can't commandeer a decent bed?'

'Who's been teaching you? You're learning to be a soldier.'

'And we're going to commandeer you some decent clothes as well. There must be a tailor here who'd like not to be hanged for a Republican rat.'

More footsteps, running up the stairs. Hammering. Calling, 'Open up.' Threats to break down the door.

They dressed themselves and opened the door to find three furious officers on the landing. 'We have finished,' Hester said. 'We are leaving as soon as Major Vernet is packed.'

'Leaving? Finished?' The man who seemed the senior of the three was staring into the room in horror. 'The beds! What have you been doing?' He peered at Hester more closely. 'You—you are a woman! A woman! Major Vernet! What——'

'She is my wife,' Michel said. He had a leather sack and was stuffing books and a few clothes into it. 'We are going to find married quarters.'

'The beds!'

'Wretched things. If I knew who made them I'd shoot him. Come on.'

They pushed their way past the three staring men and clattered down the stairs and into the courtyard. There were still men on sentry duty, or rather officers, but the day's hurrying had died away and there was little about the street outside to tell that this was a captured town, and a war had begun.

'Where are the soldiers? I thought you would have ten thousand men here.'

'They've gone home,' Michel said. 'They think it's all over. They wanted to go home to their wives.'

'We can hardly blame them for that. But if the Republicans come back?'

'We'll get them together again. Whether it'll be in time is the question. What about this house?'

It was dark and shuttered. After five minutes' hammering a man opened the door, trembling. 'We're all good Royalists here, they've been telling you lies——'

'Then you'll be glad to give us a room. Two rooms.'

'And a lot of bedding,' Hester said. 'And the means to wash ourselves. And some supper. Two bottles of wine and some roast chickens would do.'

The man twisted his hands together, began trying to say that the house was full, they were poor people, there was no food, and no one to cook it if there was.

'We shall pay for everything,' Michel said. 'We are not Republican thieves.' He put the man aside and took his candlestick from him. 'Show us our rooms.'

The house in fact was empty except for the man and an old woman crouched in a servant's cubby-hole beyond the kitchen. There was a lithograph of Marat on the kitchen wall, and a Republican newspaper on the parlour table. A Republican house from which the owners had fled, leaving two servants to try and protect it.

'There is nothing here,' the manservant said, 'I swear it. They took everything, money, silver. We have been starving, we were afraid to go out into the streets.'

'Then you are lucky we came,' Hester said. She pulled a bundle of *assignats* from her pocket, her share of the booty from Garnache. 'Go and get food for all of us. Chickens, meat, bread, wine, everything. No one will touch you. Say you are buying for Major Vernet of the Headquarters Staff. In two hours I want there to be a feast on this table. You, old mother, see to the best bedroom, light a fire, put warming-pans in the bed. I hope it is big enough for two?'

The old woman nodded in terror and scuttled away.

'And you fellow. Is there a good tailor in the town?'

'A tailor—why—the Sieur Cambon—he——'

'Is he a Republican?'

'No, oh no! He prays every day for His Majesty, I know it! As we do, old Agathe and me, God save the King, I swear——'

'His portrait is hidden behind Marat's in the kitchen? Well, if Monsieur Cambon is a good Royalist he'll be delighted to make a uniform for my friend. Tell him to be here in half an hour, with his best cloth, and three apprentices. He'll have to work all night. Oh, and shirts, a dozen of the best shirts he can find, and everything else for a tall gentleman. Agathe! Agathe! Heat water for a bath. Hurry woman, a good Royalist bath with the best scent and soap and the finest towels.'

'A bath? Monsieur—Madame? A bath?'

'Don't Republicans take baths? Then a wash-tub, old mother, anything in which my friend can clean himself. And I shall share it with him if it's big enough.'

'You?' The old woman's eyes as round as apples. 'Lord save us!'

But half an hour later they were taking it in turns to soap each other, a wooden wash-tub steaming in the middle of the cool-room floor. Pummelling and drying one another as if they were children in a river pool.

'As my teacher said, if we're to die young, let's die with clean skins and underclothes. And well fed.'

The tailor, expecting his throat to be cut. Not three, but at least one apprentice, eyeing his master's terror with a happy malice. Bales of cloth, a pile of shirts and stockings.

'This filth?' Hester said, kicking the rolls of serge. 'Saxony wool, man! The best cloth you have, I said, not stuff for peasants' trousers. You're to make a coat for a King's officer, you wretch.'

'Madame, monsieur I mean——'

'I am madame, you fool, don't you know what a woman looks like?'

The apprentice sniggered. Hester looked at him.

'Send that boy for some decent cloth before I cut his throat. You've ten minutes to bring it back.'

The tailor's hands shook so much that he could not measure properly, and Hester must help him. That made his terror worse, but in the end the job was done. The boy came back with a roll of woollen cloth so fine that the tailor gave a cry of pain at seeing it. A bale of silk for lining.

'That's what we need,' Hester said. 'Now, what time is it? Ten o'clock? That gives you another ten hours till eight o'clock tomorrow. Bring the coat and breeches at eight, you can leave this stuff here, we'll choose when we've eaten. And bring a boot-maker with you.'

'Madame!'

'Hurry, man, you're wasting time. If I need to fetch you tomorrow——'

They were alone.

'What's happened to you?' Michel said.

'War has happened to me. And I'm myself again. Where is that woman with our dinner?'

To eat. To drink. To lie in a great bed piled with down mattresses and pillows. To sink in it. Like warm snow.

'I shall show you whether I can be a friend,' she said.

Chapter 15

April. May. June. Three months of triumphs. Town after town taken. Chalonnes, Chemillé, Bressuire, Thouars, Parthenay. Tearing down the Tricolore, raising the Lilies on town halls, on churches, châteaux. Bonfires in the market squares, fed with Republican dossiers, the mass of papers of a Revolution that seemed to live on paper-work; lists of suspects, lists of condemned, lists of assets of *émigrés* to be confiscated and sold. Letters, reports, proclamations, God knew how many proclamations. Feeding the bonfires, bringing out oath priests and haggard patriots from cellars and attic hiding-places, throwing them into their own jails with kicks and curses.

But no looting. No killing when the fighting was done. No massacres such as that bloodstained imbecile Souchu had conducted in Machecoul, with his wild men from the marshes. This was a crusade. Prayers before battle, Te Deum after it. The Republican soldiers that they took prisoner released with no more than their heads shaved, and an oath that they would not fight against the King again. If they broke that oath, their shaven heads would betray them, and then beware. 'But go now and tell your comrades that God is come into France again, and Christ and His army.' The Great Catholic and Royal Army. Sweeping all before it. Nobles for leaders now. D'Elbée, Bonchamps, Rochejaquelein, whom his men called the archangel, Lescure, Donissan, Marigny, Talmond the beautiful. And Cathelineau the carter, the travelling carrier and packman, also become a general. His men called him Saint as well as General. The Saint of Anjou. Christ and His saints riding. And Stofflet the terrible, the Huntsman.

Such leaders and such men as no army had before in history.

An army of holiness. Whose peasant soldiers ran home after every battle to tend their fields, and change their shirts, and love their wives and children. To rally again with their parish captains when the call came to fight for another victory. Timid as sheep and in the next instant lions. Attacking cannon with bare hands and pikes. Throwing themselves to the ground when they saw the lighted matches of the cannoneers swinging and flaring towards the touch-holes of the guns. Crash of fire, cannon-shot screaming above their flattened bodies. Then up and race for the cannon, '*Rembarre, rembarre, rembarre!*' Nail the cannoneers to their guns if they had not the sense to run for it.

Sweeping the landscape clean of Republicans. Running behind the hedges to cut off the helpless Blues in the narrow roads and lanes, beating the woods for stragglers. Marching against towns whose garrisons shook with fear to hear the sabots coming, crash of wooden sabots, ring of steel, voices ringing. Singing the Royalist Marseillaise.

'Allons, les Armées Catholiques
le jour de gloire est arrivé!'

Taking La Chataigneraie on its steep hilltop, sweeping in so fast that they found the guillotine still wet with blood in the square, the executioners fled for their lives. Freeing the surviving prisoners who would have been dead in another hour. Glory be to God on high.

Taking Fontenay after the first check and rout.

Taking Saumur.

Taking Angers.

O sing unto the Lord a new song, for He hath done marvellous things. His right hand and His holy arm, hath gotten Him the victory.

Cathelineau the peasant, the carter, now General in Chief, and the aristocrats taking orders from him. A Grand Council set up in Châtillon to rule the reconquered countryside in the name of the King, Louis XVII, the Child of the Temple, the Royal Prisoner. A Bishop led the Council, the Bishop of Agra, the Pope's own ambassador, with the Abbé Bernier for Secretary. No longer a mere rising, but a Civil War, and one that they were winning. With an army that grew in strength and experience day by day, victory by victory. Artillery, captured from the enemy. A General Staff. Divisions. Brigades. Companies. Each parish under its elected captain providing a company, to rally within hours of a summons, sent by courier, or flags from church towers, or tocsins ringing, or the sails of the windmills tilted this way or that in semaphore.

Only the officers and a few men stayed permanently under arms. And some women. And some of the cavalry. The cavalry as scouts, as shock troops, as couriers. The Prince de Talmond commanding. It was not a marvellous cavalry. Plough-horses for the most part, cart-horses, half-broken ponies. But within it there was a small body of real cavaliers, perhaps two hundred of them. And Michel and Hester rode with them.

'If no one else but you and that mole can make lists, what does it matter if they are never made? Leave them to Monsieur Mole. You and I are going to ride together.' He had not argued. Now they led the scouts, the élite within the élite, twenty of them, eighteen men and two women, Hester, and a girl of nineteen, Anne Guerry. Her father and her husband and her baby had been murdered by the Blues, and she rode like a destroying angel, looking for death in every battle.

A time of glory.

They made it a pride to dress like princes. Silk and velvet, lace and silver. Hester began it, and Michel, and the others followed, even Anne Guerry, who scarcely spoke, and lived only to kill again. They wore white sashes, and silk cockades, white and black and green, and over the weeks of fighting, as they captured towns and tailors and found cloth, they fitted themselves with a uniform of kinds; hunting-green jackets, and breeches of soft grey buckskin, black boots coming high up to guard their knees. White silk shirts and black silk stocks. Green hats with white plumes. Cross belts and sword belts worked in silver. The finest weapons. Against the rough disarray of the peasants in their long brown coats and mud-stained gaiters they looked as brilliant as summer lightning, and lifted the army's hearts as they rode.

At the end of June they were to attack Nantes. The greatest battle, the greatest city in the West. The key to Brittany, the key to the war, to real victory. With the port of Nantes open to the English fleet, supplies could flood in from England. *Emigré* troops could land there. One of the Princes could come, must come. If not the Regent, then Artois, or at the least Condé's son.

They sent an Ultimatum to the Republicans of Nantes, and

messages to Charette, to co-ordinate his attack from the south with theirs from the east and north, along the right bank of the Loire. If the Blues did not surrender by the twenty-eighth of June, then the city's destruction was on their heads.

'It's a mistake,' Michel said. Four of them had ridden within three miles of Nantes along the right bank, the Breton bank of the Loire, and found no Republican outposts, no signs of troops. 'We should have attacked at once. All we've done is give them nine days to get ready for us.' They rode down to the river and out onto a sandbank. The water low and slack between them and a wooded island that hid the far bank. 'And the Bretons have done nothing.'

'They'll rise when we take Nantes.'

'Ah. When.'

'We shall take it!' Defeat impossible.

But they were defeated.

When they were already in the town. Savage fighting, such fighting as they had not met in all the war. Street to street, house to house, riding against bayonets, leaping barriers of dead men. Driven back, the peasants like Royal Guardsmen, heroes, but driven back. And then the cavalry thrown in as a gambler's throw, turning the tide, sweeping into a wide market square. Cathelineau himself, the General in Chief, the Saint of Anjou, riding with them, knee to knee with Michel, with Hester.

'God and the King! Rally, rally, God and St. Louis!' Cannon fire, smoke, houses burning, the peasants rallying, the Blues retreating, across the square. Men falling, firing as they fell, fighting with their last breath, fighting as death took them. She could not see for blood. Blood running from her forehead, masking her eyes. Clearing them with her sleeve. In a loft window, high up in one of the surrounding houses, she saw a man taking aim with a long-barrelled gun. He is aiming at me, she thought, in that endless moment one has when one looks at death and cannot move.

But he was aiming at Cathelineau. She saw the smoke of the shot, thought she could hear it. And beside her Cathelineau swayed back in the saddle.

She tried to hold him up, and could not. Fury of battle round them. Crash of cannon, musket fire like the crack of flames in timber.

[174]

'Get him under cover,' Michel screamed. 'Back with him.' And as they carried him out of the fighting the peasants saw that their Saint was fallen, and they broke, and ran. They ran like deer, like sheep when the wolves are on them. 'He is dead, run! The Saint is dead!' Nothing could rally them for a mile, and ground that had cost five hundred lives and hours of fighting was lost in minutes.

They were rallied at last, and fought again, but the spirit had gone out of them. The Saint of Anjou lay unconscious in a cart that slowly carried him eastwards, along the river towards safety. A new attack from the north, and for a moment the Blues broke again, at the Barricade de Vannes. Tried to fly. And Talmond, Talmond the beautiful, the imbecile, prevented them. Threw all his troops into blocking their path, when to let them go, let them spread panic, would have opened a roadway into the heart of the town.

'May God save us from our leaders,' Michel said, and hid his face in his hands.

They went on fighting until dark. But there was no more hope. Bonchamps withdrawing. D'Elbée, after a last attack. Talmond, proud of his imbecility to the end. Riding east. Defeated. And behind them, Charette's guns, still firing into the town from across the Loire. It was two days before they discovered that no one had sent word to Charette that they were withdrawing. No one had thought of it.

That same day, the first of July, Westermann rode into the Vendée at the head of the advance guard of a new Republican army of 60,000 men, and took Clisson. Two days later he took Châtillon, the Royalist 'Capital' where the Grand Council sat and issued its orders and its proclamations. The Councillors fled for their lives.

'We have lost,' Michel said. 'It is all over.'

The Republican army leaving a trail of flames behind it. Châteaux, farms, villages, churches. And a trail of murder. Killing prisoners, killing the wounded. The moment of despair they had felt turned to a deeper hatred, and strength came back. They caught Westermann near Châtillon and destroyed his force and almost caught him. Defeated Menou and the gross, grotesque Santerre at Vihiers. Fought, and broke and fought again and broke the enemy. Heard that Cathelineau had died of his wound, and wept with grief, an army weeping.

Hester and Michel and Anne Guerry and three more of their people rode to find Charette and invite him to the Council that was to elect a new chief. They found him holding court at Légé, like a king, keeping festival in the fields and woods. A court of women, of dancing, of triumph. Triumph that whatever was happening inland, here near the coast the country was theirs, untroubled by the Republicans. Triumph, and an air of contempt for the army of Anjou, that had betrayed them at Nantes. And fury that Michel and Hester only arrived at Légé the day before the Council meeting that was to elect a new General in Chief.

'You honour me too much by informing me like this,' Charette said, reading the letter. Reading it aloud in a harshly mocking voice so that his officers and the surrounding women could hear it. 'I am glad to hear of your plan.'

'And your answer, General?' Michel said.

'My answer?'

Charette's voice beginning to shake with anger. 'My answer is that this is an insult, Major. Go back to your Holy Catholic army and say your prayers. Here we are more interested in fighting.'

Laughter from his court.

They refused an invitation to stay and dine and dance by torch-light in the open meadow that formed the dancing ground. At any other time, Hester realized as they rode away, she would have admired them. Had admired what she had heard of them. His women not only danced but fought. His own sister, Mademoiselle Charette; Madame Bulkeley, Madame du Fief, Sophie and Céleste Couëtus, Madame de Monsorbier, Mademoiselle de la Rochette, Madame de la Rochefoucauld in the moments when she was not quarrelling with Charette and fighting her own private war against the Blues. All of them had fought in battle, hand to hand. More than once Hester had thought that Michel's and her own real place was with them, rather than with leaders who seemed at times more like priests than soldiers. That only Charette was fighting a war not for an old, lost world, but for a new one, in which she herself could be happy, one in which women would have a real place. Or was it simply that he attracted women as sugar attracts flies, and used them as he would use a weapon or a scarf? Women who followed him like slaves, fought for him, died for him. Not only his aristocrats, but peasant girls, like Marie Lourdais who had come more than once to Châtillon to bring messages, sometimes only insults veiled in Court language, and had risked her life fifty times over to do it. Or Madeleine Tournant. Or Marie Chevet who was already dead, taken long ago and executed.

But everywhere it was a war of women. As though the women had driven their men to take up arms, and now felt that they must share the danger. Even in the army of Anjou with its piety, where most of the women knelt in the nearest churches during a battle, praying for victory, and for their men, Hester and Anne Guerry were far from alone as women soldiers. And not merely soldiers for a moment, for an hour of crisis, but always under arms. Renée Bordereau, the peasant girl called the Angevin in tribute to her courage; Marie-Antoinette Adams, whose husband was a grocer and a Republican, and who had fled from him and his politics and his malice to take service under General Sapinaud, and become his bodyguard. Jeanne Robin who had been killed in the thick of the battle of Thouars. The tall girl Regrenille, who had been a novice with the Ursulines, and now rode with Hester and Anne Guerry in the cavalry.

Women whose fame was already spreading across four provinces, shaming men who had not brought themselves to fight. Hester herself had lost the name of 'the greyhound' and won that of 'the chevalier'. At times she was so proud of what she had done, what she was doing, that she wanted to lift in her stirrups and shout for joy. 'I am free! I am free!' As no women had been free since time began. When she met one of her sister warriors, and they recognized one another, she wanted to embrace her, could have wept for pride. And as the times darkened, she took still greater care to be splendid. To keep the lesson Madame de la Rochefoucauld had taught her. The whitest silk for a scarf and sash, the most beautiful lace for collars. Coat and breeches cut to sit without a crease, like skin. And to eat and drink as if they were in London.

She and Anne Guerry saw to it that their mess was always the best furnished. The oldest wines, the best cook they could find or capture. Their table became so famous that the Prince de Talmond took to inviting himself there, pretending that he was 'roughing it with his men'. Although he was still in his twenties he suffered already from gout, and sometimes after a second bottle of wine had to be lifted by Michel and Hester into his saddle, cursing his foot, and them, and wine, and his life.

'He comes to see you,' Michel said, after a fourth visit in four days.

She stood still, watching the prince ride away towards his quarters.

'You don't seem to mind that,' he went on, when she did not answer.

She looked at him in astonishment. 'That great toy?' she said. 'Do you think I am flattered if such a fool looks at me?'

'He's a duke's son. Other women have felt flattered.'

She could not believe what she was hearing, and was tempted to laugh, and then to be angry. 'What is the matter with you?' And then, 'You are jealous! Michel!' She did laugh. He swung on his heel.

'Michel! Have you gone mad? What is the matter with you? Michel!' When he did not turn his head she ran after him and caught him by the arm, swung him round.

He tried to put her aside.

'I won't let you go! Michel, what's happened to you?'

He touched her face. 'Nothing,' he said. 'It would be only natural if—if you were flattered. I—I'm sorry.'

They made it up, after a fashion. Made it up completely, as far as it could be made up. But it stayed in her mind, and she knew that it stayed in his, also. That nothing was quite the same. Yet why? Why? Was it so monstrous in him to be jealous for a moment? She did not understand it herself, and yet the fact was there. Nothing between them was the same. They began to be too watchful of how they talked to one another. Too carefully courteous. And again and again she wanted to bring it out into the open. And said nothing. More than once she found herself glad of reasons to be sent away from him, on a separate duty. Anything. She wondered sometimes if that was what happened to all lovers. That love had so short a lifespan and grew cool and courteous so quickly. And knew too that that was not the answer. Or—but she was afraid to look too deep for answers. She told herself she was a fool. That she should be grateful to God and Michel that she was leading the life she had dreamed of since her childhood. To live as a man lives. To ride like a man, fight in battles. To be treated by men as their equal, as a comrade. What more could she ask from life, or from Michel? He was kind, in his way of being kind. Kinder than a thousand, ten thousand men might have been.

Even in such a woman's matter as getting pregnant, that would have destroyed everything for her, he had understood, and had taught her ways to avoid it. Not the unpleasant French way, but an Indian way, with herbs that grew along the hedges. He is a man in ten thousand, she told herself, and I deserve to be punished for wanting more. She told herself that she did not want it, there was no more to want.

In August they heard that the Convention in Paris had decreed the total destruction of the Vendée. Destroy the harvests. Destroy the farms. Burn everything that can be burned. The woods, the houses. Let the Vendée be cut from the map of France like a gangrene in the body politic. Let it be sown with salt.

To make sure of the destruction, another eighteen thousand Republican troops, the garrison of Mayence under Kléber, were already marching west.

Soon after they heard that news they attacked Lucon again, and were routed again. The new General in Chief D'Elbée's second humiliating defeat. The days of endless victories were gone. And the new Republicans were closing a steel ring round the Vendée.

At the Royalist Headquarters they began to talk of breaking out into Brittany. An envoy had come from England, with promises of help if they could seize one of the Channel ports. An English fleet would land supplies, troops, weapons. The Prince de Talmond told them what was happening. For weeks she had avoided him. If he came to their mess she made excuses to dine elsewhere, or simply stayed away. So much so that Michel told her she must not make her dislike so obvious, and must treat Talmond like any other guest.

She sat now watching him, on a mid-September evening. Fifteen of them round the long table, as the Prince moved salt cellars and wine glasses, knives and crusts of bread to represent Republicans, themselves, towns and villages. He was, she thought, if one did not know what a fool he was, a very beautiful creature to watch. His hair golden, like curling flames. Tall as a prince should be, and still slim enough, only his face rounded and smooth, almost babyish, except for the air of race about it, the eagerness, the command. His hands were beautiful, and she watched them move this and that, crush a piece of bread as though he was destroying an enemy column. Laugh, his teeth white and shining, like a child's teeth, his lips red.

'Kléber and Canclaux mean to come down this way. And here is Grouchy to the east. Rossignol there. If we give them too much time—what do you say, Major?—delays, delays, delays! They will ruin us. Attack here, smash our way through to the Loire, and into Brittany. To Laval, where I can raise ten thousand men by lifting my hat. It is my own city, my own countryside, my own peasants. Ten? I've promised them twenty thousand in two days. And then to the north, to the Channel. I swear to you, if I was commanding!'

One or two of the officers flattering him absurdly. The kind of flattery, the kind of blindness to everything but rank that had brought France to destruction. She was half aware of it as she listened. Tried to catch Michel's eye. But he was arguing about something with another officer, and instead of his eye it was Talmond's that she caught.

'What do you think, ma'am?' Talmond said, in English, which he spoke well enough, and liked to use.

'I think my business is to carry out orders,' she said.

He did not answer her. Only looked. And as he looked, he was not a fool, not the man who gave wrong orders, and insisted on disaster. But a man who knew women as a fine rider must know horses. Like being touched. Very gently touched by a soft yet strong hand. She could feel it, knew what his hand would feel like, and felt her body trembling. But not the way it had trembled for Michel. A soft shivering. With Michel it was like two fighters stripped for fighting, the shivering of a hound on leash that strains to let go. A hard excitement, fierce, masculine. This was so different that she did not recognize what it was. A shivering almost of fear, fear of yielding, longing to yield, to give herself, be taken. She wanted to look away from him, and could not.

When at last she did turn her head, she saw Michel looking at her. As if he knew what had happened. She turned from both of them, made herself look contemptuous. Afterwards Michel said nothing. She wanted him to accuse her, longed for it. Grew coldly, savagely angry at his silence. Did he not care? Or did he think—what did he think? That she—or was he waiting for her to explain, beg forgiveness? For what?

'I am going to the stables,' she said. He did not offer to come with her. There was nothing to do there. It had all been done before supper.

She had been there ten minutes when she heard footsteps, quick, yet quiet. He has come to make up, she thought. She stayed where she was, hidden in one of the stalls, by her own horse, the great black she called Bayard the Second. His skin like silk. Footsteps. Her heart beginning to beat, to beat, as it had not done for weeks. He has come. He has followed me.

A voice whispering. 'Are you there?'

She hid her face against Bayard's neck. Hardness of muscles, roughness of mane, smell of horseflesh, of grooming. Rustle of straw behind her, a hand touching her.

'I have found you,' Talmond said.

And for another moment she did not move. As if—as if——

She swung round then, shaking with fury. Not able to speak. Lantern light. Shadows. He had hidden his uniform under a cloak. Had taken off his hat. His hair golden, his face soft-rounded, smooth as a boy's. He took her hand and kissed it, before she could prevent him. His mouth warm. She could not move. He touched her cheek, looking into her eyes. He did not smile. He looked sad, as if he was looking at something, someone, a long way off, beyond reach.

'Feel my heart beat,' he whispered. He held her hand against his coat.

'You must go,' she said, her voice shaking. No longer with anger.

He went down on one knee, held her hand against his lips, turned it so that he could kiss the palm of it. Pressed his face against her body. 'For the first time,' he whispered, 'I am lost. Utterly lost.'

She tried to make him stand up, to lift him.

'Let me kneel,' he said.

'Prince! I beg you! Someone will—they may have seen you——' None of it what she had meant to say. As if—as if that was her only concern, that someone might have seen him, might see them both.

'The first time I saw you, I knew. If I must die for it. Have mercy on me.' He came to his feet, caught her face between his hands. 'I have gone mad, I know it. I implore you to be merciful,

[181]

I cannot sleep, I cannot think. One kiss. One. That I can remember all my life. If I live to be a hundred, I shall whisper to myself, once I was happy, once I kissed her mouth.'

Trembling so much she could not move. Then, as his mouth came close it was as though she was waking out of sleep. She gripped his shoulders, forced him back against the timber partition of the stall. Behind her Bayard stamped and tossed his head in anxiety. The other horses shifted their hooves, rustled their straw.

'How dare you follow me? If my husband saw you!'

'I told you, I am willing to die for you. Let him call me out. I should not raise my hand against him. You and I,' he said, 'there is something between us beyond marriage.'

She wanted to shout at him, strike him. Fool, madman! All the words fell away as she looked at him. He was made for love as Michel was made for war.

'God meant us to be together,' he said. 'I won't move. Touch my face. You know we were meant to meet, meant to love one another.' His voice as sad as if they were lovers parting for ever. She did touch his face. Gently. Held the soft round curve of his chin in her palm. She knew that he had had a thousand lovers, and it did not matter. If Michel had been there in the doorway she could not have taken her hand away.

Very slowly he put up one hand and held her wrist. Drew her towards him by the pressure of a finger, pressing down on her wrist very slightly so that her arm bent, and she came to him. As if she was drunk, as if she was sleepwalking. She held his face and kissed him, his soft, yielding, lover's mouth.

'My love,' he breathed.

They stood breast to breast in the darkness, the lantern throwing its weak light beyond them, onto the smooth timber, onto Bayard's black glistening flank.

As if they were already lovers. He did not do anything. Did not open her jacket, touch her breast. Only let his lips rest on hers, not pressed close. The beat of his heart against her breast.

'There's a hunting-lodge near here,' he whispered. 'La Grotte du Lac. There's no one there. Tomorrow night. At midnight.'

His breath warm in her mouth, in her throat.

'No!'

Closing her mouth with his. Very softly. Smoothing her hair

[182]

from her forehead, touching the scar she had got at Nantes, and that was not yet healed. 'We have so little time to live,' he whispered. 'You and I.'

He was gone. As if he had never been there. A sense of loss. I am insane, she thought. What has happened to me? Oh God help me, please. Kneeling with her forehead against Bayard's flank, while he blew through his shining nostrils against her hair, his head turned puzzledly towards her.

Chapter 16

She did not go to La Grotte. Did not think for an instant of going there. But she lay all that next night awake, thinking of his being there, waiting for her. Saw his face. His hands. Felt his mouth kissing hers, his hands touching. Lay in terror beside Michel, in terror that he might touch her, and know from the trembling of her body what she was thinking, feeling. And that it was not for him. She felt tears running. I am gone mad, she thought. It is the war. The fighting. Seeing death so close.

We have so little time to live, you and I.

Oh God, take this temptation away from me. I have chosen my love. Chosen my friend. To destroy everything for—that soft mouth? She lay crying, sleepless. I am a weak fool, she told herself. Like a child crying for the moon.

We have so little time to live. Tomorrow? The day after? Out of the twenty they had been at the beginning fifteen were left. How long before it was her turn? Or Michel's? She wanted to touch him then, as if by the mere thinking of temptation she was somehow endangering their friendship. Friendship? Love. I love him! Did I not choose him? Take him for mine? No one made me, he did not take me, I took him, and now—suppose he was to be killed? Tomorrow? Next week? Every day, every fight they were in, he tried to shield her. Suppose he was killed in doing that? And Talmond came to her afterwards? What would she do?

I am insane! That fool, that soft-skinned boy! To measure him against Michel! To think—to imagine—she got up from the bed and went in her shirt to the window. Black trees. White moon. Was he still waiting for her? La Grotte du Lac. Imagined the house. A log fire. Panelled walls. A pile of furs in front of the hearth. She bit her knuckles until they bled. Four o'clock striking. She went downstairs, still in her shirt, barefooted, barelegged. There was a river running behind the house where they had their quarters, and she waded into it, knee deep, waist deep. Lay down in the cold embrace of it, under the surface, until her lungs hurt with the strain of holding her breath. Came out of the water and ran through the nearby fields until she was dry. If a sentry saw her? Shot at her? She thought that she did not care. But no one challenged her, and she came back at last, walking slowly, to the house, the stairs, the closed, stifling room. The window was open, but it was still close and the air unbreathable after the night air of the fields, the cold cleanness of the river.

Michel was awake. She knew it. Waited for him to ask her where she had been. But he lay still, pretending to be asleep. She lay down beside him, suddenly cold. Wanted to touch him, wanted him to make her warm. In that moment if he had turned to her, held her, everything would have been like the beginning, the best of the beginning. Talmond, folly, madness, would have vanished out of her mind like the chill of the river. But Michel lay quietly breathing, pretending he was not awake. After another moment she turned her back to him, and they both lay sleepless until the dawn allowed them to end concealment, and get up.

That day, and for days after, there was more than enough to keep both of them from their private wretchedness. Eight army corps of the enemy were driving into the heart of the Vendée, burning as they advanced. It was no longer necessary to use the windmills for semaphores. The smoke of burning villages and farms and woods told where the enemy was. And the windmills themselves were being burned. Because they had been used by the Royalists for spying and signalling. Because without them to grind grain the Royalists would starve. And the countryside would starve with them. There was to be no shelter, no food, no refuge, no escape. All the prisoners, all the wounded to be killed. All suspects. Men. Women. Children. All put to the sword.

The Vendée was no longer fighting for victory, it was fighting to survive. Town by town lost to the Republicans. Charette was driven from the coast inland, begging for help, begging at last to join forces with the Grand Catholic Army. And for a brief moment they did join forces, and turned on the Republicans like wounded lions. In three September days won five victories that sent the Republicans reeling back in panic. Torfou, Pont-Barré, Montaigu, Clisson, St. Fulgent.

'No prisoners, no quarter!' There was too much hatred now to show mercy. The days of releasing prisoners, only their heads shaven, long, long gone. Burned farms, burned villages, burned women to avenge. Such fighting as there had never yet been. Riding, fighting, blind to everything but the narrow space in front of her as she rode knee to knee with Michel, Anne Guerry, Regrenille, the others. Charging against a line of men, a grey blue line like smoke, and the flash of gunfire, bayonets, scream of shot, of horses dying, men falling, hacking, thrusting, Bayard kicking and rearing, screaming in battle fear. She saw a musket levelled at Michel and rode it down, the man falling, saw with a kind of dazed astonishment that the man was black, a Negro, that the line of men they were breaking was a line of Negroes.

'God and the King, God and the King!' Through the line, riding for the guns. Michel ahead of her, Anne Guerry. And in the next instant Anne's horse was riderless, galloping, Anne fallen, vanished. And they were on the guns, striking, striking, men running. The deafening, blinding smash of cannon fire as one gunner stayed by his gun, brought his match swinging to the touch hole. Michel's horse staggering with the shock of it, and then they were through, the Blues were running, flying, like hares in a field. 'Ride them down, ride them down! No quarter, no prisoners!'

When it was finished she rode back to where Anne had fallen. She lay in the stubble, still breathing, still alive. Hester got down and tried to lift her, and Anne clenched her teeth against the pain of being moved. 'Let me go,' she whispered. 'They are waiting for me.' A few minutes later she was dead. Hester kneeling beside her in the field.

Perrine Loiseau died in the same battle. They buried them side by side, two women who had shown many men what courage means.

'We lay their bodies in a narrow grave,' Father Barbotin said. 'But their souls are already in Paradise, before God's throne. Do not weep for them. Envy them their glory.'

Talmond was there at the burial. She did not look at him. Afterwards Michel said to her, 'Go to Mervent. See to your father. There may not be another chance. Try and get all of them into safety.'

She tried to read in his tone, in his face, what he really meant. To get rid of her? For how long? Because of—because of what might happen in the next few days? Or because of Talmond?

'I don't want to go.'

They were on foot, apart from the others for a moment. He was pulling on his gauntlets before mounting. 'I'm giving you an order,' he said. 'You've done enough.'

'You mean—you are—you want to send me away?'

He made himself busy with the saddle girth of his horse. With the length of a stirrup leather. 'This is no longer a time for women fighting. If it ever was. I am telling you to go.'

'I will not go!'

He swung round and caught her by the collar of her cloak that she had worn for mourning. 'I'm your husband,' he whispered. 'For good or bad. And by your choice. As your husband I am telling you to go. Whatever's between us, do you think I want you to end like that?' He jerked his chin towards the two graves, and the wild flowers that lay on them, the wooden crosses fresh sawn, raw in the sunlight.

'What do you mean, whatever is between—what do you mean?'

'Don't make me say it aloud. Just go. This is not your war, not your country, not your king. Go, I tell you.' Tightening the collar of her cloak until it was hard to breathe. 'You're not fit to lie beside those two.' His face tight with rage, with something like hatred.

'Tell me what you mean!' She gripped his arms, held him. 'You have gone mad!'

Talmond mounting his beautiful mare. A shimmer of black boots, white buckskin, gold. Black silk cravat. White leather gauntlets. The long skirts of his black coat swinging as he sprang into the saddle. Lifting his tall black hat with its great white cockade, saluting the graves, the priest, the mourners. Turning his eyes for a fraction of a moment towards her.

'To leave my bed for that! That!'

She felt in the pressure of his hands that he would have liked to kill her. Before she could answer the priest was beside them.

'Leave the fastening,' Hester said. 'It does not matter.' The priest walked with them, trying to console her for her friend. And before he left them, Michel made an excuse to ride away.

'You will be gone to Mervent before I'm back,' he said. 'Carry my respects to your father.'

'But I am not——'

'I have business in Charette's camp,' he said, as if he was talking to a stranger. 'There is trouble again, and he's threatening to leave. Did you hear of this already, Father? I may be two days. Unless of course you wish to stay here without me, for any reason?'

His face like iron.

'Michel!'

When she could think clearly again, she was alone.

She rode south that night as if she was blind. Not seeing where she was going, letting the horse guide her. Anger rising in her like waves in a storm, each greater than the last, until she shook with it, wanted to drive her spurs into Bayard's sides and ride until he threw her down from his back and she could lie in a field as Anne Guerry had done, and feel the end coming.

Anger, and then a coldness like terror. Despair. What have I done, what has happened? How can I go on?

Early darkness. Forest. She began to ride carefully, out of habit, and to spare her horse. Somewhere in her mind she knew that she must find a place to sleep. A farmhouse, somewhere. Must keep alert for any Republicans who had escaped from the last battle, and might be hiding, looking for revenge on a lone enemy. And in the next instant welcomed the thought of that. Let there be ten of them, twenty, and we can make a fine end of it. She cried tears of anger as she rode, tears of despair, and was ashamed of crying, and could not stop. Cried then for Anne, who lay quiet in her narrow grave. Or else perhaps, God let it be so, was truly with her husband, and her child, and her father, as she had longed to be.

God keep her soul. Anne who had never been beautiful as a woman. Thin, yellow-skinned, sandy, long-nosed. A wonder she had found a husband, unless it was for her goodness he had married her. And then to see her riding, transformed like sea foam on a wave, the flower and bravery. Anne the fearless, the stainless. Oh my friend.

Riding, blind with tears.

She heard the hoofbeats behind her, and took no notice. Let it come. A horse galloping. One. She swung Bayard round, drawing the long pistol from her saddle holster, took aim.

'I surrender!' Talmond cried. A dark shape in the darkness, but his voice unmistakable, like champagne, clear and joyous. Lifting his hands, his broad white muslin sash a pale mark for her to aim at. And for a second she was tempted to pull the trigger, to put an end to him, to herself, to everything. He was beside her, the muzzle of the pistol resting against his thigh. Bending towards her.

He did not say anything. Not a word. Only took the reins of her horse in one hand and began riding beside her. They came to a cross path in the forest and he turned the horses' heads to the right. His knee close to hers, his gauntlet holding her gloved hand, clenched on the reins. The horses walking quietly. Moonlight through the trees. Flakes of silver on fallen leaves, on wild flowers that had lost their daytime colour, and were black and silver in their turn, as if they belonged to the moon and not the sun. As if the day had lost all power in this silver darkness, and the things of daytime had no meaning.

They rode in silence for an hour. Soft fall of hooves in the rustling bed of leaves under the trees. An animal's eyes in the dark, red as fire. Green as emeralds. An owl's cry, an owl's shadow, drifting. She felt she had known him for ever, since the beginning of all things. For now. For now. The trees fell back and they were on a broad sweep of meadow beside a lake, the shape of a building in front of them.

She knew that it was the hunting lodge. Had been here before, that night in her sleeplessness. Like coming home. The stables. The water trough. She slid down from the saddle and they gave the horses water, and armfuls of hay, left them there. He took her to the front of the house again, by the hand, like a child. The sound of the key, door creaking, dark. The scent of an empty house. But not of neglect. Of welcome, of waiting. Candlelight. The shadows as he moved, took logs from a huge basket beside the fire place, twigs and kindlings, woodshavings. A tongue of flame, small and delicate. The scent of wood burning. There were trophies on the panelled walls, horns of deer, of stags, a wolf's head, wild boar.

All the while he was laying the fire she had stood quietly where he had left her, not moving, scarcely breathing. He turned, still on his knees, took her hands, drew her down until she knelt face to face with him. Took off her riding hat with a slow gesture of revelation, loosening her hair. Held the dark copper mass of it in the palms of his two hands, pressed it against his mouth. Began with infinite slowness to undress her, lace by lace, fastening by fastening. As if to touch her clothes was itself a lovemaking. She had to shut her eyes, bite into her lip to prevent herself from making a sound, crying out with longing. Her cloak. Her coat, button by button, unprisoning her breast, her waist. He laid his forehead against her body, breathed in the warmth of her. She longed to touch his hair, stroke his face, his neck, do to him what he was doing to her. And at the same time wanted to stay still, to let this ecstasy of waiting go on, go on for ever, until she must scream with desire for him, for what would happen. Felt the blood run on her lip as she bit harder, warm, salt-tasting, iron. Slowly twisted her head from one side to the other.

Her coat loosened from her shoulders, drawn down, over her arms, her hands. Unfastening her shirt. The fire had grown, flowered, lit the dark gold of his head, the smoothness of his back. Sky blue cloth, dark blue collar. Tight black stock. She had to touch him, touch the nape of his neck, the hair soft and warm, silk. Bend forward, hold him, hold him against her naked breast. His hands touching her waist, loosening the tight band of her breeches. The fire warm against her nakedness, the shadows moving, horned shadows of the trophies, wolf's head snarling, white curve of boar's tusks in savagery, like wild laughter.

If I must die for it, she thought. He made her lie face down on the thick sheepskin rug, and knelt beside her, running the tips of his fingers down her spine to the top of her thighs, drawing the breeches off, her boots, not as Michel had done, with a fierce urgency, but slowly, as if each movement was wonderful, its own ecstasy. Until she lay naked, her cheek against the shaggy softness, the luxury of the skins. The skins themselves were padded underneath with fleece, to make a bed for loving. A scent of wood smoke, of wildness, of the night.

He touched the hollow of her back with his mouth, tasting her skin, drawing in her scent as he breathed, his own breath warm on her, his lips scarcely touching her. Up to the nape of her neck, lifting her hair away with his hand, fastening his mouth suddenly and drawing back again as she shivered, drew in her breath between clenched teeth, her eyes still shut. The soft warmth of his mouth against her side, her hip, down to the calf of her leg, her foot. His hands touching her, here, there, so gently it was difficult to be certain that he was touching her, and the shivering of her skin went deeper, her muscles began to tremble, she had to bury her face into the softness of the rug, into the yielding, scented wool, bow her shoulders, clench her fingers on the thick fleece under her.

Another second and she must scream, tear something, she could not endure another breath, she would die of this. And he touched her again and her nerves quietened, like breath too long held going out in a long sigh, and she lay limp and dazed. Until once more he touched, and stroked and kissed. Those light, almost untouching kisses, and she began to lift her head, arch her spine backwards. Force herself up on her hands, cry out. And he slid his hands under her, held her breast in the palm of his hand, lay down beside her.

She looked down at him as he lay. He was not smiling. Only a look of longing, and at the same time of command, drawing her to him, drawing her soul out of her, so that she had no will, no mind. Possessed. She unfastened his coat, his stock. Began to undress him as he had undressed her. He lay watching her face, his own face golden in the firelight, the candlelight. His body smooth as a boy's, satin. Nothing that she knew about him mattered. The lovers, the folly, the attacks of gout that must make him a cripple before he reached middle age. None of that mattered; belonged to someone else, to a Prince de Talmond of the daytime, of the army, of the court. This was the reality, the only one.

She drew off his long, shimmering boots, the leather cold against her breast as she held first one and then the other, laid them aside, knelt over him. He held out his arms for her. Drew her down to him as if she was being drawn down into a deep pool of love.

Chapter 17

She woke at dawn as she did always. The fire had died to grey ashes and charred and blackened logs. A thin grey light from an uncurtained window. The trophies dead shadows on the dark walls. The black sheen of wine bottles on the table where they had had supper. The bread and cheese she had brought with her. Wine from the cellar.

They had slept by the fire on the sheepskins, covered with other skins, rugs of fox and wolf skin, lined with silk and wool and velvet. Velvet cushions. Had made love again in that fur-lined, firelit warmth. Slowly, gently, like tasting wine. And fallen asleep and woken to make love again. The fire dying. This time making love with hunger, almost with terror, as if there was no time left for love, the day was too near. Touching her face, whispering, breathing against her mouth, her body, holding her. Falling asleep still holding her, his breath warm against her throat, his head heavy and golden on her shoulder, on her breast.

He had rolled away from her since, and lay on his back, his mouth slightly open, breathing heavily with the wine he had drunk. By this cold light there were shadows under his eyes, and a softness of flesh round his chin, under it. She pushed herself up onto her hand and looked at him, not in horror at what she had done, but half sadly, that it was over, and the day had come. As if her real lover had gone with the dark and the firelight, and this man lying here was nothing to do with her.

She got up quietly and went out into the grey morning. The lake still as glass. She waded out into the crystal water until the coldness reached her waist, like a girdle of ice, and then lay forward and swam to the far side. A soft sliminess of weeds wrapping fingers round her ankles. She turned and swam back, waded out. A pile of leaves had drifted against a rock and she

[192]

took handfuls of them and scrubbed herself dry, the leaves crumbling to golden dust, harsh against her skin.

He was still asleep. She dressed herself and went out again. She had no wish to wake him, to say goodbye, say anything. As if truly the man lying there asleep had had no part in anything. Had been only an instrument of something, someone else. She did not think of Michel, of betrayal, guilt. Closed the door gently. Took her horse, rode away. She thought for a moment of Talmond still sleeping, of his waking, finding her gone. Smiled thinking of it. After a mile or so she sang as she rode, not caring if anyone heard her.

'*Quoi! des gueux d'hérétiques*
Feraient la loi dans vos foyers?'

Tried to turn the verses into English. 'What! That scoundrel heretics should dare to make your laws?'

Her voice high and ringing in the dawn, in the woods. Laughed at herself for what she was singing. Stood in her stirrups, and cried, '*Aux armes, Poitevins!*' She, from Sussex, from the quietest countryside in England, a Protestant who scarcely believed in God! Although she had never felt that she belonged there, in Sussex, or in the quiet grey village church. As if all her life these woods, this countryside had been waiting for her. As if they were her true home, and she was not in exile, but come back to them from far away. She drew her sword and held it glittering in the pale sunshine, lifted it above her head. Sang the song of the guns. 'The Blues are there, the cannon growls, say, my friends, are you afraid?'

Michel, Talmond, all the world. Let them go to the devil. 'I am alive,' she sang, 'I am alive, alive!' Like a bird singing. As if she had the morning in her voice, the sun in her heart.

I will find the Countess, she thought. I will ride with her.

She felt such strength in herself, such freedom, that it was like being drunk with wine. She spurred Bayard to a gallop, thundered under the arched roof of the branches, oak leaves brushing her bent shoulders, the plume of her riding hat. Rode until Bayard's breath threw flecks of white foam back into her face, and his huge strength heaved and strained under her, his lungs bursting. She let him walk, fondling his heavy neck, his ears that sprang and twitched under her hand.

'I am myself,' she told him. 'I belong to myself. I am free! No man owns me. No man ever will again. You and I, Bayard, comrade. Allez, les gars, le canon gronde!'

She rode like a knight in a fairy tale, alone in a forest. Came to a clearing. A cottage. What had been a cottage. A dark ring of ashes, the stumps of timber posts like blackened fingers. It was not the first burned cottage she had seen, but it threw a chill on her, and she rode quietly after that, no longer wanting to sing.

Once Father Barbotin had said to her, 'We are fighting for God against the Devil. I never thought that I should bless a woman who took up arms, who went out to kill. A woman, whose business in the world is to give birth to life. But you, and all the others, have taken the mantle of Saint Joan. You fight as the angels fight, against the Prince of Darkness. May God strengthen you.' He had blessed her sword, and given her a rosary, a small chaplet of beads and crucifix like the ones the peasants wore in their button-holes. She had smiled at it, but had kept it, and she felt for it, in the inner pocket of her coat. Took it out and said a prayer for whoever had owned that burned cottage and was now homeless or dead. 'Our Father.' And the 'Hail Mary' that she had now heard so often it was as familiar as her own childhood prayers.

The woods came to an end, and far away to her left, across the rolling, forest ridges, she saw smoke rising. Thick, ugly pillars of smoke, black and grey like twisted ropes unravelling. She began to ride carefully, stopping to listen, to reconnoitre a valley before she rode down into it; to avoid showing herself on the crest of a ridge; to avoid the farms. Twice she saw peasants, but they ran like sheep before she could ask them for news of the district. Another burned house. More smoke rising, nearer. An emptied landscape, emptied of life. The cattle gone from the fields. She was within ten, fifteen minutes' ride of Mervent, and the vast spread of forest. At least they were safe there. But even from the dark seascape of the forest ahead of her she thought she could see plumes of smoke coiling up against the pale sky.

She came to the edge of a wood, an outlier of the forest. The horseman's path she had been following became a narrow lane between deep hedges and fields, curving down into a valley. And out of sight below her she heard a woman screaming. She rode down, drawing her pistol, her heart beating hard and fast. If there was a troop of Blues—the images coming before she could prevent them. Images not of death, but of what could happen before it. I am afraid! she thought in horror, and set her spurs to Bayard's flanks. Was deep in the lane. And ahead of her one horseman, and a woman tied with a rope behind him, dragging along the ground. She must have screamed as she had fallen.

The man heard the galloping behind him, turned, levelling a musket. And Hester was on him before he was certain whether she was friend or enemy. Driving the butt of her pistol into his mouth as he began to shout, 'Hold! Hold!' His musket falling, his body swaying back in the saddle, and she was gone by and turning, slow to turn in the narrowness of the lane, the thorn hedges tearing at her knees, her arms. He was lying stretched by the woman, his face welling scarlet. Black uniform, skull and crossbones in silver on the collar. One of the Hussars of Death. She put the barrel of her pistol against his head. He opened his eyes and looked at her. Bewilderment, then terror.

'Turn on your face,' she said. She could not shoot him while he looked at her. He did not move. Because he could not, or dared not, or did not understand. She had broken his teeth, and the blood ran down his chin, onto his throat, like red satin. She could not pull the trigger now, in cold hatred. She backed away from where he lay, drew her sabre and cut the rope that bound the woman's wrists to the saddlebow.

'Has he raped you?'

'He has killed my mother,' the woman said. 'He has killed my mother, he has killed my mother.' She would have gone on repeating it for ever if she had not choked with tears. She stood swaying, holding out her bound wrists, staring at Hester without seeming to see her, or know what had happened. A young peasant girl, her face bruised, bloodied, torn and filthy from being dragged along the ground. Her dress ripped open showing her breasts. Hester untied her wrists.

'Can you bind his hands?'

Very slowly, stupefied, the girl did what Hester told her, while Hester aimed at him.

'Mademoiselle de Richeteau's *manoir*, do you know it? Is it still safe?'

'He has killed my mother,' the girl said. 'He has killed my mother.' She began searching along the hedge.

'What are you looking for?'

The girl did not answer, but she found a stone, the size of a man's head, and brought it back. 'He has killed my mother,' she whispered. She lifted the stone as high as she could. The man saw what she was going to do, and screamed, a high wailing shriek of terror.

'No!' Hester shouted, and pushed her against the hedge as the stone fell, struck the ground by the man's shoulder. The man gabbled, trying to shriek for mercy through his smashed teeth.

'Let him be judged,' Hester said. 'Take his horse. I give it to you. Any money that he has. Everything. But don't—when he is——' The stupidity of what she was saying came back to her, and she wanted to laugh, and then be sick. Remembered Michel's spy. She had not felt like this in battle. Never. She took the end of the rope and kicked the man onto his feet.

'I should leave you with her,' she said. And to the girl, 'Can you ride a horse? Give me his musket.'

They rode at a canter, the man running, stumbling, at the end of the rope, crying out to her to stop, to go slower, pleading. She took no notice. When he fell she dragged him fifty yards before she stopped to let him get to his feet.

'For God's sake!' he whimpered. 'Have mercy, I have a wife and children, don't kill me, let me go. I have money. Gold.'

'Search him,' Hester ordered. The girl got down and began to strip the man's pockets. Gold watches, ear-rings, pendants, coins, rings. 'His boots,' Hester said. When the man tried to resist Hester aimed her pistol at his head. 'Lie down on the ground.' He was slow to obey and she jerked the rope. He fell. 'On your face.'

The girl pulled off one boot and then the other. More jewellery. Bundles of *assignats*, a heavy purse. A gold chain, long and massive. 'Take them all.'

But the girl was sitting on the ground, pulling the boots onto her own feet. She had found a knife in one of his pockets, and she cut the band of the man's breeches, so that when he stood up they fell round his knees. She began cutting his coat from his back, until he stood in his shirt, shaking with fear. A thin, gaunt man with black moustaches that should have looked fierce and soldier-like and that now gave him an air of pathetic foolishness. His hands bound, in a dirty shirt, like a Spanish penitent walking in procession, barefooted.

'I know where to take him,' the girl said. She seemed to have regained her senses. She hoisted herself into the saddle, torn dress and long black boots. She took the rope from Hester and rode ahead. Now and then the man turned his head, trying to plead with Hester. She would almost have let him go.

'Where is your regiment?'

He jerked his head towards the east, lifted his hands to emphasize the direction. 'Far over there. A long way.'

She knew he was lying. He could not have strayed so far and survived. He had gone a mile or so in search of more loot and a woman, while his comrades were bivouacked. A mile at the outside. He seemed to be recovering confidence as they rode on into the forest. As if they were very near his comrades, riding into a trap. And they could not be half a mile from the *manoir*. The trees opened for a moment, a narrow clearing that allowed them to see the sky. Smoke rising, ahead of them, thick coils of black. She thought she could see flames.

She began to ride as if it was a race, under the trees, galloping, thinking of nothing except the smoke, that her father was there, the *manoir* was burning and he was there. She came to the edge of the trees, the wide spread of lawns, fields beyond, the forest again. And the *manoir* in flames. Fifty, a hundred soldiers. Horsemen. Black uniforms. The Hussars. Who wore their Death's Heads like a badge of honour. As she looked they were forming ranks. Pioneers still smashing windows along the terrace, to let air into the fire. Flames leaping thirty and forty feet above the roof. Smoke billowing.

Shout of orders. Silver shrillness of a trumpet. The last men running to join ranks, remount. The trumpet calling 'March'. Riding towards her.

Instinct made her draw back, deeper among the trees. The girl with the prisoner was behind her. She held up her hand, gestured to their right. 'Soldiers,' she whispered. She sensed rather than heard the prisoner readying himself to yell to his comrades. She turned in the saddle and kicked him hard in the face before he could make a sound. They dragged him whimpering back among the trees, forcing their way through undergrowth, until they were fifty yards from the path. She drew her sabre and set the edge to his throat, holding it with both hands from behind his back, and lifting, so that he had to tiptoe to avoid having his throat cut.

'One sound,' she breathed, her knee between his shoulders.

The soldiers riding, singing as they rode. She heard their voices, happy, laughing.

'Quand in n'y aura plus d'brigands,
nous nous en irons en chantant,
au nord et au midi,
Tuer nos ennemis,
Dansons——'

The song fading.

She leaned down beside the prisoner's ear. 'My father was in that house,' she said. 'If he is dead——'

The man was crying, shivering with fear. She left him and rode towards the *manoir*. No one could still be alive in it. She sat watching the flames. Like a furnace. They must have set fuel in all the ground-floor rooms. Brandy casks stove in. Barrels of oil. There was no wind and the smoke rose lazily, thick, oily black. A beam fell, crash of timber, sparks flying upwards like a universe of shooting stars. The girl was beside her, the prisoner. She turned and lifted her sabre to kill him.

'I know where they will be if they escaped,' the girl said. 'That's where I was going. The wolves' valley. They will have hidden there.'

'My father was in there,' Hester said. 'They have killed him like your mother.' But she let the girl lead her away, beyond the *manoir*, to the right, westwards, across the farmland that was the home farm of the estate, into the forest again. Two miles. Three. After the first mile they had to dismount and lead the horses, the paths were so narrow, the branches so thick and low overhead. After another mile there were no paths at all. Rocks. Picking their way down into a deep combe, a stream hidden below them, the sound of a waterfall.

'I'll go ahead of you and find them,' the girl said, 'or they'll be frightened.' She gave the prisoner's rope and the reins of her horse to Hester, and vanished among the rocks, and the thick gorse and broom, and the thorn trees that grew like a wall there. Within two minutes she was back. 'They are there,' she said, 'the people from the *manoir* are there.'

Hester stood for a second, not believing her, almost unwilling to believe her, as if she feared being tricked. And then ran, forced her way through, tore her face, her hands, was in a tiny clearing, a pocket of grassy hollow beside the stream. Twenty or more people clustered together, kneeling, sitting, some of them wounded, lying down. And her father. Léonie. Euphemia. The three of them the centre of the group as if the others were clinging to them for protection. Servants from the *manoir*. Peasants. Old men. Old women. Four or five young girls, children in arms.

'Hester!' Mr. Broadhurst cried. 'They have burned——'

'I know. I know.' She held him, smoothed his hair, reassuring herself that he was there, that he was safe. Léonie clinging to her arm. The peasants staring, afraid to question and then a flood of questions tumbling one on the other, incomprehensible. An old woman throwing herself on the girl that Hester had saved, crying, 'Perrine, Perrine!'

Her father crying. Touching her face.

'Sit down, Papa, rest yourself.' Holding Léonie's hands for a moment. Looking at Euphemia. Remembering. Her warning. She looked round for the steward of the *manoir*, and knew that he was not there. Knew what had happened to him. Saw her vision again, the old man hanging in the deep fireplace, the flames leaping.

The girl Perrine had dragged the prisoner with her. The peasants were round him now, by the stream. The old men. The women. There was a high, shivering scream, rising and rising and then cut off, choking. When Hester reached the centre of the group the man's body was lying in the water, his naked legs still on the bank, his throat cut and the stream running scarlet.

'What have you done?'

'We judged him,' Perrine said. Her grandmother, if it was her grandmother, slowly cleaning a knife-blade on a handful of grass.

Chapter 18

They hid there all that night. Perrine, Perrine Louveteau the peasant girl, and Hester, took turns to watch. They had carried the body of the dead soldier as far down the stream as they could, but his spirit seemed to be still with them in the clearing, like a thin scream of cowardice and horror. When it was her turn to watch she sat wrapped in her cloak against the night chill, the musket balanced across her knees, trying not to think of him, of what he had done. Of the *manoir*. Of the steward. Of all that had happened. We are fighting for God against the Devil. Was it true? As if such evil was loosed that only belief in the Devil could explain it. Imagined the Devil of the picture books, horns and tail and fangs. But what she saw was a tall, thin man in a black coat, with sunken, bloodshot eyes and crooked teeth, and bowed shoulders. Creuzot. She had not thought of him for a long time.

If we had never come to France, she thought. It was difficult to imagine it, not to have come here. What would she be doing now? Asleep, in her room. White bed. Shelf of books. She would still believe in Rousseau, in Diderot, in Liberty. Wake to argue with uncle George, with Henry. To annoy her mother by arguing with them instead of helping in the house, 'being what a girl should be.' What her mother had wanted was a daughter like an English version of Léonie, who would marry a nobleman's son and keep a London mansion and a carriage, and thirty servants.

Sussex. London. Her mind drifting, not homesick, but looking with amazement at that long-ago self, who had known nothing, nothing about anything. She thought of Talmond. Last night! Only last night! And that too seemed as far off as Sussex, the self who had lain shivering with love as far from her as the noisy fool who had quoted Voltaire at breakfast and fought with Henry in the stables. She had a sense of becoming something else, someone else, moment by moment, without knowing how or why, or what it was she was becoming. Like walking step by step in the dark towards an unknown place.

And as that night-walker might fall helplessly into a hidden pit, or over a cliff's edge, she felt herself falling mentally. Sick and dizzy with loss. Bent her head down to touch her forehead against her knees, clenched her teeth. I have lost him, she thought And he was there in front of her, in her mind, everything about him, her whole life with him, in the one instant of seeing her loss. Michel wounded. Stumbling along the rue du Bac. Lying on the mattress in Madame de Richeteau's attic, his eyes shining in the dark. Michel in Creuzot's loft. In the courtyard. Michel riding. Taking her by the throat in fury. Laughing. Calling her his 'great fool'. And then 'my cavalier'. And once, only once, only once, speaking to the men who had forced their way into the room, 'my friend'.

Lying beside her in the straw of a barn, holding her. Sitting in the shelter of a hedge, sharing a loaf of bread and a bottle of rough wine. Riding with him in battle. Twenty battles. And always guarding her. Yet leaving her free. After that one quarrel at Cholet, when he had taken her horse, tried to keep her from fighting, he had always left her free. Free as another man, as a younger brother perhaps, but still free.

And now I am free of everything, she thought, and felt despair, a coldness at her heart like dying. He never loved me. Never. Did he even want me? As a man wants a woman? A great fool. She tried to think what it must be like to be Léonie, to have every man desire you, lust after you like a dog after a bitch. Was that better? And felt that it could not be worse than the way she felt. To be alone. Alone. Alone.

What shall I do? The thought of Talmond, of remaining his lover, scarcely crossed her mind. It was done. Finished. Like a day that has gone by and cannot come back, one would not want to come back. Her father had said before she got him to lie down and sleep, 'We must go home, Hester. This is no place for us. We must take Léonie home with us, I have made up my mind.'

She imagined it. If it was possible. It was not, but she still imagined it. Saw herself walking in the gardens, wearing skirts, taking tea, listening to the Fairfax girls talking about fashions, and beaux, and what their eldest brother was doing in London.

I will join the Countess, she thought. We will ride together. And one day there will be an end of it, and we shall lie side by side in a field. If there is a God we can ask Him why He has allowed all this. And if there is not, at least we shall lie quiet.

But she had not the sort of mind that can endure that kind of thinking very long, and she stood up and shook herself, and walked about. She would almost have welcomed it if there had been an alarm, so that she could fight, and not need to think. Why? she kept asking herself, her teeth clenched. And was not sure whether she was asking that of her own life, her own unhappiness, or of all that was happening round her. And the two seemed combined, and to be one unanswerable question.

She sat down again and bent her head, biting her lip against crying. There was the faintest of sounds at her back and she whipped round, levelling the musket, her finger tight on the trigger. Eyes shining. Teeth white as bone.

'Madame Estairre, do not kill me.' The voice mocking.

'What do you want?'

'We must make plans,' Euphemia whispered, coming close, pushing aside the barrel of the gun. She crouched down, facing Hester. 'We must be friends, you and I. We belong together.'

'You belong to the Devil,' Hester said, her mouth dry, afraid the girl would touch her. She wanted to find the rosary, felt for it in her coat.

'You believe in the Devil? Oh wise Madame, who believes in the Devil but not in God. Perhaps you are right, all the world belongs to the Devil.'

'Get away from me.' She had the small chaplet of beads in her hand, the crucifix. She held it tightly between them. Euphemia laughed.

'I will give you something,' she said. 'I will give you what you have been crying for.'

'I have not——'

'Madame, madame!' The cold hand touching her cheeks, very softly, drying away the traces of tears. And as the hand touched her, it no longer seemed evil. She had the feeling of great power surrounding her, alien, and yet not wicked. Very old. Very great. So that the beads in her hand were like a child's toy, a thing of the morning. She let them fall Euphemia picked them up, made a necklace of them, and put them over her head. 'Wear them,' Euphemia said. 'They will help you. They will guide your Tovodun to you. They will make you strong.'

'What do you want from me?' No longer challenging her, simply asking, as if she was waiting to be given orders.

'You must take us to your army. Tomorrow. Keep us with you.'

'I cannot. I'm not going back. I'll bring you to Charette, to Légé, you'll be safe there.'

'You must do what I tell you. You know that.' The hands touching her face, touching her eyes, her mouth, as if they were taking possession. Touching her throat. 'You will take us north tomorrow.'

'I cannot!'

'I will give your man back to you. Poor madame, crying in the dark. He too is crying. In his fashion.'

She wanted to laugh, to say, 'You are mad! Michel?'

The fingers touched her eyelids, her forehead. She saw him, not as she had imagined him just now, a picture, a shadow, but *saw* him. In front of her. Lying on his back, his eyes open, staring into the darkness. She knew what he was thinking, feeling. She is gone. She will not come back. I have driven her away. He was so close, so real, she tried to touch him. And for a second he looked at her, his eyes wide, *seeing* her. Pushing himself up on one hand, beginning to say her name.

'Don't touch!' Euphemia breathed, and when she still reached out to touch him, it was like her hand being burned, not by fire, but by ice, her hand fastened there so that she felt the flesh would tear if she moved, flinched back. The vision was gone. Euphemia took her hand between hers, and chafed it.

'Madame has met love since I last touched her. Her flesh is different.'

'No!'

'Why do you deny it? Don't be ashamed, don't be sorry. It was needed for you, you had to learn something. And now you can bring that something to your friend.'

'What are you?' And she knew the answer without being answered. Saw Euphemia grow tall in front of her, so tall that the sky was hidden. A huge darkness, chained. And there was only Euphemia kneeling there, the first pallor of dawn in the east.

Euphemia thin, and black and supple, kneeling in front of Hester as if she was a suppliant, her hands joined, her eyes full of mockery, and then submission.

'I beg madame to take us north.'

Perrine Louveteau joining them. Shivering in the cold, stamping her boots. Big and strong and natural, like a young tree.

'What will you do now?' Hester said to her.

'If you are going north I will come with you. Where else is there to go? They will all go with you if you'll take them.'

'You see, madame?' Euphemia said. 'You are our salvation.' Hiding her eyes.

Chapter 19

They made their way north on foot, towards Châtillon. The old women and the children took turns to ride the two horses. Even in the few days since Hester had ridden south, everything had changed. Burning farms, burning villages, dead cattle. They spent half of each day gathering food, trying to find grain to beat into a rough paste and cook in ashes. Dig potatoes out of a bank beside a field, and eat them raw. Water from streams and ditches, hoping it was not poisoned by carrion.

It took them three days, Léonie limping and crying, half carried by Euphemia and Mr. Broadhurst. Hiding in a wood for half a day while they watched a Blue patrol burning a farmhouse and the corn stacks and searching for peasants. The Blues caught one, perhaps it was the farmer himself, hiding nearby to watch his life being burned. He screamed for a long time before they hanged him on the branch of a tree.

'Good God!' Mr. Broadhurst kept crying, 'we must do something! Hester, give me that gun!'

She had to hold him back, she and Perrine. 'They would kill us all,' she said. 'And we could not save him.'

She learned a great deal in those three days. What it is like to command. To have to command. To know that life and death hangs on a decision. Not one's own life or death, but that of twenty others. Who grumbled, cried with the cold at night, lying uncovered in a wood, children crying with hunger, old women wanting to do stupid things like following a road because they were barefoot the way they had run out of their homes, and the thorns and the stones were tearing their feet to pieces. Going ahead to a ridge of ground to watch for the enemy, and to see nothing, nothing but tree-tops, and another ridge, and a column of smoke here, another there, and to decide which way to lead her helpless followers.

And when at last, the third nightfall, she brought them into Châtillon, she could not leave them. None of them. She had to find them food, somewhere to sleep, bedding, clothes, in a town already swollen with refugees, an air of disaster hanging over it like thunder. There was no sign of Michel. Someone had told her that all of the cavalry that could be gathered had ridden west two days ago, towards Montaigu. There was no bread. No blankets to be had. Not even fodder for the horses. No one knew anything except that the Blues were closing in.

It was past midnight before she had her people settled. By bribery and threats she had found rooms for her father, and Léonie and Euphemia; two tiny rooms in a cottage that only possessed three in all. An old woman and her four small grand-children would sleep in the other that was also the kitchen. Hester and Perrine found a shed to stable the horses, and slept beside them.

The next day her refugees found her as though by instinct, and she had to get food for them again, and clothes, and sabots. Clothes and weapons for Perrine. Things for her father and for Léonie and Euphemia, who had brought nothing but what they stood in. And that had been torn to rags on the journey.

Léonie held up the woollen gown that Hester had brought her and stared at it as if she did not know what it was. 'You don't expect me to wear this?' Staring at Hester with her great blue eyes, astonishment becoming amusement. Laughing her silvery peal of laughter. 'First you make me sleep on a bed that has stones in it, I swear, and now look at this—this *thing*! Euphemia! Did you ever see such an object? And I am sure there are fleas in it. Hester!'

'Then go in rags!' Hester cried. And in the next moment her father was demanding a barber.

She went and opened the window and leaned out to breathe deep and control herself. In the street below Perrine was surrounded by the old women and the children they had brought here, and a dozen others, clamouring for news from the south.

'There must be someone who can shave me!' Mr. Broadhurst was saying. 'Or I could even do it myself if you would only find me some razors.'

A man was riding into the street, riding hard, scattering the cluster of peasants.

'What news? What news?' they shouted, trying to stop him.

'Get out of my way. Where is the Council?' And then, as he forced his way by, 'We have lost Montaigu.'

'Major Vernet?' Hester shouted, 'Have you news of Major Vernet?'

He looked up briefly, shook his head, and was gone. While the peasants ran, spreading panic as they ran with their news of disaster, magnifying it as they ran and told: until the army was destroyed, the Blues were within a mile of Châtillon. Panic spreading like fire.

Hester turned back into the room and took the woollen peasant's gown from Léonie, who was still holding it this way and that, absorbed in her contempt of it. 'Put it on!' Hester said. And when Léonie began to laugh again she took her by the shoulders, gathered the ragged silk, the remains of her *manoir* dress, in her two fists, and ripped. The rags fell, leaving Léonie in her shift and slippers, staring, one hand going to her breast.

Hester reached for the top of the chemise, tore it down like a curtain. Lifted her hand again to strike. Euphemia was between them, quick as a shadow, forcing Hester away. Léonie standing naked except for her torn stockings, her stays. Pink and white and honey gold, spilling out of the whalebone and satin, soft curves of flesh, golden hair, mouth shaping to cry in outrage.

'Good God, Hester,' Mr. Broadhurst cried, 'what are you doing?'

If she could kill her, beat her, stamp on her. She felt for a second that she would kill her, that nothing on earth could stop her. But Euphemia had pushed her back into the doorway, was forcing her down the stairs, had the door shut.

'I will see to her, madame,' she said. 'I will see to your Papa, to everything. Only do not touch her. Go and find your man and we shall wait for you here. When you come back I will have made her different.'

She almost ran from the house, and found Perrine waiting in the shed. She had fed and watered the horses, and was eating some bread. Hester gave her what money she could, and then saddled Bayard and left the town by the Nantes barricade, making towards Montaigu.

[207]

Before she had ridden a mile she met horsemen flying from the battle. Like men in a race for life, their heads down, no sign of their weapons, of anything but terror. 'The Blues!' they shouted, 'the Blues are coming, les Hussars!'

But there was no sign of any enemy, then or for the next hours of riding. Only scattered bands of fugitives, on horseback, on foot, the wounded dragging themselves along, a broken pike staff for a crutch. When she asked for news of Michel they stared at her with blank eyes, or cursed her for trying to hold them back.

She rode on into a bright stillness, nothing moving, like a green desert. Until she saw a man coming slowly towards her across a field.

Michel, she thought. Michel! Without reason, without any cause to think it. Pushed her heels into Bayard's sides, began to gallop. The man staggering as he came down the slope.

'Michel! Michel!'

But it was not. An officer, holding both hands against his side as if he was trying to close a wound. He stared at her. She had seen him before but he did not recognize her.

'Give me some brandy,' he whispered.

'I've none.' She had ridden out without so much as water or bread, not thought of bringing anything. 'Where is the army, which way is it retreating?'

He lifted an arm and pointed vaguely north. 'The Blues are everywhere,' he said. 'You'll never reach it. Save yourself.' He began to stagger on down the hill.

'Major Vernet!' she shouted. 'Did you see him in the battle?'

'He is dead. I saw him fall. Save yourself.'

'He cannot be!' She began to ride after him, and stopped, afraid of hearing it again. He could not be. Looked round her, and nothing had changed. Not the hedges, not the sky. Michel! *Michel*! She turned her horse, set him to a gallop, bending forward, racing, until the folly of it made her slow down, fall to a canter, a walk. He cannot be, he cannot be. Tried to say prayers.

If I had been there, she thought.

Another hour. And she was on the battlefield. Could tell before she came to it, the crows circling. Not a battlefield with drawn lines that generals love, but the wreckage of disaster, running men cut down, their bodies lying, one here, five there. Face down in a ditch, or caught up in a hedge like Absalom, or lying spread-

[208]

eagled in the furrows, eyes wide, staring blindly at the bright sky. Weapons. Dead horses. Mile on mile of death. She got down from the saddle and began walking, stooping, searching the faces of the dead. Here and there men still living, whispering, 'Help me'. But there was nothing she could do for them.

'Major Vernet?' she asked them, and went on, trying not to hear them calling after her, 'Water, for God's sake, water.'

She did find a stream, and brought water to some of them in her hat, tilting the brim towards their mouths. But there was no hope for them. The Blues would come soon enough, the murder squads. 'Major Vernet? Did you see him?'

Searching until she could not think, could scarcely see, scarcely stand up again after stooping over a dead man, turning his face to the sky. Twilight. One of the wounded told her he had seen the Major and his men fighting their way towards the north, towards a wood. Had seen him surrounded and cut down.

She came to the wood. A dead man lying against a tree. A man she knew. Had known. She had ridden beside him a hundred times. One of Michel's men. She shut her eyes and leaned against Bayard. At least I shall bury him, she told herself. They'll not find him.

She began to search, slowly, her mind like a stone. When she had found his body, brought it back to Châtillon, she would begin to feel again. Another dead man. A third, she could see where he had tried to crawl into shelter, hiding from searchers. She parted the leaves, bent down. It was Michel.

He lay on his side, one arm twisted behind his back, his cheek and throat blackened with gunsmoke, his coat torn by sabre cuts. She knelt down and touched him, touched his face. Felt for his heartbeat. He was alive, alive! And in the next instant thought it was her own pulse beating in her hand, in her ears. She laid her cheek to his mouth, thought she could feel the warmth of breath, the stir of it against her skin, and again was afraid to believe it, that death was cheating her. She took hold of the arm twisted behind him to straighten it, felt the broken bone grinding, and he cried out with the pain of it. Cried out! He was alive! Alive! Lifting his shoulders, his head, kissing his bloodied, smoke-blackened forehead, holding his head against her. He groaned again as his arm moved.

She tried to control herself, laid him down again, gently,

gently, easing his arm until it lay on a bed of leaves. 'Michel! Michel!' Breathed into his mouth as if she could give him her own strength, her own life. Listened to his heart beat, stronger, breathed with him again, chafed his face, cradled his head on her arm. Until he opened his eyes and saw her. He did not seem to think it was strange that she was there. Only looked at her. 'My arm,' he whispered.

She tried to think what to do, could think of nothing. It was almost dark. A doctor? The thought was so stupid that it came and went in the same instant. She held her head with both hands, bent down, touched him, kissed him. 'I must bind your arm,' she whispered. 'Wait.'

She drew her sabre and began looking for a branch to cut; thin enough to cut, strong enough to be any use. It took more effort than she had thought possible. She took off her coat, and tore her shirt into strips. There was barely enough linen to pad the splints. I'll find more cloth,' she said, touched him again, as if she was leaving strength with him.

There was only one way to get more cloth. She stripped two bodies, praying for them as she did it. 'Christ keep them, Christ take them.'

When she came back he was trying to drag himself up, to lean his shoulders against a tree. 'I'll tell you what to do,' he whispered. 'Take hold of my wrist, turn my hand palm up, and pull. Give me something to bite on.'

She gave him a piece of the cloth. He told her where to put the splints, and then stuffed the cloth between his teeth, nodded. She had to clench her own teeth before she could do it. The sound of bone on bone. She could feel it, as if her own arm was broken. Felt him go rigid, lose consciousness again. Bind tight. The break was above his elbow. If it was splintered there was no hope for the arm. Not if there were ten doctors healing it. She knew that. Tried to feel with her finger-tips. Forced herself to probe. The break seemed clean. Bend his forearm. Make a sling. When she finished she was sodden with sweat. She knelt beside him, propping herself against the tree. If I tried to stand, she thought, I should fall down. And somehow she must get him onto Bayard.

She made herself stand up.

It took five minutes that seemed like an hour. But once he was in the saddle he seemed to get stronger. She led him out of the wood. 'I'll mount behind you,' she said. 'Hold steady.' Like herself, Bayard had already covered almost thirty miles since morning. It was madness to think he could take them both to Châtillon. But if he could not—she led him under an overhanging branch at the edge of the wood, and swung herself up behind Michel, trying not to touch his arm. Reach round him, gathering the reins. Kicking Bayard into a tired but willing canter. Michel swaying. She had no stirrups to steady herself, no saddle. Nightmare. Bayard stumbling, and then half rearing at the shadow of a body, the smell of death.

But he was alive, alive. She held him, her arms round him, her face against his shoulder. When she touched his face it was cold as ice, wet with sweat, and then feverish. If she let go of him he would fall.

Picking their way, trying to remember directions, the shape of a wood, the lie of a field, of a stream. She began to talk to him to keep herself awake. And found she was repeating the same words over and over, meaningless. 'Let me be your friend. I love you. Let me be your friend.'

The moon hidden. A thin rain falling, drenching. Bayard with his head lowered, stumbling at every second step. She had to jerk him up to keep him from going onto his knees, throwing them forward. She slid down from his back and walked beside him, holding Michel up, the reins looped round her forearm. God knew if they were going in the right direction. South-east. She could not see anything, not a star, not the shape of a ridge. Now a path, now a road, now nothing. Fields. Woods. Hedges. She wanted to let herself fall. Lie down. Five minutes. But if she did she would never get up again.

The rain thickening, running down her face, down her neck, under her coat. Her breeches sodden, chafing her legs raw as she walked, Michel's boot bruising her side, as she held him in the saddle. As if she was walking in her sleep, in a nightmare. A voice crying, 'Halt, who goes there?'

She did not answer. The challenge again and then the flash of a musket shot, the whistle of lead ball over her head.

'Don't shoot, you fool! Friends, friends. Major Vernet.' A man catching hold of her. 'His arm, mind his arm.' She pushed them away. A lantern shining in her face for a moment. 'It's Le Chevalier, and Major Vernet, I know them, let them pass.'

[211]

Stumbling among houses, someone helping her. Shaking herself free. 'I'm all right. Leave me alone. Leave me to look after him.' Bayard leading them to the shed, to Perrine. Getting him down from the saddle, holding him against her. Easing him onto straw. Kneeling. 'I'm here,' she kept whispering to him, 'I'm here. I have come back.' Stripped herself, and lay beside him in the straw, under a blanket that Perrine gave her, warming his body with hers.

When she woke it was light. She was still holding him and he was looking at her, his eyes sick and feverish, but urgent, as if he had been watching her for a long time, wanted her to wake. In her sleep she had dreamed of this, of his looking at her while she slept. His eyes full of accusation. But there was no accusation there.

'I want to tell you something,' he was whispering, his voice hoarse with fever.

She wanted to stop him, she was afraid of what he was going to say.

'I know it was not true,' he whispered. 'That night—that night you got up and left me——'

She had to shut her eyes in case he should see into them.

Chapter 20

She found herself become more shepherd than soldier. Michel sick with fever. Finding a doctor for him. A surgeon who could mend his arm. There were not half a dozen Royalist doctors in the whole army, in the whole of the Vendée, and they were blind with exhaustion, scarcely able to stagger from one patient to another. Wounds, dying men, fever, dysentery, women in labour. A broken arm? The surgeon she did find at last reaching for a bonesaw before he heard another word.

'No!'

Persuading him to come prepared to heal and not amputate.

And all the time her flock of refugees following her, waiting for her, depending on her. Her father, Léonie, Euphemia, the *manoir* servants, an old man and seven women who had escaped and come with them; a dozen peasants, old people, children. In rags, without money, starving. No one wanted to help them, feed them, clothe them, shelter them. Useless mouths.

And three days later Châtillon itself was attacked and they had to escape northwards, towards Cholet. Thousands upon thousands of refugees. Officers' families in carriages, antique *berlines*, *turgotines*; the wounded crowded like bales of straw in peasant carts, or helping one another along the road; or no longer able to move and crying helplessly from the ditches, 'Sauvez-moi! Sauvez-moi for God's love.' To leave anyone behind was sentencing them to death. And yet there were hundreds left behind. Their cries for pity following the dust cloud of the refugees and the rearguard like the cries of birds in winter.

She took any she could. She had commandeered a cart from three servants who were loading it with furniture for an officer's family that was already fled north. She and Perrine found them. Loading the cart with mattresses, armchairs, velvet curtains neatly baled, tables and dining-chairs and kitchen things, trunks of clothes.

'What are you doing?' Hester shouted at them. 'There are people who will die for lack of a cart and you're taking armchairs to Cholet?' They saw she was a woman and tried to drive her out of the courtyard. She drew her sabre and they fled for their lives.

A cart and two horses. And their own two horses. They kept the bales of curtains, and the mattresses and some of the kitchen pots and pans, and threw the rest into the yard. Michel, protesting savagely, rode in the cart, and seven children with him, and three wounded men they picked up along the road who could no longer walk. What space was left they gave turn and turn about to the oldest men and the old women.

Léonie limped and cried, holding on to the tail of the cart. Euphemia walked beside her, now and then supporting her. The rest of their band kept up as best it might, Hester leading her horse with a pregnant woman balancing and swaying in the saddle and two small children clinging to her, one behind, one in front. At the rear of the small column Perrine kept guard, with her horse carrying a wounded man.

'It's only for a day,' Hester comforted the woman on Bayard. 'You can rest in Cholet, your child can be born in safety.'

Even while she was saying it she knew it was a lie, and the woman knew it too. There was no longer any safety. Anywhere.

And while the refugees choked the narrow, muddy roads, the army tried to fight. The guns could not get by the carts, the soldiers could not make way against the torrents of poor wretches they were trying to defend. Retreating towards Cholet, beyond it, to the Loire. Rumours running that the army meant to abandon the Vendée and cross into Brittany.

Defeat at La Tremblaye. Defeat at Cholet.

She fought in that battle. She could not keep herself back. She left Perrine to look after their people and rejoined the cavalry. Somewhere in her mind the thought that if she was killed it would solve everything, at least for her. And he thought that she had not forgiven him, and accepted it so humbly, accepted all she did for him with such gratitude, that it was like a knife twisting in a wound.

[214]

They fought for six hours. Fought their way down into the town, into the streets. They had set fire to the bushes as they came, the wind behind them, and the smoke rolled forward with them, blinding the enemy. The Blues falling back, breaking, the incredible happening, the peasants with their scythes and pitchforks, their hunting guns and long knives become giants again, heroes, their old battle cries lifting again in triumph. '*Rembarre! Rembarre!*' Marceau, Danican, Westermann driven and routed, only Kléber holding.

'We have them!' Talmond yelling, 'Follow me, follow me!' She rode close behind him, forgetting everything but battle, Bayard leaping, turning, kicking, Blues falling. Fighting between the narrow houses, on the stone steps to the upper storeys. Men locked together like wrestlers, too close for weapons. Crash of cannon balls against houses, stone splinters whistling in the air, death shrieking. Rattle of musket fire, peasants yelling, 'Tue, tue! Kill and kill!'

'God and the King!' Talmond was screaming, 'Follow me, we have them running!' Close by him. A black Hussar fighting towards him. Lifting his sabre.

She drove at the Hussar, parried the down swing, struck him across the side of the head with her sword hilt as their blades crashed and slid, saw him sway and fall. And the next instant saw a line of horsemen charging, counter-attacking. She and Talmond alone in front of them. She caught the Prince's bridle, dragged him away.

'Leave me!' he shouted at her, 'Let me face them!' But they were already in a side lane, turning a corner, galloping side by side down another street, and they were with their own men again, but all of them running, attack and victory turned into rout, the peasants flying, throwing down weapons, the horsemen galloping in panic, the Blues behind them, driving, harrying, killing, seizing victory out of defeat, one last battalion of Blues turning the battle, discipline against the wild furies and sudden terrors of the peasants. The word spreading that D'Elbée was wounded, Bonchamps, the two generals dying. And Lescure already dying after Tremblaye.

Triumph turned to disaster in ten minutes of fighting, when victory was in their hands.

'Rally!' Talmond shouted, 'Rally, curse you!' Trying to stop the rout with the flat of his sword, beating men across the shoulder. Hester with him, trying to turn them, hold them, make them stand.

Nothing could stop them. 'To the Loire!' the peasants shouted. 'To the Loire, to the river! Save yourselves!'

Falling back on Beaupréau, where she had left her refugees, and Michel. Riding with Talmond and a dozen officers, trying to bring order to the chaos of retreat. Expecting the Blues to follow up their victory, drive on Beaupréau before they could defend it.

They rode through the dreadful debris of the battle, the fiercest battle of the war. Dead men, smashed guns, carts lifting their broken shafts in the darkness. Pale rags of clothing fluttering on charred and blackened bushes, on the branches of trees. The hedges burned, the crows wheeling and croaking in the night sky.

Talmond rode close to her, put his hand on her arm. He said nothing. Not that she had saved his life, or anything about their last meeting, her leaving him. Only grasping her arm and holding it as they rode. As if he was saying, 'We are together again. How right that is.' And she let him ride with her like that. Only thought, why did I not stand my ground there, and let them kill me?

It was Talmond who showed her that she was wounded. He held his hand in front of her, dark with blood. Hers. He made her stop and bound up her arm with his scarf.

'It's nothing,' she said. 'A scratch.' But she let him do it, while the others rode on in the dark, leaving them alone, side by side.

'Where have you been?' he whispered.

'With my husband.'

Someone else beside them, urging them on. She made herself ride apart from him. Prayed for strength. Not to think of him, not to think of his hands touching her, of—his scarf tight round her forearm, the sleeve of her coat hanging loose. With my husband. With Michel. Michel.

He was waiting for her when she reached St. Pierre and the barn where she had left them all. He was still feverish, but he was crouched by the fire, showing two of the children how to keep it safely alive with small pieces of wood. There was a great stirring as she came in, heads turning, lifting, hope springing, depending on her. Like a weight, like chains fastened round her. They had already heard of the defeat, long ago, and had their bundles tied and ready, waiting to take to the roads again, for her to lead them. When all she wanted in the world was sleep.

'You're wounded!' Michel said, and tried to make her sit down, wanted to look at the wound.

'Leave me alone!' she whispered, the whisper savage, so bitter with savagery that he looked at her in astonishment, and then a depth of hurt that made her close her eyes, try to close her mind against him. If there had been no one there! No one else! If she could have knelt down in front of him and told him the truth. But the barn was full of people, her father, Léonie; women, children, Euphemia, Perrine, the servants, the old men, the wounded they had saved from Châtillon, crowding round her. A dreadful submissiveness of waiting to be saved again, told what to do. A child crying, hushed by its mother as if to cry in Hester's presence was a dreadful thing, like crying in church. The darkness of the barn. The firelight and the lantern making the shadows darker.

'We are going to cross the Loire,' she said to them. 'The army is going into Brittany. I do not know what will happen there, or even how we will cross the river. But if you stay here you know what will happen. Maybe some of you could save yourselves, get back to your homes if you scatter, two or three together.'

A murmur rising at that, almost of indignation. As if she was trying to escape from them, or suggesting that they abandon her.

'We'll cross the river with you. Into Brittany. Into Brittany!' As though that was salvation. A sudden excitement, movement, hope.

'I have to sleep for a little,' Hester said. 'Give me two hours.' She lay down on some straw and shut her eyes. But Michel was beside her.

'You have to eat,' he said. 'And you must let us look at your arm.'

She wanted to shout at them all, 'Leave us! At least go outside for a little, leave us that much privacy.' But she said nothing, kept her eyes shut. Hands undoing the scarf. Euphemia. Michel watching. The black hands delicately untying the knot. Unwinding the bloodstained muslin. A long, crimson cut, from wrist to elbow. Euphemia lifted Hester's arm, put her mouth to the wound. Coldness of her lips. Like ice. And the throbbing grew less, grew quiet. Her arm began to lose all feeling. She grew dizzy, it was hard to see what Euphemia was doing. Taking something from under the bodice of her dress, square and dark, like a small, narrow box on a string, a black string holding it round her neck. Laying it beside the cut, binding the scarf over it, round and round. Knotting it. Whispering as she touched.

'Now Madame is safe,' she said. She put her mouth close to Hester's ear. 'Safe with her love binding her.'

Michel making her eat. A gruel of half-ground corn boiled on the fire. She fell asleep while she was eating. Dreamed she was with Talmond. Lay under him, longing, beginning to feel the shivering, the breaking of that flood of ecstasy, when they were waking her, shaking her out of her sleep. Voices shouting 'The Blues are coming! The Blues are coming!' Michel asleep beside her, starting up, trying to make them quiet.

'Let her sleep, damn you!'

But they would not, and even if the alarm was false, it was madness to stay there any longer. She went outside and the darkness was full of movement. Refugees, carts, horses, detachments of soldiers half under command and half at breaking-point, only holding together as long as their captain led them towards the Loire. Shouted orders, curses, trying to clear the road, trying to stop panic, while other voices shouted that they had seen the enemy, the Blues were on them, that they would be cut off from the river. Run! Run! The rearguard at Beaupréau had broken, everything was lost, run for your lives, run!

She got the cart loaded. Michel insisted on walking, and led the way, her father beside him and Léonie and Euphemia clinging close. The horses behind them, Perrine leading and guarding them, armed with an iron-bound cudgel. Then the peasants and the servants, carrying what they could; a child, an armful of blankets, kindling for the next fire, a few potatoes knotted into a torn sack. Behind them, Hester leading the horse and cart, the two most able-bodied of the old men with her, armed one with an axe and the other with a heavy stick, its point sharpened and hardened in the fire.

And all round them, seeming to stretch for ever in the darkness, ahead of them, behind, running, stumbling, crying out for help, for safety, for someone lost; thousands upon tens of thousands of the refugees. A mass of shadows, stumbling, jostling, forcing their way along the narrow road between the broken, trampled hedges. Spreading out into the fields, struggling through the heavy mud, breaking gaps in the hedges as they came to them, wider and wider like a flood that carries all before it, twenty, thirty, fifty thousand refugees, driven by fear of death, by near madness. 'To the Loire! To the Loire!' As though it was the Red Sea, and behind them Pharaoh's chariots and horsemen. How they would cross the quarter-mile of water they neither knew nor thought of. Only to run, escape, force their way past a broken wagon, a horse that had slipped and fallen, an old woman collapsed and dying in the road, her family trying to lift her, save her. 'To the Loire! The Loire! The Blues are coming!'

Down the long slopes of the ridges, and then the slow climb up the next. Surely, surely this one was the last, they would see the night gleam of the river? But only another valley, another ridge. Three hours of stumbling forward, threatening to shoot fear-maddened men who tried to seize their cart, their horses. Soldiers, some of them, broken and useless, terror-stricken, only dangerous to the weak and the helpless. The real soldiers, those of the peasant army that had kept their courage, were far behind, still holding the line at Beaupréau against the Blue cavalry. She knew that she should be with them, with her comrades. But how could she leave these miserable wretches, her father, Michel, Euphemia, Léonie? Within minutes horses and cart would have gone, the children and the old women would have been trampled into the ruts of the road.

Another ridge. And someone shouted, 'There's the Abbey! There's St. Florent!' The dark outline of a steeper hilltop, what might be a building. Down a last slope, into the village of St. Florent, a swarming mass of people slowly forcing their way towards the river, to the water's edge; test the depth for wading, out to the first island only fifty yards from the bank. Already there were camp fires burning there, as if the first-comers had felt that even fifty yards of water meant safety for them, and they could rest, sleep, eat something. Men shouting for boats, for rafts, for ferrymen. Horses swimming across, their riders swimming ahead of them, or clinging to the saddles.

'Get them across to the first island,' Hester said to Michel. 'It's not too deep, look at that woman wading. They can hold on to each other. When you're there, go to the other side of it, and wait for me. I'll try to find a boat. Unload the cart and carry everything across.' And all the while more refugees arriving, pouring down the slope towards the river, across the meadows, spreading out along the bank, all of them searching for boats, for anything to take them across the broad, slow-moving flood of the Loire to the Promised Land of Brittany. Already the river was dark with the mass of swimmers. Such boats as there were, making their heavy way against the current, oar blades flashing silver, struggling yard by yard to reach the far side beyond the island, each stroke of the oars missing a swimmer's head by inches.

When a boat came back it was filled before the boatman had steadied it. More than filled, so many crowding into it that it seemed it must sink the moment it was pushed into deep water. She waited for an hour before she saw her chance, and waded out to meet a boat coming in, lifting herself over the gunwale before the boatman could prevent her. A man tried to follow her and she pushed him back into the river. 'Swim,' she said, and to the boatman, 'Make upstream, head for the outer side of that island.' The boatman began to argue and she drew her sword and held the point to his throat. 'I've twenty people needing to be saved. It's your life or theirs.'

He sat to his oars again, while she steered, and fended off swimmers who tried to cling to the sides of the long, narrow boat. The boatman heaving, groaning with the effort of pulling against the current. They seemed to be losing rather than gaining ground.

'Pull, curse you, pull, you weakling! What kind of boatman are you?'

'Monsieur, monsieur! I am not a boatman at all, I am a priest. I cannot go on, I have crossed four times already, my arms are breaking.'

'A priest?' She made her way forward beside him, and took one of the oars. 'Priest or boatman, pull!' Beginning to gain against the stream, the tip of the island within reach, sliding towards them, past them, the low bluff of the bank above them, eight, nine feet above the brown surface of the river. A few trees. Michel. Backing water, the prow scraping mud and gravel. Michel sliding down the bank, reaching with his good arm to grasp the gunwale, holding them fast. The priest bent over his oar as if he had fainted. She pushed him upright. It was Father Bernard, a young priest whom she had seen in Châtillon, a protégé of the Bishop of Agra. Dressed now in a ragged boatman's smock, a peasant's broad-brimmed hat. He stared at her without recognizing her. 'Let me rest,' he said.

'Why are you here? Doing this?'

'I wanted to save myself,' he whispered. 'But I couldn't. And now I'm finished.'

They filled the boat with the old women and the children. Léonie tried to get in and Hester struck her across the face as hard as she could. 'Wait your turn.' She beckoned one of the servant-girls who looked strong. 'Can you row a boat?' The girl nodded, and she and Hester took an oar apiece while Father Bernard steered. Slanting across to the far bank, letting the current help them. The girl must have been from the marshes because she rowed like a man, with strong, even strokes.

They landed far down-stream, and got their passengers ashore, shivering now with fear at being in a strange place.

'Stay together. Wait for me.' An old woman trying to prevent her going back into the boat, clinging to the boat's side as if she now wanted to return into the Vendée, go home, no matter what happened to her. 'Madame, come back to us, don't leave us. Mary most Holy, bring her back to us.' Children crying for cold, for hunger, for the contagion of fear.

The crossing, there and back, must have taken the best of two hours. It was already light, a sick, grey dawn. Both banks of the river crowded. The island thick with people, too exhausted now to fight over the boats as they came and went. Sitting or lying huddled together, waiting, waiting. Michel had taken command, growing stronger as things grew worse. He had brought the horses onto the island, and the load from the cart. There was no way of bringing that.

Two more crossings. Bringing two of the horses behind them each time, their eyes showing white with fear as they swam. Hours of rowing, until her back, her arms seemed broken, and she must still row. Until, miraculously, they had all reached the Breton shore, there was a fire burning, potatoes boiling, Michel and Perrine walking the second pair of horses up and down the bank until they were dry again. A hundred, a thousand fires burning like their own, a great whispering of relief among the saved. And more boats crossing, re-crossing, men and horses swimming, staggering on shore, bringing new rumours, new fears.

In a cottage near them General Bonchamps was dying, messengers coming and going. The army was on the far bank now, building rafts to bring over the guns, the stores of food, of ammunition. And there were Republican prisoners, five thousand of them, that the army had brought with them from Beaupréau.

'They are going to kill them!' Father Bernard said. He had slept for an hour and then had insisted on rowing back to the Vendée side again, and had brought over another boat load of refugees. He came to recover at their fire, and eat a piece of bread. But he could scarcely eat for exhaustion, and for the thought of the prisoners to be slaughtered. 'They say the Blues have killed our wounded in Beaupréau, but we cannot, we cannot! They are in the Abbey, in the Gabelle tower, everywhere. They are lining up cannon to slaughter them. They cannot do it!' He put his head in his hands, and then grasped Michel by his good arm. 'You are an officer, you cannot allow it. We cannot let five thousand helpless men be murdered.'

'I can,' Michel said. 'What do you think they would do to us if they had arms in their hands and we were at their mercy?'

Father Bernard looked at Hester in despair. 'I must go back,' he said. He began running to the boat, so weak that he fell as he ran and Hester lifted him. 'Let me go! Have you forgotten that you are a woman?'

'There's nothing we can do.'

'There is, there is! We'll go to the General. Come with me, hold me up.'

She supported him along the gravel shore, to humour him more than help him. She was too tired to think of anything. Five thousand? Massacre? Prisoners? The words had no meaning. Michel followed them, took the priest's other arm.

'The general!' Father Bernard kept repeating. 'You are an officer, take me to him, make them let me talk to him.'

The men round the cottage made reluctant way for them. 'No one can see him,' a man said. 'He is dying, a priest is with him.'

'I am a priest,' Father Bernard said. 'In the name of Our Saviour I command you, out of my way.'

A tiny, stifling room. A dozen men crowding it, crowding round a narrow, peasant's bed. The general lay propped up with pillows, his chest bare, sweating in the closeness, bandages tight round his stomach where he had been shot, death in his face.

'Let me speak to him!' Throwing himself on his knees by the bed, beside another priest. 'General, as you hope for mercy, give mercy to the prisoners. They will listen to you, send word to spare them, I beg of you, I beg of you.' Clinging to the dying general's hand.

'What is it?' Bonchamps whispered. Blood on his mouth as he tried to talk. Father Bernard told him his story, his voice rising as the men in the room tried to silence him.

'You who are on your way to God, bring Him this gift. Five thousand lives!'

'Grace for the prisoners,' Bonchamps said. He tried to speak louder, lifting himself from the pillows, stretching out his hand towards one of the officers beside the bed. 'Tell them— d'Autichamps, tell them they must spare them. They must! It is my last prayer! Tell the Council that if they will not listen to me I will have myself brought back across and I will die with the prisoners.' The blood ran down his chin, onto his body. Father Bernard kissed his hand, stood up.

'Quickly, there is no time to lose. I have a boat.'

Dragging General d'Autichamps with him. Michel, Hester, two or three of the others following. Father Bernard pushing the officers into the boat like captives, dragging Michel and Hester with him as if they were all agreed in this; putting the tiller into Michel's good hand. He and Hester rowing.

Past the tip of Moquart. Past Batailleuse, round its narrow point, into the main shore. An officer stayed with the boat, to use his authority and his pistol to guard it for them. Running up the steep hillside, between old stone houses. The Abbey, and the great plaza in front of it, cannon there, and a thousand, more than a thousand soldiers drawn up in lines, forming an avenue between the great doors of the Abbey and the guns. A crowd of women was trying to stop the mouths of the guns, beseeching the cannoneers not to fire, not to massacre the prisoners. Kneeling before a group of officers, generals. The Bishop of Agra there, the abbé Bernier, all the Council.

Father Bernard ran forward waving his arms, shouting, 'Grace! Grace for the prisoners, General Bonchamps demands it!' And the women echoing the cry, 'Grace for the prisoners, you cannot kill them, Glory to God on High for His mercy.'

There was a long colloquy, the generals still arguing, but the ranks of soldiers began to break, move forward to close the avenue. The gunners trod out their burning matches. Someone ran to the abbey doors and began to unfasten them, a hundred joined in, the doors swung back.

'You are free, free, General Bonchamps has freed you!' The prisoners stumbling out into the daylight, still afraid, looking at the soldiers.

'You are free!'

Hester and Michel went down the hill again, to the boat. After half an hour Father Bernard and General d'Autichamps and the others joined them, and they rowed slowly across to the far bank. Lay down and slept for the remainder of the day. By nightfall the whole army had crossed the river, there was no one left on the Vendée bank, except the freed prisoners and the people of St. Florent. They could see Republican patrols already at the water's edge and on the island of Batailleuse, staring across. About eight o'clock the word ran among the camp fires that General Bonchamps was dead.

Chapter 21

A whole people marching. A hundred thousand men and women, children. A vast migration stretching for miles along the road north towards Laval; choking it, making it impossible for the army to deploy, for the advance guard to know what was happening behind it, for the guns they had managed to bring across to do anything but make the confusion worse. If the Blues attacked—but God seemed to show mercy to these helpless fugitives and there were no more than skirmishes on the flanks, small forces of Blue cavalry easily driven off. The army took Château Gontier. Took Laval. The Prince de Talmond's city, where he had promised to raise ten, twenty thousand men. But there was no rallying, neither of townspeople nor peasants. Only a thousand Bretons joined them from the north, dark, savage men, with long shaggy hair and goatskin jackets, alien and secret. They seemed even more alien, more frightening than the Blues.

There was fighting, bitter, tremendous fighting, and for the simple-minded there seemed to be victories. Westermann defeated, the men of Mayence he had brought into the Vendée destroyed as an army, shattered, annihilated. But Hester knew from Michel, and from others, that the victories were hollow, that each one cost them men they could not replace. Out of the hundred thousand there were scarcely ten thousand real troops. She and Michel were riding again, together, with the half dozen of their troop that still survived. Good horsemen so scarce that they were in the saddle twelve and fifteen hours a day, scouting, guarding, fighting. And all the time, whenever they came back to the main column, to wherever they were camped, her refugees were waiting for her, like birds to be fed, to be comforted, saved from despair.

Supplies of any kind became a nightmare. Sabots wore out and could not be replaced. Men marched barefoot, or their feet bound in bloody rags. No ammunition unless they captured it. No bread. Buying potatoes from the Breton peasants, giving them Royalist *assignats* in exchange. The water in the streams fouled before the first night in a camp was over, and dysentery spreading. Only the hope of the sea, of the English fleet, keeping the army's courage high. That and their new General in Chief, Monsieur Henri de la Rochejaquelein. A boy of twenty, twenty-one, younger than Hester, but long before this 'The Archangel' to the army. Monsieur Henri, who when his peasants came to him in the first days of the rising, begging him to lead them, had drawn his sword and cried, 'If I advance, follow me. If I retreat kill me. If I die, avenge me.' He had only to ride into the thickest of a fight for the peasants to take heart again, drive the Blues back, scatter them to the wind; that harsh north wind of Brittany, the Galerne, that already in November cut through rags like a knife, froze the wounded as they lay.

Not that the wounded lay long. The Blues killed them as they found them. In the ditches. In the fields. In the makeshift hospitals of the towns the Royalists abandoned as they tramped northwards to the sea. Killed the wounded, killed the sick, the pregnant women, the children too small to march, too weak to keep going. Each day, Hester gathered her people. Helped by Perrine, Michel, the abbé Bernard, Euphemia. Even her father found strength from somewhere, and helped the ones who were weaker than himself.

During the days Perrine and he acted as shepherdess and shepherd, keeping the now forty or fifty of their refugees together, keeping their hearts up, finding them more food, begging from the peasants along the road, organizing the children and those who were strong enough to gather wood for fires, dig up roots that could make a kind of gruel. As things grew worse Mr. Broadhurst seemed to grow almost young again. His flesh fell away, he grew gaunt as a skeleton, but he could march all day carrying a child, and at night would sing English nursery rhymes to the children and make toys for them out of straw and scraps of wood. When Hester came he would draw her aside and talk of their reaching the sea, and of the English fleet that was to meet them.

'Only to think!' he said. 'In another week or so, a month at the outside, we shall be home again! How your mother and your Uncle George will stare at us! As if we shall have come back from the dead.'

She had not the courage to tell him that she would not go with him when the time came. And not even because of Michel. Because of the refugees. Each night when she came to them, and they looked at her, gathered round her, seeming to think that once she was there the night was safe, at those times she almost hated them, and knew in the same moment that she could not leave them. Could not sail for England, and know that they were standing on the beach, staring after her, waiting to be killed. Because they would be killed, there was no doubt in the world of it. No hope that any English fleet could bring enough help to save the rising, turn catastrophe into victory.

I am bound to them, she thought. She did not know why, could not imagine what ultimate good she could do for them, and yet she knew that she must stay with them to the end. As if they were truly her own people. Her father, Léonie, Euphemia, they must go. But she would stay. With them, and with Michel. She did not discuss it with him. They rode together, fell into the straw side by side, if they were lucky enough to find straw to sleep on, and slept for what seemed like minutes before they were roused again. They talked together of almost nothing but what had to be done; of the news and rumours of the day, of finding supplies. As if they were both afraid to talk of anything closer to themselves. Were walking carefully in each other's company, to avoid dangerous things.

He never spoke of Talmond, of being sorry, of making amends. But she guessed that that was never out of his mind for long and in a hundred ways he showed what he did not say. He had become very gentle with her, and did things for her that long ago she had used to do for him, as if their roles were reversed. He would find food for her, and insist that she eat it in front of him, so that he could know she was not giving it to one of the others. He got a needle and thread from somewhere and set himself to mending her coat one night, while she slept. They were both in rags again, but she woke that next morning to find her coat and shirt neatly darned and patched. He must have spent half the night at it, and she wanted to hold the mended cloth against her face and cry for shame.

[227]

And she in turn served him in everything possible; not as she had once done, as a follower, a younger soldier serving an officer; but as a woman does. Not that there was much room for womanhood in such conditions, but by a tone of voice, a look, a touch; by heaping the straw for him, by taking his now mended arm and massaging it where it still hurt in the cold; by cooking his food when she was so tired she would rather have lain down starving, and slept. Like a contest of courtesy. And of love. For as she acted love for him she found that she did truly love him, more than she had imagined possible. So that it seemed to her that in the long-ago times of their marriage, and their first companionship, she had not known what love was.

One night, one early morning, she tried to talk about it to Father Bernard. She had woken and could not sleep again because she was too tired, and it was too near dawn. She went out of the shed they had slept in into the cold darkness, the fierce glitter of the stars, and found Father Bernard already up, remaking the fire. All round them fires dying or rekindling, shadows moving. The sense of the camp stretching, spread for miles across the countryside.

'What will happen to us?' she whispered, shivering and trying to warm herself at the small tongues of flame.

'God will show mercy to His people.' Father Bernard kneeling, his face lit red by the fire. Like all of them he had become thin as bone, sweated dry with fever, drained by dysentery, exhausted. And yet he looked happier than when he had walked about Châtillon as sleek as a young cat, a pet for the generals' wives.

'We shall be killed,' Hester said. 'There is no hope for us.'

'Perhaps that is His mercy.'

She found herself talking to him about Michel, about herself. She wished she could have confessed to him, and suddenly was confessing.

'My child,' he said. He was scarcely thirty years old, younger than Michel. But she knelt in front of him as if she believed in his God, in his Sacraments.

'Tell me what to do,' she whispered.

He laid his hands on her head. 'Love him,' he said.

'What does love mean?'

'Love is giving. Love is surrender of one's self. Love is love.'

'I thought I loved him. And yet—when that man—how could I have done that if I loved Michel? I think I love him now—and yet if—it was to happen again—I do not know what I would do. As if—what I feel for Michel is not real love but—only friendship, comradeship—and the other—the other has my soul.'

'You think love is of the body,' Father Bernard said. 'Love is not even of the mind. That is friendship, that is comradeship. True love is worship.'

'I do not believe as you do,' Hester said. 'I cannot understand. I cannot worship Michel.' And thought, if it was Talmond we were speaking of——

'You must worship God in him, and through him. And he must worship God in you. That is love.'

The burden of it lay on her, like her tiredness and hunger. And she thought then of how near death was, and was ashamed of thinking whether she loved one man or another, instead of thanking God that she was still alive, that she had a friend. To set Talmond beside him! Near him! 'God forgive me,' she whispered, and Father Bernard touched her head again with both hands, giving her his blessing.

They reached the sea that day, a grey mist swathing the horizon, the vast stretch of the Bay of Mont St. Michel flat and level as a dulled mirror. Woods, and then the dunes, the smell of the sea and mud and the sour sea grasses. The Mount no more than a grey cathedral-shape in the mist, far away to their left. In front of them the rock islet of Tomberlaine, like a crouching lion. And further out, to their right, sails.

'They are there!' Hester cried. 'The fleet! The English fleet!'

'They are French ships,' Michel said. But she would not believe him, and they rode north along the dunes, hoping against hope that Michel was wrong, or that beyond that menacing line of Republican frigates out of Brest, they would see the English, see them bear in and scatter the French fleet like chaff. But beyond the frigates there was only mist and nothingness.

'Tomorrow,' Hester said, and they rode back to report, deceiving each other with false hopes. As the whole army deceived itself, and the whole mass of refugees. Believing that Granville would fall like Jericho, to the sound of their trumpets. That the English would come. That Brittany would still rise. That one of the child-king's uncles would stir himself in his luxurious exile, and come to lead his devoted servants, come to risk death with them.

That night she lay for a long time watching him as he lay beside her. Was he awake? He lay very still, too still for sleep. And it was too cold to sleep. 'Michel,' she whispered. If he did not answer her—but he stirred, pretended to wake, turned to her. His eyes reflecting the embers of their fire.

'You know that if—when—the fleet comes, when—my father goes—I mean to stay with you? You know that?'

For answer he put out his hand and touched her cloak. A long time went by. 'I would have to send you with him,' he said at last.

'Michel!'

He rolled over onto his elbows, his face, his eyes hidden from her by his hands. 'You could be happy again,' he said, his voice muffled. And then, clear but not harsh, not bitterly, he said, 'I know you cannot be happy with me. This——' he made a gesture with one hand embracing the camp, the army, all its future, '—what has this got to do with you?'

'Michel!' She sat up, knelt by the fire and began pushing the half-burned remnants of wood into the heap of ashes, to make some sort of blaze. She wanted him to help her, to kneel beside her, so that their bodies might touch, she might have an excuse to touch him. But he stayed where he was.

'I made you marry me,' she said. 'It was my doing. Do you think I would leave you now?' The words were wrong, she knew it as soon as she had spoken them. If it had been Talmond there, what would she have said? But they would not have needed to say anything. She turned and caught Michel by the arms, shook him and was then afraid for his mended bone, that she had hurt him. 'Michel, I am your wife!'

'Look into my eyes,' he said, 'and tell me you love me. Tell me that I am your whole life.'

She tried to do it, said the words. He smiled, and looked away. 'My father and mother hated one another,' he said. 'Words like "wife" and "husband" don't create love. You made a mistake, but it doesn't have to last for ever. I give you your freedom. Take it.'

'Michel!'

'You're still young, you can marry again, marry a man that knows what you want, how to give it to you. A man with a soft skin and——' the bitterness welling up against his will. She knew that it was against his will. She bent her head, accepting it. Tell him, something cried out in her. Tell him now. But he was already kneeling in front of her, holding the knuckles of her hands to his forehead. 'Forgive me, forgive me, I swear I know you are as loyal as—I know I was mad, vile mad to think it. I'm like my father, ruining his life and my mother's. Like a cancer, like something eating one's heart.'

'Michel,' she whispered, 'I am not—not what you——'

He pressed his hand over her mouth. 'I never learned to talk to women. My grandfather believed in work and prayer and Hell, and that women were man's damnation. He hated my mother too. He used to beat me because he could no longer beat her as he had used to. He'd tell me he was beating her devil out of me.'

'Michel—I must tell you something——'

'I've never spoken to a living soul about it from that day to now, I swore I would never tell you a word of it. And now you've made me so weak that I'm like an old woman in confession.'

'Michel——'

'My real father was one of the Trémouilles. A second cousin of Talmond's. That's why—that's part of the reason why——' He stood up suddenly, and pulled her to her feet. 'Your hands are like ice,' he said. 'Let's get ourselves warm and we'll try and talk reason.'

They made their way between the outer fires, the lines of sleeping men, the sentries. The sentries themselves half asleep, huddled with cold over a few smouldering branches torn from the gorse bushes of the hillside. Beyond the last of the fires the darkness stretched for ever. Clouds hid the stars. The war a thousand, ten thousand miles away.

He put one arm round her, held her close against him. 'When I saw you first,' he said, 'I thought, what would it be like to tame her? You were so strong, and so arrogant, I imagined taming you like breaking a beautiful wild horse that has never been touched by anyone's hand. When I was lying ill and you were nursing me, I'd think of that, and then I was ashamed, because you were so good, and so foolish, and so innocent, and I wished I knew how to please you, to be young with you.'

'Did you want to marry me?' Whispering, seeing that long ago time like a distant, distant landscape.

[231]

'I never thought of marriage. I knew that all this was coming, that—and I knew I wasn't a man to make a husband.'

'Nor I a woman to make much of a wife. My poor, poor Michel.'

'I've been very rich,' he said. 'Much richer than I deserved. And that's why I'm going to send you away. Again. This time for love. And the last time, that was a kind of love. I hated you because I loved you too much.'

'I won't go. If you try to drive me away I'll follow you, like your greyhound bitch. If you throw stones at me I'll wait till you go on and still follow you to the end.'

He stood still, and made her face him. 'Why? Why?'

'Why do you fight for your king?'

'I don't know,' he said. 'As God is my judge I don't know.'

'Perhaps that's my answer too.' All round them the frost had begun to glitter on the iron ground, like silver.

Chapter 22

Granville did not fall. The peasants fell back, on Avranches, on Pontorson, Dol de Bretagne, the enormous, unwieldy train of refugees recoiling on itself, destroying discipline, magnifying terrors. Panic at Dol, as they fought to save themselves. The whole terror-stricken mass of refugees running, the narrow street of Dol choked with people fighting to escape, trampling one another down, the living trampling the dying, falling themselves to be trampled in their turn.

A priest stopped the rout, climbing onto a mound of earth in a graveyard, lifting a crucifix above his head and shouting the Vexilla Regis, the Standard of the King, in a voice to raise the dead who lay sleeping under his great peasant sabots.

'Hail, our Cross, our only hope——'

Until the fugitives stopped, knelt, began to sing with him, '——in this day of our suffering, grant to the just a richer grace, and from the sinners, wash their sins away.'

All the voices lifting, thousands, then tens of thousands, a whole people singing, their voices lifting to the cold stars in that kind of hope that is closest to despair.

She heard the singing, she and Michel, as they rode back from what had been in the last outcome victory. Heard the huge swelling of the hymn, and held hands as they rode. The panic, mindless and terrible, told them that the end could not be far away. For some of their own refugees it had already come. Two of the children, three of the old women trampled to death. One of the old men with his leg broken. They found a household that would take him in. Perhaps he would survive.

South again. Word followed them that two days after they had fallen back from Granville, the English fleet had come. But the peasants no longer cared. South! To the Loire! To the Vendée!

Home! Dragging their way like a great serpent with a broken spine. Still fighting, still dangerous, but as dying creatures fight, desperate with hatred, with no hope of living.

Of the hundred thousand that had crossed the Loire two months ago, thirty thousand were now dead. The column thinned out and faded by the day. Clusters of the helpless sheltering under a hedge, waiting for death. The quick mercy of a sword, or the slow freezing of the nights. Flurries of sleet beating against rags. No food, no clothing. Bare feet torn by the frozen ground. And they still fought. Without hope, without reason.

Except that if they must die, then they would die defiant. Sick voices whispering, 'God and the King' as they died.

Defeated at Angers. Two thousand killed. Hunted by Westermann's cavalry like sick wolves.

Le Mans, and worse massacres, the Blues triumphant, killing every living creature they could reach, the townspeople of Le Mans as well as the rebels and the refugees. The roads choked with terror. Laval, where the townsmen tried to drive them away. Craon. Segré. Candé. Another day and they would see the river and a beginning of hope ran in them like warmth, like the sun. To reach their homes, see their fields, their woods, their church towers, kneel on Vendée soil. One more day. One!

Even Léonie took heart. She had almost died. Of dysentery and then of fever. Only Euphemia had saved her. Boiling the corrupted water from the ditches for her, cooking her food when there was no means of cooking anything, no food to cook. Fighting for her like a black leopard for her sick and dying cub. Conjuring bread out of nowhere, making tisanes from the weeds and herbs she found by the road. Finding a place for her in a cart. Carrying her. Walking beside her barefoot, half naked, thin as blackened bones. While Léonie grew almost well again, almost sleek, coming to join them at night to share their food and tell her miseries. Euphemia had even managed to find soap for her and her face and hair and hands were clean and her rags mended.

As for Hester's refugees, there were not many left. Two women servants from the *manoir*, Perrine, an old peasant woman, a little girl. And Euphemia. And Léonie. And her father. He was still alive, still able to walk, but that was all. After Granville he had withered into himself, his mind wandering. Sometimes he remembered the prison in Paris and woke in the night shouting, 'Hester!

Hester!' and she must lose her own few hours of sleep to comfort him. More than once he began trying to tell her a story of when he was young, and travelling with her mother. But it became garbled, mixed up with another story of when she herself was born. There had been a midwife. An old woman like a witch. 'I saved you from her—I have never told you, Hester—I thought it best——'

'Hush, Papa. Hush. Try and sleep.'

His mind wandering again. He seemed to think he was somewhere among mountains. Snow. 'Such a damnable bad inn—and we heard her—your mother screamed all night——'

'Ssh. Try and sleep.'

'I have to tell you—I know I haven't long now—you ought to know.'

'Know what, Papa?'

'I always loved you. Like a daughter. A true daughter?'

'More than that, much more, Papa.'

'I've tried. Your poor mother—where—we never knew where she—they took her away, you know.'

His mind wandering again. So that she cried for him, holding her fingers against his mouth to hush him.

One more day. And they were stumbling, falling, staggering down the hillside towards the river. The Loire! The Loire! The river swollen, twice the breadth it had been two months ago. Swollen by the rains of November, rolling swift and hostile, icy beyond hope of fording, or swimming. The wind like a sword. The soldiers down at the shore, hunting for boats. The refugees in a dark mass, waiting, spreading out among the fields, looking for roots to eat, wood to burn, a corner to shelter them from the wind. No more than thirty thousand now, but how many boats would be needed, how long would it take to bring all of them across that river? And how long before the hunters came? A few hours? A few hours of safety?

Tied against the far shore they could see a line of barges, loaded with stacks of hay. And there was a sudden stir and excitement down by the shore, men carrying a skiff and another boat; General Rochejaquelein leading them, Stofflet with him, Michel.

'Who will go over with me to take the barges?'

She saw Michel getting into one of the boats and began to run down the slope to join him. Euphemia caught hold of her arm.

'No, madame, no!'

'Let me go! Let me go to him, damn you!'

Euphemia clinging to her, her fingers like steel. 'Michel! *Michel*!' He looked towards her, lifted his hand, called something she could not hear. The crowd of refugees between them, everyone crying out, 'The barges, they are going to bring the barges over!' Everyone gathering to watch, the whole hillside dark and massed with people, hope binding them together. She saw the two small boats nosing out into the stream, men bending forward, straining, caught by the current and driven sideways, twisted round, threatening to overturn. '*Michel*!'

Yard by yard through the brown race of the river. Half-way. Three-quarters. General Rochejaquelein standing in the bows of his skiff, leaping on board one of the barges, beginning to throw the bales of hay into the water. They could see the bales floating, twisting away downstream. She could see Michel on another barge, was sure it was Michel although he was half a mile from her. The second boat almost there, men standing in her, ready to grapple themselves to a barge. And the sound of firing. The sounds reaching them after they saw the puffs of smoke, the swift rush of horsemen. A Blue patrol. The few men on the barges running, leaping for the shore, firing their pistols as they ran, out of sight behind trees. '*Michel*!' Running down to the shore like a madwoman, ready to throw herself into the water, try to swim. Someone was holding her back, not Euphemia, a man. She turned and it was Talmond.

She had not seen him for days. He had grown haggard, all the soft beauty gone. His uniform in rags, the plumes of his hat broken and filthy. But his eyes still held her. 'Are you trying to kill yourself?'

'Let me go to him!'

'No one could swim that. Are you gone mad?'

'Michel is over there.'

'Then he is a dead man. Look.' They saw the second boat trying to escape, row back into the middle of the river. Musket fire. A man fell overboard, was carried away by the current. The boat was sinking. Gunwale-deep, the men throwing themselves into the river, heads showing for a few moments, vanishing. The Blue cavalry riding fast along the far bank, levelling muskets, firing across the river.

'Monsieur Henri! The General! The Archangel is gone!'

Talmond drawing her away towards a ridge of ground, pushing through the crowd, hurrying her, not letting her gather herself, resist.

'Where are you taking me? What are you doing?' She began to struggle, force him to stop.

'There,' Talmond said, pointing to the woods. 'This is the finish of it, it's everyone for himself now. I know people who'll get us to England, Germany, anywhere out of this cursed country.'

'No!'

'He's dead, I tell you. Come with me.' Tugging at her, trying to make her move.

She freed herself, and began walking back the way they had come. More refugees were running now, towards her, past her. Towards the woods. Looking for hiding-places, looking for boats? Or simply running? Where was there to run? Michel. Dead. She had almost forgotten Talmond. She heard him calling after her and turned to look at him. He was following her, slowly at first, and then with swift strides.

'Are you not going to escape?'

'If you can die here, I can, I suppose. Your servant, ma'am.' There were people round them, listening to them, thinking that a prince, a general, must have some plan to save them.

And Talmond played his part, saluting her as if she was one of his staff and they had been planning victory. He called some officers to him, and they walked away together, half a dozen ragged figures, but still with their white sashes, their broken plumes, one of them carrying a standard; the Crown, and the Lilies. God and the King. The wind lifted the white silk, torn at the edges, battle-stained and darkened. After another hour the same standard led them away from the river. General Fleuriot leading them. Skeleton horses. Skeleton soldiers. Shadows. Dragging themselves towards new calvaries. Niort. Blain. The promise of a new crossing-place. Beyond Nantes. Savenay. The name running through the camp, down the column. We can cross at Savenay.

The column fading, melting away as they marched. Peasants surrendering, and the sound of musket fire a long way off as they were killed kneeling for mercy. Men slipping away by ones and twos and dozens to make their own escape, or try to. Take shelter

[237]

with the Bretons. Swim the river. Hide in a wood. Freeze as they lay hiding.

The last of her refugees died on that march to Savenay. There were no tears left to cry for them. The horses died. Bayard had died long ago, at Le Mans. They huddled over the fire that she and Perrine had gathered. Euphemia, Léonie, Hester, her father, Perrine. There was nothing to eat. Enough wood for an hour's warmth. They did not talk, because there was nothing to talk about. Léonie sat stunned with misery, Euphemia holding her. Hester and Perrine tried to warm Mr. Broadhurst between them, shelter him from the wind. The whole camp silent. A shadow made its slow way between the fires, came to theirs. It was the abbé Bernard. He had become old in these past weeks. His once thick brown hair had turned white, and fallen out to leave him half bald. His face like a skull.

'Are there any dying here?' He had his crucifix in his left hand and the rags of what had once been peasant breeches were white with frost where he had been kneeling. He had no coat, and his grey, stretched skin showed through the torn linen on his shirt. He recognized them, and sat down, slowly and stiffly like an old man. 'Have you a cup of water?'

Hester gave it to him. 'What news, Father?'

He held his crucifix towards her. 'Only this,' he said.

They slept. Woke with the cold. Made themselves move about. The dawn came. Father Bernard said the rosary. Everyone within hearing joined in. 'Holy Mary, Mother of God, pray for us sinners now and at the hour of our death, amen.' Knowing that it was this hour, or the next. Away to the north, where the outposts lay, they heard firing. The last battle beginning.

Chapter 23

In that battle of Savenay the last remnants of the army were destroyed. Thousands died where they fought. Thousands more, of the wounded, the fugitives, the refugees were slaughtered as they ran. Drowned trying to swim the flooded Loire. Shot, bayoneted, sabred as they lay in ditches, behind hedges, crawled on their knees towards imaginary shelter. A landscape of death. The last remnants hid in the forests, the woods, tried to disguise themselves as Bretons who had taken no part in the rising. Hid in the vast marshland of the Brière.

Hester took her father there, and Léonie, and Euphemia, and Perrine, and the abbé Bernard. Stumbling, running, crawling, dragging Léonie, half carrying her father, Perrine supporting Father Bernard who had been wounded in the face by a sabre slash, and was half blind. Seven, eight miles of running, hiding from the cavalry that were hunting for them. Praying for the dark to come. Hearing shots, screams behind them, the swift rush of horsemen, the shouts of triumph as the hunters found another victim.

She could see the huge expanse of reeds, tall cane reeds the height of a man where they could hide for ever, if they could find food. The soil growing spongy underfoot, then soft black mud, clinging to their feet. Ankle deep, knee deep. A narrow channel of black water, weeds clinging to them as they waded, a pale green scum that broke before them, closed behind them. Léonie cried with terror. In the dark behind them a man shouted, 'There they go! In there!' Léonie whimpering as the mud sucked at her.

'Be quiet, you fool!'

But she would not be quiet, and Euphemia clamped her hand over her mistress's face, stifled her crying. They waded forward.

Keeping to the water so that they would not betray themselves by the noise of the reeds breaking.

'Swim,' Hester breathed. Leaned forward, drawing her father with her, half walking, half swimming, deeper into the marsh. Behind them horses whinnied in terror, feeling the mud give under their hooves. The sounds of men leaping from their saddles, crashing among the reeds, cutting to left and right with their sabres.

'A torch! A torch! Burn the reeds!'

Deeper into the marsh. The stench of the mud. A swift glare of light behind them, the reeds flaming, marsh gas burning, smoke rolling.

'Lie under water,' Hester said, 'only your nose above it.' Her father staring at her. She tried to press him under, and he gave way as if he was going to let himself be drowned. She held him, whispered to Perrine, to Euphemia, 'Under the water, all of us.' The blaze growing, lighting the dark with blue and crimson flames, the smoke boiling, bellying up, then rolling towards them like a fog. The shapes of their pursuers black as devils in the glare. 'Under the water!'

And as she went under she heard Léonie screaming, '*No, no! Save me!*'

The hunters plunging towards them. Hands gripping her hair, dragging her upright. A flash of steel lifting.

'Bring them out!' a voice commanded. 'They'll know where there are more.'

Dragging them, Léonie still crying in terror, 'Save me! Save me!'

A dozen men dragging them. At the edge of the marsh a troop of soldiers gathering; an officer on horseback, his face lit by the flames. Thickset, brutal, his long moustaches grey and drooping. He sat waiting, looking down in triumph and contempt at the drowned, mud-blackened creatures his hunters had found. Pointing to Hester. 'You, where are the others? Where are your generals?'

'They are all dead.'

He cut her across the face with his whip. 'You've ten seconds to answer,' he said.

'I tell you they are dead.'

'Then join them.'

A man drew his pistol, put it to Hester's temple.

'Don't waste powder and shot, you fool. What's your bayonet for?'

The rattle of sabres drawn, men levelling bayonets, while their captors held them upright, their arms twisted behind their backs.

'Christ take us into His keeping,' Father Bernard shouted. 'God and the King!'

Léonie screaming, her screams echoing, piercing. '*Spare me, spare me!*' She flung herself forward before any of the men could stop her, knelt by the officer's horse, caught at his stirrup, his foot. 'We'll tell you everything, she knows all the generals, she knows where they are. They all escaped! She knows everything that's happened. Only don't kill me now.' Pointing towards Hester, clinging to the officer's stirrup again, pressing her forehead against his boot.

He touched her with the point of his whip.

'You're a fine brigandess,' he said. 'Are they all as brave as you?' But she had caught at the whip, was drawing it towards her, whimpering with terror. He freed himself from her, kicking her away. 'Maybe they know something. All right. Bring them along.'

'What about the priest, Citizen Commandant? And this old man?'

'Kill them.'

Hester threw her arms round her father. Perrine held Father Bernard to her.

'Kill us all,' Hester said.

The Commandant rode close to her. 'So you're a different breed?' He stared down at her, frowning. Wheeled his horse sharply. 'Bring them all,' he said. 'Forward march.'

Men tied their hands together, with long ropes like leashes. Remounted, set their horses to a trot, and they must run or fall. But Léonie screamed so loud that the Commandant ordered a man to take her up onto his horse, in front of him. Father Bernard fell, and fell again, was dragged unprotesting, without a cry.

'He is blinded,' Hester shouted. 'Why don't you kill us now?'

A man hit her with the flat of his sabre. 'Shut up, you bitch. He won't need eyes where he's going.'

But the trooper dragging Father Bernard stopped long enough to let the priest stagger to his feet again, and after that, whether from a kind of pity, or because the horses were too tired to do more, the company fell to a walk. And even that was terrible enough. The long miles back to Savenay. Up the hill. Everywhere, as they neared the town, companies like their own, small columns of prisoners who for one reason or another had been spared immediate execution. Among houses, people staring, whispering, pointing. In compassion? Horror? Every cellar, every building that could hold prisoners turned into a temporary prison.

In the market square, hundreds more penned in like cattle, crouched on the ground, silent in despair, while their captors kept guard over them with levelled muskets, bayonets, drawn swords.

The Commandant had Léonie and Hester and the others brought to the house he had commandeered. 'Bring 'em in. The two men down below. The women in here. Let's see what we've got. My oath, they stink of mud. But we'll give them a good Republican bath tomorrow. Let's see the pretty one. And that one's really black, eh? Who likes Negresses? Strip 'em off, lads.'

He sat in a wooden armchair, his belly released from belt and buttoning, hanging over his breeches, his short, thick legs in their mud-encrusted boots spread out. An orderly brought him wine and a glass, and he drank as he watched Léonie stripped naked in front of him. She stood like a slave on the auction block, but strangely not ashamed. Offering herself as something wonderful. The dried mud flaking from her skin like a serpent shedding its last year's scales, here and there the promise of her whiteness showing, of the softness of flesh, of her breasts that were still full and firm-shaped, fed by the milk and meat and bread and wine that Euphemia had begged and stolen for her.

'Turn her round.' A soldier turned her, his hands fondling.

'Keep your filthy paws to yourself, my lad. She's mine, remember, you can draw your lots for the others. That's a pretty shape of a bottom. Come and pour me my wine, Countess. Or is it Marquise? And don't spill any, or you'll pay for it.' Flicking her across the stomach with his whip. 'Kneel down when you offer it to me. That's right. Now strip the nigger girl and let's see what she's like. Lads who've been in the Caribbean say they're better than white women when you put the candle out.'

Euphemia naked. Impassive. As if there was nothing they could do that would shame her, make her feel anything. Léonie kneeling, holding the wine bottle.

'Now the tall bitch. My oath, what a she-wolf. Tell me about your generals. Which ones escaped? Or would you like to hang up by your thumbs first?'

He heaved himself to his feet, balancing his hanging belly, trying to draw it in. Wiping his moustaches with a thick, furry hand. Outside the stamp of feet, a sentry crashing to attention. A quick hurry of steps, a man in black in the doorway. Stooped, rusty, eyes sunken and red-rimmed, crooked teeth. Stooping like a rusty crow. The Citizen Creuzot.

'And who——?' the Commandant began, voice rising at seeing a civilian pushing into his presence unannounced and unwanted.

'I am the Representative on Mission, Junius Brutus Creuzot, with plenary powers from the Convention.' He stood in the doorway, looking at Léonie, naked, holding the half emptied wine bottle. At Euphemia, Hester, Perrine still only half stripped of her rags. The soldiers stood to attention. The Commandant tried as unobtrusively as he could to rebutton himself, fasten his belt. The shadow of denunciation, the guillotine, seemed to travel along the dirty wall of the room as the Citizen Creuzot stooped his way round the table, towards Euphemia, Hester, Perrine.

'Upon my soul—I know some of these people. This one. An Englishwoman, let me think of the name—Broad——? Some name like that?'

'I am the wife of Michel Vernet,' Hester said. 'When we last met——'

'It is sometimes a mistake to remember last meetings,' Creuzot said. 'A mistake. Leading to uncomfortable consequences.'

He sat himself at the table, while the Commandant shouted at his men; Léonie, Euphemia, Perrine, Hester pulling their rags together as best they could. The Citizen Creuzot watching Léonie from the corner of his eye, his mouth sneering as if he found flesh contemptible, but still interesting.

'I have orders from the Convention to discuss with you, Commandant. Can we postpone your interrogation until later? Or even tomorrow?'

The Commandant shouted orders. They were taken away, down stone steps to a cellar, cut out of solid rock. Hester's father and the abbé Bernard already there.

An hour later the men came back with torches, and took Léonie and Euphemia away.

Chapter 24

They were taken from Savenay to Nantes, their arms bound behind them, walking and running behind the horsemen who held their ropes, dragging on them to make them fall when they felt like a trifle of amusement. Hester, her father, Perrine, the abbé Bernard. Still in their rags, bare feet bleeding. But at least they had had food, water, two nights' sleep.

Léonie and Euphemia rode in an ammunition cart. Léonie had been given clothes, a peasant woman's cloak to cover her. She sat beside the man driving the cart, and even talked with him. Once Hester could hear her laughing. Euphemia crouched behind her, looking at no one, her body tense as a spring, as if her whole mind and will and soul were being concentrated on a purpose.

At Nantes another house, another cellar. But they were given straw, and better food.

The sounds of fusillades punctuating the night, and the next day. One of the guards told them they were shooting prisoners. The guillotine was too slow.

That night the soldiers took Perrine away, and brought her back before daylight, unconscious.

'You're lucky,' one of them said to Hester. 'The Representative's given orders you're not to be touched. But maybe he'll change his mind later. When you've put on a bit of flesh, eh?'

Outside, the shooting stopped. She heard afterwards that it had cost too much ammunition to shoot so many, and they had begun to drown them, instead.

Two days after that she and Perrine, and her father, and the abbé, were brought up into the daylight. The troop that had captured them ready to march. Léonie and Euphemia in the ammunition cart. Léonie flushing, looking away as Hester saw her. The Commandant shouted an order, and they began to march, down the long hill towards the river.

The air itself smelled of death. The river seemed swollen with it as they crossed over to the other side. To the Vendée. To begin the final cleansing.

'You shall be our guides,' the Citizen Creuzot said, his mouth sneering.

But there was no need for guides. They marched for days on end without seeing a living soul. Without seeing a house that was not in ashes. The carrion crows had grown so heavy that they could scarcely lift themselves into the air as the column passed.

'Give us some throats to cut!' the Commandant shouted. And as though it was a prayer which the Goddess of Reason in Her wisdom answered, they came the next day to a village, a small town, untouched by the war. The one misfortune being that it was a patriot town, ardently Republican, that had by its own prayers and miracles survived the Royalists, the white terrors, all that had happened since that first battle of Cholet a thousand years ago.

The authorities came out in festival procession to greet their heroes, drums and fifes playing, tricolour sashes fluttering in the icy wind, the people following, a crowd of patriots greeting their deliverers. The mayor held up his arms to salute the Commandant and began a speech. The Commandant gnawed his moustaches for a minute or so. Shouted, 'Enough. Enough, man. Are all your people here? Every living one of 'em?'

'There is not a babe in arms would have missed this moment, Citizen General! We salute you! Saviour of your Country! Saviour of the People.'

The Commandant gave an order. His men spread out in a long line facing the procession and the crowd. 'Open fire.' The volley crashed. A stench of gunsmoke. A fraction of an instant of near silence, filled only by the echoes of the firing. Then the screams. The mayor, untouched by the first volley, ran forward, tried to grasp the Commandant's stirrup. 'We are patriots! Republicans! Have you gone mad?'

'The Republic'll know its own,' the Commandant said. He drew his sabre and slashed the mayor across the head, the mayor's tricorn hat tumbling, his bald head shining ivory for a second before it grew crimson. 'Reload!'

From behind the wagons Father Bernard tried to run forward. Was brought up short by his rope. And lay against the wheels of the guns, shocked into stillness. Perrine shouted, 'Kill the bastards. Kill them all! Death to the *patauds*!' She laughed like a maniac all the time the firing continued, and after it, while the soldiers searched in the crowd for survivors, and bayoneted them.

Hester stood with her hands bound in front of her, fastened by the neck to the cart in which Léonie and Euphemia rode. She shut her eyes against the killings, but she could not shut out the sounds. They went on for a long time. I am in Hell, she thought, without having died. As if God slept.

In the cart, Léonie was crying and twisting herself about in an agony of fear. After a time she began to be sick, lying face down on her straw pallet, among the barrels of gunpowder and musket balls and wadding. Euphemia soothing her, whispering in Créole.

If I could find that much ease, Hester thought. And then—if I could die. But she could only stand there, listening.

There was wine and food in the town. Stores of grain. God knew how it had all survived. The soldiers found the wine, and by dark the town was bedlam. The Citizen Creuzot and the Commandant, with the few under-officers who were still more or less sober, conducted searches in the better houses. Everything portable of any value went into sacks and saddle-bags. Plate, jewellery, candlesticks, coin, paper money. The soldiers had already stripped the dead of valuables and by now were bartering gold watches against unbroken bottles of wine or brandy. Some of the houses were burning.

When the searches were over the Commandant and the Citizen Creuzot held court in the mayor's house, with Léonie and Euphemia for Mistresses of Revels. But already the Commandant had become the real master, and the Citizen Creuzot had been forced back, or had chosen to step back, into the shadows behind his thick, barrel body, his heavy shoulders, his wide planted stumpy legs. This was a time and place for soldiers, not civilians.

The next day they burned the town and moved on. The days ran into one another. The weeks. They found a second Republican oasis, and destroyed that, although this time they kept the women for the night, intending to kill them in the morning. But the Commandant and the Citizen Creuzot changed their minds, and the women were spared to become camp followers, shared out among the soldiers.

But they burned everything that would burn. Anything that still survived. When there were no houses they burned the woods, the hedges. Their advance a lengthening zigzag trail of fire, of ashes, of destruction. Hester and Perrine marched now behind the supply wagons, no longer bound, Father Bernard walking between them. Mr. Broadhurst rode on one of the ammunition carts. His mind was quite gone. He thought he was in Sussex, and had long conversations with Uncle George, and with Mrs. Broadhurst, about the scenery. Or he sat quiet, staring at his hands. The soldiers had grown fond of him and called him grandfather. His hair was very long and completely white. Otherwise he looked quite well, and became stout again on Hester's feeding. Léonie rode with the Representative Creuzot in a carriage, sleek as a cat, and had become a convinced Republican. The Commandant had had Euphemia dressed as a drummer-boy, and he kept her beside him like a fierce toy.

All the days marching. This way and that. Hunting for fugitives, for a nest of brigands. For some brigands had survived. Charette had survived. And he still held the forests. And Stofflet, who had survived that day when he had crossed the Loire with the others, before Savenay. They had gathered refugees together, formed new armies. The Vendée began its resurrection, a ghost of itself, and yet still powerful, burning for revenge. They hid in the deepest forests, in the marshes; fell on small patrols of the Republicans and cut their throats, took their weapons. The war that had been over began again, fuelled by hatred, by the cruelties of the flying columns, the insanity of destruction. The fierce yelling of '*Rembarre! Rembarre!*' rang in the dark once more, and the Republicans shivered in their camps, imagined the pitchforks at their throats.

It seemed to Hester as if it was a thousand years since she had been free. As if that had been another lifetime. And she was truly dead, only her body was walking about. Like the dead men and women Euphemia told her of, brought out of their graves for slavery. How lucky Michel was that he had not lived to see all this.

Sometimes she prayed for him. And then it would seem like blasphemy to pray for one dead man when there were so many dead. And who was there to listen? What kind of God are you? she whispered, as she lay awake in the night. Seeing again the things she had seen during the day, like waking nightmares. And yet the abbé Bernard still believed, stumbling his way through a darkness that for him had no morning. He still believed, and prayed, and when he could, brought comfort to the dying.

It was already March. April. The burned woods trying to turn green. May. Summer. Four columns like their own combined to sweep the Forest of Grasla, hunting for Charette. Behind the advance guard the troops in battle order. And safe in the heart of the columns, Commandant Piré and his three colleagues, three other commandants as unwilling as he was to end their lives in this obscene twilight.

But there was no firing. No trace of the brigands. They had captured two peasants and tortured them into becoming guides to find Charette's camp. They went hobbling now on their burned feet ahead of the columns, pointing this way and that to paths that seemed always to twist back on themselves, and lead nowhere. The men of the column began to grumble that they were being fooled, led into a trap by two wretches who were obviously spies.

'Hang one of them,' Commandant Piré said. 'It might brighten the other.'

Soldiers fetched a rope and threw an end over the low branch of an oak. The younger of the two men began to weep with fear. The older, his father, sat down and stared at nothing. Euphemia, in her drummer-boy's uniform, said, 'Let me talk to them.' She went and took the hanging noose of the rope and put it gently round the boy's neck, as if it was a scarf, stroking his face as she did it. 'Poor young man,' she said. Then she whispered to him. She stroked his face again and he shivered with terror and began to tell her something. Euphemia came back to the Commandant.

'We can find it now. I will go with him, and you can follow us, it will be quite safe.'

Black drummer-girl, peasant boy, old man, leading the way. They went as straight as the thickets would allow. And within ten minutes came to a wide clearing. Rows of huts built from branches, mud. A whole village of huts that could have belonged to the ancient Gauls. Two or three hundred of them, almost a town, with streets, and pits for rubbish, and rough ladders leading up into the thickness of the tallest trees, like watchtowers. And in the whole clearing, no one.

But the ashes of the fires were still warm. In one hut that Hester looked into there was a dish of milk on the earth floor, and four snakes were drinking from it, their viper heads like black arrows struck into a round white target. Euphemia came into the hut behind her and knelt down.

'Little friends,' she whispered. Three of the snakes left the dish and came writhing towards her feet. The fourth lifted his head and turned it and looked at her. Euphemia picked it up and stroked it. It hung limp in her grasp and then very slowly coiled itself round her wrist.

'I will give him to Arnoulde,' she said. 'Do you think he will like him? Why did you not come to me, you idle, false creature? Do you not know who I am? That I am your friend?' She put the snake into her pocket, and buttoned the flap. The other vipers were nuzzling at her foot, rubbing their soft throats against it. 'Go quickly,' Euphemia said, bending and touching them each in turn, 'hurry to your safe places, or the men will kill you.' The tongues flickered, the tiny mouths opening and shutting, the jewelled eyes unblinking. She picked them up in a writhing cluster and held their heads against her mouth, breathing on them. Hester felt sickened with horror, and yet could not look away.

'Greet them,' Euphemia said, 'stroke them.'

Hester backed until her shoulders touched the mud plaster and rough branches of the wall, the curve of the roof forcing her to bend her head forward. Euphemia held out the handful of coiling death towards her. So close that the poison spittle from the adders' mouths made drops of spray against her face.

'Big strong Madame Estairre,' Euphemia said mockingly. 'And little, little snakes. They would be your friends if you would let them.'

She was alone in the hut. The dish of dirty milk lay on the floor. Out in the sunlight Euphemia was talking to the guides, who had been tied to a tree. She knelt down between them and took their feet one by one into her lap. Two hours later, when the soldiers had finished searching the brigand village, the two men were standing up, quite easily, seemingly without feeling any pain. The four Commandants discussed burning the huts. They had found almost nothing in them. Only a pile of half-shaped musket stocks, some iron moulds for bullets, grinding stones for flour, and a few handfuls of spilled grain. A pulse made of leaves in a wooden tub, as if it was there to eke out the grain for bread; oak and beech, and young sweet chestnut leaves, and hazel. And what looked at first like glass beads, scattered from a broken necklace. They were the small, almost transparent bulbs of spring flowers, bluebell and wild garlic. Did they eat such things? Roots and leaves? She took up a handful of the bulbs, cold and greasy against her fingertips. To feed pregnant women? Men, who must fight to keep them safe? Children?

'If we burn the huts,' Commandant Piré said, 'they'll want revenge. We won't get out of this forest alive.'

It was already twilight. Among the trees it would be dark. The other commandants agreed, and they led their thousand men away.

'The guides,' one of the commandants said. 'At least we can hang them.' But the two peasants had gone, no one knew how or when. Euphemia had taken a fife from one of the soldiers and she played tunes on it as they retreated through the forest. 'Mahlbrouk,' and 'Auprès de ma blonde', and then strange tunes that made the flesh creep, until the Commandant Piré cuffed her across the side of her head and ordered her to stop.

'My love,' Euphemia said. That night Hester heard the Commandant screaming in a nightmare.

'Take it away from me! Take it away! The snake! The snake!'

When she brought in his breakfast coffee, and Euphemia's, the Commandant lay hollow-eyed and grey-faced, even his stomach seeming to have collapsed.

'What the Hell did you and that other bitch give me to eat last night? I'll have the skin off your backs. I've had such dreams all night.'

'Quiet, my precious,' Euphemia said, rubbing her cheek against his belly, coiling about him. 'Drink your nice coffee.'

'Curse this bloody Vendée. Even the wine's poison, it lies on my guts. Where the hell is Creuzot? He's been gone more than a week. Lying in a soft bed somewhere with that fat trollop of a *ci-devant*, and eating decent food, while I'm living like a pig and being poisoned on top of it. Come here, you English bitch.'

He made her kneel while he drank his coffee, and flung the

dregs over her. Euphemia lay between his fat thighs, playing with the hairs of his stomach. And suddenly, from under his limp sex the black viper pushed up its broad, flat head, began to writhe onto his groin, onto the grey white mound of his belly, rustling, whispering. The Commandant felt the movement, the strangeness of it, unlike Euphemia's hand. Heaved himself up to see what it was, and screamed.

Men came running, sentries, orderlies. Searched the bed, when the Commandant could tell them what they must search for, his breath gasping, his colour like rancid mutton fat. Searched the floor of the tent. Nothing there. The Commandant standing beside the bed, in his heavy, shaking nakedness.

'You saw it!' he shouted at Hester, at Euphemia. 'It was real, curse you! Didn't you see it, the snake, a black snake?'

'I saw nothing,' Euphemia said. 'What was it like?' Laughing at him. The Commandant lifted his fist to hit her. Turned on Hester. 'You, you whore, didn't you see it?'

'I saw nothing that Euphemia didn't see.'

'You're playing tricks! I'll have you flogged! Take her away! Tie her to a tree and let her wait till I'm dressed. Flogged? I'll have you hanged, you bitch! It was you let those spies escape yesterday, damn you for a brigand whore! Fetch me a rope someone! A rope!'

Men came running, brought a rope, noosed it. The noose round her throat, rough and unyielding against skin. Like the boy yesterday. She knelt quietly, waiting for the noose to tighten. She was not even afraid. Now it has come, she thought, and almost welcomed it, like something she had known for a long time must happen.

She wondered if she would find Michel, and began to be afraid of that. God have mercy on me, she thought. Let there be nothing. Only to lie down and rest. And thought then of her father, and was suddenly and piercingly afraid. Wanted to cry out, 'My father, my father! What will you do with him? What will happen to him without me?'

The noose tightening, a soldier beginning to drag her to her feet.

Euphemia coiled herself against the Commandant's legs, caressing his great bulge of stomach with her thin black hands.

'Arnoulde, my love! It was nothing, a shadow, you were

thinking of your bad dream, there was nothing there. Send the men away, let your Euphemia make you comfortable again. You got too hot riding yesterday, that is all. You should spare yourself for your poor slave.'

He allowed himself to be quietened. The men freed Hester. Were dismissed. The incident was over. As if nothing had happened. The Commandant laughing, lying back on the heaped pillows while Euphemia stroked his gross white belly, winding its long black hairs around her fingers. Hester fetched more coffee, and rolls and honey, and had to kneel again while the Commandant fed himself and Euphemia with alternate honey-dripping lumps of bread. Letting the honey run into Euphemia's navel, onto her purple nipples.

An hour later the Citizen Creuzot came back. Fifty dragoons escorting two heavy coaches. Léonie with him and a young man dressed with a cold, Parisian elegance. Sky-blue satin coat. Snow-white cravat. A vision from the Tuileries, or the Palais-Royal. Using a gold lorgnon to survey the camp.

'Where is the Commandant?' the boy said, lisping slightly. 'Have him fetched.'

The Commandant Piré came limping forward, staring at this infant popinjay.

'Stand where you are,' the boy said. 'Arrest him.'

'Arrest——?'

Six of the dragoons had already dismounted. They moved forward and surrounded the Commandant.

'Creuzot, damn your soul! What is this? A joke? By God I'll——'

'He is an emissary from the Citizen Robespierre,' Creuzot said. He wiped his mouth with a corner of his lace handkerchief. 'Those are two of the women I told you of, citizen. The black one and the tall one. And there is another somewhere, a peasant girl. And two men.' He beckoned a soldier. 'Find the other prisoners, you know the ones. The priest, and the Englishman, and the girl who cooks. Put them in that coach.'

Euphemia and Hester surrounded. Hester stood open-mouthed. Looked at Euphemia. Euphemia smiled. Looked away. The Commandant had begun to rave.

'Silence him,' the boy said in his cold, exact, whispering voice. And then, coming close in front of the Commandant, who stood

[252]

with his hands twisted behind his back, a soldier's rag of neck cloth stuffed into his mouth for a gag, 'Animal. Traitor. Royalist.'

At the word 'Royalist' the Commandant heaved against his captors, seemed on the point of breaking free. More men held him. Soldiers from all over the camp had run towards the scene, were forming a wide, deep circle of astonishment. Robespierre's name whispered among them. The dragoons, most of them still mounted, formed a guard, a phalanx round the Citizen Creuzot, and Léonie, and the young man, and the prisoners.

The Commandant grunted like a wild beast behind his gag, now struggling, now limp with shock, and then struggling again.

'You'll need to chain him,' the Citizen Creuzot said. 'I doubt if the others will require it.'

Chains were brought, manacles and leg-irons. The Commandant was lifted into the first coach like a sack of corn. Hester and Euphemia and Perrine pushed in with him. Out of the side window Hester could see her father and the abbé Bernard getting into the other coach.

Euphemia leaned forward and patted the Commandant's cheek, his mouth no longer gagged. 'Royalist!' she said. 'How you have deceived me!'

He roared so loud that the dragoons gagged him again.

Chapter 25

The Convent of the Ursulines, become a prison. The weeks
dragging by. July now. As if they had been forgotten. She and her
father. Perrine. The abbé. No news of Léonie, or Euphemia, or of
the Citizen Creuzot, or the Commandant. No news of anything.
Only the prison rumours, the lists read out each day for the
Tribunal, for the guillotine. The daily meeting with her father
and the abbé Bernard, at the common meal in the courtyard,
which was the only meal of the day. Thin soup, and bread, and
sometimes a piece of meat that she gave to her father. Walking
with him beside the fountain in the courtyard where the women
who still had a change of linen washed it every morning, trying to
keep clean.

'What is this place, Hester? I wish we could go home, my dear.'

'We shall go home very soon, I am sure of it.'

He said the same thing every day, almost as soon as he and the
abbé came into the courtyard, with the other men. Until there
was one day that instead of coming slowly towards her, leaning
on the abbé's arm, he came almost hurrying, his face quite
altered.

'There is news! News!' And then looked at the abbé and the
other man as if he had forgotten what news it was that he was
bringing.

She thought, I am sent for, I am to go today to be tried. And
against every expectation that she had had she felt a shock of fear,
as she got up from her place to meet them. Like cold, an icy
shivering of the skin, at the nape of her neck, and had to clench
her fists to regain her courage and smile, and say, 'Tell me.'

It was the abbé who began to tell her. 'My dear,' he said,
feeling for her arm, 'your husband——'

She felt herself sinking down, fainting, as she had not fainted since she was a child. Dizzy with hunger, and the vile air. 'Michel?' Half expected to see him there, and then to hear details of his death. But she knew that he was alive, thought that she had known it always. Had never believed that he was dead. 'Michel!' And fell against the stone side of the fountain.

Perrine bathing her face.

'What has happened?' Father Bernard was crying, staring round him at the shadows that were all that he could see. The man who had come into the courtyard with him knelt down beside Hester.

'Your husband is alive, madame, he is with Charette. I saw him three weeks ago. In the forest of Grasla, they are living there.'

'Does he—know that I am alive?'

'I can't tell you, madame. I saw him only as I was being given a message to bring to Paris, and someone told me his name. And when I was arrested and brought here yesterday I was put with your father and this priest, and they told me of you. But at least I can bring you that much news. Let me give you my arm. We should have prepared you better.'

'I'm all right. I promise you. You are very kind, monsieur. Please go to the table, or you will get nothing to eat. One of my friends will bring me something to my cell. Please.'

She went up the stairs slowly, supporting herself against the wall. One of the turnkeys shouted at her, but she took no notice. The cell. Forcing herself to climb up into her bunk. Lie still. He is alive. She put her hands over her face. I must be glad, she thought. It would be monstrous if I was not glad. As if tomorrow he would be brought here himself, and she must face him. Tell him at last. Take me first, she whispered behind her hands. Let it be finished. She fell asleep, and dreamed he was there beside her, lying with her in the dark.

'My love,' he said. 'My loyal, loyal love.'

The next day there was other news.

'Creuzot has been proscribed,' one of the Republicans was saying. Reading aloud from a smuggled newspaper. 'And they are hunting for Fouché, for a dozen more.'

'The tiger-cat is getting ready to spring again,' someone else said. 'Let them destroy each other!'

'The Representative Creuzot?' Hester asked. 'He has been arrested?'

No one answered her. All the Republicans crowding round the man with the Gazette, passionate, starving for a breath of political air, for news of comrades and enemies, of Robespierre the tiger and where he would strike next. Names shouted. 'Barras? Tallien? Collot d'Herbois? Bourdon? Fréron?' While on the other side of the fountain the aristocrats walked arm-in-arm making their jokes, their salon repartees, gossiping in the stifling July heat of the courtyard as if yesterday a dozen from this courtyard alone had not been taken to feed the guillotine, and today, any moment now, a dozen more would be called. The turnkey with his daily list and his hoarse shouting was late this afternoon, and the trestle table for the common meal was already dismantled and being carried away.

She heard him beginning his call-over of names. 'Mercier, André, *ci-devant*. Citizeness Vignaud, Sophie——'

The tightening of nerves that she could not help, each day that he began calling. As if in spite of herself she still longed to live. In spite of everything. A week ago she had heard that Madame de la Rochefoucauld was dead, with Thomazeau. Betrayed and taken, and shot on the sand dunes of Sables d'Olonne. They said she had begged for mercy, gone down on her knees to her executioners, offering herself to anyone if they'd only spare her. Was it true? After all that magnificence?

How will I come to it in the end, she wondered. Not like a battle. To ride in a cart with one's hands bound, and the mob jeering. To stand waiting. Lie down on the plank. Would she be afraid? Show it? Sometimes she prayed to be made strong. And sometimes was ashamed that she needed to pray for such a thing, after seeing so much death. She never prayed to be spared.

One of the turnkeys had said to her, 'When your turn comes, tell 'em you're pregnant. They won't top you then. And as for getting that way—the cell up the end there's empty and I've got a bit of time to spare.' Drawing down his eyelid with a dirty finger-tip. Winking. It had seemed only an ugly joke at the time. She had even smiled at it; at the turnkey Antoine who made it. He meant it kindly, after his fashion of kindness.

But the thought stayed with her, as if—as if she and Michel had—and the child had joined her dreams.

there? But there was no sign of him. And already the last prisoners were seated, made to stand, seated again. A thin, pallid man hurrying into the well of the court, a long paper in one hand, a reading-glass in the other. Rattling of papers from the table, more men entering. Judges? Tricolour sashes, red bonnets, tricolour cockades. All sitting, except the pallid man, in his long black coat, his greasy black hat.

'Citizen judges, citizens of the jury,' he began, in a thin, brittle voice. 'You see before you more sweepings from the infamous Foreign Conspiracy conjured by the arch-villain de Batz, and paid for with English gold. I need not tell you your duty. It is to crush conspiracy as you would crush a snake. You love the Republic. You love the Revolution. You are good *sans-culottes*. These vermin have plotted and acted against all of us. They planned to murder all of us. Such creatures must not be left alive to sully the earth.'

He rustled the paper in his hand, coughed, looked about him. He seemed ill at ease, and spoke as if only half his mind was on what he said. 'Citizen judges, there are six witnesses for the prosecution. They will tell you that of their own knowledge these prisoners are guilty. I call the witnesses.'

Six men shuffling into the court, or rather five shuffling, and one waddling, stamping, his eyes bulging, his face scarlet. The Commandant Piré.

Hester stared at him, scarcely believing what she saw, thinking it must be someone like him, or that he was somehow mistakenly among the witnesses for a moment, instead of on the prisoner-benches. And as she stared, the evidence was already being taken. A slouching man whose mouth twitched as he talked was saying something incomprehensible. Pointing to this and that prisoner. Dates, names. Sometimes he came to a halt and had to be prompted, like a stupid scholar who has learned his lesson very ill. He sat down, and one of the others was questioned. None of the names meant anything to Hester.

'—told me he planned to murder all the members of the Convention. He said he was given fifty louis in gold. They was foreign coins which I saw in his possession.'

One of the prisoners, no one Hester knew, stood up and shouted, 'The fool is lying, prosecutor, can you not see that? He does not even know that a louis is a French coin!'

'Make the accused sit down!'

'I protest! In the name of Justice!'

'Silence that man!'

'Commandant Piré. Give your evidence. Do you know any of the accused?'

'Aye, curse their filthy souls! That one, and that one, and that one, and that one—and those two women, that black one! Guillotine the bitches! I wish I'd shot 'em when I first saw them.'

'Did you discover them to be conspiring against the Republic?'

'Yes, every one of the cursed swine. I'd like——'

'Did they tell you they were directed in their criminal acts by foreign agents?'

'Every one of 'em!'

The Commandant made to sit, looking furiously surprised, as if he wished to say more and thought that someone might escape justice because of his being silenced. Another witness. Another interruption, from a prisoner who shouted, 'He is lying like the filthy spy he is. He never saw me there, I have never been in Clichy in my life, I come from Chartres, I was in Paris for a day——' He too was silenced. The last of the witnesses rattled off his evidence, or his lesson. The Prosecutor turned to the prisoners, held up his list to the light from a high window. In that place it was as grey as winter, although the heat was terrible.

'The Citizeness Creuzot, did you conspire with the *ci-devant* Baron de Batz against the Republic?'

'I implore you, citizen——'

'Answer the question! Yes or no?'

'No no *Nooooo*!' Trying to fling herself forward at the prosecutor's feet. Her manacle, and a guard's reaching hand, held her back. She was forced down beside Euphemia, weeping.

The same question, forty-six more times. Hester. Perrine. Euphemia. The abbé. Hester's father not answering until the guard shook him, and then bellowed on his behalf, 'He says he's guilty, the scum.'

The last name. The paper folded.

'Take them away. Citizen jurors, do your duty.'

They were taken into a large, empty room. Kept from talking to one another. Hester said to her guard. 'When does the defence begin?'

'Defence?' the man said, looking amazed. 'What defence? You're going to get the verdict now. About five more minutes, I reckon.'

She was glad of that. What defence could she have made, except for her father? And they would not have listened to it. It would be over the quicker. A voice shouting, 'The prisoners, bring the prisoners.' Filing back to their benches. The jurors entering. The names called again.

'The Citizeness Creuzot. What is your verdict?'

'Guilty.'

'*Noooooo!*'

Forty-eight times over, guilty, guilty, guilty. And then the sentences. All of death. It took a quarter of an hour from the first call of 'Guilty' to the last death sentence of the forty-eight.

'Take them away. Justice has been done. Long live the Republic.'

Forty-eight of them crammed into a corridor, sitting on long benches, waiting, like passengers for a coach. At the far end a group of men with shears and ropes, hacking off the women's hair, binding their arms, shearing away the necks of their dresses if they were too high. The ropes still bloody from yesterday. Piles of hair falling on the dirty stones, kicked aside. Binding the abbé's arms behind his back. Mr. Broadhurst's. There was shouting outside. Uproar. A man being carried through the narrow doorway, his face bandaged, blood streaming.

Someone called out, 'It's Robespierre! Robespierre's been arrested!' Others shouting, 'Make way. Make way for the Citizen Representative Barras.'

A tall, handsome man, booted and spurred, fist on sword hilt, striding in, looking at the prisoners. 'Halt all executions,' he said. 'Halt all trials in process. In the name of the Convention. Clear these people away, take them below. Prepare for the trial of the tyrant Robespierre and his accomplices. Nothing else is to be done here today. Where is the Citizen Prosecutor?'

They heard his voice bellowing up the stone stairs, echoing and fading. His staff following him, clatter of iron-nailed boots, of sword scabbards striking stone. 'Citizen Prosecutor!'

The executioner and his valets staring, shears and bloody cords in their hands, questioning one another. The same voices, the same ring of boots and steel returning. 'Take them below, damn you! Clear this place. I hold all powers from the Convention.' He disappeared as he had come.

They were taken below and put twelve together into cells. In the cell next to hers, Hester could hear Robespierre groaning in agony. After an hour or so men came and carried him away.

Chapter 26

They came back to their own prison of the Ursulines like a resurrection. Unbelieving faces, hands touching them as if they might be ghosts. Going to lie down at last. She did not know what she thought. What she felt.

Nothing. Almost nothing. Drained of everything.

The turnkey Antoine brought them some soup, almost showing himself pleased they were still alive. 'You missed your dinners. I brought you some from ours. And some bread.'

The church bells ringing, and far away, very faint, drums. 'They're taking the tyrant off to the little window, the Devil keep him. And his filthy crew with him.'

That evening the courtyard was full of it, full of these different deaths. Robespierre. St. Just. Hanriot the drunken monster. Couthon the cripple. More than twenty of them. And the crowd had screamed at them as once it had screamed at Danton, at the Widow Capet, at all the others. 'Kill them, kill them.' More blood.

The killings went on for days, and the rumours, the news now, not rumours any longer, came to them by the turnkeys, and then by the Gazette, brought in openly. The prison spies, the *moutons* who had once been all-powerful, who had denounced their fellow-prisoners to save their own lives, were denounced in their turn, and taken away and killed.

Days going by and weeks. The end of August. September. October. The prison emptying only to be refilled with the enemies of the new régime. Terrorists. Montagnards. Jacobins. What had changed? Except that the guillotine had grown lazier, and then grown still.

She did not wonder why she was still in prison. She lived as if she was asleep, thinking of Michel, and afraid to think of him. Of what would happen. If—walking round the courtyard with Perrine. Day after day.

Someone calling her name. 'The Citizeness Vernet?' Two men dressed in civilian clothes, but with the air of soldiers about them, or of policemen who had once been soldiers. Antoine with them, pointing her out.

It is my release, she thought, and felt a second of panic, of wanting to say 'No!'

But they did not tell her she was released. They did not manacle her, but they brought her out of the prison between them as if she was still a prisoner, and put her into a closed *fiacre*, sitting one beside her, one facing her, saying nothing. And she asked nothing, sitting in her man's clothing that had become rags. It was already evening, November twilight. Almost dark. Streets. People. Not many. An atmosphere of hunger, a slowing down of life. They passed long queues of silent women outside the bread shops and the stalls that sold horsemeat. Across the river. The Champs-Elysées. A gateway, wrought iron gates drawn back, a gatekeeper smoking a pipe. The two men got down and one of them offered to help her as she got down herself. She ignored his hand.

A manservant opening a door. Lamplight. 'We have brought the Citizeness Vernet,' one of the policemen said. If that was what he was. 'Go inside, citizeness.'

The two men stayed outside with the *fiacre* and its driver. The manservant beckoning. And behind him Euphemia. Dressed as she had used to be dressed, in crimson silk. A gold chain round her throat, shaped like a serpent, heavy, massive gold, its eyes made of rubies. Gold bracelets. Gold anklets. Her feet in velvet embroidered slippers. A crimson silk scarf wound round her head, hiding her crisp, Negress hair. Gold ear-rings. She flashed and glistened as she moved forward in the lamplight.

'Madame Estairre!' Bending her mocking black head in greeting. She led the way up a pretty staircase. There were wall panels of painted silk, and bronze statues in two small alcoves, holding the lamps that lit the stairs.

'My mistress is waiting for you,' Euphemia breathed. 'And the Citizen Barras.'

As she said Barras' name the pride, the sense of triumph

[264]

glowed in her voice like fire. 'It is done!' she whispered. 'She will rule as I knew she would, she already rules!'

She opened a door that was silk panelled like the walls. Warmth and perfume as she opened it. The room inside dazzling to prison eyes. Léonie lying on a couch. A tall man sitting on a chair beside her, getting up as Hester was brought in. Barras.

'Madame Vernet! What a pleasure!'

Léonie holding out her soft, jewelled hand. Gold hair tumbling, silk and fur and satin. A satin cloak edged with white ermine fur, thrown back to show her bosom. Muslin gown clinging to her, a silk shift hiding nothing, moulding her hips. Roman sandals with gold pegs, gold laces.

'Hester! My dear!' Making a mouth that was almost reproachful, as if Hester had been neglecting her. 'You are here at last!' And turning to Barras. 'Did you ever see anyone so tall?' She caressed his arm as she said it. Barras bent over Hester's hand.

'Madame's reputation goes before her.'

Euphemia knelt down beside her mistress, on a black velvet cushion bound with gold thread. Léonie's other hand played with the gold snake round Euphemia's neck.

'Why have I been brought here?' Hester said. She was conscious of her prison smell.

'I have a mission for you,' Barras said. 'The pleasantest of missions for a lady, surely? To bring peace? I want you to go to Charette and make our peace with him.'

The manservant had brought in a silver tray. There was already a table set in the window alcove of the room.

'But before we talk of business, let us have something to eat and drink? Ma chère?' Giving Léonie his hand. Bowing to Hester, offering her his arm. 'I have a partiality for champagne myself. I hope you share it. Madame Creuzot has acquired some exceptional vintages in this last week or two.'

The manservant taking a magnum from a silver bucket, pouring. Crystal champagne glasses, tall and slender as flowers. Silver. Linen. Euphemia knelt at Léonie's side, holding the silver dishes for her, and then for Hester. She did not know what she was eating. She had forgotten what good meat tasted like, and fine white bread, and fresh cheese, and fruit. Before the meal was half ended she felt sick. The heat of the fire. The scent. The food. The champagne. She wanted only to be taken back to her cell.

[265]

'You will leave tonight' Barras said. 'If that is agreeable to you? It will be best if you travel at night, at least until you are well clear of Paris. To your health, madame. And your success.'

Chapter 27

They released her at the edge of the forest. Almost where she had entered it with the Commandant, and the Republican columns. They had brought her by coach from Paris, dressed as she was, still ragged. Keeping her out of sight at the inns where they stopped for food, or a change of horses.

'I trust your parole, citizeness,' Barras had said. 'But accidents happen, circumstances arise. I would not wish your poor father to suffer because of such things. Nor your friends.'

The two men repeated the warning now. 'Remember, citizeness. You are on parole. We will return here tomorrow for your first answer, that you have made contact. And to learn how long you will need. It must not be very long.'

Barras had said that too. The Convention needed peace in the west if it was to survive, and quickly. It would pay a great price for it, if it must. The greatest price. It would even pay with the young King. And freedom for the priests, for the churches. Everything could be discussed. Only peace first. A secret, unannounced truce. Then peace. Then payment.

'Tell Charette he has my promise as a gentleman that I mean all I say.' The swarthy face, the cat's eyes looking into hers as if they wished to mesmerize her into believing him. 'Bring me back his equal promise, and negotiations can begin within weeks, almost within days. We can have peace by the New Year.'

'And my father? My friends?'

'You shall have freedom for all of them. And yourself. And of course your husband.'

'I do not know if he is still alive.'

'We will pray that he is.' He had looked almost as if he would pray for it. And now——

She stood at the forest's edge while the coach drove away. Acorns and beech mast underfoot, wet leaves. She smelled the rain that had been falling, smelled the wet branches, the November buds that seem to believe November is already spring. The sky hidden by the oak branches overhead. A grey twilight of afternoon, grey-green. Quietness.

She walked for a quarter of an hour before they stopped her. Two men with pistols stepping out from behind trees. 'Who goes there?'

'I am Madame Vernet,' she said. 'Wife to Michel Vernet if you know him. I have been released on parole to bring a message to the General-in-Chief Charette.'

The two men stared at her, one of them slowly lowering the barrel of his pistol.

'Madame Vernet?' he said, his voice unbelieving, and then believing, shouting. 'Madame Vernet! You are still alive! They told us you were dead, you were guillotined the day the tyrant fell: *It is Madame Vernet! It is the Chevalier come back!*'

He ran and embraced her and she stared at him in astonishment.

'Don't you recognize me? Don't you remember? You ran by my stirrup when we took Cholet. Don't you remember me?'

She had to pretend that she did, and hold him to her and allow herself to be held, to be put at arm's length and looked at, stared up and down like a ghost, like a new Lazarus. 'You are alive! The colonel—your husband—Colonel Vernet——'

'He is here?'

'He is, he is! Oh what will he do at such news? Run, Pierre, run, run—no, I will go, you stay. Oh Madame! Chevalier! Madame!'

If she could have, she would have run away. Instead they brought her to Michel.

Let me love him as I should, she prayed. Please, God, please I beg of you, unfasten my heart. And as she saw him in the distance, among the trees, saw him turn to look towards her, uncertain at first, unbelieving, she felt her legs growing weak, beginning to tremble, so that she was afraid she would fall, would have to stand still, lean against the nearest tree trunk to support herself.

Michel.

He was coming with swift, long strides, breaking into a run, his face still unbelieving, calling out something to her that she could not hear, could not understand.

'Michel,' she whispered. And he had taken her by the arms, he too was holding her at arm's length from him, staring, laughing like a madman, and then holding her close, and at arm's length again, shaking her in his disbelief and joy. Holding her against him.

'We—we heard you were dead.'

She kept her face hidden, her cheek resting against his. I must tell him, she thought. While men surrounded them, stared at her, laughed with the joy of men who have seen ten thousand deaths and so few resurrections.

'And I—' she said, 'I thought that you——' She wanted to laugh and to cry, to stay holding him and to run away. She would have given her soul for Talmond never to have existed, that stupid, stupid, cruel betrayal never to have happened.

'But how are you here—when—what has happened?' He held her at arm's length again, looking at her thinness, her cropped hair, her rags. Everyone coming close, wanting to touch her as though to make sure that she was real. Others running towards them, calling, 'It is the Chevalier, the Chevalier has come back, she is alive!'

Women coming, and among them one that she recognized, tall and thin as herself. Regrenille. And at the sight of her, her small, fierce head with its crown of curls, her long stride, her look of surprised arrogance that hid her humility, Hester felt her knees truly giving way, and had to hold tight to Michel to prevent herself from falling. All the battles, all the memories coming back, surrounding her, deafening her. '*Rembarre! Rembarre!*' And the thundering of horses charging, Anne Guerry, Perrine Loiseau, the Countess de la Rochefoucauld. All the women. All the men. All the long march to the sea, and the terrible return. Savenay.

'Regrenille! You are alive too!' Each life like something holy, rescued from the Kingdom of the Dead. Unbelievable. Unimaginable joy. They clasped each other, not saying anything, and Michel and the men drew back to give them that much privacy. The two of them crying. And then other women she knew. Madame de Bulkeley, grown older, but still laughing, stout and handsome and finely dressed, as finery went at that time in that ruined forest. A white sash and a white cockade, green silk at her throat and her coat carefully mended. Gripping Hester by the shoulders, laughing with her great teeth glistening. The small, neat Madame du Fief came running, and Madeleine Tournant, and Marie Lourdais— until there were a dozen women surrounding her, laughing and crying, asking questions, and more questions again before she had time to answer anything.

[269]

Michel had to rescue her, saying that she must come to the Headquarters, to see the General-in-Chief, the Chevalier de Charette.

'Indeed I must go to him,' she said. 'That is why I am here.' In a low voice she told Michel the outline of her mission as they walked towards the village of huts in the clearing, everyone still surrounding them, following them.

'And if he does not agree?' Michel said, his stride hesitating.

'Then I must go back to Barras and tell him so.'

He stopped, turning to face her, to hold her by her arms again. 'You can't go back! Are you mad?'

'I have promised.' She freed herself from his grasp, avoiding his eyes. 'One way or the other I must go back. That was the condition.'

'But—' He stopped himself, and they went on into the clearing, and to the Headquarters, a hut not much larger, not much grander than any of the others. Except that there was a layer of cut branches making a pathway to the door of it, through the mud, and the sodden drifts of leaves that lay everywhere.

He was sitting at a table, dictating a letter, two young men taking copies, their quills racing to keep up with the General's metallic staccato of dictation. '—if this unauthorized issuing of Royalist Assignats continues——' He looked up, narrowing his eyes against the light from the doorway as they came in.

"It is Madame Vernet, my wife, General. She has come from Paris, from Barras, and the Convention. Released from prison to bring a message to you.'

The General sat very quiet for a moment, his eyes still narrowed. He had laid his great plumed hat on the table beside him, his head bound round with a white scarf, and the buttons of his coat undone. He smoothed a knuckle along the thin, curving line of his moustaches, stood up slowly, unsmiling. In his elegance, his magnificence of uniform, he was unchanged from when she had last seen him, as if only a minute ago he had stepped out of Monsieur Boetz's shop in Nantes. His coat a soft splendour of green and gold; of crimson facings; high silk cravat like white foam on a wave; gold-fringed sword belt; gold-mounted pistol thrust into it like a challenge. How he kept himself so immaculate in that forest, in that swift, sudden warfare, only he and his women knew. She had heard stories of women risking their lives a dozen times to bring him a

[270]

length of silk from Nantes, to fetch him a new coat from Chez Boetz, or a pair of the long, soft leather gaiters that he always wore in preference to high boots.

And his face, and his eyes; like a great cat. As her own eyes adjusted to the shadows of the hut she thought she recognized something more recently familiar about him, as if she had seen his likeness only a short time ago. And thought, Barras! He has the same eyes as Barras. The same cat smile, cruel and self-absorbed. And thought in the next instant how unjust that was, to compare this stainless man to Barras, the butcher of Toulon and Lyon. Perhaps only men with such eyes could ever achieve power, for good or evil.

He was offering conventional greetings, expressions of pleasure at once again meeting someone of such a magic reputation. She answered him as best she could, stammering with embarrassment, and then almost harshly breaking off, and beginning her embassy.

Charette held up a hand to prevent her continuing, and made a gesture for the two secretaries, and the others who had followed Hester and Michel into the hut, to leave them. Michel turned to go.

'You stay with us, Colonel. Close the door.' He pointed to a bench for them to draw close to the table, and sat down himself. 'Now.'

She gave him Barras' message, and proposals, and promises, and he listened without a word of interruption, his elbow on the table, chin resting on his fist, his eyes fixed on hers, narrowed and intent. His face had aged twenty years in the year and a half since she had seen him last. He could not be much above thirty, as young as, younger than Michel, but he looked fifty, his features carved out of grey stone now that he was no longer smiling and vivid with movement. She had imagined this moment a dozen times as she travelled with her taciturn companions on the road from Paris. Imagined it utterly different. A group of men listening, growing more and more joyful as they realized that it was peace that she was bringing to them. An end to killing, and end to hatred and war and burning and destruction. She had imagined someone shouting, 'Peace! Peace at last!' and had nursed that picture closer and closer to her heart as she came nearer to Grasla, and to her meeting with Michel, and—she wanted now to turn and look at him, to see what he was thinking. Surely he——

But Charette held her eyes and she could not look away from

him. 'He gives you his word as a nobleman that he will keep all the conditions he has told me to offer you.' Her voice dying away. Silence. The noise of laughter outside, talk and movement. Inside the hut, nothing. Charette sitting still as a cat watching a bird on a branch. Not a sign of what he was thinking.

'His word as a nobleman?' he said at last expressionless.

'Yes.'

He laughed then, sharp as metal striking metal, the laughter ending as suddenly. 'That bloodstained assassin? A nobleman?'

She felt irrationally angry. 'I am to say one thing more,' she said coldly. 'Everything can be discussed. Everything.' Barras had told her not to speak of the King until Charette did.

'And if I want to discuss nothing?'

'Then I go back to Paris as I came. And tell Monsieur Barras what you have said.'

He did not protest at that as Michel had done. Did not even nod in acceptance. He continued to look at her, his fingers slowly fondling his chin, and then moving up his cheek to smooth his long sidewhiskers and at last to pull gently at the big gold ear-ring that the wore in his right ear, a memento of his years at sea. 'Everything?' he said at last.

'Everything.'

He stood up violently, pushing the table away. 'That jackal! How dare he offer us peace! After the Vendée has been destroyed! Do you know how many dead there are? How few are still alive? You could not count the dead! And he sends you to talk peace, now?' He strode up and down the narrow space behind the table, his hand grasping at the butt of his pistol, half pulling it from his sword belt, and forcing it home. 'It's no more than a trick to weaken us. Tell him we shall never weaken. Tell him when this began I swore on my sword that I would not stop fighting until we had a King again.' He drove his fist into the palm of his other hand. 'Have you spoken of this outside?' He jerked his head towards the door.

'No. Are you afraid that I might?' She did not know why she said that, except that she was angry, and scarcely knew why she was. Had he not the right to say what he was saying?

Beside her Michel said, 'Perhaps Barras' *everything* includes the King? Does it?'

Charette stopped his pacing and swung round on her.

'Yes,' she said.

After what seemed a long time Charette sat down again. 'I don't believe you.'

She felt too tired to argue or persuade, or insist. She spread her hands, and shrugged.

'He cannot mean it,' Charette said. 'They could not dare release him.' And then, 'Is he even alive? Have you seen him?' He leaned across the table and gripped her arm. 'Have you?'

She shook her head, and Charette leaned back on his bench, almost triumphantly. 'I thought not. After Robespierre fell there was a story the King had escaped, had been smuggled out of the Temple. Another story was that he was dead already.'

'He is still there,' she said.

'How do you know?'

There was no answer to that and she shrugged again.

'Would Barras send him to me? Send the King?'

'Everything can be discussed,' she repeated. 'Everything.'

'I don't believe it!' But this time he said it like a man who wants to be contradicted, is ready to contradict himself. 'You, Vernet? Do you think——?'

'I think they're as tired of fighting as we are,' Michel said.

'There are bread queues in Paris,' Hester said. 'And no bread. No meat. No candles. Nothing. I beg you to believe him. Why should he not send you the King?'

'Because the King is the one card he has. Once he's played it he has empty hands. And he offers freedom for our priests? And the Church?'

'Yes.'

'And for the *émigrés* to return? Here in the Vendée?'

'Yes.'

'And the guarantees?'

'I tell you he means what he says.'

'Suppose he does. The Girondins wanted to treat with us, and they're all dead now. And Danton, the Hébert, and Chaumette, and Robespierre. How long will Barras last?'

She had not thought of that. There had seemed to be such an air of permanence about that small, luxurious room where Léonie played hostess, and Barras drank champagne out of a duke's crystal goblet.

'And they would release my sister?'

'Immediately you begin talks.'

He stood up like the spring blade of a knife snapping open. 'We'll talk again in the morning,' he said. 'Now to welcome you not as a messenger from those damned villains, but as a comrade in arms.' He went to the door and threw it wide. 'Wine!' he shouted, 'fetch wine and food for Madame Vernet. And for me, I'm starving. Tonight we dance, eh, Vernet? A ball in honour of your wife. Send out word'—he shouted again—'that we dance tonight. I want every girl in reach to be here without fail, dressed in her finest. Marie! Madeleine! Madame Elizabeth! You three make the arrangements. We'll begin at moonrise and may we be ashamed of ourselves if we end before sunrise. Where's my wine?'

Madeleine Tournant brought it, running, the bottle clutched to her thin chest, her face alight with joy to be doing anything for her General, her master, even to fetch wine for another woman to drink.

'A ball?' Hester said. All she wanted to do was to lie down and sleep.

'You and I shall open it,' Charette said. 'Have they forgotten how to dance in Paris?'

'I don't know. We didn't dance in the prison, and I've not seen much else of Paris.'

The glasses came, and they drank to one another, and to the King, and victory. Not to peace, until she suggested it.

'Ah,' Charette said. 'Of course. Peace. Why not?' But he made a perfunctory thing of it.

He dismissed them then, calling for his secretaries to come back, and for messengers. She guessed that he meant to send out word to the other Royalist leaders, to tell them the news she had brought, and summon them to discuss it with him. She and Michel freed themselves from the press of well-wishers still wanting to greet her and overwhelm her with questions.

'Tonight,' Michel said. 'Later. Give a husband a chance to greet his wife first.' She would have kept the others round her like a protection. She felt herself beginning to shiver again, her knees to tremble with that weakness of nerves. How long had she been thinking of this moment, and dreading it? And she was still no nearer to knowing how to face it. What a coward I am become, she thought savagely, and wanted to hold his arm to steady herself, and dare not touch him. He touched her instead, putting his arm through hers, and she allowed herself to lean against him.

[274]

'I've ten thousand things to ask you,' he said, when they were alone among the trees. 'Are you too tired to walk?'

'No.' She waited for him to say something and when he said nothing tried to find words to begin what she must tell. And could think of nothing but his name. 'Michel——'

They were away from the clearing now, hidden from anyone in the village who might have been looking towards them. He stopped, and took her face between his hands. He is going to kiss me, she thought, and became terrified of letting him kiss her before she had told him. And when she had told—he would not want—and she—?

'No!' she said. She put up her hand between their two mouths. 'I must tell you something. I don't know how to, but—'

'There's nothing you need to tell me.'

'Nothing? You—know?'

He put her hand away from his mouth, and held it imprisoned. 'He is dead. And he died as a prince should, which very few princes do. What do either of us need to say about him, except God rest his soul?'

'But——'

'I want to tell you something,' he said, 'and then you can tell me anything you like. I've a confession to make.'

'A——?'

He closed her lips with her own fingers, pressing them against her mouth. 'Let's walk,' he said. 'These trees remind me of America, of the forests there. D'you remember asking me once about—Red Indian women? And if—'

'I remember,' she whispered.

'There was one,' he said. And then, laughing slightly, 'more than one, but—one that—was more than the others.' He said nothing else for a long time, and she began to feel the cold laying itself round her like a mist. Under her shirt, against her skin, her bones. It would soon be dark. 'I'd remember her in my dreams,' he said at last. 'She had soft, soft skin. Like velvet. Pale gold. And hair that hung down below her hips. She could dress herself in her hair. Black as midnight. She used to scent it with something, I don't know what. Her whole body smelled of it. It was beautiful Am I—am I hurting you?'

'No,' she said, with dry lips.

'She loved me, I think. And—I think that I loved her. The way that you love beautiful things. I knew that in ten years she would be an old woman. That it was all insanity, but there was a time I would—I would have given my soul, just to keep her. I'd have turned Indian—anything. I was very young of course.' He smiled sadly, and touched her face. 'As young as you,' he said. 'It was a long time ago.'

She waited for him to go on.

'What—happened?' she said when he stayed silent.

'An Indian chief took her. And she went to him as if I'd never existed. I went on dreaming about her for a long time. For years. That's my confession. Are you—angry?'

She put her head down beside his, laid her forehead against his shoulder. 'And my confession?' she whispered.

'You've made it. It's stupid to tell things twice. Charette is mad to want to dance tonight. We'll freeze to death. Come and see my hut, and I'll get a rug for you and a cloak. You look as though you need to sleep.'

'Michel.'

He laid his fingers against her lips. 'D'you remember when you made me sleep? In Montaigu that time? You sat outside the door with a drawn sabre? I met a man not long ago and he was remembering that.' He drew her along with him, holding her against him. 'What we have between us,' he said, 'nothing can break. Unless we're such fools as to want to break it. God has brought you back to me. That's all that I want to know.'

Chapter 28

She had thought that she could not dance. That she had neither the heart nor strength for it. And instead she stayed dancing until six in the morning, the November stars already losing their sharpness overhead, the bonfires dying, embers, piles of crimson ashes, the last couples sinking into exhaustion in the nearby huts. She was not aware of the cold, or tiredness. It was like a victory ball, Charette leading it. Old country dances, old dances from Versailles; minuets and pavanes; wild Breton dances. And the bonfires blazing along the village street, tables set out with wine and food, the best that could be found. Rescued from burned *châteaux* and *manoirs*, from ruined villages. So much courtesy, so much gallantry, that at first she cried. As she danced with Charette, with Michel, with the other officers, with the men. She thought afterwards she must have danced with every man there, and again and again with Michel. Down the long line of partners, holding his hand high above their heads, stepping gravely, stepping swiftly. Turning to change one partner for another. Cross hands, curtsy.

Everyone in their finery. Old court dresses rescued like the wine from a burned and looted *manoir*. Fine coats brought from Nantes or Angers at the risk of death. For the King in the Temple. For the Bourbon Lilies, and the Crown. Here there were no rosaries, no Sacred Hearts, no priests. Another kind of courage, another devotion. Only to the Throne, and Charette. Charette, their second King, their talisman. He danced like a wild buck, tireless, as fiercely joyful as if he was in battle. He never rested, danced every dance, partnered every woman. Drank a glass of wine as he passed one of the long, rough tables, and went on dancing. There were violinists sheltering in the doorways of the nearest huts, playing like madmen for the country dances, swift joyous music to race the blood, and then slow and sad for the pavanes, as if there were ghosts among the dancers. In one of those slow dances she thought for a moment that she saw Madame, the Countess de la Rochefoucauld; could have sworn it was her ghost. But it was Madame de Bulkeley, laughing and splendid, her hair made black by shadows.

Even Regrenille danced, tall and awkward as a long-legged bird, a crane stepping delicately among stones. She smiled at Hester as they passed one another, bending her head to her in greeting. Does she regret the Convent, Hester wondered? The quietness and the prayers, the holiness? Charette took hold of Hester, crying out that they must dance the new dance, the waltz, that he would show it to them. And before she knew what he was doing or would do he had her grasped round the waist and was swinging her round until she was dizzy and could not breathe. His body pressed against hers, his eyes looking up into hers, those cat's eyes that possessed women as if they were conquered villages, laughing, his teeth white under the black moustache, his age fallen away again to thirty, twenty-five.

'Faster!' he shouted to the violins. 'Faster!' And swung and led her until she began to catch the rhythm of the steps, long strides and short swift steps, her feet flying, her breath catching at her ribs. As if the grey air of prison was being wrenched out of her and her lungs filled with freedom. The guillotine, and Paris, and Barras, a thousand, ten thousand miles away. There was only freedom, only the forest and the sky and the pale, sharp light of the stars and the setting moon. The waltz in her blood like singing. And they were singing, the *Chanson de Charette*, forty or fifty of the men who had no partners, beginning the song that had become famous even before she was captured; 'Quand nous sommes à Belleville, Remparts et bastions—' Beating the rhythm on their knees with their hands.

Charette spun her round a last time so that she found herself in Michel's arms, the General-in-Chief sweeping his hat off in salute to her, the white plume touching the ground, stamped flat and hard and almost polished by the dancers' feet.

She was finished, she could not dance another step. Could scarcely walk. 'I must lie down,' she said to Michel, 'or I shall fall asleep here.'

He took her away to his hut, and she fell on his bed without being able to worry about where he would sleep. He covered her with wolf and fox skins, and his cloak. She tried to protest, mumbling that he would be cold, and was already floating away, waltzing into the darkness, arms holding her, swinging her fiercely, dizzying. She danced in her dreams, but all the dancers were shadows, dead men and women. Madame de la Rochefoucauld and Thomazeau at their head; Talmond and Perrine Loiseau, Anne Guerry; a hundred, a thousand others. She cried out in her sleep, half woke, and someone was holding her, smoothing her face, whispering to her. She slept again, and was in prison, Barras hunting her among the cells and courtyards, all the other prisoners laughing and cheering, hallooing on the wild chase. And she was hiding in a cell with Robespierre. He lay bandaged and groaning only to spring up, free of his pain, to cry, 'Death! Death to her, to the guillotine with her!'

'Hush,' Michel was whispering, 'Hush now, it's all right, I'm with you, you're with me, sleep, sleep quietly, it's almost daylight.' He held a glass to her lips and she drank from it. A sharp taste of herbs, hot liquid. She fell into sleep again like stone dropping into deep water, down and down into blackness. No more dreams.

When she woke finally the shadows were already lengthening, and she sat up shocked and bewildered, not knowing where she was for a second, and then remembering the men who had brought her there, the two police, who would be waiting——

'What time is it?' Calling out, knowing that he would be near her. He came in from where he must have been standing outside the door. He said nothing, only knelt down by the bed and took her hands, and she wanted to cry with joy that he was there, and shame. And then the cold knowledge that she must leave him.

'I must go. I have to meet them—what time is it?'

'Four o'clock.'

'I'm late! I'm late! I promised— where are my clothes?' He must have undressed her while she slept. Dragging on her breeches, her boots, her shirt, her hands shaking. Why? Because he was there, and she must leave him, and she had only—only found—she was crying stupidly, sitting on the bed, holding her jacket, bending her head down over it. She who had not cried since Savenay. Or long before that. He knelt in front of her, pulled the jacket away from her face, lifted her chin with his knuckles so that she must look at him.

'I am so ashamed,' she whispered.

'I shall be angry,' he said. 'You are the Chevalier. You have no right to be ashamed.'

[279]

'No right?'

'You should hear them talk about you,' he said. 'Like Joan of Arc. Do you think it mattered if Joan—had a woman's heart for someone—just for a few moments? Would you set up that against—all the other things?'

'I am not Joan.'

'You could have ridden with her and she would have been glad to have you there.'

'You—you've learned to talk since—since we last——'

'I've practised talking to myself. I'd imagine you were there, and I'd tell you all the things I never—never managed to say when—you were really there.' He was stroking her face, her hair, her shoulders.

'When I heard you were still alive,' she said, 'I was afraid of——'

He laid one finger over her mouth. 'It's all done with,' he said. 'D'you want me to court you all over again?'

'You never did court me. I courted you, didn't I?' She began to laugh, still crying, tears running. She stood up, struggling with the sleeves of her jacket, her arm refusing to go into its proper sleeve. She did not know whether it was inside out or back to front.

'I must have the General's answer,' she said. 'And then——'

'He needs forty-eight hours more. Let them wait.'

'I can't. I gave my word.' She had almost to break away from him, and he ran after her, and they went side by side to the meeting-place. The two men were already pacing up and down, one of them with a great silver watch in his hand, looking at it as she came into sight of them. The carriage with its two forlorn horses fifty yards off, the horses straining their heads down to crop the withered grass.

'I shall be here again in forty-eight hours,' she said. 'With a firm answer. You can depend on it.'

They saluted and turned away to their coach. She had half expected them to demand that she came with them, then and there. And she went back to the village thinking. 'Forty-eight hours, forty-eight hours.' One moment it was a lifetime, could never end. And the next it was like minutes, it was almost better to have nothing than so little, so small a time to – to become friends again? Lovers again? Man and wife again?

He had put his arm through hers, and steered her away from the village, following a winding, narrow path among dripping

[280]

branches, the leaves underfoot still frost-bound from the night, crackling like frail glass as they were stepped on. 'I'm going to come with you,' he said. 'You know that? We're not going to lose one another now, not even for a day.'

'No!' she cried, her voice rising without her knowing it. 'You cannot! They would—I'm still a prisoner, they might arrest you——'

'Then we could still be together.'

'No, Michel! No!' Forty-eight hours was nothing, nothing. Worse than nothing. She could hear the slamming of the iron doors, the bolts grinding. Could see the blade of the guillotine. 'I've no safe-conduct for you, oh, why didn't I ask for one, I never thought—he said that if Charette signed a truce, then you would be—it was so rushed, he never gave me time to think——'

'He wouldn't do anything to——'

'He would! Oh please, let me know that you're still safe, still here.' She thought that she had never loved him until now. She stood facing him, holding his arms for the sake of touching him. She wanted to touch his face, his body, feel the warmth of his body against her hands. 'Don't talk of it, please. We've got two days, two nights, they'll last for ever. And if they agree—if they agree to talk peace then—then he may send me back here. He must. And give you your safety. All of you. And you—you can come to—come with me—we can——' She did not know what she was saying. Although he had put his cloak round her she was shivering with the cold. They began walking once more, back towards the clearing, and the village. Down the long space where they had danced, among the huts. The bonfires had left broad circles of blackened earth, and grey ashes. He took her to their hut. Inside it smelled of earth and smoke. She remembered the vipers drinking from the dish of milk, Euphemia holding them writhing together in her hand. Her head brushed the curve of the roof as it had done then, and she had a sense of the world being utterly different to the world she had thought she knew. For a second she understood it, was actually grasping its reality in her mind, its meaning; all the deaths she had seen, all the suffering. Like a flash of lightning in the blackness of a storm, and one sees the shapes of the storm-clouds piled and driving in the black sky; one sees the trees lashed by the wind and the rain, and one knows why it is happening, what is happening; that it will end, and the earth will drink the rain, and the old trees that fall will give place to others, young and strong; the sky will clear by morning. The sun will rise on a new world washed clean and wonderful.

And then the image was stupid, irrelevant, nothing. She understood nothing. He was taking the cloak from her shoulders, opening her coat. He began to undress her, not with the old haste and violence but slowly, as though he had thought about it for a long time. And she stood as once she had stood for Talmond, but quietly, not shivering except now and then with the cold. When she was naked he lifted her in his arms, one arm behind her knees, one behind her shoulders, and laid her among the furs on the bed.

'Where did you sleep?' she whispered, knowing the answer.

He nodded towards the door. 'I kept watch,' he said.

'There was no need.'

'I know. Except that I wanted to.'

It was almost dark inside the hut. She shut her eyes, heard him moving, the rustle of cloth. He was lying down beside her, carefully, his hands cold as they touched her. She began to be afraid. That he—that she—that a shadow would lie between them. She almost turned her head away. Kept her eyes shut. He touched her eyelids, opened them with the tips of his forefingers. His own eyes unsmiling, his face carved out of shadows, dark bronze.

'Give yourself back to me,' he said, his voice very low. And for a moment she could not answer him, could not move. And she knew that if she stayed still another moment, it was over, there would be nothing between them ever. And she still could not move. Like fear. Like being so afraid that one cannot move, cannot lift one's arm. And she had to use every fragment of her strength, all her courage, to make herself turn, smile, open her arms to him. And then it needed no effort at all. Like being released from chains, her body soft against his, her arms round him, her face hidden against his shoulder, against his neck. No bones in her body, no strength except to give in, to surrender.

'There's not much of me left to give,' she whispered. And the shadow was gone from between them, she could not remember why it had been there. Talmond so far away that he belonged to another life, like a dream she had had that was fading as she thought of it, was almost gone, was gone entirely and she knew only that she had dreamed of something but she could not remember what. Lay and let herself be taken. Like a first time, like a marriage night. Like a bride who had been frightened of being hurt and finds the hurt turn to joy.

Not the way they had made love before, like two athletes stripped for a contest, so that each lovemaking was a victory, and at the same time a defeat. But a giving, a surrendering, a quietness. She lay holding him against her, whispering stupid things, her mouth touching his.

'D'you remember when we first rode together?' she whispered. For the joy of remembering. The nights they had been too tired to make love, and she had lain holding him like this, while he slept. She thought now that then she had known the secret and afterwards had forgotten it again. That deep possession, that tenderness of loving, wanting nothing but to love. And yet the secret was like smoke, dissolving as she tried to grasp it, and she thought of Euphemia slipping away from her, and of how many secrets Euphemia knew. 'So much love. So much death.' How had she known? And that sense of the world's hidden reality came back, and she clung to Michel in the dark.

'Why were we spared?' she whispered.

'Hush,' he breathed. Smoothed his hand on the flatness, the almost hollow of her stomach, down to her lap. And she thought of Euphemia again, so velvet-dressed in her nakedness, so complete. Had the Indian girl been like Euphemia? Pale gold instead of velvet black. Hair like a curtain of black silk, a cloak, surrounding her, dressing her. Oiled and scented so that her whole body was scented by her hair. How had she made love? And she imagined soft suppleness, yielding and gentle. Her body——

She wanted to ask him, and could not. Felt even her breast burning with the shame of it, as if she had indeed asked him. Felt the shame turning to something she did not recognize, like a pain catching under her heart. She pushed herself up onto her elbow, looked down at him as he lay half asleep. Was he—did he remember—think of—that girl when he was——? He opened his eyes and looked at her, and she searched in them for what he was thinking, whether he was laughing at her. Wanted to shake him, force the truth out of him. Only for a moment. In the next moment she was crying, her face down beside his, buried against the hard pillow.

'Is it because you're going back?' he breathed.

She wanted to say, 'Come with me, no matter what happens, come back with me.'

'Yes,' she said, 'that's what it is. Are we friends? Are we truly friends now?' He looked astonished at her, lifting her head with his hands so that he could see her face.

'What do you mean?'

'You said—you said once——'

'What did I say? Why d'you remember things? We're so much friends that——'

'—we could say anything to one another? Ask anything?'

'What d'you want to ask?'

'Nothing,' she whispered. 'Only—sometimes I wish—I've been wishing that I was—I was like other women. Like—Léonie, or—Euphemia?'

He stared at her for a second as if he thought she had gone mad, or he could not remember who Léonie and Euphemia were. Then he did laugh, holding her so tight she could not breathe. 'Oh, my love,' he said. 'My dear, dear fool. My dear, dear friend.'

Chapter 29

It was a silent journey to Paris. Her escort treated her more kindly, even with respect, seeming almost surprised that she kept the terms of her parole, and admiring her for it. But she answered their occasional politeness very briefly, and they were still concerned that no one should see more of her at their stopping-places than was essential. She was still a prisoner, and a secret one, and they travelled through the ruined landscape as fast as the starving hacks of the posting stations could take them. Still all the signs of war until they had left the Vendée well behind. Columns of troops, guns, baggage wagons; sentries and patrols at the outskirts of every small town, unless it was one that had been abandoned to the Royalists. In those it was her turn to be ready with Charette's *laissez passer*. Twice they were stopped by Royalist bands, one of them giving allegiance to Stofflet, and not Charette.

The men who had halted their coach eyed the two policemen savagely, as if they guessed who and what they were. 'Your business?' one of the patrol said.

'The King's,' Hester answered him, and after another hesitation they were allowed to pass. The senior of the two policemen wiped his mouth with his handkerchief and did not look at her again until several miles had gone by. Then they were out of the Vendée and into the sad countryside of the Republic. Here there were no burned woods and farms. Only hunger. The two policemen breathed more easily and relaxed mile by mile, laughed once or twice at their own conversations, and tried to be kind to her. The younger man even intended to be gallant.

'That was my husband who was saying good-bye to me,' she said, and after that they left her alone. She tried to sleep, the jolting of the coach now lulling her, now waking her with a savage lurch into a pothole or over a great stone or a frozen rut. My dear, dear friend. My dear, dear friend. It had been worth all things to hear those words. All the prison. All this journey. If I never hear them again, she thought, it has been worth while. And then the thought of not hearing them again gripped her heart and threatened to stop its beating.

'You must see the King,' Charette had said. 'With your own eyes. You say you'd know him again. He can't be changed that much in two years. And question him. Ask him about the time you saw him, what he was doing in the *Manège*. I want to *know* that it's the King. They could have put any child in there, the King could be dead long ago.'

'They wouldn't——'

'Wouldn't have dared? Are you a fool? They've killed his father, his mother, his aunt, do you think they'd stop at killing him if it suited them?'

'I know.'

'See him. Talk to him. When I *know* that he's alive and that they'll send him to me, then I'll talk peace.'

'And if Barras hedges?' Michel had said.

Charette had spread his hands. 'We go on fighting.'

'And my wife?'

'I'm sorry.'

Charette and Michel had looked at one another for a long moment, and then Michel had gone out of the hut, and she had found him walking slowly towards the trees.

'Barras will make peace,' she said. 'I know it.'

'If he doesn't—if he puts you back into prison——'

'He won't——'

'—I'll come to Paris and I shall kill him, if I have to shoot him from the dark like a murderer.'

'Michel, Michel, I shall be back here within days. I swear it. I know it!' She hunted for arguments, persuasions. 'Euphemia!' she said. 'She promised me—she promised me everything would be well. As I was going down the stairs——'

He did not trouble to answer her, and shortly after that it was time to go, to the rendezvous with her escort and the coach and this journey. At the last moment he had still wanted to come with her and it had been the policemen themselves who had prevented him. 'If you step into this coach,' the senior of the two had said, 'you are

[286]

under arrest. And under sentence of death, to be carried out immediately. We would have no choice.' He had opened his cloak and showed the heavy pistol he was carrying beneath it. Even then she had had to thrust Michel away from her, and climb into the coach so hurriedly she realized afterwards they had never said good-bye to one another, never so much as touched hands.

Perhaps that was as well. She might not have had the courage for it. And she stayed silent in her corner of the swaying, lurching, straw-smelling coach, hugging the cloak round her that Michel had given her. And the more than cloak of 'Dear, dear friend.' She felt tears coming, strangely enough not of sadness but of happiness, and was afraid the two men would see her crying and misunder-stand. She turned her head away to look out of the misted, dirty glass of the window at the frozen landscape. Trees, hills, farms, hedges, woods. Not much different to the countryside she knew by now like her childhood. More open, sweeping. But something of the same shape to it, to the villages, the houses; the same look to the peasants, the occasional thin cattle.

Then she thought of her father, of Perrine, of the abbé Bernard. 'I'll not say anything until he frees them,' she thought. 'Not a word.'

Angers. Le Mans of the massacre, of the dreadful memories. She shut her eyes as they rumbled through the narrow streets, up the hill and down again onto the road for Chartres and Paris. Day. Night. Day.

It was almost night when they entered Paris at last. Soldiers at the barrier. A crowd of peasants waiting to leave. Others waiting to enter. Carrying baskets with a few eggs, a loaf, a scrawny hen past laying. To sell on the black market if they could get their treasures past the barrier without the soldiers' taking them. Into the unlit streets. Piles of refuse, beggars raking among the piles for some-thing to eat, something to wear. But as they came to the centre of the city, near the river, she sensed a difference about it, she could scarcely tell what it was at first. Lit windows. A mansion blazing with candlelight. Coaches. Not many, but with lanterns; she saw a coachman in livery, footmen behind. Saw a *Traiteur's* Dining Rooms and a group of people going in, laughing, the women in feathered headdresses and fur cloaks. Then they were gone by them, and the street was grey and cold again. But the image of laughter and freedom remained.

Like a rainbow after storm. A promise that the fear had gone. And, she thought suddenly, we shall live. Euphemia was right. As she's always right. Everything will be well again. She had to shut her eyes for a full minute, needing the darkness to hold that image of light and laughter safely in her mind. When she opened them again they were rolling up to Léonie's gates and courtyard, turning in. But they could not enter, the small courtyard was already full of carriages, blazing with torchlight. They had to leave the coach outside and get down.

'Come,' the senior of the policemen said. They went in among the horses and carriages. Coachmen and footmen and the link-boys standing about in the cold, slapping their arms against their sides. The house brilliant with light, music playing. The front door was open, and a man dressed like a major-domo, black coat and knee-breeches, powdered wig, staff of office, with footmen in velvet coats and white silk breeches ranked behind him, was receiving guests.

A woman going in, leaning on a man's arm. Swathed in a crimson shawl, a nod of ostrich feathers above her head, dyed like the tricolour, one red feather, one white, one blue.

'We'd best go round the back,' the policeman said. He gripped Hester's arm roughly, the sight of so much elegance seeming to remind him that she was his prisoner, and not deserving of any courtesy. But there was torchlight outside the kitchen quarters, too, and a brightness of candles in the windows, in the sculleries, everywhere. And not tallow candles, but wax. The kitchen full of servants, drinking hot toddy and cognac, smoking cigars, eating pasties from a tray handed round by two women servants, fat and laughing and rosy-faced. A servants' party to echo their masters' and mistresses' pleasures upstairs. And as the two policemen took Hester into the broad kitchen, pushing their way between tall footmen, other servants came pressing behind them, the men they had seen in the courtyard released now from their duties until they were called again.

'Something hot to drink, for the love of Heaven!' one of them shouted. 'I'm froze with the cold. There's a turn-out for you. I haven't seen the likes of it in years, it's the old days come back.'

'I must get a word to your master,' one of the policemen was saying to a servant of the house. He whispered something, and the girl stared at Hester, looking alarmed. She seemed to be protesting at the impossibility of disturbing any of the greatness overhead, the policeman insisting. He came back, and beckoned Hester through the crush, into a stone passage, itself bright with candles set in wall candleholders. The girl went ahead of them and up a short flight of stairs. They could see the hallway, and the main stairs, a throng of people trying to go up, and others trying to come down. Women's bare shoulders, jewels, laughter.

The girl pushed them into a small room full of cloaks, men's hats, walking canes, shawls, furs, and closed the door hurriedly as though she was ashamed of them. The two policemen stared round them and then determinedly at nothing. Hester sensed that they disapproved of everything they had just seen. She was not sure that she approved of it herself, remembering the beggars raking among the heaps of refuse.

They waited a half hour. The younger policeman said, his voice bitter, 'It doesn't take them long, does it?' The older man silenced him with a look, and a swift glance at Hester. Now and then the door opened, and one of the footmen of the house laid another armful of cloaks and shawls wherever they could be laid, staring at the three of them down his nose. At the policemen's serviceable dark clothes, at Hester's obvious raggedness. She felt like putting on her cloak again in spite of the heat of the small cloakroom. They could hear the music, and the growing uproar of too many people enjoying themselves in too small a house.

Three quarters of an hour. The door opened, and it was Euphemia. Dressed in white. White muslin so thin and fine it showed her blackness through it. She seemed to have on nothing at all under the gown. And she was wearing a broad gold collar and heavy gold bracelets, the collar joined to the bracelets by gold chains to emphasize her slavery, and the richness of it. Her hair was hidden by a turban of white muslin held together in the front by an emerald brooch set with an egret's feather.

'Give me your prisoner,' she said to the older of the policemen. 'I am to take her to General Barras.'

The policeman began to say something, and bit off the words, his face darkening. Euphemia did not trouble to hide her contempt for him. White rubbish, her eyes said, her narrow smile, the insolent carriage of her head. She looked at Hester. 'You cannot come through the house looking like that.'

'I could put on my cloak,' Hester said.

Euphemia wrinkled her nose. 'Here.' She took up one of the fur

[289]

cloaks from the pile beside her. Ermine and sable, lined with silk. She put it round Hester's shoulders. 'Big Madame must learn to dress again. Now come with me.'

The crush on the stairs had eased. People were dancing in a long reception room. She had a glimpse of it through the open doorway. Mirrors, chandeliers like hanging diamonds, like ice in sunlight, a waft of heat and scent and wine and burning candles. Ten million miles from the Vendée, ten thousand years from Robespierre and the Terror.

Another flight of stairs. The room she had been brought to before, its doors open, people laughing, drinking, eating from trays held by footmen, women with painted fans. She saw Léonie for a second as Euphemia hurried her past the doorway. Léonie in green silk, a red ribbon round her white, beautiful throat, a jewel hanging from it, her hair a cascade of gold half caught in a net of emeralds. Her voice at once loud and languid, crying, 'This house is unendurable! It is a hovel! One cannot have fifty people here without a crush. Thérézia! My love, are you being looked after?'

Down a short passage, a bedroom, Barras heaving himself up from an armchair. Silk curtains draped round the bed, a fire burning. Barras lifting her hand to his lips, bowing. 'Your servant, madame.' He made a gesture of mocking resignation at the bedroom. 'There is nowhere else to receive you in privacy, I'm afraid.' There was a tray of wine and *friandises* on a table by the fire. 'If you'd like something more substantial after your journey?'

She shook her head.

'And your news?'

'I must see the King,' she said. 'Myself. I am to be allowed to see him and speak to him. And return to General-in-Chief de Charette to assure him that it is truly the King. Then he will treat with you. But he will want the King promised to him, into his own hands. That before all else.'

Barras had sat down, slowly. He waved her to another armchair, on the other side of the fire. She took off her borrowed cloak, not knowing where to put it. Laid it on the bed, and sat down.

'You won't like what you see,' Barras said.

'Is he—ill?'

Barras nodded, a look of grave and serious regret coming over his face like lights being extinguished in a theatre. 'You are an Englishwoman. You never saw him—before all that has happened.' He spread his hands as though all that had happened was nothing in the world to do with him, except as a tragic matter for general sorrow. 'And I—' his voice deepening. 'I'm still of the nobility, it's in my bones, in my emotions. My ancestors for a thousand years—it's a terrible, terrible thing. Robespierre!' He shook his head, his brown hair shining in the firelight.

She was on the point of saying that she had seen the King when he was still Dauphin, and stopped herself.

'You won't realize what he once was,' Barras said. 'A happy, innocent child. It's a dreadful business. I've done what I can. Medicines. Toys. Care. Kindness.' He woke himself out of his reverie, and sat forward. 'Let me pour you wine, madame. What else did the Chevalier de Charette tell you to say to me?'

'Before we discuss that,' she said, 'I want something in exchange.'

'Your freedom?'

'And my father's. And two other prisoners who were with me in the Ursulines. And a safe conduct for my husband to be with me anywhere in France. I want your written order for these things.'

'My dear Madame Vernet,' Barras said, 'You shall have all that and more. If what you've brought me is worth bringing. You and I, we are not shopkeepers to chaffer over a bargain. Tell me everything, and you shall have everything.'

She found herself believing him. The room, the silks, the fire, the wine. The big, elegant man in his long blue military styled coat, sitting so easily across the hearth from her, sipping his Burgundy like a red jewel in the cut crystal glass. Even the way he sat underlined his difference from the Jacobins, the revolutionaries, the policemen downstairs. Like a gentleman. He held his glass like one. As if he belonged to the Vendée and the Royalists, and not to Paris. Was he trying to tell her that, without putting it into words? That he sympathized? That he was trying to amake amends? For the massacres he had ordered in Toulon and Lyons? For voting for the King's death? He had brought Robespierre down. Ended the Terror. Did he now mean to end the Republic? Restore the throne? Why not? Why else had he sent her? Told her she could discuss the child King?

She hesitated for another moment. But how could she bargain? What had she to bargain with? She told him all that had been said, slowly, picking her way between facts and suppositions. Careful to say nothing that might give the impression that any of the Royalists wanted peace at any price. 'They will go on fighting for ever, unless you can meet their terms.'

'You spoke of additional guarantees,' he said, refilling their glasses. 'Did he describe what those might be?'

'He would want to keep his own troops under arms. And the Republican troops out of the Royalist districts.'

Barras held his glass up to the light of a candelabra above the fireplace. 'He is asking for a Kingdom within the Republic.'

'And for the King's sister to be sent out of France into safety. To Vienna, or to her uncle, the Count of Provence.'

'He wants all our cards.'

'He would want money too. And supplies. Materials. Everything. To rebuild the Vendée. Do you know what's been done there? In the name of the Republic?'

'All wars are terrible,' he said. 'Civil wars worst of all. Why do you think I want to end it?'

He leaned forward, and touched his glass to hers. 'You shall see the King,' he said. 'And you shall have your father's freedom. And the others'. You have my word for it.'

She felt half drunk with the wine, and the firelight and the warmth, and the closeness of the room. He seemed quite different from her remembrance of him. Kind and good and generous. His face noble. Vivid and sincere.

'You'll need somewhere to stay,' he was staying. 'And clothes and money. Leave it to me.' He stood up, and tugged a red velvet bell-rope beside the fireplace. 'Are the fellows who brought you here below, still?' She nodded.

Euphemia came gliding in, her gold chains shimmering, clinking softly like gold bells, or coins.

'A bedroom for Madame Vernet. And supper. I make you responsible for her comfort. Tomorrow she is to have dressmakers. Everything that she wants. Send for Leroi. Tell him to have his people bring all a lady might need, a dozen choices of everything. The bills to me. And send up one of these fellows below, I'll give him an order for your father's release and the others'. We'll arrange an apartment for you.'

'Madame de Richeteau's,' she said, bewildered by so much sudden victory. 'If—if she's still alive—and willing to have us—in the rue du Bac. I——'

'Arrange it,' Barras said, his hand resting on Euphemia's bare black shoulder, fondling it. He lifted his glass again in courteous dismissal. 'I hope that very soon you'll be my guest in gayer circumstances. Laughter is coming back to France. And you're helping to bring it to us.'

Chapter 30

Leroi came the next morning before she was awake. He came himself, with a young man assistant, and a middle-aged modiste, and half a dozen sewing girls. A chattering and mothswooping and whispering of young women; swathes of silk, of satin, muslin; huge baskets of stockings, ribbons, hats, shoes, slippers, sandals; a trunk full of dolls, each doll dressed in a fashion of the moment, wax face and glass blue eyes; black-haired, flaxen, chestnut; dolls able to stand by themselves, set out on the dining-table like a fashion show. A mist of scent and powder; chypre and cologne, Quatre Voleurs, Grey Lady, Venus Water. As if Monsieur—impossible to think of him as Citizen—as if Monsieur Leroi was Aladdin, and he had rubbed his lamp and transformed Léonie's dining parlour into fairyland. Crimson silk, snow banks of muslin, a rainbow of ribbons shaken from their rolls, flung here and there with a magnificent carelessness.

She had slept until ten, until she was woken by Euphemia to tell her that the dressmakers had arrived. She had sworn to herself that she would wake at six, and be at the prison before seven when the gates first opened for visitors, and she had slept like a drowned woman until Euphemia came in to shake her awake. 'Up, up, Big Madame, you are to be turned into a woman today. I am responsible for you." She had taken off her slave chains and collar, and was dressed in what passed with her for négligée, wrapped in green silk that moulded her body like tight smooth shining leaves wrapped round a dark, tropical fruit.

Since their time in the Vendée she had grown sleek-fleshed, with rounded hips and the suggestion of a bosom, her skin like black satin, and even her pretence of humility that had never been more than a pretence was vanished. She gave Hester no more time than to rub her face with a sponge and pull on the silk night-robe that she had given her the night before. It barely reached to Hester's knees and made her feel more ridiculous than if she were naked.

'I cannot——'

'It is General Barras' orders. Come quickly.' And when Hester still protested she seized her by the wrist and took her to the dining parlour like a captive. 'Here is your client,' she said. She did not trouble to curtsy to Monsieur Leroi. But the King of Fashion bent himself in half in his bow of welcome and, straightening up, clasped his hands together, looked at Hester, looked up at the painted ceiling for inspiration, and cried: 'A Greek goddess! Pallas Athene! I see you in Tyrian purple. A purple velvet cloak. White silk for the lining. Marcel, the velvets!'

The young man burrowed among piles of cloth, lifted a swathe of velvet like a dark banner and came and draped it round Hester's shoulders. Sewing-girls crawled round her feet, pinning and arranging. It was impossible to interrupt. Monsieur Leroi had new inspirations. Pale muslins. Flesh-coloured tights. She seemed to be crying, 'No!' And 'I cannot, I have nothing on!' again and again, and no one took any notice of her, as if she was a lay figure, one of the dolls standing with wax faces and glass eyes on the dining-table. Standing half naked in a room with two men and what seemed like countless women, now wrapped in silk, now in her shirt again, now draped in velvet, muslin, cashmere shawls, a linen toga, Monsieur Leroi and his assistant greeting the toga with cries of, 'A Vestal Virgin! Magnificent! Merveilleuse!'

Léonie had come in as they were trying on the toga. She did not share their enthusiasm. 'Oh Hester! It makes you look so—so manlike. I don't think it suits her at all.' The toga was put away.

'My father,' Hester said. 'And my friends. I must go to the prison at once. Have the orders been given?' For the past quarter of an hour she had been looking for the opportunity to interrupt him. But it took another hour before she could get rid of him, or rather escape from him. Silks and muslins held against her, slashed with scissors in a frenzy of creation, pinned and draped and tucked, while she tried to protest that she had no money, that she wanted nothing but a warm woollen gown and a cloak, and some underthings.

'Underthings?' Monsieur Leroi said, incredulous. 'But no one wears *underthings*! The shift has disappeared this three months at least. As for the chemise!' His assistant clasped his hands in disgust at the chemise. 'The waist-stocking is still permitted beneath the lighter muslins. You shall have two or three of those. But I doubt if true Society will tolerate them much longer.'

She did not dare to say that she had no intention of appearing in Society. And she escaped out of the room at last, dressed herself in what now seemed like a beggar's cast-offs, hid herself as best she could inside Michel's cloak, and crept down the stairs, afraid that she would meet one of the sewing-girls, or a footman, or the major-domo. Into the courtyard. Euphemia had ordered a *coucous* for her, and paid the fare in advance.

'He will take you wherever you wish. And here is money. One of the footmen has been to Madame de Richeteau. She is expecting you.' Pressing a thick wad of *assignats* into Hester's lap. 'It is difficult to buy food even with money. I'll have things sent to you. This afternoon.' As she was closing the door of the *fiacre* she leaned in a last time and whispered, her voice deep with triumph, 'The world belongs to us! All of it!'

Leaning back against the greasy cushions, closing her eyes. Monsieur Leroi. Euphemia. The bundle of notes as thick, thicker than her fist. Michel. Barras. The prison. All that had happened these last days. Last night. She had not had breakfast, and last night she had been too tired and tight-strung with nerves to eat. Difficult to buy food. Papa will be hungry, she thought, and I shall have nothing for him. And the abbé. And Perrine. As though to give them food was more important than to bring them freedom. And then she was terrified that they would not be freed, that the order would not have come, Barras would not have kept his word.

She beat on the glass window in front of her, wanting the driver to go faster. But his horse was starving, and swayed from side to side as he walked, threatening to fall between the shafts before they crossed the river, let alone reached the Ursulines. But they came there eventually. 'You must give that horse something to eat,' Hester said. The driver stared. He did not seem to be in much better condition himself. She looked at the bundle of notes that Euphemia had given her. Five livres. Ten. How much would a livre buy? She had no idea. It had used to be a day's wages for a workman when they had first come to Paris. Now? She gave him ten livres. 'Will this buy food for both of you?' He looked at the note stupidly, like someone who did not know what it was. 'Wait here,' she whispered, and within another second had forgotten him, his horse, everything in the world but her father.

Knocking at the gate. The familiar iron sounds. Familiar stenches, voices, echoes. But now gatekeepers and turnkeys were springing to their feet, welcoming her, bowing, creaking with fat and leather as they led her to a chair. 'The Citizen, the Citizeness's father – the Citizen Curé—the Citizeness Perrine Louveteau—they are being brought here, at once, at once. General Barras' orders—they have been given breakfast—is the Citizeness comfortable in that chair—would she take a glass of wine? Does the smell of tobacco offend her?'

'I was in prison here,' she said. 'You can't have forgotten me. It's only a few days.' But those few days had transformed her into General Barras' friend. Had set such a gulf between her and turnkeys that they could not see her features across it. They laughed, gruffly uncomfortable, afraid of her, afraid for their jobs, perhaps for their lives, in such a time of vengeance. They laughed again in relief when Mr. Broadhurst, and the abbé Bernard, and Perrine were brought to the *guichet*. Obsequious farewells. Agonized refusals of ten livres' drink money, so that she had to push the crumpled *assignat* into the gatekeeper's fist. Hugging her father who stared about him in wonder.

'Are we going somewhere?' he said. 'Are we going home?'

'Papa! Papa!'

Hugging Perrine, the abbé. Outside. Into the *fiacre*. Slowly, slowly towards the rue du Bac. She did not care how slowly. Holding her father's hands against her, touching his face. Touching Perrine, the abbé. 'They are sending us food. Oh Papa, you've grown even thinner. Perrine, has he not been eating?'

'He missed you.'

Crying. Laughing. The rue du Bac. More money for the starving horse, the starving driver. Old Anne the servant, crying in wonder, in disbelief, running towards the stairs, calling up to her ancient mistress on the broad landing above: 'It's really them, it's them, and two strangers, a priest, a priest!' Running back to them, curtsying. 'Monsieur l'abbé!' Kissing the abbé Bernard's hand, while he stared about him at the shadow forms of the hall, blinking his wounded eyes. They were all crying. Madame de Richeteau tottering down the stairs. 'Where is the General? Where is the General, Anne? He must be told.' Frail as a ghost in ivory lace. Smelling of lavender. Kissing Perrine with great fondness and saluting her as 'Cousine'.

'We must tell the General at once, that you are come.'

It was a moment or so before Hester realized that she was speaking of her long-dead husband, and not of Barras. 'It doesn't matter,' she said to Perrine, who was trying to correct the mistake about her cousinship. 'Let's go upstairs and cry in comfort.'

But that was not allowed, and they had to sit for an hour in Madame de Richeteau's drawing-room, among the clocks, and the Sèvres shepherdesses, and the two stuffed cats, and the little gilt tables and chairs, and drink ratafia and eat stale sweet biscuits.

'There have been such dreadful things happening,' Madame de Richeteau said. 'It is a mercy that you did not come here sooner, you would have been quite alarmed. Men came here one day with guns, right into this drawing-room! I told the General to complain to the King about it, and he must have done, because they never came back.'

Perhaps it was the best way to celebrate their freedom, and their being together again. In the late afternoon another *fiacre* arrived, heaped with supplies, Euphemia guarding them like a djinn from the Arabian fairy tales. White bread. Wine. A joint of beef. Eggs. Butter. Cognac. Milk. Coffee. Sugar. Soap. Candles. And with them the first instalment of Monsieur Leroi's genius. A long lacquered and painted box like a wedding *corbeille,* packed with the velvet cloak, two gowns, stockings, Roman sandals, silk and velvet bandeaux for the head, ostrich feathers, a fan of painted silk, a small red velvet jewel box.

'Open it,' Euphemia said. Inside the jewel box there was a red ribbon, and a gold pendant. The pendant was a model of a guillotime, miniature but perfect, with a silver blade that slid up and down between the gold pillars.

'Is—is it a joke?' Hester breathed, holding the tiny, murderous thing on the palm of her hand, feeling the hairs rise at the nape of her neck. 'Someone's dreadful idea of a——'

'It is the latest fashion,' Euphemia said. 'Everyone who has lost a relative is wearing one. Or who just survived, as we did.' She laughed, and put the red ribbon round Hester's neck, like a line of blood. 'You are to wear it tonight, to the Récamiers. I am to call for you at half past seven.'

'Tonight? But—I have no intention—my father——'

'It is General Barras' desire. I think the toga truly suited you best, madame. I told them to include it. The rest of your wardrobe

[298]

will be delivered tomorrow and the day after. Now do I have your permission to leave you?' Her cold fingers fastening the ribbon close, the pendant heavy against Hester's throat.

'I cannot come tonight. Tell him——'

'If you want to see the King, madame.' Touching the jewel, one finger lifting the tiny blade, letting it fall with a faint click of silver against gold. 'I shall come for you.'

To see the King. Remembering the boy in that cramped hutch in the *Manège,* playing with the bandalore, leaning against his father's knee. The Queen. The courtiers. How many of them were still alive? Or was the child King the only one? He would be ten now, eleven. What had they done to him?

Dressing herself in her old room, the shutters closed against the cold. 'What have they given me?' she cried to Perrine who was helping her to dress, and exclaiming over the silks and the crisp muslins and the gossamer stockings that covered one from foot to waist, at once flesh-coloured and almost transparent. The toga was the only gown that was not transparent. Fine white silk with a gold border. When it was correctly draped it hung to her heels behind but rose at the side to show one leg to above the knee. And it was supposed to reveal the opposite shoulder and most of the bust, the folds and drapes fastened with an enormous cameo set in gold. Gold sandals. And the purple cloak, purple velvet lined with oyster satin, the velvet dark as midnight, and then the lining like a flash of moonlight as the cloak swung open for a moment. She could not help being pleased with it. She stood in front of the cheval glass that had been in Léonie's room and turned so that the cloak would swing again. Smoothed the velvet with her finger-tips, feeling the soft resistance of its deep pile. She had never worn such velvet. How much could it cost? Perrine was fitting one of the bandeaux round her hair. Monsieur Leroi had almost wept at the way her hair was cropped.

'*A la victime,* madame, yes! But with art! With finesse! That looks as if Sanson himself had hacked at it.'

'He did, or at least one of his assistants.'

Monsieur Leroi had turned pale.

The feathers. Like a Red Indian chieftainess. They made her look nine feet tall and even more ridiculous than she felt already. 'I can't go dressed like this. I won't!'

'Oh madame, you must. You look so fine!'

Madame de La Rouchefoucauld. 'You have sworn me a comrade's oath to be as splendid as you can.' She swung the cloak open, and then flung a corner of it over the left shoulder. It was certainly magnificent. There was a knocking at the door, old Anne's voice calling, 'Madame, madame! The black girl is here, and your *fiacre.*'

The streets already dark. Icy. Empty except for shadows. Then the lights and rattle of a coach. Here a lit window, there link-boys with torches. The river. Notre-Dame like a black cliff. Rumbling north towards the Temple. She felt her heart beginning to beat hard with excitement. Scarcely allowed herself to believe that it was true, that she was going to see him, the child King they had fought for so long and terribly. Did he know? Had he been told of the Vendée, of all the battles, of all those who had died for him? Or had they kept all that from him?

The Temple courtyard, soldiers. Euphemia showed a paper through the window. Rattling across the cobbles. Stepping down. More soldiers. The mass of the Great Tower heavy and dark above them. A door grinding. Grinding shut behind them. Stone stairs. The entrance to a guard-room, soldiers, men in civilian clothes wearing the tricolour sash and cockaded hats. A dark, quick youngish man greeting them, hurrying them away from the entrance, up more stairs. 'I am the Citizen Laurent,' he said, his voice low and husky, with a heavy Créole accent. 'I am the guardian to the Capet children. You must stay outside,' he said to Euphemia. He was unlocking an iron door, relocking it as soon as they were inside on a narrow landing. Unlocking another door, heavy timber this time. To keep one child secure? They were in an empty room, nothing in it at all except a large, rounded porcelain stove, against the far wall. 'Stay here,' the guardian Laurent said again to Euphemia. 'We go this way.' Leading Hester through two more rooms, and a corridor, each door locked and bolted. They seemed to be going round the circuit of the Tower. Into a square room, lit by one hanging lamp, full of shadows. She saw the dark shape of someone hunched over a card table. There were cards scattered, folded, fallen onto the floor. The boy held his head in his hands and did not look round even at the sound of the door opening, at Laurent's voice.

'A visitor, monsieur.' He put his mouth close to Hester's ear, drawing her down to his level. 'You were told you would be shocked. It was not our doing. You should have seen this room when we first came here, after the tyrant was executed.' By 'tyrant' he obviously meant Robespierre, and not Louis XVI.

The boy still ignored them. The room seemed clean enough. There was a handsome bed, another table, an armchair. Toys here and there. A bird-cage on one of the deep window-sills that were like alcoves carved into the walls high up. 'He was covered with lice,' Laurent said, 'and the room was like a jakes. No one had cleaned it for six months and he was never let out to—it was terrible.'

'May I speak to him?'

'He won't answer you.'

She felt her throat closing. 'Monseigneur,' she whispered. Went slowly up to the table, and stood in front of the boy. He was dressed neatly, in a grey sailor suit, with a darker collar. His face was hidden by his hands and his hair hung forward. Much darker than she remembered it. Perhaps that was the light, or it had darkened with illness and imprisonment.

'Monseigneur, I am from the Vendée. I bring you a message from your loyal subjects.' She thought that Laurent might object, and said quickly, 'I saw Your Majesty once before, in the *Manège*, with the King your father. Do you remember that day? Please, your Majesty, look at me, I am your friend.'

The boy slowly, slowly lifted his head. Fine, narrow features. Fine, luminous eyes. But an imbecile's. Gaunt with illness, dead to all intelligence. Nothing there. She had to support herself by leaning on the edge of the card table. A card fell to the floor. It was the ace of spades. 'What have they done to you?' she breathed.

'Are you satisfied?' Laurent said.

She began to turn away, sick and frightened, wanting only to get away from the room, that piteous, pitiful creature. Why had they not had the decency to kill him, instead of this? But something about the boy's face, his hair—something—caught at her mind. Eleven? Sick, imbecile, imprisoned; nothing could make an eleven-year-old child look as old as this boy looked; it was not the ageing of illness, simply of growth. This boy looked sixteen at least.

'Ask him to stand up,' she whispered to Laurent, no longer able to talk directly to the boy, scarcely able to say anything.

'Stand up for the citizeness,' Laurent said, and the boy stood. Still slowly, but obediently. More cards fell as he levered himself

[301]

upright. He was astonishingly tall, but all the height, all the growth was in his legs. His body was quite small and hunched, the head too large for it. Now that his hair was closer to the lamplight she saw its colour more clearly. Chestnut. And the prince's had been gold. Fair gold with only the slightest touch of auburn. This could not, could not be the King. She swung on Laurent furiously.

'This is—' she began. And stopped herself. 'This is a monstrous thing,' she whispered. They heard a sound overhead, a chair moving, someone walking softly and lightly across a room above them.

'Madame Royale,' Laurent said. 'The girl Capet.' The King's sister. Daughter of Louis XVI and Queen Marie Antoinette.

'Have you done the same to her?'

He shook his head.

'Take me to see her.'

'Only through the spy-hole. You cannot speak to her.'

'Why not?'

He nodded towards the boy. 'She doesn't know,' he said. They went back the way they had come, rejoined Euphemia, went up another flight of stairs. More doors unlocked, unbolted. Through a small spy window she saw a girl bent over an embroidery frame. She must have sensed that she was being watched, spied on, and lifted her head. Her face drawn and tragic, but a child's face still, alive, intelligent. Hauteur in the curve of her eyebrows, the set of her mouth. They had not broken her. Hester slid the cover of the spy-hole gently across the Judas window again.

'Do you not let them meet?'

'Never.'

'You are monsters!'

Laurent bowed his head. 'The citizeness should lay the blame where it belongs. I only obey my orders.'

She thought they would never reach the air. Door after door unlocked, unbolted, bolted and locked again behind them. Echo of stairs. The King had come down these steps on his way to execution. The Queen. The Princess Elizabeth. She stood in the courtyard, breathing deep. Charette would never make peace now. Never, never, never. Unless—unless the real King was still alive. Somewhere else. Hidden. What had Barras intended? That she should see that poor wreckage and try to persuade Charette to make peace without him, laying the blame for what had happened

[302]

to the boy on Robespierre? So that there need be no talk of a King, of freeing him, or letting people know what had been done?

They got into the *fiacre* and drove the way they had come. She said nothing to Euphemia. But when they were getting out in the courtyard of the Récamiers' mansion Euphemia caught her by the arm and whispered, 'He is still alive. They will let you see him if you press hard enough.'

She was offering her hand to Hester, helping her down, lifting the edge of Hester's cloak to avoid the step, her face impenetrable. One of the Récamier footmen there, holding a torch above his head to light their way. Carriages. Servants. Torchlight. It was impossible to say anything, to ask Euphemia what she knew, how she knew it. The double doors thrown wide, a brilliance of lamplight, chandeliers, torches. The hallway paved and pillared in marble, the pillars draped with pale yellow muslin, a crush of people arriving, music playing, not simply two or three violins but an orchestra. Footmen like grenadiers in velvet and powder and silk stockings. A stout, middle-aged gentleman greeting his guests at the head of the broad marble staircase. The banker Récamier. A major-domo asking her name. Crying out, *'The Citizeness Vernet'*, making it sound like 'Madame la Duchesse.' Euphemia had vanished. The stout gentleman was clasping her hand, his own covered in white gloves. White kid, soft as skin.

'Enchanté, *citoyenne*. My wife will be ravished to make your acquaintance.'

Such a crowd in the reception room behind him as made it difficult to breathe. Was Barras here? Did he spend his life at receptions? She knew no one. People stared at her, towering above them as she did. And she in her turn found herself staring, in spite of her preoccupations. Almost naked breasts. They could have been naked for all the covering the gowns provided. One woman, surrounded by men, was dressed in a leopard-skin, or half dressed in one, her black hair cut *à la victime* to show the nape of her neck. The red ribbon round her throat and the guillotine hanging between her splendid breasts, one of them entirely bare, the other decorated by the leopard's paw rather than covered. The men surrounding her seemed barely able to speak, they were so absorbed in looking.

But she was only one of a dozen, of fifty half-naked splendours. Silk and muslin, floating draperies that only floated to reveal, and

[303]

settled again to cling close to curves and shapes of womanhood. A footman had taken Hester's cloak, but even so she felt overdressed in her toga with its mere revelation of one leg to the middle of her thigh.

If all these women had been prostitutes it would have been startling enough, but they were obviously not, or at least not in a professional way. No prostitute would be so shameless, nor would she have so many diamonds as that woman there. She was almost clothed in them. And that one. And that one. So much gold, such emerald collars; such ruby clasps to hold bright-coloured ostrich plumes; such pearls and sapphires; slender, beautiful hands heavy with jewels. And the men—they too were jewelled and scented, their hair no longer cropped *à la Titus*, since the women had taken over the cropped fashion, but with long ringlets falling to the tremendous collars of their coats, their cravats foaming above starched linen shirts studded with gold, or black pearls, or garnets. Long pantaloons clinging to their legs like another skin. Slippers with jewelled buckles. The heirs of the Revolution, of the Terror. The new aristocracy sprung like the Phoenix from the blood and ashes of the old. The bankers, the speculators, the buyers-up of Church property and the forfeited estates of *émigrés*. The men who had scooped up blood from the gutters and turned it into gold. And their women. The wealth of Sheba's mines emptied into this room, distributed by handfuls and sackfuls and barrow-loads. Champagne exploding, foaming, pouring; cries of joy at greeting, parting, toasting, drinking.

The pressure of the crowd was taking her to a doorway, a corridor, another room. A double flow of people, in and out, as though it was a museum. She was gradually pressed inside. It was a bedroom, high-ceilinged, with the bed like an altar raised up on a dais. The high bed-posts were swathed and draped in pale pink muslin. Everything that could be draped and clothed in muslin or silk or satin had its swags and coverings and bows and curving falls of pale pink and mist white. What was not dressed and decorated with silk or muslin was gilded. Or made of marble. Or padded with swansdown and pink satin, decorated with white silk love-knots, and the initials J. R.

A tall beautiful girl, also swathed in muslin, was standing on the dais by the bed. 'This is my bed,' she was saying in a clear, childish voice to someone near her, who could scarcely need to be told. 'And my bathroom is through there.' She turned and looked towards the doorway, and her face was so beautiful, so wonderful, that all criticism faded and vanished, like the absurd follies of the room, and it was impossible to do anything but stare at her. She stood poised by her swansdown altar, pointing towards another doorway, another glimpse of pale pink and white; marble and draperies and gilding; a flash of mirrors, of candlelight, of virginal purity. Hester would have been content to stand there, staring at the vision of the girl who must be the young Madame Récamier, but the crush pressed her forward towards the bathroom. There was a bath carved out of marble. Even the hot water cans were gilded and there was a soapdish of solid gold. She was swept out again on the tide of admirers. The girl was saying to newcomers, 'This is my bed, and my bathroom is over there.'

Someone close behind Hester whispered to a companion, 'They're not really husband and wife, you know, he's her father, he only married her to save his property for her if he was guillotined.' But she was outside in the corridor. Euphemia appeared beside her from nowhere, tugging at her sleeve.

'The General is waiting for you, he wants to speak to you now.'

He was in the library, where the books seemed to have been bought by the yard, for their weight of gilding. Corinthian pillars along the walls created alcoves. There were gilt and marble reading tables at which surely no one had ever read so much as a newspaper. Busts of Solon, of Socrates, of Plato, of Aristotle. Statues of Roman Emperors. General Barras stood elegantly languid beside Augustus, surrounded by women, his jewelled hand resting familiarly on the great emperor's shoulder. The women fluttered and clustered round him like butterflies. When he saw Hester coming towards him he made the gesture of a man freeing himself from children.

'Madame Vernet is coming to speak to me on behalf of a dear friend of hers. Will you permit her to be private with me for a minute or two?' He drew her into one of the alcoves, his mouth still smiling, his eyes watchful, searching her expression. 'Smile,' he said in a low voice. 'Look light-hearted. It's the fashion now.'

'I cannot,' she said. 'That was not the King.'

His own smile stiffened for a moment, curved again. But his eyes had turned to stone. 'I did not know that you knew him.' His voice very soft and dangerous. 'So?'

'I know the King is alive,' she said. 'Take me to him. If you want peace, you must let me see him. And for pity's sake, do something for that poor child in that room.'

'We have done all we could.' But his eyes avoided hers. He put one hand to his chin, a huge cornelian and gold seal ring flashing dark fire. 'As for—the other one—it is not as simple as you think. There are some who would kill him out of hand if they suspected where he was. We must both of us, you and I, be very careful. We are surrounded by more dangers than you can imagine. Wait. Be a little patient.' He said the last words in a slightly louder voice, so that anyone who was trying to listen might hear him, but without seeming to wish to be heard. And, slightly louder again, 'Trust me, citizeness, I shall do all I can for your poor friend. If it is possible it shall be done. Now, I beg of you, amuse yourself. The time for sadness is gone by.' He bowed, kissed her fingers, was surrounded once more by adorers. Hester herself was almost jostled out of the way by fresh adorers coming to sip at the fountain of power. Men as well as women. Like Versailles again, the courtiers thronging. And he stood like a king. More kinglike than most kings. Tall, handsome, brilliant in blue velvet coat and black silk breeches, white stockings, buckled shoes. The Revolution, the Terror, might never have been. Or had they only been hidden away for the moment behind the Corinthian columns, the muslin draperies?

A man plucked at her toga, stood on tiptoe to reach near to the level of her ear. 'You're a friend of General Barras, I see,' he whispered. He was small and stout, with diamond rings that flashed as he waved his hands in front of her, perhaps to let her see the diamonds. 'I've been hoping to have a quiet word with him, not in this crowd of course, but alone with him somewhere. For anyone who could arrange that it might be worth a great deal of money. A *great* deal. I know where there's enough leather to make four million pairs of soldiers' boots.'

Across the room she could see Léonie. She seemed to be dressed in a gold fishing-net. Euphemia was beside her, wearing her serpent collar and a length of crimson silk wrapped round her like blood running from a wound.

'I'm not talking about paper money,' the stout man whispered. 'Real cash. Or, if you preferred, jewels?'

Chapter 31

The days of waiting became weeks. She went every day, and sometimes twice a day to Léonie's house, to learn if there was news, or if General Barras was there, or had left word for her. She had told herself at first that it would be tomorrow, two days at the most. Or three. Did he not want the negotiations for peace to begin as soon as possible? He more than the Royalists? Four days perhaps, and then—she would see Michel again. She dreamed of him now as she had never done, not as someone seen in the distance, but close to her, touching her. She would wake thinking she felt him still there, the warmth of his body, the sound of his voice.

I am in love, she thought wonderingly. Again. Or—in so different a way to that earlier passionate hunger, that fury of possession, that it was something quite new and strange, a deep, longing need of him, so that without him she felt incomplete, was incomplete. When she came near to Léonie's house, turned into the now familiar courtyard, her heart began to beat faster; she would think; if there is a carriage there it will mean——

But there was always a carriage there, two, three, a dozen; in the courtyard itself, and outside in the tree-lined, quiet street of wealthy, discreet small houses; waiting while their owners paid their respects, their homage to the *amie intime* of General Barras, who in everything but title was now the ruler of Paris, and of as much of France as held to the Republic. It was no longer possible to see Léonie as soon as one arrived. It seemed to be more difficult day by day, the length of time one must wait grew longer. A footman with powdered hair and white cotton gloves served coffee and liqueurs in a small parlour on the ground floor, like a minister's ante-room. Anxious-looking men sitting there, talking studiedly of anything but why they had come; or women with red eyes only too eager to confide that they had a husband or a son or a brother in prison, or emigrated to England or Germany and now starving and praying to be allowed to return. Or needing a position. Or a pension. Or a passport. 'Do you think that she will help me, madame?' While through the open doorway Hester would see a heavy-set man coming down the stairs looking thoughtful, or slyly pleased, and the manservant would come in and murmur quietly, 'If the Citizen such and such would like to attend on the Citizeness Creuzot?'

These of course were Léonie's 'business mornings'. She never told Hester what happened during the tête-à-tête interviews, but the atmosphere of bribery hung like a gold mist in her dining parlour where she received her suitors. Sometimes, when Hester reached her at last, she found Léonie playing with a diamond ring, or a pearl necklace, or weighing a heavy purse in her hand like a cat with a dead sparrow. Or Euphemia would be relocking the big mahogany, brass-bound chest that stood in one corner.

Even Euphemia became hard to see, and much sought after by the minor clients. In the afternoons, when Léonie received the generality of visitors, and was 'at home to her friends', Euphemia was there like a shadow, and Hester would see men and sometimes women slip gold into her hand and whisper urgently, nodding towards Léonie in the centre of her throng of courtiers. And at a proper moment Euphemia would attract her mistress's attention and the suitor would obtain a moment of semi-privacy to make his or her petition. To sell four million pairs of boots to the army? Or forty million biscuits full of weevils? She heard a man complaining loudly at one reception that some 'scoundrel in the War Office turned down my biscuits because they were too far gone! The soldiers love the weevils, I told him, they taste like meat, but the fellow——'

'I get so tired,' Léonie complained. 'They give one no peace.' But she looked very well on it. And she would treat Hester with great kindness, like condescending to a poor and ill-favoured distant cousin. She would ask Euphemia languidly if she had remembered to send round more food for dear Hester and her poor Papa.

But the food was needed. It could scarcely be bought for money, and one only needed to walk a few yards from Léonie's house, or turn off the rue du Bac into a side street or an alleyway, to find beggars so weak with hunger that they could no longer beg, but lay on the ground dying, sheltering against a wall or in a doorway from the bitter December wind. Hester took to bringing the remains of their meals to a particular alleyway near the de Richeteau house, where half a dozen famished skeletons were always collected. It was difficult to tell if they were men or women. Like ghosts. They took the crusts, and the pieces of meat, and the rinds of cheese, and anything else that she could bring, and ate in silence, slowly, gone far beyond the stage where hunger eats wolfishly, and come to that last moment of starvation where it is difficult to eat at all, and crumbs of food seem to fill the stomach and block the throat.

One day there was something familiar about one of the shadows. A familiar hoarseness in the voice that whispered curses instead of thanks. She looked closer and it was the Commandant Piré. A ruin of bones and slack skin, an ulcer eaten deep into one cheek, weeping yellow matter, his once thick and glossy grey moustache turned dirty white, hanging like tendrils of dead weed round his toothless, shaking mouth.

'How are you—come to this?' she whispered, shuddering at him, at what he had been as much as what he was, almost frightened of him, of this walking death. He stared at her, and recognition lit a momentary fire of hatred in his dulled eyes.

'Royalist whore,' he mumbled. 'Curse your guts.'

That same night she saw a gang of Muscadins stoning the windows of a house, yelling, 'Come out, you Jacobin scum!' Beefy young men in heavy-shouldered coats, carrying knotted clubs. A workman, a *sans-culotte* in sabots and baggy pantaloons, turned the corner towards them and they saw him and abandoned their stone-throwing to give chase, like bloodhounds after a fox. The workman fled, leaving his sabots, racing for his life on bare feet, the Muscadins yelling and hallooing. The three or four hunted Jacobins who had been trembling behind the barred door of the house peered out, saw that the coast was clear for a moment, and ran in the opposite direction, shadows of fallen greatness. Six months ago the whole city, France itself, had trembled before them. Now they muttered their hatred behind locked doors and broken windows, and fled home, grateful to be safe for another night.

She went out as little as she could. Only to call on Léonie. Or to walk with Perrine and her father and the abbé for half an hour in the December sunshine. And then to call on Léonie again. And as the days became weeks, and the weeks became a month of waiting, even those visits seemed pointless. Even if she saw General Barras for a moment at one of Léonie's 'Afternoons' there was no opportunity to speak to him privately, and he made no move to draw her aside. Only once, as he was bowing over her hand, he murmured, 'Patience, citizeness, I beg of you.'

She became so inured to waiting that when at last it happened, there was the promise of an end to waiting, she could not believe it. At another of Léonie's afternoons. Euphemia saying quite casually, 'You must go to the Opéra tonight, madame, but you need not be there before eight o'clock, unless you wish to hear the singing.'

'The Opéra?' Her heart missing a beat. But it could not—she had said it so indifferently. It was no more than——

'You mean——' Still not believing it. Trying to catch Euphemia's arm, hold her. But she was gone, into the crowd. Tonight? The Opéra? It could not be——

She took the abbé Bernard for escort. And as late as they were, since the performance started at six, the fashionable crowd was only now arriving. A sea of coaches and *fiacres*, of shouting coachmen, footmen, theatre ushers; of hungry onlookers staring at the dazzle of jewellery and ostrich feathers, at the new aristocracy of riches. There was a surge and sway of excitement as a woman went into the theatre in front of them.

'La Tallien! Notre Dame de Thermidor! That's her! She brought the tyrant down, she did it, La Tallien!'

The murmur lifting, becoming a shout of acclamation. The woman turned to the ragged crowd and curtsied, diamonds glittering at her throat, on her splendid, naked arms, in her hair. Cropped black hair like polished sea-coal. Naked shoulders. Almost naked bust. It was the girl who had worn the leopard-skin at the Récamiers' reception. But not all the shouting was in praise of her.

'Our Lady of Thermidor?' a woman screamed. 'Look at her! Look at her diamonds! And we're starving! I wish Robespierre had got her first!'

The crowd dividing, quarrelling, women fighting. The Citizeness Tallien's escort hurried her inside the theatre.

Inside the foyer a brilliance of candlelight and gilding, a flash of mirrors, of women's jewels. Ostrich feathers. Silks, bare flesh, the scent of powder, perfumes, flowers. An old woman selling nosegays of hothouse violets. Ushers in black knee breeches and long green coats, theatre girls offering programmes, and little cartons of *marrons glacés* and candied fruits. The poor abbé staring about him, bewildered. An usher brought them to Léonie's box, Léonie leaning forward over the velvet-covered parapet, talking in a loud voice to the Citizeness Tallien, in the next box to hers.

'Thérézia, my dear! I haven't seen you for this age! When are you going to visit me in my poor little cottage? Such a joke of a house!'

On the stage a woman was singing an aria, but it was not possible to tell whether she was singing well or not. Only a voice half lost in the babble of conversations and greetings and farewells. Before the new arrivals had settled down the act was already over, and the audience poured back into the foyer and the broad gallery behind the main tier of boxes. A hand touched her arm. A man beside her, whispering, 'Madame Vernet? A word with you if you please.' Nodding towards a less noisy, less crowded corner of the gallery. Feeling her heart catch, and then beat faster.

'If you would stay here a moment,' she said to the abbé. Now. It had come. The man who had whispered to her was buying two glasses of champagne from a theatre girl. 'To your good health, madame.' Giving her a glass, touching his glass to hers. 'And to the King's health.'

'To—the King's health,' she answered, keeping her voice as low as his. A tall man with small, deep-set eyes, close together above a long nose, the end of it oddly tilted up, as if it was pressed against an invisible window-pane. She felt an instantaneous distrust of him, a pricking of the hairs at the nape of her neck, and was sorry that she had answered his toast to the King. And yet, if he was from Barras——

'Tell me quickly, monsieur.'

'Tell you—?' And for a fraction of a second the deep-set, cunning eyes were at a loss. 'On the contrary, madame, it is you, I hope, who will tell *me* something.' The eyes searching hers, like small swift animals, ferrets, peering out of their burrows, hungry for prey.

She was going to say, 'Then you are not from General Barras?' And the stupidity, the imbecility of that almost self-betrayal made her flush crimson.

'Some weeks ago, you visited the Temple?'

She said nothing, the pricking at the nape of her neck like a cold hand touching her. What was he? Police? A trick of Barras' to make her betray herself, compromise herself with——? Felt the prison gates closing, closing, like a weight crushing her against a wall.

'I respect your discretion, madame. No matter. You were seen by a friend of mine. I have friends everywhere.' And as if to underline that he turned and bowed to someone, smiling, lifting his glass in salute. Turned back to her. 'What did you find in the Temple, madame?' He waited, cocking his head, the odd, tip-tilted nose lifting, seeming to snuff for the truth in the air surrounding her.

'Who are you?' she whispered. Wanting to support herself against the damask-panelled wall beside her. Prison has broken me, she thought. If I have to go back——

'I pray your pardon. I am the Baron de Batz, at your service, madame.'

'The Baron——' For a moment the name meant nothing.

'I regret what you must feel, madame. My name must have unhappy memories for you——'

The Conciergerie. The trial. Fouquier-Tinville reading out the list of the accused. The heads of accusation. 'The Foreign Conspiracy' and 'the arch-villain de Batz'.

'It was a habit of the Robespierre clique to accuse me of everything. I assure you that no one is happier than I that you survived. But the Temple, madame. Was it the King?'

'I have nothing to tell you.'

He came closer still. 'I think you were brought there to identify him for General de Charette? And if it had really been Louis XVII whom you saw—perhaps you would by now be back in the Vendée again, discussing—terms?' He looked swiftly round to see if anyone was close enough to overhear them. 'Am I right, madame? Terms of peace? There are others besides General de Charette who are interested—who have a right to be interested in those terms. And in everything that concerns the King. If you are a loyal servant of His Majesty you will listen to me very carefully.'

'Monsieur——'

'Listen, I say. Are you to be brought to see the true King? But why else would you be still here, free? Neither back in the Vendée nor back in prison? Am I right?' His eyes more and more ferret-like, swift and feral and untrustworthy in their deep hiding-holes. 'You don't answer me? I tell you, great projects hang on this. For the—loyal subject—who told me where the true King is to be found—a hundred thousand livres would not be too rich a reward. Two hundred thousand. Think of it, madame.' He turned again, bowing to an acquaintance, smiling. 'We'll walk back to your party. Two hundred thousand livres. In gold. For the whereabouts of a house. A few details.'

Before she could answer him he was bowing, lifting her fingers to his lips, was gone. She saw him for a moment, giving the empty champagne glasses to the theatre girl. Powdered hair, an old-fashioned queue clubbed and tied with a black ribbon. Then he had vanished completely, like a conjuring trick. The abbé staring about him, lost among unfamiliar shadows. 'Is that you, Madame Vernet?'

'Yes, yes.' The sense of chill remaining with her. Irrationally. Nothing to fear. Only another intriguer, hunting for secrets, advantages. One of a thousand, ten thousand—but how had he known so much? Eyes peering out of dark holes, spying. Surrounded by them. There was a stir at the head of the broad staircase, and the Citizen-General Barras came slowly towards them, followed and flanked by his courtiers, hanging on his every word and step and gesture, his smile. A royal progress along the gallery.

'You look magnificent, citizeness' he said to Hester. 'Citizen abbé, your servant.' Gathering them into his entourage, the whispers running like a green fire of jealousy; 'Who's the tall girl? And "abbé", did he say? A priest? What does that mean? Where d'you say the girl is from? What a height she is! It's unnatural!'

Léonie's box again. General Barras beside her, asking for the loan of her programme, for someone else to lend him an opera glass. When he returned the programme to her there was a fold of paper inside it, pushed under the green silk cord. A single line of writing, unsigned. 'Tomorrow morning at seven. Be prepared for a long journey.'

The door at her back opened slightly, and a spiral of air touched her bare shoulders. She shivered, turned slightly, thinking someone was behind her. But there was no one. Only the door unfastened, opening in a draught.

Chapter 32

Three men came for her. In a *fiacre*, so that they were crushed together uncomfortably as soon as she got in. The two policemen who had taken her to the Vendée and back again, and a stranger, a man dressed with a nondescript shabbiness. Thin, cold features, cold eyes. A hint of fox about him, about the reddish hair that showed beneath the brim of his hat. He did not introduce himself, but gave her a limp, cold handshake and a brief bow. The two policemen seemed nervous of him, not speaking at all, and seeming uncertain whether they should acknowledge her as someone they knew already.

The *fiacre* drove as fast as its horse would take them towards the Orléans barrier and a mile beyond it. They got down at the gate of a villa and the red-haired man dismissed the *fiacre*.

'Is it—here?' Hester asked him. Wrought iron gates, tall stone pillars, coats of arms carved into the stone. He shook his head and offered her his arm.

'Walk with me, citizeness.' The two policemen followed them and they walked for half a mile. At a turn in the road a coach was waiting. In all the half mile the red-haired man had said nothing at all. One of the policemen had carried the small, ancient valise that had once belonged to General de Richeteau, and that old Anne the servant had found for her. The policeman put it in the trunk of the coach. She thought of her earlier journeys with them and tried to smile at the changed circumstances. But she found her mouth was stiff with nerves, with tension.

'We have a long journey ahead of us,' the red-haired man said. 'If you permit, I shall sleep now.'

The younger policeman had unfastened a cloth and spread it out on his knees. Bread and cheese and a bottle of wine. 'If you'd like to share with us, citizeness? There's no wine glass, I'm afraid.'

'I've breakfasted already, thank you.'

The two men drank from the neck of the bottle, turn and turn about, ate, whispered between themselves, their eyes watching their sleeping companion. She stared out at the winter countryside. Patches of snow. Black trees. Farmhouses crouched under a heavy sky. It rained for an hour, a cold sleet, making the road still worse. Midday. Evening. Dark. They had changed horses several times. At four in the afternoon they had a meal, not in an inn but in a private house. The owners of the house were not there, or not visible, only a servant woman and an old manservant. Hot punch and roast chickens. They had obviously been expected and the red-haired man at least knew the servants well. They seemed afraid of him, and called him 'Citizen Representative', scuttling to carry out his orders.

After the meal they travelled on through the night, sleeping, waking, jolted together, the charcoal stove between them making the air stifling without making it warm. She dreamed of the King, of the Temple, of the cretin there, of Michel. Of fighting. She woke up once and found that she must have cried out in her sleep, because the others were awake, staring at her in the reddish light of the stove.

'You have bad dreams, citizeness?' the Citizen Representative asked, his voice touched with something personal for the first time in speaking to her.

'Sometimes.'

He drew his hand down over his thin face, like drawing down a blind after that moment of self-revelation. 'It is a disease of the age.'

They slept again. Woke in a greasy daylight, her mouth and throat dry, her lips sticking together, her eyes feeling hot and full of dust.

'How much further?' she asked.

'We should be there tomorrow.'

All day. All the next night. Another grey, ugly morning. They were in a forest, the road even worse than yesterday, or the day before. Lurching into great holes, deep, frozen ruts. She realized that in all the journey they had not seen another coach, scarcely another traveller. The coach stopped suddenly, without warning. When she looked out of the window, she saw a man by the roadside.

Like a huntsman, a dark coat and high leather gaiters, carrying a long-barrelled gun across his shoulders.

The Citizen Representative got down from the coach, stiff and muttering, stretching himself. Cold air, icy but fresh, a blessed relief. The huntsman saluted. She heard him say, 'Everything is ready, citizen.'

'We are here,' the citizen representative said to her. He went to the coachman and gave orders in a low voice. As soon as they were all standing by the roadside and one of the policemen had taken her valise from the trunk, the coach drove on.

'I think you are used to marching? It is about three miles through the forest.'

She looked down at her sandals, at Monsieur Leroi's silk stockings and muslin gown, under the dark velvet cloak. 'I'm not dressed for marching.'

'I am sorry. You should have been warned. But there is no help for it.'

The younger policeman carried her valise. The other offered her his arm.

'I am best by myself, citizen.' And after the first few yards, the ground hard and unyielding under her feet, and then crisp and rustling with fallen, frozen leaves, her sandals, her clothes did not matter. Clean air, cold and sharp, catching her throat, her lungs, reminding her of a hundred winter mornings with Michel. On horseback, riding with the others, with Anne, with Regrenille, with Perrine, with the men. I am free again, she thought. Felt her spirits lift as they had not lifted since—since she could not remember when—since long before Savenay. It is a beginning of something wonderful, she thought. The King will be freed, and I shall—I shall be with Michel again. We shall begin again quite new, everything wonderful. If she had been alone she would have run, have gone running among the trees, would have sung. She began to hum the Marseillaise, setting the Royalist words to it in her mind. The two policemen stared at her.

'I didn't think you sang that?'

'Oh yes, with our own words to it.' She nodded towards the back of the red-haired man who had gone far ahead of them. 'Who is that man?'

'The Citizen Representative Fouché.'

She had heard the name before, but could not remember why or how. She bent down and took off the useless sandals, and walked in her stockinged feet. Let the stockings be ruined. She would have given the whole *corbeille* of Monsieur Leroi's rubbish for a pair of riding boots and breeches, and a shirt and coat. But in a few days' time!

'*Quoi! des gueux d'hérétiques*
Feraient la loi dans vos foyers?'

They glanced at her again, but without asking her what song it was. One of them fell back, and she began to have the sense of being guarded. Once or twice she thought that among the trees she could see the huntsman who had been by the roadside. Or another like him. More than one. It gave her an unpleasant feeling of nakedness, helplessness. And yet it was reasonable. If the King was here, they would not leave him unguarded.

An hour walking. There had been no path when they began, but now they had come to a cart-track. Rough, unkempt, but used. She heard a dog baying, and then howling as though someone had kicked it. The trees fell back, there was a field, unpromising-looking even for winter. A low huddle of buildings; blackened, sodden thatch; a frost glitter here and there, grey ice in the ruts of the track now that they were clear of the trees. A man slouching towards them, waving his arms and shouting. 'Go away, go away, go away! I'll shoot.' He had no gun, and when he came closer she saw that he was an idiot, his features working. An older man followed him, a heavy woodman's axe swinging in one hand. A huge dog came racing the length of its chain, was brought up short and howled. The older man kicked it as he went by and it slunk back out of sight.

The Citizen Representative Fouché ignored the idiot and talked in a low voice to the man with the axe. They both glanced towards Hester. The Citizen Fouché beckoned her forward. The two policemen stayed at the farm gate. There was still that sense of being watched, surrounded; of armed men keeping out of sight. The thought crossed her mind that they might intend that she should not leave here, that all this—because she knew too much now? Knew that the child in the Temple was not the King? Her mouth was dry again. To die on horseback was another thing. She looked at the man's axe blade, at his face, at once sour and brutal, the face of a peasant who hates all men; all women; rich, poor, neighbours, strangers, his own family who want to share his sparse food. A man who would kill anyone for another crust of bread.

The peasant jerked his head for her to follow him, the idiot cried 'I'll shoot! I'll shoot!' The dog growled treacherously from the shelter of a broken wine cask. She picked up the skirts of her cloak and her gown to walk carefully across the filthy yard. Frozen dung-heap running yellow icicles and tongues of half frozen urine. Puddles of filth, a scatter of droppings from half a dozen moulting hens. A donkey tethered to a wall that seemed on the point of tumbling into a rubble of stones and mud.

'In here,' the peasant said. She had to bend almost double to go inside the doorway.

A smell of dirt, of sour, rancid cooking, garlic, stale wine. A sloven of a woman, almost as tall as Hester, a great gaunt shadow looming out of the darkness of the kitchen, wiping her hands on a ragged skirt. The peasant spoke to her in dialect, rough and incomprehensible. The woman opened another low door and waited for them to go through.

'After you, citizeness,' the Representative Fouché said, and again she had the stupid fear that she would not leave this place alive, that someone was waiting beyond the doorway, an axe lifted, a club. But there was no one. A bare room with a table and stiff chairs. There was even a clock hanging on the wall, ticking. A staircase led up from the far corner. The woman passed ahead of her, led the way up the stairs. There were only two rooms up there. They went through one to reach the other. The first room must be where the couple slept. A big, curtained bed, a smell of staleness, airlessness. In the inner room a boy was sitting on a truckle bed, wearing only a coarse shirt, the bed looking as if he had heard them coming and just got up from it. His eyes frightened.

'People to see you,' the woman said. The boy cringed into himself, hugging his chest with thin arms. He had fair hair, as far as she could see in that light, with the shutters still closed and only a filter of daylight coming through.

'Stand up and let 'em see you.'

The boy stood, slowly, watching the woman, glancing at Hester, at the Citizen Fouché, sharp back at the woman again, like someone afraid of doing wrong without knowing it, of being struck for no known cause.

'The shutters, woman,' the Citizen Fouché said. 'And open the window.' He held a handkerchief to his nose. It was hard to tell if the smell came from the woman, or the boy, or the bedding.

[318]

Although the quantity of bedding seemed adequate enough, and the shirt was heavy flannel. In the daylight she could see that the boy's hair had red glints in it, and he seemed the right age, although grown taller than she had expected. He stood waiting, his lower lip hanging. He put up a hand and touched it, pulled it down lower.

'Leave me alone with him,' Hester said.

'That is impossible—' the Citizen Fouché began. She turned towards the door. 'Then let us go back to Paris. I have come here to speak to him alone, or not at all.'

After a moment the Citizen Representative smiled thinly. 'As you please, citizeness. It is in your own interests to be discreet. And brief. You have five minutes.'

'I have as long as I need. I have been sent here by the Citizen General Barras to act as I think right. Do you take it on yourself to contradict his orders?'

'I shall be waiting outside,' he said. He went out, and the woman followed him, staring at Hester as she closed the door. There was the sound of a bolt, or a heavy bar sliding into place.

'I am come to help you,' she whispered. 'Will you talk to me?'

The boy nodded.

'What is your name?'

'Louis Charles Capet, the son of the tyrant.' His voice hoarse, and rough. As he spoke he coughed, pressing one hand against his side. A small, dry, racking cough. His thin cheeks had an unhealthy colour, too red in patches on the cheekbones, too white elsewhere. He was very thin, and his hair hung lank and dull. She tried to stifle her feelings, keep her voice steady.

'What was your mother's name?'

'The Austrian bitch. I'm glad she's dead, curse her filthy soul.' He looked expectantly at Hester, his mouth beginning to smile placatingly, like a child who has recited a lesson well and hopes to be praised.

'Have they taught you to say those things? Oh child, oh monseigneur.' She had no doubt that it was the King, they could not have taught another child to——. But she made herself go on. 'Do you remember one day, a long, long time ago, when you were still with your father and your mother and you were taken to a great building full of people? You had to stay a long time in a very small room, very crowded. That was just before you were put in prison. You remember that day?'

He nodded suspiciously, as though the lesson was taking an unexpected turn and he was growing afraid again. 'Give me a drink,' he whispered suddenly. 'Brandy.' He plucked at his lip, his hand trembling.

She could not prevent herself from sounding shocked. 'Brandy?'

'I'll sing,' he said, wheedling. He began to sing a street song, the words vile. She gripped his hands.

'Stop that! Stop it!'

'He gives me brandy when I sing for him.'

'I have come to give you your freedom. Do you not know who you are, what you are?'

'I'm Louis Charles Capet, the son of the——'

'You are Louis the Seventeenth, King of France. You are to be King, do you understand what that means? To rule over the whole of France, to be the greatest man in the whole country. Do you understand any of this?'

He shook his head, but slowly and wonderingly, his eyes changing. He had beautiful eyes, his only good feature, large and blue as the sky, and the remains of intelligence in them. But the whites were veined and yellow, and the lids crusted with matter.

'Tell me,' she urged him, 'what were you doing that day? Were you playing?'

'I had a bandalore,' he whispered, 'I remember.' He began to cry, silently, huge tears, his face not changing. 'My mama, my mama.' He slid down off the bed onto his knees, caught Hester in his thin arms. 'They made me say it. They beat me until I said what I did, that she lay beside me and——shall I go to Hell, madame?'

'No, no. She is in Heaven, she understands, she knows what they did to you. And your sister is well, I saw her not long ago, she is neat and pretty and they are not hurting her.'

'My sister? They haven't killed her?'

'No, and she will soon be free, I promise you. And you are to go on a journey, you are to join your army and they will make you King. You shall have a horse, and brave men will guard you and fight for you if need be. But there will be no need. The whole of France longs for you to be King.' She kissed his forehead. 'Have they been cruel to you here?'

'They beat me sometimes.'

'They shall not do it any more.' She stood up, and lifted him to his feet. There were tubercles on his wrists, swollen lumps like pigeon's eggs. He began coughing, and she had to hold him up until the fit was passed. He sat down on the bed. 'We shan't let them see that you have been crying,' she said. 'Kings do not cry.' There was a jug of water on a table and she dipped her handkerchief into it and began to clean his face, and his eyelids. He seemed astonished to be gently treated, and began to cry again. She waited until he could control himself, kneeling in front of him. 'I'll leave you my handkerchief,' she said. 'As a promise that I shall come back very soon. And then, then you will be free for ever, there will be no more prison, no more rooms like this.'

She made herself leave him, thinking suddenly of the boy in the Temple, the imbecile. Who would free him? But they must, they should make it the part of any Treaty, however secretly, that the boy should live with the best care that could be had, all the remaining days of his life. And this boy would see to it, when he was King. She knocked and waited. The wooden bar slid back, the woman was there. She rebarred the door before she went downstairs with Hester. In the room below Hester touched her arm.

'If you, or your man, or anyone, lays a hand on him again,' she said, 'I will come here and kill you. Do you understand that?'

The woman looked at her in astonishment, crude anger in her face. She saw Hester's eyes and the anger turned to self-justification. 'He pisses his bed. He's a pig. The son of a pig.'

'I shall kill you,' Hester repeated. 'And bury you in your dung-heap.'

The woman took a step back, felt for the door into the kitchen behind her. They went out into the squalid yard and Hester said to the Citizen Representative. 'Tell this creature she is to treat him with respect, and with kindness. If she does not know what those are, explain them to her.'

The Citizen Fouché smiled his cold, somehow threatening smile. 'I am sure that she will do all that is correct. If you would step aside with me for a moment, citizeness?'

He took her to the gateway, and a few yards beyond it. 'You are satisfied? As to whom you have just seen?'

'Yes.'

'Then we will go back to the road, citizeness, and take our different directions. You may tell General Charette that if all goes as we wish, he shall have his King before midsummer. Within six months from today. Providing——' He began to walk away from the farmhouse towards the forest, picking his way delicately among the ruts and frozen muck of the cart-track. 'Providing that no word of this reaches anyone beyond ourselves. The citizen Barras is walking a tight-rope. So are we all who want to bring this about. One word, one rumour about surrendering that boy to you, and——' He stopped for a moment to face her, and astonishingly, made the sign of the cross. As another man might have drawn a finger across his throat. 'You understand?'

She nodded, and he walked on, saying nothing more until they were almost at the road. Most of the time he walked far ahead of her, alone, the two policemen following her, still carrying her valise. The same sense of being watched, or guarded. Although she saw no one except themselves. When they were five minutes away from the road, or so she judged, the Citizen Fouché stood still, waiting for her. 'There are two carriages waiting for us now. One will take you to the Vendée. You will travel alone. I suggest you keep this about you. I think you know how to use it.' And he gave her a pistol, of the kind that duellists use, wrapped in a cotton neckcloth. She took it wonderingly, unwrapping the cotton to look at the barrel, chased with silver. 'I am sure you will not need it, we have taken precautions to see that you are not followed. But it will remind you to be cautious. And silent. And here is the document you wanted for your husband. His *laissez-passer.*'

They went on together to the road, and the coaches. Hers small and shabby, with only two horses. But the coachman looked a vigorous man. Of the same stamp as the two policemen who were now climbing into the other coach, after stowing her valise for her.

'One last word,' the Citizen Fouché said. 'It is not only from one side that you need to look for danger.' He closed the door and stood back before she could say anything. Nodded, and her coach was moving. She stayed for a moment sitting forward, still looking out of the window. I am going towards Michel, she thought. Towards Michel. She sat back in a corner of the seat and looked again at what he had given her. There was a small powder-horn, three bullets in a twist of paper, a thin, delicate steel ramrod, and some wadding. And the pistol, lying heavy in her lap.

Chapter 33

She woke suddenly. Sharp awake, as she had used to do on campaign. Lay very still, not breathing, listening. What had woken her? The inn was silent. Even the wind had dropped. A sense of freezing in the air of the room. The fire, such as it had been, had died long ago. It must be four, five in the morning. A servant getting up? Another traveller? But there had been no other traveller. Only herself and the coachman. And he had gone to sleep in the stables, beside the horses. He was probably warmer there. She had wanted to go on, they were only thirty miles from Grasla, but the man had driven fourteen hours that day and was finished. So were the horses, wretched beasts fit for the knackers, that had had been all they could find at the last posting stage.

A step outside her door? There was no bolt, not even a latch, she had had to put her valise against it to keep it shut as she undressed. What was wrong with her? Had she lost her senses as well as her courage in these last months? A wretched hovel of an inn, thirty miles from the Royalist headquarters—what could happen here? And no one had followed them, she knew it. Day after day an empty road behind them. Scarcely a living creature coming from the opposite direction. As though France itself had died and they were travelling through an endless graveyard.

The inns each more miserable, more starving than the last. This one had been hard put to it to give her a bowl of watery soup and some vile wine for supper. There had been no bread, not even the greyish cement made of rye husks and sweepings that Paris now had for its daily ration.

She sat up slowly, turned back the covers. There was no one outside. No one, and yet—were those voices? She went softly to the door, listened again. A whispering. Very faint. They must be in the kitchen. Servants. The woman of the house. But both the woman and the man last night, and the servant girl, had shouted at one another as if they were calling sheep on a hillside. It was hard to imagine them having the delicacy to whisper because someone else might be sleeping. And that hidden nerve somewhere in her body began to quiver more strongly with the sense of danger.

She went softly to the bed and took her cloak, to cover her white shift. Took the pistol from beside the bed. She had laughed at herself for emptying it and reloading it last night. The last time. So close to Michel. One more day. Loading it out of habit, for something to do, for an echo of old days, as though to handle the powder, the bullet, the fine-made ramrod, brought her closer to Michel, helped to cleanse away another fragment of that grey stain of humiliation prison had left on her.

Weighing the pistol in her hand. Heavy, and yet well balanced. She went back to the door. The whispering had stopped. She held her breath. Not a sound. No clattering of pots, no raking of ashes that there would have been if a servant had been in the kitchen. But that sense of—a living presence near her. Coming nearer. Her heart beating, hard and fast, and then growing quieter, her breathing growing steady. She waited behind the door. The sharp, brittle creak of a stair, and the sudden deepening of stillness as someone stood frozen, waiting for the noise to die, to hear if anyone stirred, woken by it. Then the soft slithering of a step. Bare feet, or boots covered with cloth, for silence. Outside the door.

She heard the brushing of fingers touching and feeling for the latch. They must know that there was no bolt inside. Had it been taken off on purpose? While she ate her vile supper? The door pressing inwards, pushing the valise aside. At that sound the pressing stopped. She felt the draught of even colder air from the doorway. Thought she could see the outline of a hand, feeling round the edge of the door, touching the corner of the valise. Lifting. Was that all they wanted? Robbery? And as she thought of it the door was forced violently back, hitting against her, almost knocking the pistol out of her hand. A swift rush of darker shadow across the room. The sound of a heavy blow, a club, striking the bed.

'Hit the bitch again,' a man whispered, hoarse and savage.

'She's not here!' This voice loud in panic. The sounds of bed-clothes torn aside, thrown to the floor. The club rattling against the floor beneath the bed, searching. 'Let's get out of here!'

'Be quiet, curse you. Fetch a light from below. There'll be papers somewhere.'

The Commandant Piré. His voice, beyond all doubting.

She could not control herself. Fear like a sickness, like a palsy. Her finger tightening on the trigger against her will. The tremendous sound of the shot in the narrow darkness, the flash of fire. She did not know where she aimed. The man by the bed yelled in terror, ran, hit against the half-open door, fell, scrambled. Was outside. She heard him trying to leap down the stairs, falling again. Heavy steps running, the banging of a door below. Voices, a woman shouting 'Murder! Murder!' Outside more sounds of running. Then of horses. Fading.

After what seemed a long time the innkeeper came up the stairs, a candlestick in his hand, the candle flame trembling as his hand shook. When he saw her, he shook so much in terror that the candle threatened to go out.

'You had best put that down,' she said. She aimed the pistol at him, gesturing towards the table by the window.

'I swear by the Holy Virgin! Madame! I had nothing to—you're safe! I heard—I thought—'

'You thought I was safely dead. What did they pay you?'

'I call God to witness! They said—they were police——' His woman was calling from below 'Martin! What have they——?'

'They said they only—only wanted to search—for papers—what —what could I do?' The man was on his knees, his hands joined. The woman was in the doorway. Saw Hester, her husband, the pistol. Began to shriek. The servant girl on the stairs, joining her shrieks to her mistress's.

'Tell me what else they said.'

But there was nothing to be got from any of them. Only weeping, terror. The terror of poor wretches who had spent years changing sides, never sure which was the safest, how long a period of safety a new treachery could buy.

The coachman came. He swore that he had given chase to the two men. On foot? Had he not had a pistol?

'They were too far off, citizeness, before I could fire.'

Had he known? Brought her to this inn on purpose? She told him to bring out the horses at once, and put them to the coach. Told the innkeeper to give her something to eat. Long before daylight they were on the road, only thirty miles to travel. Six, seven hours. Before dark she would—how had he found her? Known she would be there? And why—why? Revenge? Hatred? But he had been looking for papers, although there had been none to find. Only the safe conduct for Michel. And to kill her. If she had been still asleep—she felt the blow of the club across her forehead. It would have crushed her skull, smashed it. She lay back in the seat feeling sick, the sour wine of her breakfast rising up in her throat. The long, long ago days of fighting seemed clean and innocent compared to this.

It was ridiculous to think like that. To die of a sabre cut on horseback, or a bullet; to die in a dirty bedroom with one's skull split open; both came to the same thing a moment afterwards. But they did not. And she saw again the famished shadow of the Commandant in that alleyway, snatching the bread and cursing her in the same instant, such a poison of hatred in his voice that it was like the handful of vipers Euphemia had once held in front of her, their spittle wet on her face. Had it been only hatred that had brought him there to the inn? And the papers only something he hoped to find, so that he could sell them? But sell them where? To whom? And how had he got money for horses, for the journey? He must have ridden fast to reach the inn before her. Unless he had known in advance? But how? Who could have told him?

An enemy of Barras? The Jacobins? Wanting to ruin the Treaty before it could be made? Ruin Barras for trying to make it? And finding Piré, starving and filled with hatred, as a perfect tool? There could be no other rational answer. She must warn Barras. But there was no way of warning him, not safely, until she herself was back in Paris. And as she lay in the corner seat of the swaying, slow, creaking lumbering coach, half drowsing as the day crept forward, grey and freezing, Paris hung on the horizon of her mind like a dark threat.

What had Fouché meant when he said, 'It is not only from one side——' Not only from the Jacobins, of course. But—who else, then? And without any conscious thought she saw de Batz's face, the ferret eyes, the white, gristle tip of his nose questing and snuffing for secrets. Saying, 'There are others besides General de Charette who are interested——' Offering her two hundred thousand livres! So that—so that he himself could rescue the King, forestall Charette and—gain the credit? The bargaining power of holding the King himself? Or—kill him, so that—someone else—?

It was not possible, not thinkable. But two, three years ago, had anything of all that she had seen since been thinkable?

And yet, de Batz the Royalist, and Piré the Jacobin, in league? Piré, eaten with hatred of everything de Batz—— But, two hundred thousand livres? How many times over would that have bought Piré's soul, and his principles, if those were what he had?

The questions going round in her mind, weaving together, cancelling one another out, melting one into another until they lost all semblance of reason, all possibility of being answered. The coach swaying, lurching, the pistol resting across her lap. The only answer to anything. Anything. Half asleep. The rattle and creaking of the wheels like voices trying to answer her. But she could not understand what they were saying. Piré. De Batz. The King. Fouché. Barras. Round and round.

She slept for an hour, woke, slept again. Dreamed of the Commandant, the snake creeping up between his fat, hairy thighs. Dreamed of the child King, kneeling by a bed, and the shadow of a club lifting, smashing down on his head. She woke sweating in the cold, in the stale airlessness, and pulled down the window-glass, drawing in a deep, deep breath of clean, frost-sharpened air. It was dark. Freezing. But she left the glass down for the sake of the cleanness of the air, of the cold that would drive away sleep, and more dreams.

An hour later they were stopped by a Royalist patrol. White sashes, white cockades. A dozen horsemen escorting her to Charette. And Michel.

Chapter 34

It was late January before they reached Paris. The Vendée already at peace, only the final Treaty to be signed, but already the reality there. Royalists walking in the streets of Nantes, the white cockade in their hats. Fraternizing with the Blues, the soldiers who had spent the past year and more hunting them like wolves. The peasants creeping back to burned farms, staring about them at ruined fields. Young women from Nantes and Angers and Saumur coming to visit the legendary Charette, to stare at his Amazons, his Court of Ladies. To look wonderingly at Hester, at Regrenille, at Madame de Bulkeley, Madame du Fief, the demoiselles Couëtus; at the peasant girls who had served him like faithful hounds and bodyguards, Marie Lourdais, Madeleine Tournant, the others. Each of them become a legend. And the leaders, the generals, the young officers. Men who had defied the whole of France, and lived, and won. Swift-moving, dancing men, who laughed, and courted, and paid compliments. And men like wolves, hard-eyed, silent. To touch them! Their swords, their guns; to think of the horrors, to feel *frissons* of delightful fears.

Dances, dinners. Cartloads of supplies found somewhere, to make the peace talks agreeable. Wine. Roast meat. Fresh bread. And the slow grinding of the conferences behind the celebrations, behind the joy of truce, of being able to walk freely in the open. She and Michel walking, talking, loving, coming to their own terms of treaty and of peace. She had no part in those other talks, except to wait to be sent back to Paris, when they reached the right stage.

It came on 21 January. 'I want the King delivered to me by mid-June. You cannot bring him yourself because you are known now as my agent. And that business at the inn—you'd only bring danger—I shall send someone for him. And between now and then,

Barras is to break the Jacobins, you understand that? I don't care how. The guillotine, arrests, exile, prison. He must so break their backs that they daren't move. When the King comes to me there must be nothing such as happened to you.' Charette's face was haggard with sleeplessness, but still alive, filled with a hard eagerness, with plans. He could not keep still as he talked, but paced the tent that the Republicans had given him. 'And I shall keep my word. No one—not my closest officers—no one shall know that the King is part of this Treaty. And after he is arrived here I'll not proclaim him King until July. Barras has that much time to prepare everything. And then——' He gripped her by the elbows, swung her round in a fury of joy. 'We shall have a king! God save His Majesty! And that bitch who has beaten him shall hang. Tell Barras to see to it, or I'll send someone to do it for him.'

And the days and nights with Michel. Like the honeymoon they had never had. The journey to Paris, thinking of nothing but that she was with him, that they were alone together, sleeping, holding one another. Tomorrow did not exist, nor yesterday, nor Paris, nor the King, nor Barras, nor Charette. Only Michel. Like discovering an unknown country that reveals itself familiar after all, moment by moment. Discovering his body. Making love. Remembering his tones of voice and finding them unchanged, the look of his eyes as he laughed, as he was quiet, the look of his face as he slept.

'It is peace!' she kept on whispering. Told him of all that had happened since they were last together. Of Léonie and Euphemia. Her father. The abbé. Perrine.

'And Creuzot?'

'He is in The Hague now, I think. They sent him to Brussels first. Léonie would be astonished if anyone mentioned him.'

But by the time they saw her again it would have been unthinkable for anyone to be so indiscreet. In the weeks since Hester had last seen her she had become acknowledged Queen. Her house was filled day and night with suitors and courtiers; *ci-devant* aristocrats jostling ex-Terrorists, Jacobins praying her help to wipe out their past and rebaptize them as devotees of Barras; army contractors; financiers; army officers looking for promotion, or reinstatment; men looking for posts in the Ministries, in Embassies; a river of gold and jewels flowing into Léonie's curved and joyous hands.

The first night that she received them she was dressed in diamonds. A mass of them round her throat and on her bosom, rising and falling as she breathed, flashing fire so that it was impossible to look at anything else, until one saw the diamond arrow dressing her coiled magnificence of hair; the diamond-studded girdle round her waist, the diamond bracelets on her plump, smooth white arms.

'Thérézia is pregnant!' she cried by way of greeting. 'Can you credit it? And by Tallien! Her husband!' Peals of laughter, echoed by the room. Euphemia beckoning Hester from a doorway.

'He is waiting for you,' Euphemia said.

General Barras. In the same small dining parlour where she had first met him, standing by the hearth. Lifting an eyebrow in welcome, smiling, raising her hand to his lips. 'So it is done,' he said. Stood while she told him all that she was briefed to tell.

'You may let General Charette know,' he said when she was finished, 'that he need no longer concern himself about the Jacobins. I have already begun with them. Long before June they'll not have a ditch left to hide in. But you understand, it is not only the Jacobins, and the one-time Terrorists, who are against the Restoration? There are a hundred factions, wanting a hundred different solutions. Between now and July I have to weld enough of them together to make us safe. But it shall be done, have no fear of it.' He himself might never have been a Jacobin. Never a Terrorist.

She became aware of the hundred, the uncountable number of factions for herself. She and Michel became as besieged in their fashion as Léonie in hers. Not openly. But in secret. Men coming softly up to them from the shadows. Whispering. At the theatre, in twilight, in her street, in a crowd. Or anonymous notes begging her to keep a rendezvous. Once she saw the Baron de Batz, or rather he saw her. Coming behind her outside the Palais-Royal.

'You have no news for me, citizeness?'

'None that you would like to hear.'

His eyes searching hers. 'Perhaps in—the summer?' He smiled and bowed, and was gone. What faction did he belong to?

She learned to guard not only her tongue, but the expression of her eyes, the movements of her hands. Even at Léonie's receptions she would be drawn aside for a moment; sudden questions whispered, hinting that the questioner knew everything and wanted only a nod of confirmation. The King was to be freed? Next month? It had happened already? He was held in Orléans, was he not? Or is it now——? And General de Charette—she knew his ultimate intentions? She was offered money. And more than money.

'I am from the Count d'Antraigues,' a man whispered to her at the theatre. 'Of the Paris Royalist Committee. The Regent has heard much of your courage, and your husband's devotion to the cause. We need such a man with us here in Paris. I am empowered to offer him promotion to colonel——'

'He is already a colonel, citizen.'

'And the Cordon of St. Louis.'

'What must he do to earn such a reward?' Trying to keep the anger from her voice, her expression.

'We need to be accurately informed, madame, of the recent negotiations with the Chevalier de Charette. Of the *secret* part of them.'

'If my husband possessed any secrets his inclination would be to keep them to himself, monsieur.'

'And the title of Baron, at the Restoration.'

'Garat is singing, monsieur. We shall miss the best of the evening.'

And outside, in the streets, the famine tightened its hold on Paris as the winter slackened. The bread ration fell from half a pound to four ounces. To two. Two ounces of vile stuff like cement, and the bread queues stretched the length of a street to obtain it. There were risings in the Faubourgs. Starving workmen, shrieking, half-demented women, invaded the Convention and were driven out by bayonets. The Muscadins swaggered in the streets like an armed force, swinging their loaded cudgels, their heavy coats and skin-tight pantaloons like a uniform. Thrashing the *canaille*, the 'starvelings', beating women with long whips. From one day to the next, people expected the Restoration. Cursed it. Hoped for it. Shrugged. Shouted 'Bread or a King! Give us bread or a King!'

'It needs only a touch,' Michel said, 'and the whole rotten building of the Revolution will fall, and we shall have won.' Lying with her in the dark, listening to shouting below in the rue du Bac. A gang of hooligans beating on doorways, threatening violence to someone. Hooligans? Royalists. The young men who would rule the city in another month.

'I hate them,' she said, astonished at her own depth of hatred for those mindless fops with their buckled slippers and their long lovelocks and their cruelty. Had the Jacobins been worse? 'I hate them! If I was Barras I would clear them from the streets like garbage!'

But Barras only shrugged, and smiled, and kissed her hand. 'All will come right,' he said to her the next afternoon, at Léonie's reception. 'You shall see.' He bent close to her. 'The fifth. We shall make the handover on the evening of the fifth of June. You shall have your King.'

That was the 31st of May, the 12th Prairial of the Revolution's calendar. Ten days since he had crushed the last rising of the Faubourgs, of the 'starvelings'. Léonie was wearing emeralds, a collar of them so high that she could barely turn her head.

'Thérézia has given birth!' she cried to someone. 'She is calling it Thermidor! Can you imagine? Poor wretched child!'

'Don't leave at once,' Barras murmured, 'not immediately after they have seen us together. Go and take supper, talk to people. Show nothing. Talk to that officer by the buffet table, he'll amuse you.'

A young, very young officer in shabby, almost ragged uniform, and gaping, ill-made boots. He was eating with both hands; with a swift, and at the same time furtive violence, like a soldier looting a food-shop. Lank chestnut hair, falling to the worn collar of his coat. He turned to look at them as they came beside him, and it was the young Italian captain of the Tuileries, who had dragged her and her father and Léonie and Euphemia into the *Manège*, that long, long ago day. Three years ago.

He looked no older. Only hungrier and even worse dressed. But he had become a general since, she saw from his epaulettes. A general of brigade.

He recognized her in the same instant, and bowed carelessly, like an old friend who had seen her yesterday. 'Your cousin keeps a good table,' he said. He waved his hand in a gesture of hospitality, as much as to say, I make you free of it, and helped himself to another cutlet from a long silver dish. A footman poured champagne for them. 'Introduce me, citeziness. General Buonaparte, citizen.'

She made the introduction, none of her mind on it, thinking, June 5th, June 5th. Seeing the farm, the boy waiting. The woman, the idiot, the man with the axe, the huntsmen guards. How had they treated him since she——? She had had Barras' assurance that all was perfect with him, that the woman had been rebuked and threatened. Just as she had had his assurance about the poor imbecile creature in the Temple. For what his promises were worth. And now?

She heard Michel talking to General Buonaparte about the Vendée, or rather General Buonaparte talking to Michel. He seemed to be lecturing him about the folly of the attack on Nantes. 'If you had only turned towards Paris, Colonel! As your army entered the gates of the city the Lilies would have floated over Notre-Dame. Within a month you'd have ruled France.'

She touched Michel's arm. 'I think we must go now. It has been a pleasure, General, but my father is not well and we must——'

They travelled alone. Only one policeman, for guide and escort, and he rode on the box with the coachman. The roads were dry, and they made better time, but it was still an endless journey, and as they came nearer to the forest she found it difficult to talk of anything, even to feel happy at what they had come to do. She turned again and again to look out of the narrow window at their backs. The road stretched empty. The fields on either side of them.

There was no one. And it was not possible that anyone should have known that they were going on this journey. Only Barras. And the policeman escorting them. And the coachman. And—who else? How could she tell, how many others there might be? But there was no one following them. She held Michel's hand in hers, and then pressed it against her side. I have become a woman, she thought. I have become what I have despised since I could remember, full of reasonless fears and stupidity. She made herself think of other things. Of her father, growing more himself by the day. He had complained bitterly that they were leaving him alone again. The valet she had found for him did not know how to clean a boot, let alone brush a coat or tie a cravat. He seemed so well at such moments that she thought that at other times he was merely pretending still to have no memory, like a child pretending not to be well yet in order to continue being spoiled. And the abbé. With one eye he could almost read print, for a few moments at a time, until his sight grew blurred with the effort. And Perrine, growing used to Paris, beginning to forget the past, or at least to put it to the back of her mind.

Am I the only one who cannot forget, cannot make terms with the present? How long ago since I thought that to have Michel beside me would be all that I could ask of God, and now——

'I wish that we were going with him,' she said, and even that, to say it, was stupidity. She could only draw danger down on him, as Charette had warned. Too many people knew her, knew what she had done. Even this—to come like this to watch the handing over herself—and yet if she did not—she and Michel—who else was there whom Charette could trust? Who knew the child?

'By tonight it will be done,' Michel said. 'We'll have a king again.'

A king? He had not seen him. And she had not told—oh, some of it, but not the way his eyes looked, the way he cringed. What kind of man would he become? What would Charette and the others do with him? Make him? To be treated as he had been and the next day to be a king. The King. To have grown men kneel to him, women flatter him. Or sneer behind his back, or cry over him. And she wished again, wholeheartedly, in spite of the danger of ruining everything, that she was to go with him into the Vendée. Could stay with him. Not for the futility of being close to a king. But because—because he had cried so childishly against her breast. Because long, long ago she had watched him playing beside his father and she had had that one impossible chance of saving him, saving his father and his mother, his sister, from all that had since happened. Because once his mother had looked at her across the heads of the crowd, and must have thought——

They were in the forest. The coach stopped where it had done before, a huntsman waiting. Did he know what this day meant? He did not show it. Saluted the policeman, Michel, went back among the trees. The coach went on to wherever the coachman intended to change horses, before he returned to wait for them, in a few hours. It would be dark by then. And the child—— The child would be on his way to Charette. She wanted to ask a woman's question: will he be all right? and gritted her teeth against it. Almost as if he was—her child.

'You'll be—I didn't tell you quite how bad he is. You won't let him see—what you think? He's so frightened of everything.'

'That's one thing his father never was.'

'His father was a grown man!' Her voice rising. She stopped herself, hung on Michel's arm. 'I'm sorry—I've thought so much about him——'

'What do you think I've done? What have we all done for these past years except think about him?' And he apologized in his turn,

[334]

and they walked on in silence. Twilight among the trees. June silence, warm and still, leaf-smelling. A lovers' time. It will be all right, she told herself, it will. It must be. So many people dead, so much ruin, for this child to become King. Nothing could prevent it now, God could not permit that. And as she walked the memories came, one by one, like pictures in a book; the old priest in the Abbaye Prison, cut down and hacked to death as he prayed; all the others; the young brothers with their angels' faces and their hunger for martyrdom; the Countess like Joan of Arc in the market square of Garnache lifting her sword, kissing the hilt in homage to this boy King; the peasants racing for the guns, armed with nothing but sharpened pitchforks; all the battles; all the graves; the last battle for Cholet, and Talmond beside her; the crossing of the Loire and Bonchamps on his death bed, whispering, 'Grace for the prisoners.' All that this boy might be King, and God be worshipped again in freedom, and all be as it once had been.

It could not be ruined now. And she drove away from her mind the thought of the Muscadins in the streets of Paris, flogging poor market women with their whips, thrashing starving workmen with their cudgels, simply because they were poor and ragged, and had cried out for bread. All for the Royalist cause and the glory of the Throne. She drove away the thought of Barras; drinking champagne and sending another convoy of his enemies to Guiana, and a slow death by fever; the thought of Léonie, on fire with emeralds, feeding her guests to suffocation while men and women and children died in the streets from hunger; drove away the thought of all the soft intriguers creeping in the shadows, who would race forward in a month or so when it was safe, and claim that they, they had restored the Throne. Who would restore the dead?

They heard the dog baying, saw the farm. Michel let go of her arm, and they went into the yard, the dog making his savage, strangled attempt to reach them, and falling back, to cringe away into his barrel as the woman came out and shouted, 'Get away, curse you.' She might almost have been shouting it at them. But she gave them a sort of greeting, and gestured them into the kitchen, trying to smile at the same time, to inform Hester of how kind she had been in the interim, and of how unnecessary Hester's threats had been. 'He's waiting for you,' she said, her voice obsequious.

He was sitting on a stool by the table, a bowl of bread and milk in front of him. He seemed to have eaten none of it, and had pushed it away from him. Could he not eat for excitement? Did he understand what was happening, going to happen? He was dressed in the same shirt, and rough serge pantaloons that must once have belonged to an adult. The idiot son, probably. And wooden sabots.

'He's sad to be leaving us,' the woman said. She tried to embrace him and he cringed, as the dog had done. Hester took her by the shoulder and pulled her aside. Michel went on one knee.

'Your Majesty.'

The boy stared at him, as frightened as he had been of the woman. 'Leave me alone with him,' Hester said, and when Michel hesitated she took his arm and the woman's and pushed them both out of the doorway. She found another stool and set it beside the boy's. 'Someone will come very soon to take you away,' she said. 'Do you know where you're going?' He shook his head. His lower lip hung and quivered.

'Am I—going to be killed?' he whispered. 'She said——'

'You are going to be King. And you must be brave. You must make your father and your mother proud of you. They will see what you do, and how you are, and every step you take, you must think, this is for my mother, this is for my dear father. You cannot think or act like other children. All your life long you must only think of others, of serving them. You are going to brave men and women who have risked their lives for this moment, for you. A thousand times. And thousands of people have died for you. Every day of your life you must remember them. You must be very brave, and very proud of what you are to be, and very humble inside because it is God who made you King, and those who fought for you, not you yourself. Can you remember all this?'

He nodded uncertainly, his eyes afraid. Of her? Of what was to happen? Of what she was saying to him? What could she say to him? And yet she felt she must, that no one else would say these things, and that he must know them, must have one chance to learn to be a true King.

'And you must learn to know your true friends. To know the good people, who tell you things you may not want to hear. To love those who serve you truly, and despise those who only flatter you. Oh child, can you understand?'

He nodded again, but his eyes had filmed over with tears. And he was only looking at her face, not listening to what she said. The tears swelled and fell. She held him against her, felt the thinness of his body, the ill shape of it, the shoulders hunched and tense with fears; years of terrors. Could he remember anything but terror? 'May God look after you. Now we'll go and walk together among the trees, and you shall get to know my husband. He is one of those who has fought for you. He can tell you about your soldiers, and all the men who are waiting for you.'

She took him outside to Michel, and for an hour they walked in the forest, slowly, because the boy coughed so much. Yet it seemed to do him good, to be in the fresh air, and away from the farmhouse and the woman. There was no sign of the man or the idiot. Nor of the huntsmen, nor of any guards. Had they been withdrawn? She sat down on a fallen tree, and Michel talked to the boy of horses and guns and battles. He might as well have been talking of the moon. He realized it himself, and stopped. What was there that either of them could say to him? The child needed a year, five years of gentleness, of being loved, and taught; instead——would Barras become his eventual guide? Proclaimed King in the West by Charette and the others. Brought in triumph to Paris. To be taken over by the politicians, the intriguers. By women like Léonie and Madame Tallien. Guarded by the Muscadins. In a year or so, would a man like Michel get near enough to him to say anything, remind him of anything?

They heard someone shouting, 'I'll shoot you, I'll shoot.'

It was the idiot, lumbering towards them, waving his arms. He ran ahead of them, back towards the farm, still shouting his war-cry. The farmer was there, and a youngish woman wearing a peasant bonnet, and an old man. The woman came forward and dropped onto her knees in front of the boy, making a great sign of the cross as she did it. Then she grasped both his hands and kissed them, while behind her the old man was also kneeling, holding his broad brimmed hat against his chest.

'God bless Your Majesty. May Christ and His angels have us in Their keeping while we bring you to your people.'

'I'll shoot him!' the idiot bellowed, jumping up and down in his excitement.

'Are you by yourselves?' Hester said. She did not know what she had expected, but one woman, one old man!

'He'll travel with us as our son.' The woman's voice trembling with pride. 'We've papers. We get the coach four miles from here.'

'Best go now if you're going,' the farmer said. 'It's nearing dark.'

'Have you a pistol?' Hester asked the old man. He shook his head.

Michel was lifting the boy's hand, going on one knee again. 'It's right that they have no weapons. If they're stopped and searched——' He kissed the boy's hand. 'God go with Your Majesty.'

The boy suddenly turned and put his arms round Hester. 'You come with me,' he whispered, his face hidden against her body, his voice muffled.

'I cannot,' she said, 'I'd only bring—danger on you.'

She had been going to say 'worse danger'.

He did not try to insist. Turned away with his hunched, rigid shoulders, his head bent, joined the two peasants waiting for him. Began walking with them towards the trees. Before they had gone a hundred yards he had to stop for a fit of coughing; and again before they were out of sight.

Chapter 35

They heard the news at the last posting-station before Paris, as they were changing horses.

'Good news, eh?' the ostler was saying to their coachman. 'The Capet wolf cub has snuffed it at last, rot his soul.'

Michel was out of the coach and had the man by the collar of his shirt while he was still laughing. Lifting him off his heels, half choking him. 'What the hell?' the man shouted, trying to free himself.

'Are you saying the King is dead?'

'Let me go, damn you. A Royalist are you? We've a Committee in this town as——'

Michel lifted a fist.

'Michel! Michel!' She flung herself down from the coach and caught his arm. 'Let him go. Tell me—tell me what has happened.'

'Blast your eyes both of you. Royalist scum. Your precious boy in the Temple is dead and buried, and may you both follow him.'

'In the Temple?'

'Aye, where the hell else?'

She got Michel back into the coach. He looked as if he still did not believe what he had heard. The coachman cracked his whip, and the half-starved horses leaned into their harness as if they were at the end of a stage rather than the beginning, but the coach moved, they were clear of the inn and the ostler's curses.

'He must have died almost the same time that we—' he began. Looked at her. She thought that he was going to leap out of the coach again and run back to the inn. Made to catch hold of him to prevent it. 'They killed him,' he whispered. 'I swear it. You said he was imbecile, but not ill? Not dying?'

'He did not look dying.'

'Barras has done this! He's betrayed us. I knew it, I knew we should never have——'

'What do you mean? God rest him, but he's better dead, poor creature. And we have the King.'

'The King?' Michel said. 'And the news shouted to the whole of France that the King is dead? That boy in the Temple that everyone still believes was the King? Why did they let the news get out if it's not a betrayal?'

'I don't understand——'

'Neither do I, but I mean to, if I have to choke Barras as I was going to choke that swine back there. You think it's just an accident, a coincidence? It must have happened the same day that we—why didn't they keep it secret if it was really *just coincidence*?' His voice savage. 'So that afterwards they could say the King had escaped? Say anything? But what they do is announce his death to the world; the son of Louis XVI is dead. So that now when the true King is announced—half of France'll not believe it. I tell you Barras has done this to protect himself and ruin us.'

'But we can prove that he's the King!'

'How? And how long will it take? When you restore a king to his throne you need to do it overnight, not by months of argument.'

'Then we'll fight for him, again. Charette——'

'Fight? With what?' He beat his fist on his knee and stared out of the window. 'We were going to bring Louis XVII to Paris, not a boy who says he's Louis XVII, and can prove it if he's given a chance. What will the armies do? Come and listen to him tell stories about his mother, as proof of who he is? Or listen to their officers who still hate our guts and say he's an impostor? What will Paris do?'

'But Barras——'

'I tell you Barras has done this. I know it. An overdose of laudanum. Or a pillow over that poor idiot boy's face for five minutes. And we're ruined, and he's safe.'

'But it was Barras who began it, wanted it!'

'He wanted peace, not a king! And he's got peace. Now he's had time to ready himself, strengthen the armies and the government in case Charette and Stofflet and the Bretons start fighting again. He doesn't need peace any more. He's used us, and we let him.' He turned towards her, slowly. 'And if the King doesn't reach Charette?'

[340]

She stared at him, 'What are you—thinking?'

'Say prayers for him,' Michel said. 'I'm thinking that there's not one chance in a thousand that he'll reach Charette. One old man? A woman? Why should Barras let them reach the Vendée? I tell you, he's had what he wants from us.'

But that night Barras received them both, his expression desolate. His explanations so persuasive that it was hard, impossible to disbelieve them. The guardians in the Temple—the doctors—the Commissioners from the Sections—there had been too many people who knew the boy was dying, that he was dead. It could not have been kept secret.

'Dying? But he——'

Barras spreading his hands wide. 'There was a sudden inflammation—in the stomach——'

'And the King?' Michel said. They were in Léonie's small dining parlour, the remains of Barras' supper on the table, the noise of fifty or a hundred guests from the rooms beyond, music, women's laughter.

'The King?' Barras echoed, lifting his handsome eyebrows. 'It is a difficulty, but one that we can overcome. We'll explain that Robespierre made the substitution. We have already spread the rumour of an escape. The Convention has even sent out orders to search for the—the boy Capet and his sister. Forgive the description, my dear fellow.'

Michel paced the narrow width of the room and came back to the empty fireplace. 'If the King doesn't reach Charette——'

The long, white, nobleman's hands spreading again in that southern gesture of resignation, courteous reproach, incomprehension. 'My dear Colonel Vernet, what are you imagining? You saw to the handing over yourselves. What should go wrong now? In a few days we shall have General Charette's acknowledgement, and then——'

Almost impossible to disbelieve him. To think of murder and betrayal, in that comfortable, rich, furnished room. The silver champagne bucket, the wink and flash of crystal in the candlelight; the tall, elegant, easy man astonished at their suspicions. He put an arm round Michel's shoulders, smiled at Hester. 'Come, you've lived with suspicions too long to trust anyone. Heaven knows, so have we all. May God grant us to re-create a France in which we can trust one another again. Now, champagne? Supper for you both?

[341]

Léonie will have someone look after you. I have to go myself. Duty, alas. But you have done your part. There's nothing to worry about. You have your King.'

He left them half convinced, more than half; to walk home to the rue du Bac, and her father's fretfulness, and Perrine's patience, and the abbé Bernard trying to read his Office, a sentence at a time, resting his eyes between whiles. Warmth and quietness. She lay that night in Michel's arms thinking of the dead boy, and of the living one who must by now almost have reached Charette. Perhaps tomorrow, the next day. And then—she prayed for him, her lips moving silently against Michel's bare shoulder.

'What are you whispering?'

'Nothing.' She held herself close to him, smoothed her finger-tips along his arm, across his chest, felt the strength of his heartbeat. 'If——' she breathed.

'If what?'

'If we—if we should ever—have a child—what kind of world would she live in?'

He pushed himself up on one hand, staring down at her as she lay in the dark beside him. The narrow bed, too narrow for them both.

'What?' he breathed. When she did not answer he said, 'You're not—are you telling me that——?' His voice urgent, different. He put his hand on her breast, as though he in his turn was feeling how her heart was beating. Brought his hand down her body to lie on her flat stomach. 'Are you?' Whispering.

'No,' she said, 'no!' For a moment almost angry with him, almost in horror of the thought, and then—— 'Would you——? Is it—something that you want? Very much?'

He did not answer immediately. Bending his head down until his mouth was close by hers. 'And you?' His voice so low that she was not sure whether he had spoken at all or she had imagined it. She felt her heart beating hard and fast. Rebellion. And behind that, something else, that she could not recognize. For a moment did not want to recognize. Thought of the boy clinging to her, the narrow, stiff shoulders, the limping walk, the fear in his eyes. If we had a child, she thought, how I should care for him! How I should care for his mind and body! For hers. It would be a girl. And she would know nothing of all this world of treachery and killing. Would live all her life in sunlight.

She held Michel close to her, against her. Touched his hair, his shoulder. How would she look? His hair? Black, black hair? His face? That Red Indian, carved face. In a girl? And thought of the Indian girl, the suppleness, the scented skin, and was furious for a moment; with him; with herself; with womanhood. And made herself grow soft and yielding, lay waiting.

Seven days later they heard from Charette that the King had not reached him. The message was in code, brought to them by a messenger who came to the rue du Bac in the dark, saluted and left without a word, without showing his face. Michel spread out the paper in the lamplight and they decoded it together, Hester with the copy of the Missal that served as a codebook, Michel writing the letters one by one as she found them, under the numbers of the code.

'He has not come. What has happened? You swore Barras could be trusted. Now he has betrayed everything. The King is dead, I know it. *If he ever began the journey*. When I discover who did this I shall kill them, *whoever they are*. And the boy dying in the Temple is part of the betrayal. But it will not serve Barras' purpose. The King is dead, but there is another King. Long live Louis XVIII. You have been Barras' dupes. The Chevalier de Charette. General-in-Chief of His Majesty's armies of the West.'

'What can have happened to him?' Hester breathed.

She sat with the letter in her shaking hands, staring at it without seeing the words, the lines of numbers, Michel's strong writing underneath them. Saw the boy walking, hunched and small between the old man and the peasant woman. Walking away into the shadows. What had happened? He had turned his head to look at her after that last fit of coughing. Had leaned against a tree, bent double, and as he had straightened up he had looked towards her and lifted one hand, very timidly, in the hint of a farewell.

'What can have happened?' Michel said between his teeth. 'They've killed him. First the idiot boy in the Temple. Then the King. Either that couple who took him away or someone lying in wait for them. And he suspects *us*! Us!'

She repeated his word stupidly, not taking in for a second what he meant. 'Us? Who——?'

Michel tore the letter out of her hands. 'When I discover who did this—whoever they are—— He means *us*! Can't you read?' He grasped about him for words venomous enough to contain his rage, and failed to find them. Smashed his fist down onto the frail table so

[343]

that it threatened to break. '*If he ever began the journey!* Damn his soul! To write like that to me! To you! Who've—if he was here in Paris I'd——'

'Michel! Please. If the King is dead——'

'If? You think they stopped on the way for a few days' rest? Lost the road? Of course he's dead.' He crossed himself, walking up and down the ante-room. 'What happened to you in that inn happened to him. Only he didn't survive it. And Charette! What does he write?' He came back to the table, snatched up the letter in a savagery of contempt. '*The King is dead, but there is another King. Long live Louis XVIII.* Have you ever seen the creature he calls Louis XVIII? D'you know what he's like? That crapulous Judas!' He read down to the bottom of the letter, his lips moving, almost snarling. '*You have been Barras' dupes!*'

She thought he would break something. Crushing the letter between both hands, ripping it into fragments. She had never seen him like this, not even when they had had the worst of their quarrels; not when she had tried to free the spy that day in the woods; never.

'Charette?' he whispered, his voice sinking under the weight of his fury. 'That dancing master!'

'But Michel——'

'Don't try and answer me, don't try and soothe me down! That—that womanizer, with his silk scarves and his lace and velvet, and—damn and damn his little, lace-edged soul to Hell. *General-in-Chief of His Majesty's armies of the West*! Because he's still alive, when the real generals are all dead! And why the devil is he still alive? Because——' He choked on his fury, had to sit down and prop his elbows on the table, hide his face in his hands. 'Why do you think I've fought so long?' he whispered. 'To put the Count of Provence on the throne as Louis XVIII? To make Charette a Marshal of France? I've fought for my King's son. And now Charette says, like announcing a dance, *The King is dead but there is another King*!' He put his head down on the table, and buried his face in the crook of his arm.

She knelt beside him, put her arms round him. 'He may not be dead,' she whispered, stroking his hair. 'God couldn't allow him to be dead. Not now, not after—we'll go to Barras. If we have to kill him we'll make him tell the truth——'

But the next morning Barras was out of Paris. Gone on a tour of the north-east, commandeering food for the city. He was away ten days, and the day that he returned the news came that the Treaty with Charette and the Vendée was finally and completely broken. Charette had attacked the Republicans at Essarts. The war was begun again.

Chapter 36

'I give you my solemn promise,' Barras said, 'I know nothing of what has happened to the boy. Do you think I saved him out of the Temple in order to have him murdered in a ditch?'

As handsome, as elegant as ever, his legs stretched out beside the dining table in Léonie's parlour, white fingers playing with the stem of a champagne glass, begging them to sit down, to eat with him, to take a glass of champagne. Once again it did not seem possible that he was lying. Could anyone lie with such a show of frankness? And yet she was certain he was lying. He had known. Had known! Slowly, she took Michel's arm, and tightened her fingers on it in warning.

'If the woman bringing the boy to Charette was indiscreet,' Barras said. 'Showed him too much respect——' He sighed, lifting one eyebrow and shaking his head sadly. 'The man who attacked you? You say you knew him as a bitter Jacobin?'

'I knew him as a murderer.'

'So. If General Charette could not do better than send one woman and one old man, travelling by public coach——'

'You know why he did that,' Michel said, freeing himself from Hester's grasp. 'You could have brought him openly to the Vendée, with a regiment for escort. Ten regiments.'

'And been in prison or dead myself, before he was proclaimed King? My dear Colonel, if I may say it to you without offence, you know a great deal about warfare, but not very much about power and politics. Could I even trust the regiments? My dear, dear Colonel——'

He put down his champagne glass and rubbed his finger-tips deep into the sockets of his eyes. 'But I make allowances for your feelings.' He looked sharply at Michel, and then at Hester. 'Have you thought that it might not have been Jacobins who—have done whatever has been done?'

'What do you mean?' Michel turning towards him with a swift movement as if he still meant to attack him, as he had threatened before they saw him.

'There are more kinds of Royalist than one,' Barras said. 'Not all of them welcomed the idea of a boy-King under Charette's tutelage. How much do you think the Count of Provence might have been willing to give to cease being merely Regent? And to become King Louis XVIII? Uncles are often less than tender towards their nephews, and the uncles of child-kings notoriously so.'

He let them consider the possibility, that between themselves they had already more than considered, watching them over the edge of his champagne glass. The house was quiet. Léonie already gone out, to someone else's reception, Euphemia with her.

'Your position, here in Paris,' Barras said, 'has become— equivocal, I am afraid. There are people—in powerful positions— who will expect to see you arrested. At the least. You were here to negotiate a Treaty and to help see that the terms of it were kept. Now it has been broken, and officially you're enemies of the Republic. Do I need to tell you that I want nothing unpleasant to happen to you?'

Michel turned towards him from the windows where he had been drumming impatiently with his finger-tips on the glass. 'What are you threatening?' he said contemptuously.

'Threatening?' Barras said, raising his eyebrows in reproach. 'You have become my friends. You have not threatened me with any attempt at making public what we had planned together for restoring Louis XVII. Why should I threaten you? But we must make provision to avoid unpleasantness. I must have a persuasive answer when I am asked why you are still free. Can I give one?'

Michel began to say something harsh. Hester stepped forward quickly, and caught his arm again, sinking her fingers deep into it.

'What answer do you want?' she said.

Barras smiled at her. 'Madame Vernet has a sense of the realities of life. Sit down, I implore you. You're both too tall to have you standing over one. Take some wine. There are at least three main Royalist groups in Paris that need to be taken seriously. I need someone who can talk to all of them. Someone who can bring their thoughts to me, and mine to them. Who can help me persuade them to agree between themselves, and to be patient. Would you be willing to do that?'

'Patient for what?' Michel said. Although he had sat down Hester could feel him quivering with tension, with the need to do something violent. She touched his wrist, and felt him grow quieter, still tense, but in control of his feelings again.

'For the end that we all have at heart,' Barras said, offering to refill their glasses that they had not yet touched. He shrugged, and refilled his own. 'The welfare of France. And France needs a King. But Louis XVIII must learn to accept that France does not want to step back into the past. It must go forward, with a new kind of monarchy. You can help in that, too. Whatever the Paris Royalists have been telling him, I'm quite certain it was not the truth. Perhaps you could arrange for at least some truth to reach—Louis XVIII? To tell him that if he wants to leave Verona and come to Paris, he must come as a—shall I say, *democrat*?'

'Louis XVIII!' Michel began. 'That——'

'We will do it gladly,' Hester said.

Ten minutes later they were outside the house, walking under the trees. There was an empty coach waiting, and a group of men who looked like police.

'That coach was waiting for us,' Hester breathed, 'If we had not said *yes*.'

'I wish I'd killed him. He knew! He knew what had happened!'

'I think so too. But it would do us no good to be back in prison, and if we were in prison we wouldn't live very long. He'd see to it.'

They walked to the river, and along the quays, past Notre-Dame, opposite the Ile St. Louis. She stopped, leaning over the parapet, staring down into the dark, hidden water.

'Do you want to escape from here? Fight again? Join Charette?'

He cursed Charette for a full minute.

'Then let's do what Barras asks us to do. He can have his motives, and we can have ours. What else is there?'

'What motives? To help put Louis XVIII on the throne? The dead in the Vendée must be weeping in their graves to think what they died for! That!'

'Then let's do it just to keep ourselves alive!' She beat her fist softly against the parapet. 'We've lived for a King. Let's live for us now. We could get to England—to America—— But if we're in prison, dead—what's been the use of anything? I want a child, Michel. Ours. I want to give her the future. I want her to live——'

'I'm too tired to think of anything,' he said. 'Too sick at what's happened.' He put his arm round her waist, leaned his forehead against hers. 'Tomorrow. Tomorrow we'll think. Now——'

'We'll go home,' she whispered. 'Thank God we're free to go. Imagine——' But he had not been in prison to imagine it. And as they walked home together she thought she could hear the echoes, stone and iron, smell the vileness. Dreamed of it as they slept, and woke clinging to him.

They became Barras' liaison with the Paris Royalists. Like walking in black mud, the stench rising at every step. Worse than before. Treacheries, betrayals. It was July, and an army of *émigrés* from England landed in Brittany, at Quiberon. And long before the news of it reached Paris a man came from one of the Royalist committees to betray the plans of the landing.

'You may tell the Citizen General Barras that——' And all the expedition's plans spilled out, like bile. Who was coming, where they would land, what supplies they had, what the Bretons were to do. 'You may assure the Citizen General that this landing does not have the support of His Majesty. We wish to owe nothing to England. And we do not trust the leaders of the expedition. If the expedition is destroyed His Majesty will be unmoved.'

Michel waited a week, until the information was useless, and only gave it to Barras then.

'I have had this already from another source,' Barras said. 'When it was still useful.' He shook his head in mock reproof, and then apparently genuine sadness. 'I understand, Colonel Vernet. I understand your feelings. Neither you nor I can always be proud of our acquaintances. And allies.'

Léonie's receptions had become quasi-Royalist. The Baron de Batz came there openly, and although not at the same time, his enemy, the Count d'Antraigues of the Paris Royalist Committee also came there, foppish and mincing. With information, petitions, sly bargains to propose. Others of the Committee came and went like shadows. Men and women from opposing groups. And spies, messengers, envoys, returned *émigrés* disguised under false names and papers. Men sent by the English agent Wickham, in Switzerland, offering English guineas. Men sent by the Count d'Artois in

Germany, intriguing against his brother, now Louis XVIII. Men sent by the new King, from Verona, warning against his brother Artois, and against England, and against the Baron de Batz; offering Léonie the title of Countess, and Barras a dukedom, the day Louis XVIII was installed in the Tuileries. Offering Michel money, an estate, the rank of general, as well as the already offered barony, and the Cordon of St. Louis. Like an auction mart of treacheries and counter-treacheries. In the Vendée Stofflet was betrayed and killed. They said he was betrayed by his own political adviser, the abbé Bernier.

Only in the apartment of the rue du Bac was there any possibility of a momentary ease of mind. And even there the intriguers and the spies followed; some of them, she was sure, *agents provocateurs* employed by Barras, giving her false information to see would she bring it back to Barras. One informer, soft and grey-skinned, came to tell her that two of Charette's agents were secretly in Paris, and offered to sell them to her for twenty louis in gold.

'Barras will pay you five times as much, madame, but I dare not go to him direct.'

She was in the hallway of Madame de Richeteau's house. He had come knocking softly at the door under cover of darkness, and she beckoned him inside.

'Now, monsieur,' she said, and took him by the throat. He tried to scream, clawed at her wrists, his eyes forced half-way from their flat, harelike sockets, his grey face going dark. When he hung slack in her hands she dropped him on the black and white marble tiles and stood waiting for him to recover. He came to his hands and knees at last, swaying, and she kicked him hard in the side so that he fell again, and slid against the wall.

'Go back to whoever sent you,' she told him, 'and go on your knees to him not to send you to me again.' She dragged him out onto the steps. Shut the door. Upstairs her father was calling to her. 'Who is it, Hester, what is happening, what was that noise?'

'It was nothing, Papa. A poor wretch come begging.' And ran to pacify him.

He could go out by himself now, and would join the bread queues for the pleasure of telling the others there how outrageous it was to need to queue for bread. 'And such bread! In England we wouldn't give stuff like this to a horse! What is your government about?' He found plenty of sympathetic hearers, and he was arrested twice, needing to be rescued from the police with a note from Barras or one of his secretaries.

'I think we should send your father back to England,' Barras said after the second rescue. 'He would be happier there.' And she knew that it was true, and that added to her feeling, not so much of unhappiness—often and often she was happy; with Michel; simply to be free; to have food to eat; to see her father recovering, the abbé reading again, saying Mass with Perrine for his assistant, old Anne and Madame de Richeteau and some of the neighbours for his congregation. Sometimes she went to his Mass herself, with Michel, and knelt in gratitude for all that had been given back to her. No, not unhappiness, but—tension, a cruel stretching of the nerves; a constant feeling of dangers surrounding her that she could not see, could not fight against; expecting something worse to happen, she did not know what, or when.

A new revolution? A new Terror? She had become the protector of a wretched family in the Faubourg St. Antoine; a beggar woman with a baby a few weeks old and three other children who went begging with her, skeleton children with swollen bellies and hollow, black-shadowed eyes. The mother coughed blood and looked like a sick animal, helpless with misery. Standing on the Pont Neuf in all weathers, holding out a thin, filthy hand to the indifferent crowd that passed her by.

The day that Hester found her it was raining, but the woman and her children stood there as if they were unaware of it; unaware even that the crowds had gone, had taken shelter, and that they were almost alone on the bridge.

Hester stopped beside her to give her money and speak to her, and the woman looked at the *assignat* and at Hester, and as if kindness had broken something in her she sank down onto the wet pavement and sat there, crying. Hester called a passing *fiacre* and put the woman and the children into it. 'Where do you live?' It took a minute for the woman to gather her mind enough to tell her.

'I will come with you,' Hester said, not trusting the driver to take them where they wanted to go, if she did not go with them. And found herself a quarter of an hour later in the depths of a wretchedness she had not imagined could exist. Not the hunger of beggars who had never worked, or known any prosperity. But of good workmen who could not find an employer; of ruined shopkeepers; of craftsmen who had had to sell the tools of their trade to buy bread; of women who had nothing left to sell but their own bodies.

She went several times after that to bring the woman food, and to try to find work or help of some kind for her neighbours. Badgering the guests at Léonie's receptions, or Madame Tallien's, or Madame Hamelin's, to give her commissions to have furniture made, or curtains sewn, or rooms repainted. But half of Paris was starving, and men and women would work all day for the price of a loaf of bread. Anyone who needed the price of two loaves, or three, because they had children, stayed unemployed. And starved. While Léonie, and Thérézia Tallien, and Madame Hamelin, and their friends, and Barras' friends, rode through the streets in diamonds.

On one of her visits to the St. Antoine a crowd of women gathered round her *fiacre* and began shouting at her because she was well-dressed. But the strength they had had when the Revolution began, when they marched on Versailles, and took the King and Queen back with them to Paris; that was gone, and Hester faced only a weak and starving hatred, too weak to do more than curse her, and back away from her as she got out of the *fiacre* and walked towards them, carrying the basket of food for her protégée.

That night she saw Barras at Madame Tallien's reception, and told him what she had seen. Barras shrugged, and smiled, and spread his hands.

'They are always starving,' he said. 'They make a habit of it.'

'But you must give them work! You have peace now, there is no more fighting.'

He sighed, as if genuinely the thought of starvation saddened him, and set down his champagne glass on a table. 'It is easier to make war than to make peace. All governments discover that. Perhaps we need war after all.' He recovered his good humour and smiled at Madame Tallien who was passing by in a state of almost naked splendour, her hair rippling like liquid ebony.

'There,' he said to Hester, 'goes one reason for unemployment. If you women insist on abandoning almost all your clothes, where can the weavers and the sewing girls find work?' He took up his champagne again, as a signal that that was enough of political economy for such an hour of the night.

'How is monsieur your father? Does he improve?' And without attending much to her answer Barras bowed and left her for less serious company. A moment later she saw him with Madame Tallien.

And I too, Hester thought. I am drinking champagne, and eating the best of food. If I bring a few crusts of bread to the Faubourg St. Antoine, does that absolve me from everything? What are we all doing, what are we hoping for, waiting for? Louis XVIII? And if he became king in fact, what would he do for those women? Although he could scarcely do less than Barras and his colleagues were doing for them. Could anyone do more?

She grew sick of thinking of such questions in such a place, and went home, to see to her father, and renew the slow, cautious argument about his going home, and leaving her here in France.

She had had to tell him that the possibility existed for his going home; that Barras would find the means for it. And he accepted that as the most natural matter in the world, as though the packet boats sailed every day from Calais to Dover, carrying English travellers to and fro. But he assumed that she would be coming with him.

'And Michel, Papa?' she had said gently, the first time she had told him about it, feeling her way towards explanations, to telling him that she could not come.

'Michel?' He looked uncertain for a moment as to who Michel was. 'Oh, let him come if he likes. The house is big enough. We have stayed here too long, child. Those estates of Léonie's—but all is settled now and we should be at home. It will be the shooting season in a short while, and I must be there. I seem not to have had a gun in my hand since I can remember. It is becoming very selfish in you, Hester, to go on wanting nothing but pleasure and gadding. Your mama——'

'Mama does not want me home, Papa, you know that as well as I do. She's delighted that I'm married, and that she need never trouble herself about me again.'

'Your mama—' he began once more, his eyes growing uncertain. 'I wanted to tell you something about her.' He scraped at his few remaining hairs with a corner of the book he had been reading. 'You have put it out of my mind with all your objections to going home.'

But it was the Baron de Batz who told her. Not long after her rough treatment of the grey-faced informer he came up to her in the foyer of the Théâtre Feydeau, rubbing his hands together with an

[353]

air of triumph. 'Things are marching, madame. These new elections! In a few weeks we shall have achieved by the ballot-box what all Charette's fighting could never do. Although I hear—' he whispered in a lower tone, looking slyly at Michel, and then at Hester's hand that he was still holding—'I hear, madame, that you have recently taken up arms again. Or should I say throats?'

'Was he an acquaintance of yours, monsieur?'

The Baron smiled. 'You are like your mother in more ways than one,' he said. 'Strength of hand, and sharpness of tongue. No, he was not my acquaintance, I am happy to say. You and I should be friends, madame, we fight for the same cause. Did not our illustrious General Barras mention to you that we of our persuasion were all to be like one united family?' Smiling again, like a cat playing. Claws hidden. It was only a moment later that she realized what he had said.

'My—mother? But she is—how do you know anything of——?' The sharpness of tongue was true enough.

The Baron was looking astonished, truly or falsely, and then sly, glancing at Michel. 'Madame, madame! I am desolate! I have—perhaps I have stepped on—delicate ground?'

'What are you trying to tell me, monsieur?'

'Why, nothing, nothing at all, an idle compliment, no more.' He made to bow and turn away. She caught his arm and held him, the theatre crowd eddying round them. 'Madame, I beg of you, you are drawing attention to us.'

Michel took him by the other arm, and said, 'If you have something to tell my wife, we shall be more comfortable outside. Come, monsieur, walk with us, let's at least seem like friends, as you suggested.'

In the street they went a few paces from the lights of the doorway, turned a corner into an alley. The Baron made a sudden effort to free himself. They held him until he was still again. Michel pushed him against the wall. 'Now, tell us, without any fear of interruptions.'

The Baron looked from one of them to the other, his face no more than a dark shadow, his eyes glittering. 'You do not know your parentage? I swear to you, if I had thought that you—that your husband——'

Michel put his hand on the Baron's neck, fitted a thumb under the jawbone, and pressed hard. 'I said, tell us. Don't trouble to

[354]

explain why you didn't want to spread poison. Just spread it, and we can judge what it's worth.'

'My parentage?' Hester said.

'If your husband would take his hand from my windpipe—— Let us at least behave like gentlemen. Thank you, monsieur. I assumed that you both knew. That your mother was Mademoiselle Anne de Montbéliard and your father was—on reflection it was an indelicacy on my part to refer to the matter, and I offer you my profound apologies. Now, may I cause myself the displeasure of leaving you, and return to the theatre?'

'And my father? Who is my father?' She had him by the lapels of his coat and shook him so hard that his head rolled and struck against the wall.

'You'll kill him,' Michel said.

'Your father is dead,' the Baron whispered. 'Your—grandfather had him—had him shot. They were going to run away together, and get married——'

She was shaking him again. 'What was his name?'

'A young officer. In—the Queen's Guard. Madame, please! A Swedish officer, Axel—Axel Dahlstierna—madame, I implore you!' She let go of him and he lay against the wall, rubbing his throat with one hand and holding the other between them, half fending her off, half in a gesture of surrender. 'I swear——'

A patrol came by in the main street, and as Michel and Hester turned to look, the Baron slid sideways along the wall and was gone. They heard his running footsteps for a few moments. Then only echoes, and the tramp of the patrol marching. They turned back towards the theatre, but without needing to speak of it went on beyond the entrance and began walking in the darkness towards what had become their chosen place for being alone together, along the quays near the Ile St. Louis.

She did not want to talk, and Michel sensed that, and they walked in silence. What did it matter what his motive had been in telling them? To see if it might give him a hold over them? Revenge, for her not sharing her secret with him, about the boy King? Or one pawn's move in a game of chess about which they knew nothing? To try to tie them to one faction or another, make them distrust someone, hate someone else? There was no way of knowing. One handful of mud more or less, that was all, as far as he was concerned.

But for her? It did not cross her mind to disbelieve him, and she thought how strange that was as soon as the realization came to her that she had not doubted him, not from the first second. So much falling into place. Her mother's—no, not her mother—her foster-mother's dislike for her, at once veiled and bitter. What had happened? How had she come to—her father's story about Switzerland—that she had thought was only his mind wandering. He had tried to tell her half a dozen times. The coach, her mother being taken away in a coach. And the old woman, the midwife. What was the truth of it, what had happened? Her—her mother—the word unfamiliar suddenly, embarrassing, so that she flushed as she thought of it—her mother running away? Driven out of her home? The birth happening too soon? But who had taken her off in the coach? Why had they—why did she leave me behind?

She stood still. 'Let's go home,' she said. She began walking fast towards the rue du Bac. If she had been alone she would have run. When they reached the house she did run, up the stairs, three at a time. Her father reading in bed, his hair on end, his nightcap fallen unnoticed onto the floor, the candle flame guttering as she flung herself into his bedroom.

'Hester! What—what has happened—what is the matter?' Putting his hand to his heart, lifting himself in the bed.

She forced herself to be calm, seem calm, went down on her knees beside him. 'Nothing, Papa, nothing at all. I came home to—to see that you were all right.' She made him lie back, settled his night cap on his head. 'Papa——' And thought, he is not. He is not my father. And did then want to disbelieve it, wanted to cling to him, to not knowing. But she had to know. 'Papa, several times you began to tell me something, do you remember? About Switzerland. The day I was born.'

'The night,' Mr Broadhurst said. 'It was a damnable bad night, your mother kept us awake for hours, poor wretch.'

'Tell me what happened.' Keeping her voice very low and calm so as not to frighten him, and drive the memory away. And he told her calmly, as though it had all happened only a few days ago, to a friend. Coherently. The inn below the St. Gotthard Pass. The screams that had woken him that night. The storm. 'I remember, I opened the window, and the shutters, and a great heap of snow fell into the room against me. I thought I should catch my death of cold from it. But she was a splendid-looking young woman, the little I

[356]

saw of her. She must have been near as tall as you, my dear.' And then, 'Of course, she was your mother. That accounts for it. Where are my spectacles? Where have you put my spectacles? I cannot do without them since Doctor Maupuis gave them to me.'

'Here, Papa. Here they are, with your book. And did you—did you never hear of—her again? The young—the young woman——' She could not yet bring herself to say 'my mother'. And she was afraid that that might confuse him, too, and set him thinking about Mrs. Broadhurst.

'No, no,' he said. 'Never. Monstrous people! To have wanted to kill the child! It could not happen in England, thank God.' And the mist drifted over his mind again, almost visibly. 'We are going home soon, are we not? This life of theatres and dancing is not good for you, my dear, you are looking peaked and you have shadows under your eyes. Good Sussex air and English food is what we both need. Your mama will be so anxious for us——'

But what more was there to learn?

Such little as there was she learned herself over the next days. And it was no more than she could have guessed. The young officer with no money and no prospects beyond a handsome figure, hoping to make his fortune in France. The girl of a great family. Very great. Nine of the Montbéliards had died in the Terror. Her grandfather, her grandmother, aunts, cousins. A dozen more were with the emigration, in England or Germany. And her father's family? No one knew anything of it. A poor family of country gentlemen in Sweden, sending its sons abroad because they would starve at home. A young man towering above his comrades of the Queen's Guard. A lover, a duellist, a horseman. 'He was a magnificent fellow, madame,' an old *ci-devant* vicomte said, searching his memory. 'But why does a young lady of today wish to know of him?'

'No—no reason beyond—beyond that I have heard stories of him, monsieur.'

'Oh, stories! Those there were! And the Montbéliard girl! Like two mad creatures. One could do anything in those days in our circle, or almost anything. But not as they did, right in the full light of day. Like Héloïse and Abelard. As if they had lost all their senses except passion. It was the talk of Versailles. And then—what could one expect? The old Marquis was not the man to tolerate that kind of humiliation for very long.' He smiled the sweet, reflective smile of a man tasting old, old wine and remembering his youth. 'She was a beautiful thing to see, Mademoiselle de Montbéliard. Not unlike you, madame, for height and figure.' He looked at her with a sudden sharpness in his tear-faded, hooded eyes, the fine, delicate nostrils flaring at the scent of an ancient scandal revivified.

'And—she, monsieur? Do you know what—happened to her?'

'She died in Italy, I heard, madame. In childbirth, presumably. Or soon after. As to the child——' And his eyes probed again for secrets.

But she scarcely minded if he guessed. Did not mind. She carried away with her that image of two beautiful, passionate creatures so much in love that they risked death by their indifference to it, courted death.

And I am their child. She seemed to know them for a moment, see their faces, see them walking in sunlight on a wide space of lawn while others watched them from shadows. Arm in arm, one fair, one dark, both tall, heads bending towards one another, touching.

I shall always think of them like that. Not—not as she was afterwards, in Switzerland, and the inn, and the servants, and the storm outside, and her crying out with the pain, and with loss. Like Héloïse and Abelard. To sacrifice everything for passion. Everything. 'Right in the full light of day.' Nothing ashamed, or secret. She went home and the abbé Bernard was saying his Office, walking up and down the ante-room.

'Do you say Masses for the dead, father? To help them if they're in purgatory?'

'Why, yes, yes, of course we do.'

'Then—would you say two Masses for—for two people who—were once very close to me? Would you need to know their names?'

He shook his head wonderingly. 'I will say ten, my dear, a hundred for you. For your intentions.'

She went to her own room and knelt and prayed for them. And long after her prayers were finished stayed kneeling, thinking of them. And thought suddenly, they are still alive! In me! Held out her hands in front of her. My mother's hands? My father's? The blood in my veins is theirs! A horseman and a duellist.

Even Talmond—even that insanity, that sense of being released from all laws, all morality, of being driven on a flood of passion that nothing could, nothing should resist, even that seeming to fall quietly into place in this newfound scheme of things. 'As if they had lost all their senses except passion.'

[358]

She lay face down on the bed, touching the pillow where soon Michel would be lying beside her. I belong here, she thought. I belong. To him. To France. To—what? What part of France? The Muscadins? Barras? De Batz and the Royalist Committees? Where do I belong? Where does Michel belong? And fell asleep before she could see any answer, any beginning of an answer.

Chapter 37

August. September. Paris, half of France turned Royalist. More than half. Shouting 'A King or bread' as once it had shouted for the Revolution. The army itself had grown sick of the Convention, of the Léonies and Madame Talliens and Madame Hamelins, of arrogant luxury and shameless corruption flaunting themselves while the country starved and conscripts tried to defend France with ill-made, half useless weapons; marching in cardboard boots, shivering or sweating in ragged, wretched uniforms; while the army contractors made their millions.

'Give us a king or give us bread!'

Léonie's receptions had taken on a flavour of Versailles, in opposition to La Tallien's Republicanism. She had begun to demand etiquette, and she enjoyed discussions of genealogies, while her guests, if not rich, were expected to be witty. Hester found her one day thinking aloud to Euphemia about the problem posed by Creuzot's existence, in this new scheme of things.

'Could he not be an absentee duke?' Hester said, 'Just as he's been an absentee Terrorist all these months?'

'He was never a Terrorist!' Leonie cried. 'He was always a Royalist! In the Vendée he saved everyone, we both did, we were almost guillotined for it! How can you be so cruel?'

But by the end of September there were other things to concern Léonie, besides her husband's acceptability as a duke. The rumour that Hester had heard once or twice had become a certainty; that Barras had grown tired of Léonie, and taken on Madame Tallien as his official lover. And the flow of suitors, courtiers, petitioners; bribe takers and bribe offerers; the corrupted and the corrupting; the unemployed aristocrats and frightened Jacobins; all the tide of gold and despair and hope that had filled Léonie's house to bursting, began to slacken.

The army contractors had already abandoned her, sniffing the wind while it was still an infant breeze, and she had thought that it was merely their humility, afraid to approach her now as a soon-to-be duchess, and she had sent reassuring messages to the more valuable among them, letting them know that she had not become proud or unapproachable, no matter what the future might hold.

But now the desertion was like the *sauve qui peut* of a sinking ship. It was possible to walk quite easily from one room to another, and hear oneself speak. Only the very slow in the uptake were there, and those who liked free champagne and would go on to La Tallien's house later, to do real business. Barras himself still came, but only briefly, to show languid surprise at Léonie's tears and threats, and hysterics. The hope of becoming a duchess vanished with her recovered honour. With the bleak prospect of becoming no more than Madame Creuzot again.

It was during one of those scenes that Barras proposed Saint-Domingue as a solution; to send Creuzot out there as Representative on Mission, with orders to solve the problems of the slave rebellion, and the mulattoes, and the white Royalists, and white Republicans. 'Just for a few months,' Barras said, stroking her hair. 'You would be like a queen. And I am quite sure that the richer planters would be——' pursing his lips, '—suitably grateful for any small favours you and your husband could do for them. Quite frankly, my dear, I'm offering you a goldmine.'

It was Euphemia who described the scene to Hester, acting it out with a dark, swift humour, her eyes burning like molten jet. 'It has come at last! We are going to free my people!' She reached up and took Hester's face between her hands. 'We must say good-bye to Big Madame. And there are great things in waiting for you too, I see them. For your man. Great, great things. One day he will truly be a duke, not like my poor mistress!' She laughed, her voice husky, fierce with mockery and impatience.

'A duke?' Hester said, laughing too. 'You think the King will be so grateful to us?'

'Not the King,' Euphemia said scornfully. 'Someone much greater than a king. An emperor!'

Hester stared at her, wondering if it was a joke that she did not understand. But Euphemia was too full of what was to happen to explain anything. 'We shall free my people!' she whispered. 'Do you know what it has been like for us? For them?' And she drew her nails slowly and gently down Hester's cheeks. 'Do you know what the whips are like?'

Léonie calling her, her voice hysterical, Barras hurrying down the stairs.

Hester waited until he was gone, and went slowly up to the small dining parlour that was now Léonie's room for scenes, as it had been for bribery. She was on the Persian hearthrug, writhing like a wounded snake, clawing at the rug and sobbing, her hair spread round her in a tawny magnificence of ruin. The hairdresser had been with her that day for four hours and now his work might never have been done, except for the perfume and an air of expensiveness about the desolation, the weeping misery of pink satin negligée and golden curls. And for a moment the thought touched Hester's mind that there must be more, even to Léonie, than a heap of silk and ruined beauty. But the thought went as swiftly as it came. Euphemia was kneeling over her mistress, trying to lift her by the shoulders.

'Up, *ma cocotte*, it is not the end, it is the beginning! Come, listen to Lalitté, listen to your *matelotte*, they will fill your hands with money, they will cover you with jewels. This has been nothing, nothing! Wait until we are on the island, wait until you see how we shall make the white men sweat their gold out! Oh, let them see what we shall do to them!'

'Let me die!' Léonie wept, 'Leave me! Leave me! Everyone else has gone, you go with them. Go to her, that fat bitch Thérézia! *Go to her!*' She tried to beat her head against the floor.

'Get up,' Hester said, and when Léonie did not answer she picked her up like a doll and set her into one of the arm-chairs beside the fireplace. Euphemia smoothed down the satin; pale pink, dark red velvet bows from throat to ankle, pink lace at the cuffs, the neck, round the hem; a mistress piece from Chez Leroi. Léonie's weeping became hysterics. She flung herself from side to side of the chair, and then forward against Hester, beating with her fists now at herself, now at Hester, clawing at her own hair, at her négligée, ripping away the lace from her neck, and flinging it into the fire, throwing herself back into the depths of the chair and screaming, 'Leave me alone! Both of you. He's gone, he's gone!'

The screams like glass shattering, short and powerful and

calculated. Hester leaned forward and swung her open palm, hit her across the face as she had done once before, at the crossing of the Loire. Léonie fell sideways, her mouth still open in mid-scream, the scream cut off. She looked for a moment as though her neck had been broken. Sliding gently onto her knees. And Euphemia was there, pushing Hester away with a soft yet terrible violence, frightening in its strength and its control. Her eyes—and then Hester was nothing to her. Going down onto her own knees beside her mistress, gathering Léonie against her breast, gold head against black shoulder, red silk, black hands touching, fondling, smoothing the round, porcelain cheek that was now turned crimson, already swelling.

Hester leaned against the mantelpiece, shocked herself at her violence against that soft and foolish creature.

'Help me to lift her,' Euphemia said. 'Take her to her bed.' As if she was commanding it, not asking.

And Hester obeyed her as if she had the right to give commands. The soft, perfumed weight lay in her arms, golden head fallen back, white, full throat contriving to look beautiful even in unconsciousness.

'Bring her in here,' Euphemia said. Opened a door into a small ante-room, another door. The bedroom. Almost darkness. Hothouse warmth. A wide, low bed like a vast seashell filled with down and satin, a soft glistening in the firelight. Hester eased Léonie onto the centre of the bed. Eyelashes lifting, huge tears rolling.

Euphemia came close, wrapped her cold finger round Hester's wrists. Drew Hester down until they were both kneeling by the bedside, facing one another. Her eyes holding Hester's, jet black, shining. She lifted one hand, fitted her palm and fingers against Hester's cheek, very softly, very cold.

'Oh, madame!' she said. 'She needed that. But I could not like to see it happen. Do not be afraid of me.'

'I am not afraid,' Hester breathed, and she did not know if that was true. Felt as if Euphemia's eyes were drawing her strength out of her. Felt herself swaying forward, falling, and knew that she had not moved, was still kneeling upright. And yet that sense of falling, inside her mind. The room was still there, the dark, the firelight, and at the same time a bright landscape, so bright with sun that it was cruel. Cruel green of forest. Cruel sky. Black gibbets against the fierce blue. Rows of them, so many she could not count. Birds wheeling, slowly, gorged with eating. Blue sea, gold sand, black corpses hanging.

'That is Saint-Domingue,' Euphemia's voice was whispering. 'That is my home. Those are my people. That is where we are going. To set them free. I am not your enemy, Big Madame. Only their sister, their friend. We are going to set them free, my mistress and her man. I will make them do it. And you have helped us. I am not your enemy.'

'Let me go,' Hester said, her own voice far away.

'I have never kept you prisoner,' Euphemia whispered. 'Only to make you help us when I needed you. Go free, Big Madame. Go free to your own life.'

And the same sense of falling although she was still kneeling there. Again there was a blaze of light, but candlelight, a long room crowded with men and women, such a splendour of dress and uniforms and jewels as she had never seen, a slow magnificence, a stateliness about the way they moved. One of the men Michel, although it was difficult to recognize him. His hair grey, and a long scar from one temple down to jaw bone. Wearing a uniform she had never seen, never imagined for its splendour, the collar very high and thick with gold; stars and orders on the breast of the coat, an enamelled cross hanging from a broad crimson ribbon round his neck, a heavy blue sash across one shoulder and a great white and gold star fastened to it. A tall bearskin cap held under his arm. Looking towards her, smiling. Turning to someone else, bowing. A small, stout man, something familiar about his face. Also glittering with stars and orders, a hush of reverence surrounding him, women sinking almost to the ground as they curtsied, men bowing. He looked at her, his eyes pale grey, icy and yet burning, like a falcon's eyes. The little general. Grown so magnificent it was beyond believing. Grown stout. Grown arrogant. But the same eyes. General Buonaparte. Become—what had he become? 'Sire,' she heard her own voice saying. And she was curtsying—falling—falling——

Euphemia holding her up, cold hand against her face. How long had she knelt there?

'That is your road, madame. Go. Go now. Leave me with her.'

She could not remember going down the stairs. Found herself in the courtyard, drawing in deep breaths of the cool, night-scented air like someone who has been drugged, or stifled, moving uncertainly so that she needed to stand for a moment in the gateway. Needed to be certain that nothing had happened, nothing had changed, that the street was as it had been—how long ago, when she came through this gateway to visit Léonie? Tried to grasp what she had seen, to understand. But she was no longer sure that she had seen anything. Only the blaze of light was left, now sun, now candlelight.

Buonaparte. The little general. The ragamuffin general of brigade, feeding himself with both hands at Léonie's buffet. Starving. Become an Emperor?

And then even that was gone.

She was so tired when she reached the rue du Bac that she fell asleep long before Michel came home. He had left a note saying he would be late, that he had gone to meet 'some people you know about!' Royalists. One of the Royalist committees. Eager to betray some other Royalist committee. Or to betray the Royalist rising that was being planned so openly it did not need betraying. She tried to stay awake for him, set out their supper in their bedroom, swore she would stay awake. And lay down and fell into depths of sleep as though Euphemia had truly drugged her.

She woke to find Michel beside her, the candle already snuffed, only the smell of wax and burned wick telling that the darkness was no more than a moment old. She touched him to tell him she was awake. Wanted to tell him she had dreamed about him, dreamed something very strange, but before she could remember what it had been, turn it into words, the dream was gone, dissolved.

'I dreamed about you,' she whispered.

He was sitting on the edge of the bed, a shadow. And yet even in the shadow there was despair. 'If you could have heard them. Royalists! Like rats! Tiny, treacherous minds, scrabbling in a sewer. And I've had to listen, and listen, instead of killing them. The Vendée was clean compared to this. I'm sick of the very sound and sight of them. They make me want to vomit. The rising starts in five days' time and already they're drawing up lists for the guillotine, for when they've won. And half the names on the lists are better men than any of these swine will ever be.'

'Shall you tell Barras?'

'They've asked me to. They're offering him a dukedom and ten million louis to betray the Convention and proclaim Louis XVIII.'

'Do you think he——?'

'I'm sick of thinking. Sick and sick and sick. I'd like to see all the Royalists and all the Jacobins and the whole stinking tribe of politicians driven over a cliff into the sea. But he'll probably do it. The Royalists look like being the winning side. Once they start they ought to have Paris in six hours and the whole of France in a week.'

More than Michel thought that the victory was already certain. All through the city Royalist flags, Royalist cockades were being made ready for the day. Men were marking down their Jacobin enemies for denunciation and reminding neighbours of how they had always loved the King in secret and always hated the Revolution. To hear the talk in the bread queues, in the streets, the Convention had not a friend in Paris. The National Guard was Royalist and bourgeois to a man and the government had so distrusted the regular troops of the army that it had sent the garrison out of the city and passed a law against any troops returning. For fear of treachery it had made itself defenceless.

Whereas the Royalists could call on sixty thousand armed men. They had only to surround the Convention in the Tuileries, and demand its abdication, and the thing was done.

The Convention knew it. On the 4th October it broke its own recent law and called in troops under General Menou. Ten thousand men. Marching into a sullen, hostile Paris, the rain lashing the streets, as the columns closed on the Royalist Headquarters in the one time convent of the Daughters of Saint Thomas. And incredibly one man defeated the ten thousand. One man. De Lallot, the youngest of the Committee, going out alone on the Convent steps to face Menou. 'The Law forbids you!' he cried. 'You will not pass this doorway except over my dead body. Your presence in Paris is illegal, and the whole city is amazed at your violation of the law. Touch one hair of my head and your name, General, and yours, soldiers, will be infamous for ever. Your country's eyes are upon you. Your country will judge you. In the name of the Law I command you to withdraw.'

And General Menou drew back. Marched his ten thousand men away in the drenching rain. He was cashiered that night for failing to carry out his orders, but the victory remained with the Royalists. All they needed to do was act. And instead they talked. The streets full of messengers, patrols of the National Guard. De Lallot riding from place to place, whipping up the zeal of supporters, placing entries. De Batz organizing, trying to organize, tomorrow's *coup de main*, the march on the Convention in the Tuileries, as he had organized everything else. Appointing General Danican to command it. Or perhaps General Danican appointed himself. No one was quite sure who had appointed whom to do what. And all of them talked, and made speeches, and went on talking.

While Barras and the Convention, waiting moment by moment to be besieged in the Palace of the Tuileries, as once the King had been, drew their breath and began to recover courage.

Hours earlier Barras had sent Michel, and Hester with him, to talk to de Batz, and they were there when Menou arrived, and saw him driven back by the force of de Lallot's character. Barras' instructions had been to get what terms and concessions they could from de Batz, and although Barras did not say it, it was clear enough that he meant for himself, and not for the Convention. If de Batz won, he would still need politicians to make his victory a reality and not merely a return to chaos, and General Barras and a number of his closer colleagues were ready to assume this new burden for the sake of France.

'Perhaps this is the way it must happen,' Barras had said, shrugging almost indifferently. There was an odd languor in his manner, as if he was bone tired, and was almost happy to have decisions made elsewhere, and simply to float with the irresistible tide. 'We shall have a king a few months, a year or so earlier. It will come to the same thing in the end. But if you can find a way to stop him—the Treasury is empty, but we might find a few million livres here or there. If de Batz creates the Restoration, Heaven help France.'

There were no terms to be made. And they were not sure that they wanted to make them. Hester herself was no longer sure of anything, except that she hated de Batz, and hated Barras, and was sick to her heart of intrigue, and sicker still at the thought of more killing, more useless, useless killing. For what? To overthrow one clique of scoundrels and set up another. She could not allow herself to think of all the dead, of all the bravery that had gone by. The time of the first fighting in the Vendée, all that blaze of hope and of ideals was like a remembrance of the Gospels, of a Calvary seen far away, and wonderful, haloed by light. And here, black mud, clinging to the soul.

Menou marching away. The rain lashing, drumming on the roof of the one time convent. Men talking, shouting, arguing. General

Danican precise and fussy as an old woman, spreading out maps of the city, stabbing with his old woman's finger here, there.

'One column by the rue du Dauphin,' he was saying. 'Two columns must cross the river by the Pont Neuf, and return by the Pont Royal——'

'The man is an imbecile,' a voice said at Hester's shoulder, and she turned to find General Buonaparte beside her. As shabby, shabbier than ever, his face gaunt, and at the same time still far too young for his uniform, his oversized boots, his rank of general of brigade, his overlong, trailing sabre. He looked like a boy dressed up in an older brother's worn-out uniform.

'He seems to know what he wants to do,' Hester said indifferently. Michel was still trying to deal with de Batz, without being certain what deal he wanted to make, or why he wanted to make it. Except that he knew he wanted nothing for France that de Batz could bring about. But then—he wanted nothing that Barras had created either, if he had created anything.

'What he intends to do is insane,' General Buonaparte said. 'To attack the Tuileries by the rue du Dauphin and the Pont Royal? Ten men and a cannon could hold either against an army. Take me to de Batz and I'll tell him what he should do.'

She smiled, and then took him to the Committee's inner meeting room. Why not? She was tired of listening to General Danican and his staff, and the meaningless litany of street names and times and officers in charge of this or that. She was tired of everything. Too tired even to wonder at the strangeness of the little, shabby general being there, and wanting to serve these people. What did it matter? Michel was still talking to de Batz, de Lallot and the Committee at the other end of the room shouting at one another about the terms of tomorrow's Proclamation, and whether it should refer to new elections and a new Constitution. No one mentioned the King. Half the Committee, even in Royalist Lepeletier, still believed in the Republic and thought they were fighting for it and the true Revolution. The other half held their peace about Louis XVIII, knowing that they would have the strength when they needed to use it. The Republicans on the victorious Committees, here and in every Section, could then be quietly conducted to prison, or into exile. Officially this rising was for the Commune, and the 'pure' Republic, which meant now the interests of the bourgeoisie, and the members shouted slogans at one another, growing dark in the face with passion about words, and shades of meaning, and the exact limitations there must be on the right to vote.

'Monsieur de Batz. May I present General of Brigade Buonaparte to you, who wishes to be of service?' Neither she, nor Michel, nor the Baron, had made the least reference to their last private meeting. It merely lay beneath the surface, like a rock under dark water, making any real trust between them impossible, if it ever could have existed. 'Your general is a fool,' General Buonaparte said. 'Do you know what he's planning?'

'He is an experienced soldier,' Baron de Batz said coldly. 'I think I know your name, General Buonaparte? Toulon? A friend of Robespierre's brother? And erased from the Army List?'

'I was reinstated a week later,' General Buonaparte said, his voice rising, his Italian accent growing stronger. 'Give me the command of your forces and you shall have the Tuileries within six hours from now.'

'My dear General, how good of you to wish to serve the cause of the Commune. But to have too many generals is as dangerous in war as too many cooks in a kitchen. All our arrangements are made, monsieur.' He bowed with elaborate discourtesy, and turned back to Michel.

'Imbecile,' General Buonaparte said very loudly. Hester led him into the other room. Suddenly he broke away from her and went to the table where General Danican was still disposing of columns, and sentries, and allotting times for them to be in this place and in that.

'You are talking nonsense, gentlemen! General Danican! You will ruin your cause! Show me that map.'

General Danican turned his mild eyes on the small, quivering figure beside him. 'Citizen——? I do not think that I have had the honour of your acquaintance?'

Two of the staff officers grasped General Buonaparte by the arms and began to march him towards the outer door, their faces white with anger.

'Gentlemen,' Hester cried, 'please, the Citizen General Buonaparte is with me. Let go of him, I beg of you.'

'Then please conduct your friend outside, madame,' one of the officers said between his teeth. He too seemed to know who General Buonaparte was and to dislike him. As he released his grip he said, 'This is not a place for repentant Terrorists.'

[369]

They went outside into the porch of the convent. It was still raining. 'We will go to Barras,' General Buonaparte said. He was still shaking with nerves, as well as anger; with a fury of impatience, like a man who burns to act and does not care in what direction or for what purpose so long as he acts immediately.

'What do you want to do there?' Hester said. He was so like an ill-mannered boy that he amused her. A boy dressed up. And in spite of the ill manners something likeable about him, something alive and genuine. 'If you wait a short while Colonel Vernet and I have to go to him to tell him what we have been able to do here. You can come with us.'

'What have you been able to do?'

'Nothing, I think.'

'As I imagined. The fools! Why are they not marching now? Give me a few hours more and I'd make the Tuileries impregnable. Is Barras doing that?'

'I don't know what he's doing.'

He paced the breadth of the porch, his hands clasped behind his back, his head bent. Turned on her. 'Fetch your husband out now.' She stared at him. 'Now, I say. There's not a minute to waste. Bring him out to me and we'll go to Barras.'

'But——'

'Hurry, woman!' He stood in front of her, looking up into her eyes, his own eyes compelling her almost physically to obey him. His hair lank and dark, glistening with rain, his shabby hat dripping rain onto the shabby collar of his coat. 'Do you want those fools to control France?'

'I don't know what I want.'

'Then fetch your husband to me. He's wasting his time in there.'

She did what he told her. She did not know why. She began to laugh at him and still did as he ordered. Ran. For the sake of running, of something definite. Found Michel standing alone where she had left him a few minutes earlier, de Batz now with the group of Committee members, arguing about a message to send to another Section, and who should go. De Lallot gesticulating, crying that they were wasting time. Beginning to make a speech about it.

She told Michel what the little general had said, still laughing, and to her surprise Michel came with her immediately. 'Why not? There's nothing to be done here.' He looked contemptuously towards General Danican, still surrounded by his staff officers, still making plans as the minutes and the hours ticked by.

'—then gentlemen, we are agreed? The attack begins tomorrow afternoon, at four o'clock precisely. Precisely.'

'He's right,' Michel said. 'Our little friend is right, the man is an imbecile, he's throwing away twelve hours.' It was already midnight.

Outside General Buonaparte was stamping his feet as he walked up and down, still with the quivering of impatience to act. He seized them each by an arm and began to walk very fast, and then to run. The drums were beating across the city, a dull rumbling of menace in the rain. The drums of the National Guard, of the Sections, calling men to arms, to arms, to arms. To save Paris, throw down the mockery of a Convention, the profiteers, the Government of Whores, bring back the Commune, bring back ideals, bring back the King. But what King, and what ideals? And all in the old woman's hands of General Danican, and the orators of the Committees.

They reached the Tuileries drenched through to the skin, and found the Convention in full session, the corridors as full of talkers as the Lepeletier Headquarters; as many speeches, as many futile plans. Barras in a small room with a dozen other men, all shouting at him. He was trying to organize the defence of the Palace.

'Where the devil have you been all this time?' he said for greeting. 'And General Buonaparte. I was looking for you all day, I've sent a dozen times to your hotel. This is your chance, man, the one you've been looking for. Although what sort of chance it is—what does de Batz say?'

'In effect he offers nothing,' Michel said. 'He told me he'd talk tomorrow night, when it's all over. As for money, he expects to have the Treasury by then. He said he'll talk to you here in the Tuileries when they're in control.'

'And you'll be on his staff, I suppose?' Barras' sneer at once bitter, and weary of everything.

Michel shook his head, not troubling to be angry.

'Damn all this,' General Buonaparte said. 'Give me a dozen guns and not a rat shall reach here, except dead and on a plank. What guns do you have? Have you brought the guns from Sablons?'

'No,' Barras said, beginning to turn away to someone else. 'What guns?'

'The artillery park at Sablons! You mean to say——?'

'You should have been here hours ago. It's too late now to talk about artillery. We need men——'

'Give me an order for the guns and you shall have them inside three hours. They won't attack until four tomorrow afternoon. Give me the order, quick! Colonel Vernet, Colonel Murat there will ride for them. Your order, and some horses.'

Barras signing a scrap of paper, his mind, his eye already on something else, turning to someone else.

General Buonaparte shouting, 'Colonel Vernet, Colonel Murat! Take this order, find horses, ride as you've never ridden, kill your horses under you but get the guns. You, citizeness, you've seen war, come with me, I'll need a messenger who's not an imbecile. We need troops, gunners, we need to get emplacements ready, we've fifteen hours——'

By the end of them she was asleep on her feet. Drenched, exhausted, hungry—she could not remember when she had eaten last. The guns rumbling into the Carrousel. Already morning. The air full of thunder, of the drums, of men marching. All Paris marching against the Convention, still in session in the Tuileries. Vast columns crossing the river, forming along the quays opposite the Palace and the Louvre. The rain falling, slowly clearing. Pale autumn sunlight, rain-washed. Wet streets shining. And the guns, the guns. General Buonaparte like a weaver's shuttle in a loom, here, there, tireless; feverish with energy. From one bridge to another, and another, placing the cannon from Sablons.

Messengers riding, bringing threats from the Sections, from de Batz; commands to surrender. Sentries calling. The drums beating. The hornet murmur of thousands upon thousands of armed and waiting men, waiting for the order to attack, to fire.

Michel tried to make her go into the Tuileries, to find something to eat, somewhere to lie down. She went, but only to fetch bread and cheese and some bottles of wine, and bring them to the rue du Dauphin where Michel and Colonel Murat and General Buonaparte had their main position. General Buonaparte racing between there and the Pont Royal, staring across the river, waiting for a move. Racing back again to where the Sectionnaires had occupied the Church of St. Roch across the roadway. Twenty yards separating the two forces, the width of the rue St. Honoré. And on the other side the breadth of the Seine, the length of the Pont Royal. Sixty thousand men against the useless, untrustworthy ten thousand General Menou had led in yesterday. And the guns from Sablons, now surrounding the Tuileries in an iron ring.

Three o'clock. Half past. The minutes going. Across the river General Danican rode along the Quays, came to the head of the Pont Royal. They could hear his frail voice shouting, calling on the gunners to surrender. Four o'clock. General Danican riding back, into the rue de Beaune. The army of the Sectionnaires, of Paris, beginning to move, forward towards the bridge.

'Let them hear the sound of grapeshot,' General Buonaparte said. Two guns fired. Steel shot whistling, screaming, striking against the houses opposite. Windows shattering, the corner of an old house crumbling, dust lifting, bright steel flashing in ricochets, rolling, glittering.

The vast, dark column of the attackers shivered. A clatter of musket fire, wild and disorganized, from the front files. And then all the attackers running. Running for their lives. Melting into side streets. One officer shouting, 'Rally men, rally, over the bridge before they can reload!' But he was alone, almost alone. A knot of horsemen waving useless sabres. Forty thousand men running from a charge of grapeshot that had touched none of them. Not a wounded man.

Firing from the Church of St. Roch. General Buonaparte racing back, Hester and Michel following him, her mouth still half-full of the bread and cheese she had been eating before the guns fired. It had taken so few seconds. She thought of the peasant soldiers who had taken cannon with their bare hands, with scythe blades and sharpened pitchforks. A hundred, fifty of them would have had the guns by now, turned them against the Tuileries. And forty thousand Sectionnaires had turned tail and fled without even trying to attack.

It was no different in the rue du Dauphin. Another twenty thousand Sectionnaires paralysed by the sound of gunfire, driven off like sheep. Most of them never could have reached the guns if they had had the courage to attack. The narrow street was a defile. The weight of numbers was useless, an encumbrance, no more than a few handfuls of men at a time could do anything at all, and they did nothing, hiding in the porch of the church, behind the pillars, inside the church itself. Perhaps they were saying their prayers. They needed to. By nightfall it was over, and the impossible had happened. Barras and the Convention had won. De Batz was in hiding. And the Royalist cause was in ruin.

That night the streets were silent, except for the iron dragging of the guns. General Buonaparte's guns, moving down one emptied street after another in the darkness, to stop, and fire a round of blank, and move on. Only the powder flash, and the roar of firing. But enough to hold the city quiet and terrified. Royalist and bourgeois Paris crouching behind bolted doors, trembling. The workers', the *sans-culottes*' Paris broken months ago, and now careless of what might happen, so that there was bread. First the workers. Then the moment of the bourgeois, and the *ci-devants*, the intriguers. Now the guns. It was the soldiers' turn.

Epilogue

Late September, 1796. Switzerland. The St. Gotthard Pass. The wind screaming, snow flurries beating against the windows of the coach, whitening the heaving flanks of the six great horses as they struggled up towards the saddle of the pass. Too early for snow. They had promised her below that the road was easy, that there was no fear of bad weather. She sat muffled in the furs that Léonie had given her before she and Creuzot and Euphemia sailed for their tropic goldmine of Saint-Domingue. Perrine also in furs, holding the baby in a nest of warmth against her breast. Outside, Captain Jacquemart, Michel's A.D.C., struggling to make headway against the wind, and the sting of the driven snow that every moment gave way to sleet, his horse plodding, already white as a ghost.

She drew down the glass and called to him. 'Captain, come inside the coach, you are mad to stay out in this, you'll freeze.' But he only saluted, snow frozen to his moustaches, his side whiskers, his eyebrows and the rim of his hair beneath his Hussar's cap. Every time he had touched Hester's hand, in greeting when he came to Paris to fetch her, now on this journey, helping her in or out of the coach, little as she needed help three good months after the birth of the child; every time he touched her hand or needed to speak to her he trembled with boyish pride and timidity, blushing to the ears. General Vernet's wife! He spoke of General Vernet as though he was speaking of the Archangel Michael, and also as though he was speaking of an aged hero grizzled in long wars. He himself was not yet twenty-one years old, and already a captain.

'This is the youngest war there ever can have been,' Michel had written. 'There are colonels of twenty-three and four, and generals of brigade who are scarce twenty-five. Buonaparte himself is only twenty-seven, and Colonel Murat, my closest friend here, is only

[375]

twenty-nine. I am an old man among them at thirty-five. I think Buonaparte has promoted me general of brigade because it embarrassed him to have so old a colonel under him. You asked me after de Batz's rising, "What have we done?" I can tell you now. We have helped to give France a man who will do such things for her as no one in her history has done, unless the chances of war rob us of him. We have smashed the Austrians in a month. One month! And are in Milan as conquerors, the Lords of Italy. Nothing is too good for us, nor for the men. The Italian cities pour torrents of gold at Buonaparte's feet and he scoops it up with both hands and scatters it among us like rain.

'Murat is so fine you would not recognize him, he glitters with gold braid like the morning star, and as for his horses! He has a dozen at least. I am fine enough myself, remembering your teaching of long ago, but I save something, also thinking of you, and the child who will soon be born. The moment she is, the moment you can safely travel, come to me here, I implore it and command it, and know that I need do neither. Write me your news, every least thing. How you feel each day, how Perrine is. And the abbé Bernard. And your father. He must long ago have reached England. Have you heard from him? Write me everything.

'I write this at night by the light of a silver candelabra, in a Palace no less, with four splendid horses of my own below in the stables, and two soldier servants, and an A.D.C.! A boy of twenty, desperate to grow moustaches and look the man. I shall send him to fetch you the moment you tell me you are ready to travel. May God have you in his keeping. Your Michel.'

That had been in May. He had written every week since then. And now she was going to him, and she had still not answered for herself the question she had asked that night of the fifth Vendémiaire, of de Batz's futile, self-doomed rising. Now in Paris there was the Directory of Five, with Barras acknowledged for Chief of Men, in fact if not in title. And Madame Tallien, and Josephine Beauharnais become Madame Buonaparte, to rule Barras, and through him rule Paris and all France. And the bankers, and the army contractors and the speculators, to fasten like leeches on the Treasury. What had changed? Except that Léonie was gone, and La Tallien was installed in her place, and Ouvrard the banker was grown richer still, and Madame Hamelin had outdone everyone by walking down the Champs Elysées naked to the waist. And

Madame Tallien had riposted by appearing the next night at the Opéra wearing a blonde wig, and so thrown the whole of female Paris into a splendour of confusion. What else had they achieved?

But I have Michel, she thought. And baby Stéphanie. And in a few days I shall be with him, in Milan! Milan! She touched the baby's dark head. Like a kitten, sleeping, lying against Perrine's stout comfort. Hester was afraid to take her onto her own lap in case she woke her, and she drew her hand back and thought again of that other journey up this murderous pass. Her mother's journey how many years ago? Twenty-eight. Twenty-eight years ago. So near her time. On this road! God rest her soul. Where was the inn? They had told her which one it must be and how far up the pass. There, ahead? At that bend in the road? But when she leaned out the snow blinded her, and the wind took her breath from her throat so that she could not call out to Captain Jacquemart or the coachman. Was it over there?

But it was on the other side of the road, and she never saw it, half hidden as it was by the snow. And late that evening the coach struggled over the pass itself, and the horses took new strength as they began the long road down. Down towards Italy, and warm sunlight, and soft, flower-scented air.

The baby Stéphanie woke, and Hester took her into her arms, showing her the dark night and the stars that were already shining. 'We are going to join Papa,' she told her. 'He is a famous general, and he has fought in great battles so that we can all be together again, and there will be no more wars. You will not know even the meaning of the word, my darling. Only peace. And happiness. And love.' She held the baby against her heart as the coach rolled down the twisting mountain road, under the bright, cold stars.